ALWAYS YOU

CRYSTAL HUBBARD

Genesis Press, Inc.

Indigo Love Stories

An imprint of Genesis Press, Inc.
Publishing Company

Genesis Press, Inc.
P.O. Box 101
Columbus, MS 39703

ISBN-13: 978-158571-371-4
ISBN-10: 1-58571-371-6
Manufactured in the United States of America

First Edition 2007
Second Edition 2010

Visit us at www.genesis-press.com or call at 1-888-Indigo-1

DEDICATION

I have the best readers in the history of the written word, and I'd like to dedicate this book to all of you. I'm so thankful for each of you, but I have to give a special holler to Vannesia, who always knows just what to say before I even know I need to hear it.

*Please continue to send me your comments and questions at **crystalhubbardbooks@yahoo.com**.*

ACKNOWLEDGMENTS

Always You is something new for me, and I have a lot of people to thank for helping me pull it together. Kim H., one of NASA's finest minds, made learning about computers fun. Almost. There wasn't such a thing as a dumb question when I spoke to members of the St. Louis Police, and one of you in particular didn't doubt me for a moment when I said I didn't roll through that stop sign. Special thanks to my husband—my eyes, ears, and nose when it comes to overseas hotels. I'm also thankful to the Bureau of East Asian and Pacific Affairs for the engrossing etiquette tutorial. I'd like to acknowledge Anneliese Hubbard, creator, owner, and designer of Soul Hippi, the home of Hazel Wear fashions. And finally, I offer my thanks to the city of Chicago. The line between work and pleasure always blurs nicely there.

PROLOGUE

Hotel Sakura
Tokyo, Japan

Two butlers rigidly flanked the entrance to the Seiyo lounge. Still as wax figures in their black cutaway coats, dove-grey trousers and white gloves, they stared straight ahead, unblinking. Though they said nothing, Chiara Winters was sure that they inwardly seethed at the horrible behavior of her companion, Chen Zhou, who loudly smacked his lips after knocking back a shot of whiskey. With a sharp crack on the highly polished surface of the burled walnut counter, his empty shot glass joined a long line of others that the bartender made no effort to clear away.

"What's going on, Zhou?" she asked, her tone cautious as she eased onto the tall, suede-covered stool beside him. "I rang your room three times and your cell phone twice. We have an early flight back to Chicago tomorrow. You're not going to be in any condition to travel if you keep this up." She and Zhou had traveled extensively throughout Asia over the past few years. They were technical sales and public relations reps for United States IntelTech, Inc.—USITI, to insiders—and they were the software giant's top-selling duo. They were so successful, they answered directly to "U-City" founder and CEO Emmitt Grayson, who personally managed the accounts they acquired.

Grayson had begun working with computers as an undergraduate in Nevada's state school system. Twenty years later, he started his own software design firm built solely on the success of his patented Relay-Group Systems (R-GS) chips, which enabled linked computers to communicate more efficiently. The R-GS chip was USITI's signature product, and Grayson himself chose the clients to whom he wished to sell it.

Chiara and Chen Zhou had spent the past several years predominantly in the Far East, exclusively promoting the R-GS chips, and their hard work had paid off. If there was a major corporation between Russia and Australia without R-GS chips powering their computer systems, Chiara was at a loss to name it, and she and Zhou had just closed a multimillion-dollar sale to a Japanese biorobotics firm.

Zhou had a funny way of celebrating their success.

Japan was a culture of manners, and the concept of *shibumi*, elegance and restraint in all things, was celebrated. Zhou's loud, public drunkenness was an embarrassment for him, Chiara, and every butler and bartender in the otherwise deserted lounge. Manners and culture clashes aside, a drinking binge was uncharacteristic for Zhou, and Chiara was concerned.

"What's going on, Zhou?" she asked again.

"You." With two fingers, Zhou waved over the bartender and, in fluent Japanese, rattled off an order for warm sake. "And me. We're the problem, Winters. We don't belong here. You don't know what we've done!" His black eyes overbright with his sudden burst of emotion, he punctuated his words with sharp stabs at the counter. The bartender's impassive expression never changed, even though Zhou nearly toppled the small ceramic carafe of sake he presented to Zhou. Chiara was well schooled in the customs and traditions of Japan, so it was second nature for her to reach for the carafe and pour a dignified amount of the dry rice wine into Zhou's fresh drinking cup. When he tried to pour for her, slopping a substantial quantity of the sake onto the counter, she turned her tiny cup over in refusal.

"Finish that cup and I'll get you to your room, Zhou," Chiara said, nervously tucking a long lock of her dark hair behind her ear. "We can talk there."

"Why?" He hiccupped sharply. "So we can have privacy? There's no such thing as privacy in our work. He's made sure of that."

"Who?"

Zhou leaned in close, startling her with his fluidity of movement in the depths of intoxication. The moist heat of his words seemed to coat her neck in fumes. "Our boss."

"You're not making any sense."

He wagged a long finger in her face. "For the first time in five years, I make sense."

She took his hand in both of hers in an attempt to rein him in. "Zhou, I—"

"Do you remember what you said to me, the first time we met?"

She winced, shaking her head. Drunk was one thing. Crazy was another, and Chiara was suddenly convinced that Zhou was in the midst of a mental collapse.

"You said, 'Good morning, Mr. Chen. It is my honor and my privilege to welcome you to United States IntelTech, Inc.'"

"I did?"

"Only you said it in perfect Mandarin, and you knew to reverse the order of my name." Zhou squeezed Chiara's fingers, and with his free hand, he gave his brow ridge a tense rub. "You took one look at me and you knew that I was Chinese." He tore his hand away to raise his fist to the bartender. "I am Chinese! Not Japanese, not Korean! I am Chinese!"

He propped his elbows on the bar and shoved his fingers into the glossy black spikes of his hair. "You are the only one who sees me for what I am, Chiara.

You notice so much. What else do you see?" His fathomless eyes turned to her, and beyond the reflection of her own coffee eyes she saw raw misery.

"You're in trouble. Is it money?"

"I wish it were."

"We've worked together for five years. If there's something I can do to help, you know I will."

"The only one who can help me now is me." He slid off the stool, bobbling on shaky knees before he steadied himself. He tugged on the lapels of his tailored jacket, straightening the rumpled suit as best he could. He seemed remarkably clear and alert when he leaned in close to her and whispered, "Keep noticing things, Chiara. Keep an eye on everything."

"Zhou?" she called as he turned and took a step away.

When he glanced back, he looked exactly the way he had the first time they'd met. The tall, handsome computer software representative that Emmitt Grayson had stolen away from a rival software company had an elegant confidence that complemented Chiara's more exotic nature. She had always been able to rely on Zhou, had always trusted him. Now, as he gazed back at her with the shine of tears in his eyes, a quiver in his chin and a frightened smile on his lips, a shiver skipped along Chiara's spine.

She swallowed the thick, sticky lump suddenly plugging her throat. "I gotta tell you, buddy. You're scaring me."

"Good." Zhou blinked, and a tear fell from his eye. "You should be scared."

CHAPTER ONE

The mannered voice and clipped words of Abby Winters flowed from the speakerphone sitting on one corner of Chiara's desk. "Are you still coming home?"

"Planning to." Leaning over, Chiara brushed a speck of dark lint from the leg of her wool pants.

"I can't hear you, baby."

Chiara sat upright and tugged at her pale alpaca sweater to straighten it before tucking a loose tendril of black hair behind her right ear. "I said I'm still planning to come home next week." She crossed her fingers before adding, "I'm looking forward to spending Christmas with the family."

"Everybody's dying to see you."

Chiara heard the smile in her mother's voice, and she had to smile herself.

"There's so much going on," Abby bubbled. "John's been back for almost three months now. He still hasn't found a house yet, but it's not from a lack of trying. I think ol' Almadine's trying to sew the umbilical cord back on. Kyla had a fancy book signing downtown, and you should have seen all the local celebrities who turned out for it. Cady's pregnant—"

"Still?" Chiara joked.

"*Again,*" Abby clarified. "Virginia's almost a year and a half now, and Cady and Keren don't seem to be wasting any time about going forth and multiplying. Have you spoken to Clara lately?" The Winters family information officer didn't give Chiara a chance to answer before she continued. "Troy's got early acceptance to Stanford. He always wanted to go back to California, so I guess he's getting his wish. Danielle's dancing the lead in The Black Ballet Theatre's production of *The Nutcracker* this season, and Christopher got tickets for all of us. The St. Louis Symphony Youth Orchestra plays for the show, and Chris Jr. is sitting first chair on the violin. I tell you, my grandchildren are so talented! I know they get it from our side of the family because I was always very artistic."

"Ma, I—"

Abby nattered on, and Chiara wondered if it even mattered whether she was on the other end of the phone. "Did Ciel call you? She was supposed to. Clarence won't be returning to the fifth grade after Christmas break."

"Did he finally get expelled?" Chiara laughed lightly. "He wasn't selling book reports again, was he?"

"No, Ciel put him out of business. Let me tell you 'bout your nephew," Abby exhaled, a touch of her Southern dialect creeping into her speech. "That boy started selling book reports in September. He made up business cards on Chris Jr.'s computer and sample reports that he advertised on the Internet on a web page he and C.J. created on one of those free website providers."

Chiara laughed.

"This isn't funny," Abby declared. "That child—"

"I'm laughing at you, Ma." She eased back into the embrace of her pricey leather chair and activated one of the lower back massage features. "You sound like a computer expert now, and six months ago, you didn't even know what 'log in' meant."

"The system you recommended was just so easy," Abby marveled. "I'm down with the download."

"Don't get cocky, now. You're the same woman who interrupts my meetings because you're scared to open a mailer daemon."

"They shouldn't call it a demon if they want you to open it," Abby complained.

Chiara steered her mother back on track. "So why isn't Clarence going back to school after the winter break?"

"Oh, he's going back, just not to the fifth grade. That boy tested off the charts on his fall standardized proficiency exams. He's being promoted to the seventh grade."

"Mid term?" Chiara sat forward, for the moment forsaking the soothing hum of her massage chair.

"If his homeroom teacher had her way, he would have been moved on the first of November. Ciel told you what he did on Halloween, didn't she?"

"Yes, but you can't blame him entirely. Cady's the one who loaned him the monkey."

"Cady's paying for that animal trainer's lake house," Abby said with a click of her tongue. "If I'd married a rich doctor, I wouldn't spend all of his money renting monkeys."

"The monkeys are meant to entertain the kids on the Raines-Hartley pediatric oncology ward," Chiara said in defense of her sister. "But she should have known that giving Clarence permission to borrow a monkey would lead to disaster."

"Knowing Cady, that's what she was hoping for. She had Mrs. McNairy for fifth grade, too. She hated Mrs. McNairy."

"Good Heavens, Ma, is the St. Louis Board of Education still allowing that woman to teach? She was the worst teacher I ever had. She's as mean as a damn rattlesnake."

"I don't like to hear you use that kind of language, baby," Abby said. "I forgot you had Mrs. McNairy, too."

"Yes, and I wish Clarence had gotten the monkey drunk before he smuggled it into school. There are chimps in Uganda that get drunk off beer they steal from illegal breweries in the jungles, and then they go on the rampage, attacking people to steal food."

"Drunk monkeys, huh," Abby said with practiced disinterest. "I've just run on and on about the home-folk. Tell me, how was your trip to Taiwan? When did you get back to Chicago?"

"It was Tokyo, and we came back three days ago. It went well. We secured the contract with Siyuri

Robotics. Zhou and I did our routine—he takes the lead, explaining all the technical details of how the software is installed and what hardware is required while I sit quiet, making everyone think I'm just a secretary or something." She took a self-satisfied spin in her chair. "Then I come in with the sales pitch, showing them exactly how USITI's R-GS microchips will vastly improve communications between their in-house computer systems as well as locations elsewhere. Zhou sells the process, but I sell the merchandise itself. Then Zhou leaves the room and the clients talk among themselves in Japanese, thinking I don't understand what they're saying."

"That's deceitful, baby," Abby admonished. "How would you like it if you thought you were having a private conversation and somebody was listening to every word?"

"First of all, Ma, it's rude, even in Japan, to speak a foreign language in the presence of someone you think doesn't understand what you're saying. Second, they shouldn't presume that Zhou is the only one who speaks and understands Japanese. And third, if they wanted to speak in private, they could ask me to leave the room."

"What were you wearing in that meeting?"

"Clothes." Chiara hoped she didn't sound as guilty as she suddenly felt.

"What kind of clothes?"

"A blouse. A skirt. Just clothes."

"How short was the skirt?"

Short enough to guarantee that no one would be asking me to leave the room, Chiara thought. "I don't trade on my looks to secure deals, Ma."

"I'm sure you don't, but I'm also sure that your long pretty legs help keep attention where you want it."

"It's an ugly part of the business, Ma."

"Why do you persist in calling me 'Ma?' None of my other children call me 'Ma.' It's so…guttural."

"Would you like to hear about the rest of my trip, Mommy dearest?" Chiara asked sweetly.

"Tell me about Zhou. Is he seeing anybody?"

"Zhou went a little funny on me toward the end of the trip. He went a lot funny, actually." Chiara got goosebumps, and not the good kind, as she thought back on Zhou's odd behavior in the hotel bar. "He was at our Monday morning debriefing with Mr. Grayson, but he's been out since. I have to give him a call."

"Maybe if that boss of yours didn't keep the two of you on the road two weeks out of every month—"

"It's not that bad, Ma."

"—then maybe you and Zhou could spend more time with your families. Nothing helps release stress more than family."

"Or adds to it," Chiara grumbled.

"What?"

"It wasn't stress, Ma. Zhou loves the travel. So do I. It's the reason we both wanted to work in sales and public relations. We wouldn't have this job if we didn't love what we do."

"Well, it sounds like he's burned out to me," Abby said before launching into a familiar tirade about long lost daughters who spent more time chasing business deals in the Far East than at home with their families.

A light rap on the glass door of her office turned Chiara's attention from her mother's rant to her employer, Emmitt Grayson, who stood in the doorframe. He wore a suit, always black, and always exquisitely tailored. The elegant draping and high armholes on this particularly wide-shouldered jacket marked it as the product of one of Grayson's favorite cutters, Anderson & Sheppard of Savile Row. From the neck down, his $8,000 suit gave him the look of the idle rich masquerading as a hard-working businessman; but from the neck up, he wore the concerned expression of an investor watching his favorite stock nosedive. His square forehead creased in severe lines and his dark blue eyes were unreadable; he beckoned Chiara with a sharp hand gesture.

She nodded and turned back to the phone as she stood. "I have to go, Ma. I've been called to a meeting."

"Okay, baby," Abby said, cheerfully abbreviating her speech. "See you in a week!"

❧

Six tall, narrow, polarized windows behind Emmitt Grayson's sprawling kidney bean shaped desk revealed the choppy, bluish-black waters of sunlit Lake Michigan. The bright shine of the cold December day couldn't penetrate the dim austerity of Grayson's office, which was decorated in somber shades of blue, gray, charcoal and black.

Grayson himself, his tall, angular frame wrapped in black, was the centerpiece of the room as he sat with one pale hand covering the other atop the mirrored surface of his obsidian desktop.

Unbidden, Chiara took one of the stylized black leather and chrome chairs in front of the vast desk. Grayson's high-priced interior decorator had spared no expense in selecting the ultra-modern chairs. The stiff seats and low backs testified that style, rather than comfort, had been paramount.

As she always did when called to Grayson's office, Chiara kept her eyes on his crystal-clear reflection in the desktop. His icy gaze was less likely to turn her to stone that way.

"Chiara," he started, his deep voice a quiet rumble, "I have some news about Chen Zhou that you'll find disturbing, but before I go into that, I need to ask you a few questions."

She shifted her gaze from Grayson's reflection to his face. His pale eyes were just as cold as those of his reflection, and as he stared at her, the memory of Zhou's words started a chill creeping through her.

He watches…

"Chiara?"

She snapped out of her reverie. "Yes, Mr. Grayson, I'm sorry."

"Chen seemed rather…anxious, I would say, during the debriefing of your last trip to Japan. Did he seem all right to you in Tokyo?"

He listens…

Chiara softly cleared the lump that had formed in her throat. She chose her words carefully. "He seemed tired. We've had some long trips: India, Laos, Thailand, Malaysia, and then Tokyo. Even though we both love to travel, the long jaunts away from home begin to take their toll."

Grayson sat back in his chair. "You seem to handle the stress well. And so did Chen, until recently."

For lack of a better excuse, and feeling as though she needed to explain, Chiara said, "Chen's a lot closer to his family than I am. He really missed them while we were gone."

Grayson's long, pale fingers stroked his chin. "I was under the impression that you were quite fond of your family."

He spies…

Chiara's chill worsened, and she clamped her jaw to stave off a shudder. Her older sister Kyla was an actress, and taking a page from her book, Chiara pasted on a smile. "I love them. The farther I am from them, the more I love them."

Grayson spent another long moment studying her. "I suppose it couldn't have been easy for you, being the youngest of five. I myself am the 'baby' in a brood of seven. I had four older brothers and two older sisters, each of whom made a hobby of torturing their younger sibling. I'm sure you can imagine the pain I endured as a defenseless youth."

He smiled then, and Chiara gave in to a shudder. Behind the cobra-like gleam in his eyes, it was impossible for her to see any trace of the tortured child he claimed to have been.

Grayson sat quietly, as though expecting Chiara to regale him with stories of her own torture at the hands of her sisters, but the worst thing she could think of was the time when Cady convinced her to walk a homemade tightrope. After enlisting Ciel's help, Cady had "borrowed" Old Lady Voss's clothesline. They had tied it to one side of the fence surrounding the backyard and stretched it all the way to the opposite fence. Using a stuffed teddy bear to demonstrate, Cady showed her younger sisters the light, skipping steps necessary for the successful navigation of the rudimentary tightrope.

Convinced that she had at least as much dexterity and daring as a teddy bear, Chiara had eagerly climbed the stool Cady had furnished and stepped onto the tightrope. The next thing she remembered was a face full of dirt, a sharp crack in her forearm, a lot of screaming—her own—and her sisters scrambling for cover before their mother raced out to take names.

That was the day Chiara had learned how much power a five-year-old wielded. For the next month and a half, her sisters had been her full-time beck-and-call girls, catering to her every whim.

It had been Grandma Claire who'd put a stop to Chiara's injury-born tyranny, and Chiara almost smiled at the memory of her grandmother's sweet scowl as she'd ordered her to stop making Cady spend her allowance to supply Chiara with red shoestring licorice.

"I'm sorry to dredge up sad memories for you, Chiara," Grayson said. "You're fortunate to have found a new family here at USITI."

"U-City," as Grayson pronounced it, had recruited Chiara straight out of George Washington University. Despite the high starting salary, excellent benefits and incentive programs, her feelings about the company had been lukewarm, until she'd learned that her best friend had accepted a position at the company.

She and John Mahoney had both begun in the information systems department, but Chiara's background in foreign languages had landed her a position in sales and public relations. Until his recent relocation to St. Louis, Missouri, to spearhead the information systems department of USITI's newest hub, John had spent his days at the home base in Chicago while Chiara was sent to the farthest nooks and crannies of the Far East to peddle Emmitt Grayson's cutting-edge computer products.

Sitting in the direct line of Grayson's penetrating stare, Chiara wished more than ever that she had just stayed in information systems with John.

"Thank you, Mr. Emmitt," she muttered graciously.

"You've always demonstrated unshakable loyalty to your USITI family, Chiara," Grayson continued. "I trust you'll turn to us, should you need to, in the coming days."

"I'm afraid I don't understand what's going on." She sat up straighter, but avoided Grayson's unreadable stare, opting instead to keep her eyes on his severely slicked back iron-gray hair.

"Chen Zhou was found dead in his apartment this morning, apparently from an accidental drug overdose. Did you know that Chen was taking Valiaz and Mitrazepam?"

"Wh-What?" Chiara faltered. "Drugs?"

"Valiaz is an anxiolytic and Mitrazepam is an hypnotic," Grayson coolly explained. "Apparently Chen was being treated for anxiety and insomnia."

Chiara shook her head. As her mind grappled with what Grayson was saying, she tried to remember ever seeing Zhou take medication, any medication. A firm believer in herbal and natural remedies, Zhou was the one who had taught her the Ayurvedic concept of *vata*, *pitta* and *kapha*, the three *doshas* that governed all metabolic activities. If Zhou had trouble sleeping, he'd been more likely to take melatonin than Tylenol. As for anxiety, until their last night in Tokyo, Zhou had been one of the most easy-going, laid back people Chiara had ever known.

"The body was discovered by Chen's sister," Grayson continued. "She was supposed to have met him for lunch on Tuesday, and when he didn't make the appointment, she became concerned. I blame myself for this catastrophe, Chiara. Chen was behaving strangely after this latest junket to Japan, and I failed to delve deeper into the situation after our meeting Monday morning…"

Grayson continued to speak but Chiara's own thoughts blocked his words from her ears. Zhou was dead? He'd killed himself? It was impossible, too impossible, no matter what Grayson said. Chen had acted out of character in Tokyo, but he'd been in control, for the most part. He'd made sense. Nothing of what Grayson was saying was making any sense.

Grayson spoke in his usual toneless fashion, as though he were reading stock reports rather than giving her the details of the gruesome death of her partner, and Chiara forced herself to listen to him.

"We here at USITI had our suspicions, but we saw no need to drag you into the mess Chen was making of his life," Grayson said, "but now I wish that we had. Did you ever see Chen abusing drugs, Chiara?"

The numbness that had settled into her ebbed a bit, to allow a renewed burst of shock. "Chen didn't do drugs."

"Security cleaned out his office this morning and found unprescribed Valiaz." His unblinking stare held Chiara in place. "I was as surprised as you are to learn that Chen was not only using, but that he would bring such filth into our home at USITI."

"But, Mr. Grayson—"

"I understand your shock, Chiara. He was your partner, after all. If he could hide his habit from you, then how could anyone else foresee the inevitable disaster to come?"

She stood up on shaky knees and paced around her chair. "This doesn't make any sense at all, Mr. Grayson." Her voice shook with unshed tears as the reality of Chen's death sank deeper. "Zhou and I have spent more time with each other than with anyone else over the past few years. We're friends. How could he have hidden a drug habit from me? How could he have performed his job so well if he were an addict?"

"I have no answers for you, Chiara. All I have is the evidence from Security. I understand that this is distressing to you, but I have to ask you a few more questions about Tokyo." Grayson sat forward, tenting his hands on the desk. "Did Chen mention anything to you, anything at all, about his future plans with USITI?"

"He wasn't interviewing elsewhere, if that's what you're asking," Chiara almost shouted. Zhou was dead, and all Grayson cared about was whether or not Zhou planned to quit?

"I have reason to believe that Chen was engaged in activities that would undermine the integrity of USITI's products," Grayson said, his voice a degree or two cooler. "While I am indeed saddened by his tragic demise, I have a company to run, and I need to know if Chen's actions in Tokyo have put my life's work at risk."

Hot tears squeezed from Chiara's eyes and she blinked them away. "He got drunk in the bar on our last night, but other that, he seemed fine. He didn't do anything else out of the ordinary." She used the heel of her hand to scrub away a fresh fall of tears. "I'm sorry, Mr. Emmitt. I'm shocked. I…this is unbelievable. Zhou…" She covered her mouth with one hand and wept openly; all the while her mind replayed her last encounter with Chen.

Grayson spent a long moment studying her, narrowing his eyes as though he could peer directly into her skull and read her thoughts as they were born. Apparently satisfied with her response, he dropped his gaze. "I'm sorry to have been the one to tell you about Chen, but I thought it best that you heard it from me, rather than on the midday news. You're going home for the holidays, yes?"

She nodded. Words couldn't squeeze past the hard, heavy lump in her throat.

"Perhaps that's best, for you to get away for a few days. Take as much time as you need, Chiara." He turned to his right to face his computer monitor, and Chiara took that as a sign of dismissal.

"Thank you, sir." She started for the door, but halfway across the cavernous office his voice stopped her in her tracks.

"You should be scared."

She jerked around to face him, her breath frozen in her chest. "I-I'm sorry, Mr. Grayson?"

His lips pursed in mild annoyance before he repeated himself slightly louder and more clearly. "I said you should be there, at Chen's funeral. It will be the day after tomorrow, on Saturday. Chen's family is handling the arrangements. You should be receiving the details in a company e-mail scheduled to go out this afternoon."

"Y-Yes sir," Chiara managed. "I'll be there."

"Chiara?" Grayson called once more. "Your sister Kyla had a baby recently, yes?"

She nodded as she dried her eyes with the cuff of her sleeve. "A girl. Niema. She's six months old."

"She was rather large at birth, wasn't she? Nine pounds, four ounces?"

A shiver crept along Chiara's spine. Niema's newborn photo sat on one end of her desk, along with the photos of her other nieces and nephews, but Chiara couldn't recall ever mentioning the baby's birth statistics to anyone other than Chen Zhou and John.

"Family is important, Chiara, and I'm glad you'll be spending some time with yours. I hope you'll see what's important and what's worth risking. Chen failed to do that. I'd like to think that perhaps, in the end, he realized the error of his ways."

"Zhou was a good man, Mr. Grayson," Chiara insisted quietly. "I never saw him take pills, not once, in all the time I knew him. And you couldn't have asked for a more loyal employee."

Grayson tented his hands on his desk. "I admire your faith in your coworker. However, I'm afraid I can't afford such emotional generosity. You see, Chiara, Chen failed to turn in an important piece of hardware upon your return from Japan."

Baffled, Chiara soundlessly wondered what Grayson was referring to.

His icy gaze boring through her, Grayson explained. "The R-GS master chip. It's missing."

CHAPTER TWO

As always, Abby had a full house for Christmas Eve dinner. Cars lined both sides of the street of her mother's block, but Chiara's expert parallel parking ability had enabled her to squeeze her sporty rented Mazda between a gargantuan SUV and a station wagon four houses down from her mother's.

She tucked her formless suede handbag under the passenger seat before she got out of the car and activated the alarm. She then pulled her white fox fur coat closer about her and started for her mother's house. The cold night was bright with starlight and a dusting of new snow that put a fresh face on the seven inches that had fallen two days earlier, assuring St. Louis a white Christmas. Chiara's rabbit-lined reindeer-hide mukluks left indistinct footprints in the sprinkling of snow as she crossed the street and stepped onto the sidewalk. She wondered who was in attendance this year, not that she would recognize too many of her mother's and sisters' guests. She hadn't spent too many Christmases at home in recent years, and as she climbed the seven steps to her mother's front walkway, she realized how far out of her family's loop USITI had taken her.

How far I've allowed *the company to take me*, she amended. She turned and sat on the top step leading to the porch, her back to one of the brick support pillars.

The mukluks and her coat had been purchased in a small town near the Kuskokwim River, one of the colder regions in Alaska during the winter months. Her clothing was warm enough to keep the chill off the Yup'ik salmon fishermen who lived on Nunivak Island, and as Chiara shivered, she realized the chill came from within. Ever since her conversation— inquisition was more like it—with Grayson, she'd had a hard time keeping warm. And keeping calm.

Though Grayson had stuck himself to her hip throughout Zhou's funeral four days ago, he'd said nothing to her the whole time. The hopeful part of Chiara wanted to believe that Grayson's silence was out of respect for her grief. The rational part of her felt otherwise. That part of her knew that Grayson was watching her every move and listening to every word she spoke.

Everyone in sales and public relations, as well as a few other miscellaneous USITI employees, had attended the traditional Chinese funeral. Zhou's family had been there, his parents and siblings looking otherworldly in their white mourning apparel. Zhou's coffin was covered in wreaths of flowers bedecked with ribbons, a testament to the respect people had for Zhou and his family's status. Chiara herself had burned incense for Zhou, along with a pile of money, to honor Zhou's ancestors and to make sure that he had enough money for the next world.

Other than to straighten the tiny white lilies Chiara wore in her hair, Grayson hadn't made the slightest effort to interact with anyone at the ceremony. Even now, five days after the funeral, Chiara cringed at the memory of the black suit and red silk tie Grayson had worn to the funeral. Grayson had seen to Chiara's schooling in the cultures of the countries in which she did business, but he'd never bothered to learn a thing about them himself. Had he taken one of his own cultural sensitivity seminars, he'd have known that "Zhou" was Chen's first name, not his surname, and that the color red at a Chinese funeral is taboo, a symbol of disrespect toward the deceased.

Chiara thought that she'd cried all the tears she could, but sitting on her mother's front stoop listening to the sounds of her family in the warm house triggered fresh waves. As a part of life, death made sense. But Zhou's death remained utterly senseless, no matter how hard Chiara tried to find a reason for it. From their years of working and traveling together, Chiara and Zhou had become closer than most spouses, even closer than siblings; Chiara safely assumed that she knew him better than anyone. It was impossible for her to make herself believe that Zhou had overdosed, accidentally or otherwise.

Grief consumed her, and all she wanted to do was fling open the front door and melt into her mother's embrace.

The big, wide front windows, opaque with condensation, blurred the figures moving behind them and the splashes of color provided by the Christmas tree lights. The tall, shadowy figures in the living and dining rooms were adults, probably enjoying coffee and dessert. The shadows in the little room off the dining room, her mother's tiny library, were shorter and more active, indicating that Chiara's nieces and nephews were probably assembled within it. Conversations spilled from the slightly open windows, and listening closely, Chiara picked out individual voices in the dining room.

"There ain't no Chinese tap dancers an' you ain't never gonna see no Chinese tap dancers," came a loud male voice that slightly slurred its words.

"Come on, Hippolyte," responded a voice Chiara recognized as that of her brother-in-law, Lee. "Asian people have excellent body mechanics. Think about martial arts."

The drunken voice boisterously harrumphed. "Kung Fu ain't 'bout rhythm, it's 'bout reaction. That's why you don't see no Chinese tap dancers. You just proved my point, boy…"

"Clarence!" Chiara jumped at her sister Ciel's voice, which had an unusually sharp edge to it. "You get right on upstairs and check things out!"

"I'm in the middle of a game, Mama," Clarence complained from what Chiara marked as the library.

"You better get up to that bathroom," came Ciel's dark, motherly warning.

"Why do you want him to go to the bathroom?" Lee asked, clearly intervening on his son's behalf.

Chiara barely heard Ciel's growled response. "Because he smells like he wiped sideways. Now get him up to the bathroom before I go in there and choke him. He told me he took a shower today, and obviously he didn't…"

"Catch him, Keren, he's got Mama's salad tongs," Cady said, her voice full of laughter.

"Come here, Sammy," Keren called gently.

Chiara pictured him hoisting her little nephew up in his arms and gently prising the salad tongs from him.

"He says it's his bionic hand," Cady explained, her voice close to the front door. "Lee's been teaching him all about *The Bionic Man*."

"And *The Six Million-Dollar Woman*!" Sammy piped in.

"There he goes," Cady laughed over the thunder of Sammy's footsteps, which retreated deeper into the house. "That child of mine wears me out. I'd be all set if *Sesame Street* came in pill form…"

Chiara tuned out the voices of her loved ones and turned her thoughts inward. As much as she wanted to see everyone, she was in no hurry to do it all at once, with God only knew how many strangers surrounding her. Zhou's funeral and the rest of the work week had left her drained, and while she knew that only the care and concern of her family could fill that emptiness, she couldn't bear to face them with a houseful of strangers present.

She shivered and drew her warm coat closer about her. She was an outsider now, made so by her dedication to USITI. She had stayed away too long and traveled too far.

She thought about going back to the car and waiting there for the crowd to thin, but she didn't really want to hide out in the tiny rental any more than she wanted to sit on the cold stoop. Movement equaled warmth, so Chiara fastened her coat about her, flipped up her wide, rabbit fur-lined hood, and went back down to the sidewalk. Pulling on her white wool gloves, she started down the street, toward Tower Grove Park.

❧

Each step closer to the park gave Chiara a profound sense of déjà vu. Her feet traveled a path she hadn't taken in months, past houses that seemed so much smaller and shabbier than she remembered, yet still achingly familiar.

She passed the tiny brick house that had belonged to Mrs. Lafayette, who'd turn her water hose on you if she caught you snitching fruit from her heirloom cherry tree. Chiara had a vague recollection of her mother mentioning Mrs. Lafayette's death a few months back, but apparently that hadn't stopped the life-size plastic nativity scene, complete with a black Mary, Joseph and Jesus, from making its annual appearance on her snow-covered lawn.

The house next to Mrs. Lafayette's had its usual candy cane motif, with the more recent addition of a giant inflatable candy cane ridden by a teddy bear in a Santa hat. The best house, though, was near the corner of Alfred and Magnolia Avenues, right across the street from the park. This was the house that neighbors never failed to complain about, the one that people came from all over St. Louis to see.

While other families were displaying jack o' lanterns and cutouts of bats to celebrate Halloween, the Mahoneys—led by Almadine Mahoney, the daughter of a genuine hell-and-brimstone-breathing Baptist preacher—shunned all things associated with All Hallow's Eve. She commandeered her husband and two sons in a project that began on October 31 and ended on Thanksgiving: the preparation of their home for its showy Christmas display.

Every angle and window of the two-story brick house was traced in light, but Almadine didn't stop there. Every bush, tree and fixture on the property, as well as the driveway, was also draped or outlined with tiny white lights in preparation for Thanksgiving Friday, the day Almadine invited a select number of friends and neighbors to her home for what her sons John and George called "The Ignition."

Chiara crossed the street in front of the Mahoneys to get the full effect, and she wished that she'd brought her sunglasses with her. She laughed out loud, convinced that she'd seen the Mahoney house from the airspace above St. Louis as her flight had come into Lambert Airport.

When they were kids, John would complain about how the light from his own house kept him awake at night, and he couldn't wait until New Year's Day, which the Mahoney men celebrated by taking down all of the Christmas lights.

There were a number of cars in the Mahoney driveway, but Chiara couldn't pick out John's. If his mother had had her way, and she always did, John's sensible Saab was parked in the garage, squeezed between Mr. Mahoney's fat Cadillac and Almadine's prissy Mercedes. Almadine Mahoney would have wanted to leave as much driveway space as possible for the select guests she'd invited to her annual Christmas Eve dinner and prayer meeting.

John was somewhere in that house, probably playing waiter to his mother's guests. Chiara refused to call them friends. Almadine wasn't the kind of woman who fostered warm friendships. She culti-vated strategic alliances.

It would have been easy enough for Chiara to go up to the front door and knock. Almadine would have done her best to make her welcoming grimace look like a smile, and she would have admitted Chiara to the house as a demonstration of her

Christian fortitude and generosity. But she would have glued herself to Chiara and John, to prevent even the remotest possibility of what she called "hanky panky" between them.

Of course, what Almadine didn't know was that she was too late. Chiara and John had hanky-pankied in just about every room of that house but for the one Almadine shared with her husband, car dealer, Bartholomew Mahoney.

The living room drapes were pulled wide and Chiara easily spotted John's father, his pencil-thin mustache neatly trimmed, his bald spot gleaming like a freshly glazed cinnamon bun. His bulky figure was wrapped in one of the traditional holiday sweaters his wife forced him to wear. This latest one was equipped with a tiny white blinking light affixed just below his collar. The light was the Christmas star shining its brightness over the embroidered nativity scene stretched over Bartholomew's flabby torso. The heads of the three wise men peeped from Bartholomew's armpit, but the baby Jesus in his manger was sandwiched between two rolls of belly fat.

Almadine, her stick-thin figure perched stiffly in a leather and brass wing chair, held court beside her husband, who had a bottled beer propped on one knee and a plate piled high with food on the other.

Chiara glanced at the upper left corner of the house where a soft square of golden light warmed the night. If John had managed to escape his mother's gathering, he was probably holed up in that room, his old bedroom, which Mrs. Mahoney had turned into an office three minutes after John's departure for George Washington University.

In the old days, Chiara would have hidden in the shadows and crept to the side of the house and used Cecile Brunner to help her scramble up to the second floor. It had taken years for Chiara to realize that Cecile Brunner was not a person, but a variety of rose that Almadine had spent years training to climb a twenty-five foot trellis on the side of the house.

"Cecile Brunner's not doing well this year," Almadine would mutter to herself as she mixed her special fertilizer blend in the backyard. Or, "Cecile Brunner looks better than ever!" Almadine would crow. Thanking Cecile Brunner for her helpfulness in reaching the second floor of the Mahoney home undetected, Chiara would scale the trellis like a circus performer and tap on John's window.

Accepting the fact that she wasn't fifteen anymore and with no assurance that John was even in his room, Chiara didn't feel like climbing the trellis or even ringing the doorbell. Shoving her hands into her pockets, she moved on, crossing deserted Magnolia Avenue to disappear into the park, and easily found her way to the paths she knew best despite the camouflage provided by the fresh fall of undisturbed snow.

Her mukluks left the snow virtually undisturbed as she moved among the poplars and silver birches, the silent sentries saluting the night, their bare branches making puzzlework of the purple-black sky. Chiara had seen much of the world and had left her eye prints on ancient wonders, yet her snowy neighborhood park remained one of her favorite places on earth.

She passed the darkened stone tennis clubhouse and its courts where she and her sisters had spent exactly one Saturday afternoon striving to become candidates for Wimbledon; she paused at the snow-frosted wading pool where the Winters girls had spent dozens of hot summer days. Almadine associated swimming with public nudity so she never allowed her sons to play in the shallow waters, but that had never stopped John from sitting on the edge of the pool, his jeans rolled up to his knees, kicking water at a frolicking Chiara.

To the left of the pool Chiara noticed something new—well, new to her, given that she hadn't visited the park in awhile. Where there had once been a stand of evergreens stood a second playground to balance the one that had always existed to the right of the wading pool. The right side playground was for older children while the left side, with its shorter, fatter slides, squat merry-go-round and seesaw, and swings outfitted with safety bars was clearly for toddlers. The red reclining baby swings drew Chiara's eye. Even though the swings held fluffy blankets of undisturbed snow, Chiara had no trouble picturing a tiny baby bundled up and strapped into the seat for a glorious ride in the shade of the inter-locked canopies of giant oaks and elms. Shaking that image free from her brain, Chiara moved on.

She came to the wide cobbled road separating the north side of the park from the south, and she spent a moment gazing at the Turkish pavilion under which she and John Mahoney had once pretended to be guardians of the cave hiding Ali Baba's treasure.

She skirted outside the nimbus of light provided by a pair of iron lampposts on either side of the road as she crossed it, and then she disappeared behind a thick wall of well-manicured yew bushes.

Pausing, she took the time to savor the sight before her. She loved Tower Grove Park, and before her stood the ruins, one of the reasons why.

She never felt that she was truly home until she'd visited the ruins. The scene was more beautiful than she could have hoped, certainly more so than she remembered. The big willows, their feathery branches glistening with ice and snow, stood still in the windless night as they hung over the big reflecting pool with the stone fountain.

Turned off for the season, the fountain was the centerpiece of the pool, which was so full of snow Chiara couldn't distinguish the brick-lined drop-off from the even ground surrounding it.

Snow began to fall steadily and softly, and so quietly that Chiara had the feeling that she'd stepped into a postcard of the park in winter.

She broke out of her reverie to circle to the incomplete stone wall edging the far side of the reflecting pool. The wall, built from bricks salvaged from the demolition of the Lindell Hotel over a century ago, was the mock ruin that had given the area its name. Chiara automatically went to the archway in the wall and counted three bricks in and four bricks down. She had to kick away a good foot of snow to find the brick with the chink, which marked the "hidey hole," the secret mailbox that she and John Mahoney had dug out two decades ago.

The hidey hole had been created during one of their more elaborate childhood adventures, a game called Runaway to the Railroad, which had been inspired by a fifth-grade school assignment about St. Louis abolitionist Mary Meachum, a free black woman who hatched a plan to help nine runaway slaves flee the slave state of Missouri across the Mississippi River into free Illinois. John had portrayed one of the slaves, with Chiara in the role of Meachum.

John, who knew a thing or two about being treated like a captive, had thrown himself into the part with such vigor that Sybille Hasse—who'd been minding her own business sucking on a Pixy Stick before Chiara drafted her to play the role of the St. Louis sheriff who'd foiled Meachum's plan—had fled the park in tears after being directed to turn John over to slave catchers, played by twin brothers Roy and Randy Cates.

Roy and Randy, their identical blue eyes flashing, their duplicate blonde, bowl-cut hairdos swinging, had looked like bookends as they'd wrestled a struggling John into wrist shackles made of Chiara's knee socks.

Mrs. Hasse later made a visit to Abby Winters, which had forced Chiara and John to file away Runaway to the Railroad with their other banned favorites: The William Tell Game, The Electric People Game, and The Cannibal Game.

They'd grown older and abandoned their imaginary pursuits for more intimate games at the ruins, but Chiara and John had never outgrown the hidey hole. As had been her habit through the years, Chiara eagerly pulled out the heavy blonde brick and stuck her mittened hand into the hole. She broke into her first smile in over a week when she withdrew a tiny white box tied with white satin ribbon.

She and John would exchange Christmas gifts properly later, so she didn't expect anything extravagant as she pulled the ribbon free from the box. She lifted the tiny lid and laughed out loud when she saw a tiny stack of four postage-stamp sized chocolates.

The treats were frozen solid, but that didn't stop Chiara from hastily undressing one of them and popping it into her mouth. The taste of rich dark chocolate flavored with anise coated her tongue and filled her with warmth. For years, she and John had communicated through gumballs, shoestring licorice, Bazooka Joe comics, oddly colored stones and whatever else they thought would be of interest to each other. Chuckling, Chiara replaced the brick, thanking her lucky stars that John's taste in hidey hole trinkets had matured, just as he had.

She felt a little guilty, though. She was so consumed with her feelings about Zhou, she hadn't thought to bring an offering for John. Her last visit to the ruins had been in June, when she'd popped into town for two days to meet newborn Niema. John had left a tiny piece of beach glass for her, a keepsake he'd collected during a weekend they'd spent in St. Kitts. Chiara had left nothing for him, and despite that, he'd gone and filled the hole in anticipation of her Christmas visit.

The park was a favorite spot of all the Winters girls. But for Chiara, John was the reason the ruins were so special.

Chiara used her foot to kick the snow back in front of the secret brick, and she thought about the sunny day she first met John Mahoney. Every Sunday, her Grandma Claire would send her, Kyla and Cady to Magnolia Baptist Church for the mid-day service, and every Sunday, fifteen-year-old Cady would steer her younger sisters left, into Tower Grove Park, instead of right, into the church.

After pooling the offering meant for the church, they would go to the 7-Eleven on Morganford and buy Razzles and Slurpees, then go to the ruins. Usually, Cady would lie in the shade of a linden tree reading whatever book she was currently in, while eleven-year-old Kyla danced about the sun-bleached stones, lost in one of her fantasies about charming princes. At eight, Chiara was content to sit at the edge of the reflecting pool, weaving crowns made of dandelions, or making leaf tents for the caterpillars she caught.

The best Sundays were the ones when all three sisters played together, when Cady forgot to be a moody, bossy teenager and Kyla allowed them to share her colorful imaginings.

The ruins didn't belong to them, but they'd been accustomed to having the place to themselves on Sundays. On the day they discovered John Mahoney, the pastor's grandson, sitting on the wall as though awaiting their arrival, they'd each felt a sense of dread. For Chiara, who was in the same class as John at school, that dread had been mixed with fury.

"What are you doing here?" she'd demanded of the scrawny little brown boy in his austere black suit. His hazel-grey eyes twinkling, he'd said nothing as he watched Cady and Kyla withdraw to the opposite side of the ruins.

"I'm playing with you," John had told her.

Rolling her eyes, Chiara had stalked back to her sisters. But under John's friendly stare, it had been impossible to get back into the swing of their game. Every Sunday thereafter, John would sit on the wall, most of the time arriving before Chiara and her sisters, and all he would do was sit on the wall, sweating in his Sunday suit.

Everything changed the day Cady directed her sisters in an adventure inspired by her latest read, *The Three Musketeers*. She'd had no problem casting the roles of Porthos and Artemis, but she'd only managed to confuse herself trying to play both Athos and D'Artagnan.

"Hey you," Cady had called to the sweaty boy on the wall. "Do you want to be a Musketeer?"

Before Cady's inquiry was complete, John had leaped from the wall with a battle cry of "All for one and one for all!" And from that moment on, their drafted D'Artagnan had truly become their fourth Musketeer. It wasn't until months later that Chiara learned how much John's participation in their Sunday activities had cost him.

Where John was a wildly enthusiastic participant in their Sunday play dates, on Mondays, at school, he would keep to himself. While Chiara was bossing as many kids as she could in games of Freeze Tag and Four-Square during recess, John would retreat to the big sweet gum tree in the farthest corner of the schoolyard. From a distance, he would watch Chiara's games, and she in turn would peep at him, wondering how he could be so animated and imaginative at the park and such a dud at school.

The first day she joined him under the sweet gum tree was the last time she ever played at recess. She'd approached him at the tree close to the end of their second grade year. John had sat with his knees pulled up to his chin and his arms circled around his knees. He'd hidden his face in the hollow formed by his arms, but Chiara could still hear him sniffling.

"What's the matter with you?" she'd asked as indifferently as she could.

"My back hurts," John had said, his voice congested with tears.

"Did you hurt it yesterday at the park?"

Without lifting his head, John shook it.

Chiara's eyes moved over him, seeing nothing out of the ordinary until her gaze landed on the short sleeves of his St. Louis Cardinals T-shirt. The skin of his right arm, just at the edge of his cuff, was striped with painful looking red welts.

"You got a whippin' yesterday?" Chiara had asked in horror.

"My mother whips me every Sunday," John had confessed into his arms.

"What for?" Chiara had demanded angrily. "What'd you do?"

"I go to the park."

Chiara hadn't known how to respond, other than to sit close to John and bark at any child who dared come near them. The next Sunday when John showed up at the park, he and Chiara played with their usual abandon, but also with a sense of defiance that made their games more enjoyable. And on

Monday, when John retreated into his own world of hurt, Chiara willingly kept him company.

She pulled herself from the ancient memory that remained ever fresh in her heart and mind and tucked the remaining chocolates into her pocket. In coming to the ruins, she'd realized what would truly make her feel better in the aftermath of Zhou's death. Quickening her step, she made her way back to John's house.

CHAPTER THREE

Chiara had purchased the mukluks because she liked the way they looked, but as she crept around the Mahoney house, careful to remain close to the line of evergreens, Chiara was thankful for their stealth properties. The same qualities that enabled Yup'ik hunters to move about undetected allowed Chiara to hunt in secret too. Only her prey had two legs rather than four.

She peeped into the windows, ducking quickly whenever anyone turned his or her gaze her way. The Mahoney living room was large, with vaulted ceilings and wide, open spaces. It was probably twice the size of her mother's, which had been packed with family and friends.

She moved on to the next set of windows, those belonging to the dining room. Tables draped in white linen and topped with Almadine's fine silver lined one long wall. Gleaming Versailles-styled chafing dishes steamed atop the tables, and Chiara's stomach grumbled when she eyed a five-tiered tower of sterling silver platters heavy with pastries covered in chocolate shavings, powdered sugar, colorful icings and glazed fruit. There was enough food to feed the entire neighborhood, yet Chiara could count only ten or eleven people in the house.

One person stepped up to the dessert tower. He wore tailored grey slacks and a sleek black lamb's wool sweater the same dark hue as his neat afro. The sweater fit him perfectly, nicely highlighting his broad chest and shoulders and complementing the warmth of his pecan skin. Having given him the sweater a year ago, Chiara knew from experience that the sweater was as soft as it looked.

She took off one of her mittens and softly tapped her fingernails against the window.

The man swung his head from the assortment of éclairs and turned toward the window. Chiara had been looking at John Mahoney's face for more than twenty years. She knew every line, every plane, every hollow and every quirk of expression. Yet when he turned her way, his brows slightly knitted in curiosity; Chiara was struck dumb by his beauty.

Men weren't supposed to be beautiful, but John couldn't accurately be described any other way. He'd been a good head shorter than she until eighth grade, when he returned from a six-week summer bible camp twenty pounds thinner and four inches taller than Chiara. Through high school his slender frame had filled out with muscle built from playing soccer, baseball and running track.

He'd become a real heartthrob at Hamilton-Foxx High with his trademark head of wild curls. The longer John's hair grew, the looser the curls became, and girls—teachers, even—couldn't keep their hands off it, despite glares and threats of violence from Chiara.

It was Cady who'd taken one look at John's out-of-control hairdo and dubbed him Mahofro, a name that had stuck once Chiara delivered it to the rest of the student body.

John had allowed Chiara to shear him prior to the start of their freshman year at George Washington University, and he'd kept the same neat look ever since. As many times as she'd passed her hands over his soft, fragrant curls, looking at him now Chiara couldn't wait to get her hands on him again.

John's gaze traveled in her direction, but he was looking too high. Chiara exhaled a puff of air on the windowpane, producing a blank canvas of condensation. She used her fingertip to write !YEH on the glass. John's eyes instantly went to the message. His fine, full mouth drew into a tiny smile, but he made no other outward sign that he'd seen her. He set down his dessert plate. Chiara furiously shook her head, and John caught her meaning. He took his plate with him and exited into the living room. Chiara had to press her cheek up to the glass to follow his progress. He spoke a few words to someone near the stairwell before he backed a step up the stairs, then turned and bolted up and out of sight.

Cecile Brunner's thorny young vines had been cut back for the winter. Her oldest, thickest vines provided lots of sturdy hand and footholds free of thorns for Chiara to shimmy up the trellis. As she neared the roof overhanging the front porch, John's window opened. Chiara launched herself up and into his waiting arms and allowed him to help her into his room.

"The fact that it's Christmas Eve won't stop my mother from shooting you if she catches you here," John said. His dire warning was accompanied by a smile that took the last of the chill from Chiara's heart. Without a word, she locked her arms around his neck and pressed her body into his, absorbing as much of his warmth as she could.

John's arms moved into her coat to embrace her, his hands strong and comforting at her back and waist. "I heard about Zhou. I'm sorry."

Chiara's eyes stung, but for the time being, she had no more tears to cry. "It was all over the news in Chicago and Mr. Grayson sent out a company-wide e-mail about it. I still can't believe he's gone."

John sighed heavily, and Chiara felt herself move along with his body. "You never know what's going on with people," he said into the top of her head. "Everything can look fine on the surface, but underneath it might be all rotten and ugly."

She drew away from him and picked at the plate of desserts he'd brought up. "You sound like your mother. 'Everything may be all lush and green on top, but underneath you have worms sucking on filth and decay.' "

"I didn't say that," John gently corrected. "You know that's not what I meant." He reached for her.

Chiara let him take her hand and walk her to the narrow bed he'd slept on for most of his childhood. He sat her on the stiff mattress, which was covered in a frothy pinkish-white Chenille duvet that was a far cry from the western and space age motifs John had favored as a boy.

"Zhou was the real deal," Chiara insisted, her voice tightening. "What you saw was what he was. Did he ever strike you as the type who needed tranquilizers and sleep aids?"

"No, but maybe it was the medication that kept him on such an even keel." John helped Chiara out of her coat and draped it over the straight back of his mother's office chair. "You and Zhou were close, but I'm sure he drew the line at discussing his mental health issues with you."

Chiara scooted farther onto the bed to rest against the backboard. She drew one foot up to the duvet.

"Nice boots," John chuckled. "Is your woolly mammoth parked outside?"

"I love these boots." Chiara stretched out a leg and examined her big, furry foot. "I could do jumping jacks up here in these and Almadine would never know it."

John cleared his throat, his eyes tracing the length of Chiara's leg. She wore form-fitting white pants and a matching mock turtleneck. White was Chiara's best color, and she looked like a snow princess lounging on his old bed. The cold had put rosy kisses on the honey-brown plumps of her cheeks. If not for the sadness dulling the dark of her big pretty eyes, he would have crawled onto the bed with her, pulled the candy-colored duvet over them, and replaced the kiss of the cold with kisses of his own. Knowing exactly what she needed, John sat beside her and curled an arm around her.

Chiara readily nestled into his side, grateful for his solidness and concern. Her eyes moved over the gold-flocked wallpaper and blinding white moldings Almadine had installed after John left home. She didn't have to try hard to see the room as it had been during John's adolescence, when posters of planets and distant galaxies covered the walls, darkening the room to the point where Almadine referred to it as "John's cave." The hardwood floor, now covered with a plush pinkish-white carpet, had been a minefield of telltale squeaks. Even now when she had first entered his room, her feet had remembered where to step to keep the floor from betraying her presence.

Almadine had kept John's old narrow twin, but she'd converted it into a day bed. John's body was much taller and wider than it had been when he'd last lain in the bed, and his masculinity overwhelmed the extreme girliness of the room.

"What are you thinking about?" John asked.

"Work," Chiara answered. "Mr. Grayson was acting really odd before I left. Odder than usual."

"Yeah, he's a weird cat," John agreed with a yawn.

Chiara tipped her face up to his. "Sleepy?"

"My mother's prayer meeting was more boring than usual this year. Granddaddy opened the meeting with a sermon about keeping Christ's birthday holy."

"Christ was born in March, not December. How come we don't keep that day in March holy?"

"December, March, it doesn't matter," John said. "My grandfather keeps every day holy."

"Did your mom invite Mrs. Coopersmith?" Chiara chuckled.

"No, they haven't recovered from their last falling out. My mother's not the forgiving type to begin with, and when Mrs. Coopersmith told her that she liked Kyla's cookbook, my mother hit the roof."

"Why? Just because my sister wrote a good book?"

"My mother hates that your family is so successful," John said.

"No, she hates us, period," Chiara clarified. An old anger began to stew deep in Chiara's chest. Almadine Mahoney, from the first moment she'd met Chiara, had decided that she didn't like her. In retrospect, Chiara realized that Almadine wouldn't have liked any girl who'd shown an interest in John or his brother George. But when Mrs. Mahoney began actively searching for reasons to turn John against her, Chiara gave up on any attempt to earn the woman's respect or admiration.

"To this day she doesn't believe that my father was killed covering a story in the Middle East," Chiara said. "She thinks he ran off with some other woman. Remember when she came to school for our fifth-grade play? She took one look at Cady, Kyla and me and had the nerve to ask me if my sisters and I had the same father."

She drew her face into a severe scowl and pinched her voice into a parody of Almadine's and said, " 'Your sister Cady is so much yellower than you, and your sister Kyla has a much thinner build. You're half-sisters, aren't you?' " Using her own angry voice, Chiara added, "I didn't even know what a half-sister was, so I said 'I don't know,' like some dumbass."

John curled her deeper into an embrace. "Don't let memories of my mother's bad behavior upset you now." He chuckled darkly. "She's going to have something bigger to rage about soon enough. Save your strength for that."

Chiara harrumphed. Inside, she wished that she could tell Almadine off once and for all.

"How are you feeling?" John tenderly stroked her arm through the warm knit jersey of her turtleneck. "Have you told your family about us yet?"

"I haven't told anyone. I think Mr. Grayson thinks I'm hiding something, though. Right before I left, he sent me an e-mail saying that he was personally overseeing the inspection of the inventory, receipts and financial transactions made by me and Zhou on this last sales trip."

"Yes, I know," John said. "There's not much that happens at USITI that the information systems department doesn't know. We're the electronic mailroom of the whole company. We know who's getting fired, who's getting hired, and who's getting pegged for an internal investigation."

"Why didn't you call and tell me that Zhou and I were being audited internally?"

"Mr. Grayson calls for internal audits of financials and e-mail accounts all the time. They're the technological equivalent of random drug tests. You and Zhou were overdue for an audit. You're not hiding anything, are you?" John teased.

"Of course not."

"Well, that's why I didn't tell you. I didn't think it was a big deal. According to the scope of the audit, Mr. Grayson is more interested in Zhou than in you."

"Even so, I swear, that man can smell a secret."

"He couldn't smell Zhou's," John pointed out.

"I told you," Chiara insisted. "Zhou was not using drugs. I would have known. He was distraught about something in Tokyo, and he'd had a little too much booze, but he wasn't strung out or high. He was upset, and he never told me why.

"Who knows, maybe that was the secret he was keeping from me," Chiara reluctantly considered. "Maybe he did have a problem with prescription drugs. It's not like we weren't exposed to samples from just about every pharmaceutical manufacturer in North America and Asia."

John brushed his lips across Chiara's crown. "Everyone has secrets, Chi."

"What's yours, John?"

"Same as yours, baby," he smiled softly.

"May I assume that you haven't shared your secret with Almadine?"

John winced on a sharp intake of breath. "Hell, no. I've got enough to figure out without my mother screeching about hellfire and white-hot pitchforks poking at my private parts."

"Is there a problem with the new office?" Chiara draped one leg over John's and turned her hip into him, bringing her thigh closer to John's aforementioned parts. "You're the wonder boy of USITI's information systems. Mr. Grayson wouldn't have put you in charge of establishing the St. Louis hub if he thought you couldn't handle it."

"I've got USITI covered. I'm going to Chicago right after New Year's to give Mr. Grayson my December status report." He leaned over Chiara, reaching past her to the walnut end table supporting a squat brass lamp. "It's this I can't figure out." He grabbed a square of black paper about the size of a credit card and placed it in Chiara's hand. "You got me, baby."

Chiara examined the tiny black paper and saw that it was actually an envelope bearing a broken USITI security seal. She opened it and shook out a clear plastic card bearing a greenish-black square of silicon thinner and smaller than a standard stamp. She drew in a loud breath, releasing it on a shudder. Cold dread bloomed in her fingertips and spread inward until it clutched at her heart, making it difficult for her to breathe. "Th-This is USITI property," she stammered. "Mr. Grayson…Zhou must have…how did you get this?"

John sat up and turned a bit sideways to fully face her. "It was in the hidey hole last week," he explained, his forehead drawn in taut lines of concern. "What is it, Chiara?"

"It's a master chip," she told him, her voice cracking. Her head swam with nausea as sick understanding moved through her. Closing the chip in her fist, she stood up and anxiously paced the floor, mindless of the creaky areas beneath the carpet. Hands on her hips, she bent her knees and leaned forward. "I think I'm going to be sick."

John shot off of the bed, took her by the shoulders and steered her into the tiny half bath adjoining the room. He helped her lean over the toilet, and his own internal alarm system flared as he smoothed her hair back from her suddenly sweaty brow.

"It's just a microchip," John started. "What's the big deal?"

Chiara tightly gripped the edge of the pearly pink basin with one hand and bowed her head over it. "No, it's not. This is bad, John, it's really bad."

"I installed it, but I couldn't read it," John said lightly. "It's password protected. No harm, no foul, baby."

She angrily displayed the microchip. "This is it!" she hissed. "This is the chip that Mr. Grayson is looking for. Zhou took it! And for reasons known only to him, he put it in a place where one of us was sure to find it!" She collapsed onto the lid of the closed toilet and squinted her eyes behind her hand. "What was he thinking?" Tears of confusion and fear burst from her eyes. "What could he have possibly been thinking when he came all the way to St. Louis to bury this chip?"

John quietly dampened a white washcloth with cool water. He used it to mop Chiara's tears, then her forehead, before he folded the cloth in thirds and laid it across her nape. He leaned against the edge of the basin, his arms loosely folded across his chest, his head lowered in thought. Zhou's death…Grayson's internal investigation…Chiara's   distress…a   missing microchip…John raised his head and fixed his eyes on Chiara.

"Maybe this was Zhou's way of telling you that he was in trouble," John carefully suggested. "Maybe…maybe he knew that his life was in danger."

Chiara opened her hand once more and looked at the chip. Whatever Zhou's problem was, Chiara knew that she'd now inherited it.

John left her in the bathroom splashing cold water on her face while he crept downstairs for coffee. By the time he returned, Chiara had calmed and was sitting on the bed. The master chip was back in its envelope and basking in the light of the brass lamp, but Chiara couldn't seem to take her eyes off it.

John handed her a delicate bone china cup filled to the brim with steaming black coffee. "How did Zhou know about our hidey hole?" he asked, easing onto the bed so as not to make Chiara spill her hot coffee.

"I told him about it ages ago. We got to know each other pretty well during our day-long flights to the Far East."

"What do master chips do?"

"I don't know," she sighed. "We sell the R-GS chips to our clients, then Zhou programs the sales codes for that lot of R-GS chips onto the master. Once the full block of R-GS chips is sold, the master is filled up and Zhou turns it in to Mr. Grayson."

"So that thing is a form of inventory control?"

Chiara nodded. "I suppose."

"Zhou hid it in a place you were sure to find it, so he must have meant for you to do something with it."

Chiara shook her head. "Not me. You. You're the one in information systems. You're the computer expert."

"I tried to install it, Chiara. There's nothing I or anyone else can do with it unless they know the password to enable the chip. Zhou made a mistake."

Chiara sipped her coffee, certain that no truer words had ever been said.

"What do you think we should do with it?" John wondered aloud.

"I think we should turn it in to Mr. Grayson when I go back to work next week."

Something in her voice gave John pause. "What do you *want* to do with it?"

"My partner might have lost his life over that chip. He left it for us to find for a reason. I think we ought to find out what that reason is before we give the chip back to Mr. Grayson."

Gripping his head in both hands, John leaned back and released a long sigh. "I had a feeling you'd say that."

"Mama?"

Chiara quietly closed the front door behind her. Even though her mukluks were totally silent against the thin Persian runner leading from the foyer, she tiptoed, sincerely hoping not to arouse any more attention than necessary from the family and friends remaining in the house.

The house wasn't as full as it had been earlier when she'd first cased it, and she was thankful. She was even less in a mood for an onslaught of great aunts and unfamiliar family friends than she'd been before.

"Mama?" she dared once more after peeping into the living room and finding it empty, and then veering left at the empty stairwell to enter the abandoned dining room. She paused at the Victorian black pine buffet against the wall adjacent to the swinging door leading into the kitchen. Even though the buffet had been cleared, Chiara could still smell the savory scents of her mother's cooking in the air. Spice-encrusted eye of round roast, baked chicken with bay leaves and oregano, a baked ham with cloves, pineapple rings, maraschino cherries and her mother's delicious cinnamon-orange glaze…For the first time since Zhou's death, Chiara felt the vague rumblings of an appetite.

She gently pushed open the swinging door, willing the old hinges to keep their silence. Abby Winters, her matronly figure dressed in Christmas red, a linen apron embroidered with holly and jingle bells tied about her waist, stood at the sink, her back to the door and Chiara.

She hummed as she rinsed her best bone china plates before arranging them neatly in the lower rack of her big dishwasher. The tune was not one that Chiara recognized, but the warm, melodic sound started a much-needed feeling of security and comfort welling in Chiara's heart. She hadn't realized how much she'd missed the sound of her mother's voice, the warmth of her embrace. It was all she could do not to tackle Abby and wrestle her into a fierce bear hug.

"Mama," she said sharply, her nose tingling with the threat of tears.

"What is it, baby?" Abby said casually, turning.

Chiara watched her mother's eyes. With five daughters, "What is it, baby?" was Abby's rote response to the sound of the word "Mama." Chiara always enjoyed the moment of recognition, when

Abby actually looked at her and registered who she was.

"Merry Christmas, baby!" Abby squealed. In a flash, she had crossed the kitchen and had tugged Chiara into a tight but soggy embrace. "Oh, I know I'm ruining your big fancy fur coat, but I don't care," she exclaimed. "I'm so happy you're here!"

Chiara was the shortest of Abby's daughters, but she still had an inch or two over her mother. She allowed her mother to enfold her into her arms and hold her as close to her heart as she could. She breathed deeply of her mother's rose-scented silvering hair, wallowing in the special treatment she seemed to receive as the baby of the family.

Abby withdrew too soon and took Chiara by her upper arms. "You must be hungry," she declared. After helping Chiara out of her coat, she scanned her from head to toe. "Oh baby," she sighed sadly, her shoulders slumping a bit. "You've lost so much weight since the last time I saw you."

Chiara cupped her elbows and lowered her eyes. "I'm fine, Mama. Just a little bit tired."

"Yes, well, grief can wear you out." Abby hung Chiara's coat on a hook mounted on the wall near the back door before seating Chiara on a stool at the butcher-block preparation island in the middle of the kitchen and bustling back to the refrigerator. The stainless steel vault, a recent gift from Kyla and Zweli, was almost as large as those found in restaurants. When Abby swung open the door, Chiara's eyes widened at the enormous assortment of leftovers arranged on the deep, wide shelves.

"Would you like some ham?" Abby asked, heaving out the gigantic platter before Chiara could answer. "You're definitely going to have to try some of my winter squash medley. It came out so beautifully. It's one of Kyla's recipes, from her cookbook. You have a copy of it, don't you?"

Chiara nodded. "Kyla gave me one when I was home in June."

"I gave you what in June?" Kyla said, entering the kitchen from the hallway. She went straight to Chiara and swallowed her up in a hug. "Glad you made it, road runner." She glanced at the digital clock built into the stove. "And with an hour to spare. I suppose this counts as being home before Christmas."

Chiara's eyes slightly narrowed. Of all her sisters, Kyla was the one who continually gave her the hardest time about keeping away from the family so much. Chiara wondered if Kyla ever listened to the pointed comments she made—if she had any idea how they actually sounded to the person she aimed them at.

"I got here as soon as I could," Chiara said with a defiant tilt of her chin. "I work for a living, you know."

"So I've heard. Mama says that you and Chen Zhou were the top-selling sales duo at United States IntelTechnologies." Kyla half-heartedly punched the air in a fake salute to her sister's success. "Gotta peddle those microchips, come hell or high water, I guess."

At the opposite end of the prep island, Kyla leaned one elegant hand on the butcher-block top. She was gorgeous in a slinky red dress that highlighted her caramel-gold complexion and the best parts of her new figure. The birth of her daughter had given her body a lushness that it had lacked during her days as a struggling actress in California. With the recent success of her cookbook, the birth of her daughter and the post-production work she was doing on her first feature film, Kyla radiated confidence and self-assurance, the two things Chiara suddenly felt herself lacking as she continued to kindle the fight with her sister.

"It must be nice to be able to come home whenever you please," Chiara said. "Those of us with *real* jobs don't have that luxury."

"Zweli and I make the time to be with the people we love," Kyla said. "Don't get mad at me because you broke your word to Mama."

"I didn't break my word," Chiara fired back. "I said I'd be home before Christmas, and as you pointed out, Christmas is a good hour away."

"Now, now, girls." Abby turned away from the Ziploc bag of dinner rolls she had just opened. "You haven't been together for two minutes, and you're already fighting. It's time you grew out of this constant bickering."

Scowling sullenly, Chiara reluctantly agreed with Abby. She and Kyla had always been at each other's throats, usually over nothing. And usually Kyla started the nothing. "I had a funeral to go to," Chiara put in. "I got here as soon as I could."

Kyla used an index finger to gracefully tuck a lock of her glossy dark hair behind her right ear. "Mama said that that funeral was on Saturday. That was almost a week ago. You could have come home sooner."

Chiara pursed her lips. Yes, she could have come home sooner…if she'd felt like being suffocated by questions and concern from her mother and sisters. Chiara suddenly realized that John was lucky. He had only one domineering battleaxe of a mother. Chiara had five.

Blithely chewing the corner of a dinner roll nicked from the plate Abby was preparing for Chiara, Kyla blew her most lethal verbal dart. "I don't see why you went to Chen Zhou's funeral. You couldn't be bothered to come home for Grandma Claire's."

Chiara slammed her fists on the butcher block. "Zhou wasn't just my partner, he was my friend. I don't have to defend my decision to go to his funeral! As for Grandma Claire, *I couldn't come home!*" erupted from her with a furious burst of hot tears. "I tried to! I wanted to, but Mr. Grayson wouldn't let me leave until Zhou and I had signed our new clients, and by the time we were done, it was too late!"

"Why are you bringing that up, Ky?" Abby accused. "That was…" Abby's mouth went slack. "Good Lord, that was five years ago today, wasn't it?"

Kyla nodded, her jaw stiff with emotion. "I just think it's important for us…for *all* of us…to be together at Christmas."

Chiara angrily swiped at her tears. She was thirty years old, but no matter how old she got, she always felt like a helpless kid around her big sisters. "It's important to me, too," she said. "And I'm sorry I wasn't here sooner. I'm sorry I wasn't here when Grandma Claire passed. I didn't have much of a choice."

She bit back a bitter laugh. Her final statement perfectly summed up her experience working for USITI. She had never felt threatened, exactly, but she'd always felt pressured to place the job above all else. She hadn't minded because she'd always been able to balance the pressure against her level of success. She'd enjoyed the travel and knowing that she was the best at what she did. Above all else, USITI had given her the chance to thrive well out of the bright light cast by her overachieving big sisters. But as she stood facing off against Kyla, her longest and most beloved adversary, Chiara wished that she'd found her spotlight a little closer to home.

Abby rushed to Chiara and crushed her into a hug. As though she was five years old again and crying over a skinned knee, Chiara clung to her mother and sobbed, her petite frame shaking.

"Baby?" Abby questioned, her concern evident in her voice. "Oh my Lord, child, what's gotten into you?"

"Guilt, probably," Kyla muttered.

"Would you just shut the hell up?" Chiara shouted in a wet spray of tears.

"Hey, ladies, what's going on in here?" Zweli Randall, Kyla's husband, hurried into the kitchen. "I just got the baby down and I'd like her to get a good night's sleep. She's going to need it tomorrow for her first Christ—" He spotted Chiara, who raised her face from her mother's shoulder.

"Hey, Zweli," Chiara said, drying her eyes on Abby's shoulder.

"Chiara," Zweli greeted warmly, stealing her away from Abby to give her a long, tight squeeze. He pressed a loud kiss to her forehead. "Good to see you, baby sister."

"At least one Randall is glad to see me." She shot a dark look around Zweli at Kyla.

He released her and stood between the two sisters like a referee, a very well dressed one, Chiara noted. Zweli wore his holiday finest, a pair of sleek trousers in grey worsted wool belted at his trim waist, and a crisp white shirt of Egyptian cotton so fine it looked like silk. He no longer had his stubby dreadlocks, and instead wore his hair in a longish but well-kept wavy afro. His green eyes sparkled as he looked from Chiara to Kyla.

"I'm glad to see you, Chi," Kyla said. "That's the whole point. I'd like to see you more frequently. You said you were moving home ages ago, and you still haven't done it."

"Speaking of home, Mrs. Randall, when does your husband plan to take you and your baby to yours? Soon, I hope?"

"I am home," Kyla said simply. "So are you. You'll be a lot happier once you figure that out."

CHAPTER FOUR

Her belly full after being permitted to eat in the kitchen in peace, Chiara quietly made her way upstairs to find an empty bedroom. The first bedroom she came to was her mother's. Abby was still in the kitchen clearing away Chiara's plate and drinking glass, despite Chiara's willingness to do it herself. The room across from Abby's was occupied, and Chiara could just make out three female voices, shrilly whispering.

"Don't put any tape on that corner, you'll make it bulge," came the first voice, which Chiara recognized as that of her thirteen-year-old niece, Danielle.

"It'll get out if we don't tape it up all over," fiercely whispered nine-year-old Abigail, never one to cower before her older cousin.

"What if it chews through the paper?" wondered Ella, who at seven seemed to be literally the voice of reason among the three.

"It doesn't eat paper," Danielle said. Chiara pictured the condescending roll of the eyes that probably accompanied Danielle's declaration.

"It might rip up the paper with its claws, though," Abigail offered.

"Maybe we should put tape all over it," Danielle considered.

"But poke some holes so it can breathe," Ella reminded them.

"Clarence is gonna love this present!" Abigail said.

Probably, Chiara silently agreed, acknowledging her eleven-year-old nephew's fondness for anything with fangs, fur, feathers, venom or claws.

Even though a seam of soft light shone at the bottom of the door of the room adjacent to the girls' room, Chiara thought it was probably empty. It was Abby's habit to leave table lamps burning in the rooms in the front of the house, especially on holidays. She stepped closer to grip the doorknob, but Kyla's quiet utterance of her name stopped her. Just as their bickering had carried over into adulthood, so had Chiara's tendency to eavesdrop at doorways. She kneeled in the corridor and gently pressed her ear to the keyhole.

"...not fair," came Zweli's voice. "Chiara's a grown woman, but you and your sisters treat her like she's still a ten-year-old in pigtails. I'm not sure I'd come home that often either, if folks jumped down my throat the way you did tonight."

"I couldn't help it," Kyla protested. "Christmas is still hard for me. Mama does the house up so nicely, and so many people always turn out for Christmas Eve and Christmas dinner. I should be happy, but I want all my sisters around me at the holidays. It keeps me from missing Grandma Claire so much."

"I know, honey."

"Chiara acts like she doesn't miss her at all," Kyla argued. "Grandma was so sick for so long, and Chiara didn't bother to show up once."

"People handle grief in different ways, baby, you know that. You were here when Claire passed, but you have to admit…you acted pretty stupid most of the time."

Kyla made a noise of indignation.

"You know you did, Ky. Has anyone thrown your behavior back in your face?"

"No," she grudgingly admitted.

"It's because we all knew how hard it was for you, dealing with Claire's death. We didn't hold your foolishness against you because we knew it was your way of dealing with everything."

"Chiara dealt with it by not dealing with it at all, and I'm supposed to respect that?" Kyla suggested testily.

"She did deal with it," Zweli said. "I was there a few times when Chiara was on the phone with Claire in the hospital. Claire's the one who told her not to come home. Maybe there were some things your grandmother knew about your sister that you didn't."

"Like what?" Kyla scoffed.

"Like maybe Chiara wouldn't have gotten through it as well as you and the rest of your sisters did. Chiara might just be one of those people who are better off alone, doing their own thing, instead of being in the thick of everything."

In the next moment of silence, Kyla seemed to contemplate her husband's words of wisdom. "Chiara's always pulled away from us," she said.

Not pulled, Chiara thought. *I was pushed.*

"All right," Kyla sighed. "I'll let it go. This is Niema's first Christmas. I don't want her hearing her aunty and her mama fighting."

The light under the door disappeared with a faint click, and Chiara heard the bedsprings twang in response to the movement atop them.

"You'd better go to sleep, Mrs. Randall, or Santa won't bring you any presents," Zweli said.

"Santa won't mind if we stay up a little longer," Kyla replied. "Not if he knew what I plan to give you tonight."

"I don't want to wake up Niema," Zweli protested weakly.

"Then you'd better be quiet, Dr. Randall," Kyla whispered. The rest of her words were too soft for Chiara to hear, but there was no mistaking the meaning behind Kyla's silky laughter and Zweli's moaned responses. Embarrassed by her intrusiveness, Chiara moved on to the second set of stairs.

Abby had remodeled the attic, converting most of it into a spacious bedroom suite complete with a master bath, and the rest of it into well-organized storage area. Chiara recalled the e-mail her sister Cady had sent her, bemoaning the loss of the chaos of disarray and dust-covered junk that she had loved all her life. Once she reached the top of the attic stairs,

Chiara saw that Cady hadn't been too distressed by the renovation since she and her family were firmly settled in the "penthouse suite" for the night.

After knocking softly on the trapdoor and receiving permission to enter, Chiara raised the unlatched door and climbed up. Keren and Cady, snug in the new brass queen Abby had bullied two deliverymen into transporting up the two steep, narrow staircases, both held index fingers to their pursed lips. Chiara followed Cady's pointed look toward the opposite side of the room, where Cady's three-and-a-half-year-old twins, Samuel Keren and Claire Elizabeth, slept in the matching brass trundle bed. Cady regularly sent Chiara e-mails containing photos of the twins. Seeing Sammy and Claire nestled together like a yin and yang symbol—to Chiara's eyes—the twins couldn't possibly look more adorable.

The contents of the ancient crib next to Cady's side of the bed quickly stole Chiara's full attention. Virginia, almost a year and a half old, slept on her chest and knees with her tiny round backside pushed into the air. Cady's youngest had her mother's honey-gold complexion and her father's full, sculpted mouth in miniature. Her black curls were all her own.

"She's so beautiful, Cady," Chiara sighed, thinking that the baby looked as compact as a packaged meat-loaf in her long-sleeved Onesie. The side of the crib, the same crib she and her sisters had used in infancy, squeaked in protest when Chiara rested her forearms on the rail and leaned on it.

"Let sleeping beauty lie," Cady advised in a soft voice. "If she wakes up, the twins will get up and think it's time to open presents."

"Time to open the ones they haven't already opened," Keren said, closing the book he'd been reading. He moved a pair of heavy, black-framed glasses from his nose to the crown of his shaved head. "Clarence organized a raid of the tree after dinner tonight. Abigail, Ella and the twins had opened half their gifts before we found them in the basement under a mountain of wrapping and ribbons."

"Santa won't look too kindly on that," Chiara said absently as she lightly brushed her fingertips over Virginia's silky black curls.

"One of Santa's elves took all the rest of their presents and hid them," Cady said as she fluffed her own multi-colored curls with her fingers. "They're going to be awfully surprised in the morning when they don't have anything to open, the little brats."

"They aren't brats," Chiara said, her eyes fixed unblinkingly on Virginia. "They're angels."

"Angels with no appreciation for delayed gratification," Cady said. "Are you all right?"

Chiara looked up from the baby to see Cady peering at her, her eyebrows drawn together.

"I'm fine." Chiara quickly straightened and moved to sit on the foot of the bed. "I'm just a little tired. It's been a long week."

"I'm sorry about your partner," Keren said. He reached toward the rocking chair beside his night table and drew forth the navy pajama top he'd discarded. Chiara couldn't help staring at the stack of chiseled abdominal muscles moving beneath her brother-in-law's mahogany skin as he put the top on. The attic was always a bit too warm, as evidenced by Cady's simple sleeveless cotton nightgown, so Chiara knew that Keren was dressing for her benefit.

"When did you start wearing glasses?" Chiara asked, forcing her tone to be lighter than she felt.

"About a month ago," Keren grumbled. He pulled the glasses off, carefully folded them and set them on the nightstand.

"Keren turned forty this year." Cady hid a smile behind her loosely curled fingers. "They always say that the eyesight is the first to go."

"I see just fine, woman," Keren stated emphatically. "There's just too much fine print in the world."

"Lower your voice," Cady said softly. "Let Wynken, Blynken and Nod get a good night's sleep."

"What are you going to call the next one?" Chiara asked, shifting her gaze to the light flannel blanket covering Cady's midsection.

"No idea." Cady set her hands over her abdomen, and Keren moved closer to her, to cover one of her hands with his. "It's an inconclusive at this point."

"A what?" Chiara wondered.

"My twenty-week ultrasound was inconclusive. The baby's legs are folded, so the technician couldn't get a clear picture of the gender."

"It's a girl," Cady remarked as Keren said, "It's a boy."

Chiara wistfully gazed at Virginia. "It doesn't matter."

"So," Cady started, "what were you and Kyla shouting about downstairs?"

Chiara stared at her, wide-eyed. "You heard us all the way up here?"

"We heard *you*," Cady said. "You've always had a voice that travels. Kyla's the trained actress. She knows how to moderate."

Chiara snorted. "I don't know where she gets off telling me how to live my life. I'm not the only one who's spent a lot of time away from home. Clara lived on the West Coast and you lived on the East Coast for years, and Kyla…that dumb chump traveled all over, too, filming her stupid *Lifeguards* television show. That movie she signed on to do in June took her across half the United States for four months, and not only that, she dragged Zweli and her baby along with her! At least when I travel for my job, I don't uproot anybody! My job—" She caught up short, unable to defend anything about her job and the distance it had created between her and her family.

"What is it, Chi?" Cady asked.

Chiara shook her head, dismissing whatever she might have wanted to say.

"You may as well tell us what the matter is," Keren said. "Cady'll pull it out of you one way or the other."

"Nothing's wrong." Chiara aimed her lie at the baby's sleeping form.

"We heard the waterworks, kiddo," Cady told her. "Kyla hasn't made you cry like that since you were in braids. Something's up, isn't it?"

"It's nothing." Chiara stood and moved to kneel at the twins' bedside. "It's something at work. I can handle it." She was aware of her sister's gaze on her as she rested her hand on Sammy K.'s small back. She envied his complete obliviousness to what was going on around him. He and his twin shared the same breath, and Chiara envied that, too. She had been close to her siblings, but being the youngest, she'd never felt as though she'd been on an equal footing with them. Sammy K. and Claire had come into the world together and would always have someone on whom to depend.

She touched his freshly shorn curls, marveling at the beauty of his dark brown skin and his chubby cheeks. Sammy K. was the more active of the pair, the one who unfailingly followed his sister's mischievous schemes. Claire, with her dark honey complexion, ginger curls and long, sweeping eyelashes, could charm a saint into snatching candy from the Brach's display at the supermarket.

"Chiara?"

She tore herself from her contemplation of her niece and nephew and returned to the foot of the bed.

"They're going to be here tomorrow," Cady told her. "You don't have to fill up on them tonight. Why don't you go to bed? You'll feel better after a good night's sleep."

Chiara nodded. "I'll squeeze in with the girls, I guess."

"Mama hadn't counted on them staying the night, but they insisted," Cady said. "Clara and Ciel were glad to have them out of the way, so they could finish wrapping their gifts."

"Were the boys here tonight?"

Cady nodded. "Troy brought his new girlfriend. The girl wore him like a piece of jewelry."

"You just didn't like her." Keren nestled closer to Cady and punched his pillow before scrunching it under his head. "She was nice."

Cady glanced at the ceiling. "Nice and possessive."

"Troy seems to like her," Keren said.

"Troy is only eighteen years old, he has no idea what he likes."

"She's got big tits, doesn't she?" Chiara asked knowingly.

"They're the same size as her head," Cady scoffed.

"Then that's what Troy likes about her."

"How do you know so much about Troy's preferences?" Cady asked.

"He sent me an e-mail when I was in Tokyo. He wanted some Japanese anime graphic novels. He doesn't read Japanese, and the only other reason any red-blooded American teenager wants those books is because of the artwork. Big knockers feature prominently."

"C.J. brought his little cross-eyed girlfriend, too," Cady said. "You should have seen him. He got his license a few weeks ago, and he drove her here."

"Chris Jr. has a girlfriend?" Chiara smiled. "Do you hate her, too?"

"She's a sweetie, and I don't hate Troy's little floozy. I just think he can do better. He's going to Stanford in the fall. He shouldn't be hooking up with some hoochie." Cady lowered her voice. "She reminds me of some of Zweli's old girlfriends."

"That bad, huh?" Chiara chuckled lightly. "Hopefully, it's just a phase he's going through."

"It took Zweli twenty years to outgrow his phase," Cady pointed out.

"Yes, but look at him now," Keren said. "He's a happily married family man."

"So, Chiara," Cady started with exaggerated casualness, "have you seen John Mahoney lately?"

Chiara dropped her gaze to her feet. "I stopped over before I came here."

"Did Almadine give you a big ol' kiss and hug?" Cady teased.

"I didn't run into her."

"You're a little old to be climbing in windows, aren't you?"

"I really needed to see John."

Chiara shifted her gaze from Cady's, but not before she saw the understanding there. Cady, perhaps better than any of her other sisters, knew the importance of finding a strong shoulder—the best shoulder—to rest your head on in times of grief. Their Grandma Claire's death had been a time of unbearable sorrow, but from that painful soil, Cady's beautiful family had grown. And continued to grow, Chiara acknowledged with another glance at Cady's barely noticeable abdomen.

"John's been around a lot since he moved back here to start USITI Junior," Cady said. "He has dinner with us almost every Sunday."

"He loves Mama's cooking."

"He loves you," Cady said. "When are you two finally going to stop pissing around and get mar—"

Chiara abruptly stood. "I'm tired. I'm going to bed. See you guys in the morning."

She ignored Cady's loud whisper calling her name as she hurried to the opening of the stairwell and disappeared through the trapdoor. She bypassed the bedroom where her nieces seemed to have quieted for the night. She caught a glimpse of her mother reading in bed, but rushed by her open door without a word to her. Chiara kept going until she'd reached the kitchen where she retrieved her coat. She pulled it on as she moved through the darkened dining room and foyer. Silently, she opened the front door and slipped out of the house.

Once outside, she took a long, deep breath of the frigid air. It refreshed her but did nothing to rid her of the tension coiled in her neck and lower back. Nor did it clear away the anxiety tightening her chest. She trotted to her rental car and hopped into it. As she was pulling her left leg in, she happened to glance down.

Long footprints in the snowy street held her gaze. The new snow had erased the evidence of her movement in or out of the car, yet someone with big feet had been near her car recently. The prints were dusted over with snow, but they were clear enough to make the fine hairs at the back of Chiara's neck stiffen. She studied them closer, reading the pattern of them, and what they revealed chilled her blood.

The footprints began at her driver's side door. As if their owner had exited the vehicle soon after she had.

Chiara leaped out of the car and peered into its darkened interior. The tiny backseat of the Mazda was empty. She whirled around, her heart thundering in her ears, looking around her. Her neighborhood slumbered peacefully, a few lights in the upper floors of the houses glowing warmly into the night.

Nothing seemed out of the ordinary. Nothing other than the big footprints leading from her car to the sidewalk in front of her mother's house.

"I didn't call you to make you come here." Chiara opened the door to her hotel room wider and retreated a few steps, allowing John to enter. "You should be at home with your family."

"So should you." He closed the door behind him, then turned the thumb latch and bolted the security lock. "Your family's a lot more pleasant to be around than mine, so I really don't understand why you ended up running to a hotel in the middle of the night on Christmas Eve."

"It's Christmas now," she said sullenly. "And there was no room at the inn. My mother's house is full, and I didn't feel like bunking with my nieces." She led him into the living room section of her suite.

John whistled under his breath when he took in the view from her wall-length window. The St. Louis Gateway Arch, gleaming like a 630-foot stainless steel ornament, practically stood in her living room. "I hope you're charging this to your USITI expense account."

"I'm on my own dime tonight." Chiara curled up in an ornately styled wing chair. She'd changed into an oversized T-shirt, and the garment rode up high on her thighs as she folded her legs under her. "I asked for a standard room, but the front desk guy was feeling the spirit of the holiday and upgraded me to a junior suite." She pointed to a counter, where a black platter sat at the edge of a sink. "He even sent up a bottle of champagne and a plate of fruit and cheese, all compliments of the hotel."

John squatted before Chiara and lazily drew his hand along the bare skin of her knee. "I'm sure the booze and the cheddar squares are delicious, but why are you here, Chi? Honestly."

"I…" The lone syllable trembled from her lips, but then she shook her head and fixed her gaze on his. She had known him for so long, had shared so much with him. She willed him to see the convoluted knot of emotions strangling her from the inside out. The fading footprints had scared her, if for no other reason than they'd brought out a streak of paranoia that she'd never known herself to possess. And Kyla had been obnoxious to her, but that wasn't unusual. Why had it upset her so much more tonight than it had over the past twenty-five years of her life?

And that chip…Why did thoughts of the deliberately misplaced master microchip made it feel as though battery acid churned in her stomach?

She slid off of the chair and into John's arms, wrapping her own tightly around his neck. He stood, bringing her to her feet, and noticed the shiver in her small frame. He held her, pressing kisses to her hair and murmuring comforting words of nothing to her.

"I'm in trouble, John," she gasped, and the desperation in her confession tugged at his heart.

He couldn't stop himself from chuckling. "I wish I had a dime for every time I've heard you say that."

Her hold on him tightened. "I'm in real trouble this time, because of Zhou. Because of that master chip."

"Baby, you can't worry about that. You had no idea what Zhou was doing. From the looks of things, *he* didn't know what he was doing. You can't waste your time worrying about something someone else did."

"Someone…s-someone followed me tonight," she said haltingly.

John took hold of her shoulders and pulled her away just enough to meet her eyes. "What do you mean?"

"At my mother's I saw footprints leading away from my car. I think someone was in my rental."

John's eyes flashed as silvery grey as the Arch dominating the view. "Are you sure?"

"I saw the footprints in the snow, John. They started at my car. They led away from the driver's side."

"Maybe you just parked where someone had crossed the street. There was a lot of activity on your street tonight. Your mother wasn't the only one having a party."

"Maybe…" Chiara admitted, thinking about it. It was entirely possible, really, that she'd parked in a spot that had been freshly vacated by someone else. Her overeager imagination, already sparked to life by John's possession of the master chip, had conjured a scenario that now seemed impossible: that someone had been in her car or had followed her to her mother's.

❧❦❧

John couldn't decide which was more beautiful— Chiara as she'd been when he'd first spied her peeking into his mother's dining room window, or Chiara as she was now, lying nude in his arms, snuggled deep under whispery cotton sheets and goosedown. Her head was pillowed on his chest, her thick, dark hair blanketing his shoulder and neck. Her upper body languidly rose and fell in the telltale way of deep slumber, but John didn't dare move to see if she were actually sleeping.

He would do nothing to disturb the perfect peace of this moment.

Though he kept his gaze fixed on the grayish-pink sky which was sprinkling fluffy, fat snowflakes over St. Louis, he remained acutely aware of the woman wrapped around him. Chiara was one of the most incredible people he'd ever met, and certainly the most remarkable woman. Where she was a complete enigma to her family and even the few people she considered friends, John had always understood her with perfect, unerring clarity.

At least he thought he had, which was why he'd come to her at the hotel, and why he lay awake now, his forehead tense in thought.

Chiara, who had always been the stronger of the two of them, the more poised, the more confident, certainly the more fearless, was scared. He'd hardly recognized her at first when she'd let him into her suite. Her deep brown eyes had seemed to shine a bit too brightly; her full, luscious lips had pulled into a brittle, anxious smile. Even her body language had been all wrong. She was the smallest of the Winters sisters at a neat five-feet and two inches, but she'd always seemed taller and mightier and moved with the elegant power of a trained dancer. Tonight, she seemed to have collapsed in on herself a bit.

John shifted her in his arms. Chiara's arms and legs tightened around him, as though in sleep she was afraid he would let her go. He kissed the top of her head and locked his hands together around her shoulder, mutely assuring her that he wasn't going anywhere.

Chiara's head moved, settling more comfortably on the hard muscle of John's chest. She knew he wasn't sleeping. As often as they'd shared a bed, she could tell when he was sleeping and when he was awake. Sleep pulled at her, but she forced her eyes to remain open, to stare unblinking at the patterns the reflections of the falling snow made on the pale duvet cover. Her problem had brought John to her, and now it was keeping him from getting a good night's sleep. It wasn't fair for her to doze when he was surely turning her situation over in his mind.

John's steadiness, his calmness and his generosity with her had been a constant source of strength for her through the years. In some ways, he was the flip side of herself. Where she might have sat in the wing chair all night tearing at her fingernails in sick anxiety, John had eased back her fears with his silent acceptance of them. He'd stripped off her nightshirt and black panties and settled her into bed before piling his own clothes on top of hers and joining her there. He'd held her, covering her legs with one of his, allowing her to nestle into the solid warmth of him. He used his body to cloak her from the chill night and the scary things it contained.

Heart to heart and belly to belly, at that moment John had no interest in sharing anything more physical with her, other than his need to protect her. And Chiara selfishly drank up every bit of it even as tiny sharp claws of guilt tore at her at the thought of what she might have gotten him into, all because she couldn't pull Zhou's troubles out of him before they left Tokyo.

Zhou's actions were stuck in a permanent loop in her head. With each replay, she tried to discern what had caused him to fall apart as he had, but nothing he'd said helped. Nothing other than his warnings about Emmitt Grayson.

He watches…he listens…he spies…

The words echoed in Chiara's head until they became a sinister sigh ushering her into a troubled, broken sleep.

CHAPTER FIVE

No sooner had Chiara shoved her key into the deadbolt on her mother's front door than the door swung open, revealing Abby Winters in full battle regalia. She had one of her everyday, utility aprons cinched around her waist instead of the festive holiday one she'd worn on Christmas Eve. Both fists were balled on her hips, a long wooden spoon clutched in the left one. Her right foot, dressed in the old pink slippers she wore around the house, bounced up and down like a metronome counting out the beats of her anger.

"Where've you been?" she demanded.

Chiara couldn't tell if the hectic roses in her mother's deep brown cheeks were the result of her temper or the hot stove she'd likely just abandoned.

"Good morning, Mrs. Winters," John said smoothly, stepping into view on the front porch. "Merry Christmas."

John's presence flipped the right switch. At the sight of him, Abby replaced her frown with a wide, easy smile. She hugged him and accepted a kiss high on her cheekbone. Abby wrapped her arms around one of his and drew him into the house. She continued her tirade against Chiara, but softened it for John's benefit.

"I called the girls down for breakfast and they said they hadn't seen you all night," Abby gently accused over her shoulder as Chiara hung her coat on the full tree just inside the dining room.

"I checked into the Adam's Mark late last night." Chiara followed her mother and John into the kitchen. She undid one more button of her white and blue striped shirt in anticipation of the wave of heat that would wash over her once Abby swung open the kitchen door.

But her mother hesitated. "Wha…" Her words faded, and her face pulled into a mask of confusion. She freed John, who shook his arm to restore feeling to it. "Why?"

Chiara pushed past her mother and John, placed her ear against the kitchen door and said, "Because I'm thirty years old and I didn't feel like listening to a bunch of little girls giggle all night." She raised her head, balled up her fist and hammered it against the door. A shriek of pain sounded on the other side.

"That hurt!" Danielle cried out as she pulled the door open from the kitchen side. She bent over to retrieve her wire-rimmed glasses from the floor. "And I'm not a little girl," she protested, despite her wardrobe of hot pink Power Puff Girls pajamas. "I'm thirteen!"

"Stay out of it, little girl," came her mother's voice, carried on a burst of heat from the kitchen. "Morning,

Chiara," Clara called to her. "Have you had breakfast yet?"

Chiara slipped past Danielle and threaded her way through the congested kitchen. Half of Zweli protruded from the refrigerator, and Abby skirted around that half to drag John to the back door, to show him the plans for the new rear patio Santa Claus had given her through her sons-in-law. Abigail and Ella were propped on stools at the prep island, nursing glasses of orange juice. Still in their pajamas, the girls seemed to wriggle with the energy they were saving to open the presents heaped under Abby's 10-foot Christmas tree.

Chiara found her oldest sister, Clara, manning the pots and pans pleasantly steaming and bubbling at the stove. She embraced Clara, who had been stirring cinnamon and honey into a pot of Cream of Wheat. "You didn't have to go to a hotel," Clara said, her voice low so that only Chiara could hear her. "You know you could have stayed at my house last night. Christopher and I have plenty of room."

Chiara took the wooden spoon from Clara's hand to sample a steaming bit of the hot cereal. "I'll bet Kyla and Zweli did too, considering they holed up here last night."

"Mama told me that you and Kyla got into it." Clara began dishing the cereal into ceramic bowls. "You can't let her bother you."

"She didn't, not really," Chiara admitted. "There are some things going on at USITI. I thought coming home would help."

"It will," Clara smiled. "Once you fully acclimate. It took me a while to get used to being home, once Christopher and I moved back. I didn't realize how overwhelming the Winters clan can be when you're here full time."

"It's always been different for you," Chiara pointed out. "You're the oldest. Mama and Grandma Claire always let you do what you wanted. I always had a houseful of bossy broads telling me what for."

"Aunt Chiara hurt my ear," Danielle whined to her mother as she accepted a bowl of cereal.

"You had that coming, DNN," Zweli called as he turned from the refrigerator with a pre-made bottle of milk. "You need to stop eavesdropping on people."

"DNN?" Chiara questioned when Zweli neared her to use the microwave to heat the cup of water he'd use to warm the baby bottle.

"Danielle News Network," he chuckled under his breath. "She's out of control with the eavesdropping and gossiping."

Abby, her remodeling show and tell complete, took center stage in front of the sink. "Finish your breakfast, kids, I need my kitchen back," she announced. "We've got people coming at three and we need to be ready."

"Grandma, it's nine o'clock," her namesake said with a swing of her long, dark braids. "You have plenty of time."

"What do you mean 'you'?" Abby challenged. "I said 'we.' I still need the cranberry sauce made." She began ticking her needs off on her fingers. "I have to put the bourbon butter glaze on the turkey and stick it back in the oven, I need the russet potatoes peeled, the sweet potatoes wrapped in foil, the eggs deviled, my eggplant sweated, my shrimp shelled—"

"Are you making the ginger shrimp recipe I e-mailed to you from Thailand?" Chiara broke in.

"No, *you're* making the ginger shrimp recipe you e-mailed to me," Abby said, her response a seamless part of her litany, which continued with, "my cabbage shredded, the cherry and apricot glaze brushed onto my ham, the cranberry vinaigrette made, my squash stuffed—"

Danielle, a blush brushing her cashew cheeks in brick red, covered her mouth and giggled.

"Is there something the matter with you?" Clara asked pointedly.

"Grandma said that she needed her squash stuffed," Danielle repeated through a fresh round of giggles.

"Why is that funny to you?" Clara asked.

"It's funny to Uncle Zweli, too," Danielle said.

Zweli, his wide, devilish smile frozen on his face at being called out, zoomed from the kitchen with, "I gotta feed the baby."

Clara pursed her lips and turned back to the stove. She used a rubber spatula to stir Abby's cherry-apricot glaze. "That girl's mind has been in the gutter ever since she turned thirteen. Ever since she started junior high, all she thinks about is boys and sex."

"It's normal at that age," Chiara said. "At least she's giggling about it out in the open. You should be worried when she tries to hide it and starts sneaking around to explore things on her own."

Still stirring furiously, Clara grudgingly smiled. "You sound like a mother. I suppose you're right. But still…" She chanced a look at her youngest child, her only daughter, and her brown eyes softened. "I was hoping my baby would stay a baby just a little while longer. Instead of turning into an MTV/BET-obsessed human Bratz doll."

"Just be honest with her," Chiara said. "You always were with me, and look how I turned out."

Clara chuckled, her full lips pulling into a warm smile. "Yes, look at you…staying out all night with John Mahoney."

"I know why you didn't want to sleep with us last night," Danielle called from her stool at the prep island. "There was someone else you wanted to sleep with." She moved her index finger in a tiny point at John.

Armed with a bright red hand towel trimmed in green ribbon, Clara swept across the kitchen to shoo her daughter out of the room. "Get upstairs and get dressed!" she shouted, her words nearly drowned out by Danielle's hysterical laughter.

"Who did you sleep with last night, Aunt Chiara?" Abigail asked, her dark eyes wide with genuine innocence. "I slept with Ella and her icy cold feet."

Ella tugged at one of her glossy, blue-black braids. "I forgot to put my socks on." She put her foot on Abigail's knee. "My feet are nice and warm now."

"Ugh!" Abigail groaned.

"You two go on and get dressed, too," Abby instructed, prompting them with a hand on their backs. "The sooner you get dressed, the sooner you can open your presents."

"Aren't we waiting for Troy, C.J. and Clarence to come over?" Abigail asked.

"They should be here by the time you finish dressing," Abby smiled. "Now get a move on."

Chiara watched her nieces, their matching braids merrily swinging, exit the kitchen. When she turned to find John again, she was startled to find her mother standing directly behind her.

"So who *did* you sleep with last night?" Abby asked quietly.

John fought the need to shiver in the early darkness. When "the husbands"—Christopher, Lee, Keren and Zweli—went to the back porch after dinner to collect beers from Abby's big coolers, John had decided to accompany them, rather than remain in the living room with the wives, children and Winters family friends.

The husbands had barely popped the caps on their bottles of gourmet brews before they began to interrogate John as to whether he'd popped the question to Chiara.

"Abby said that she had a feeling you were going to," said Christopher Holtz, Clara's husband. Even though he'd had laser surgery to correct his vision, Christopher still had the habit of pushing at the bridge of his nose, as if he still wore the glasses John was so used to seeing propped there.

"It's a hard step, I know," Zweli said, his breath condensing in the freezing air. "Believe me, I know. But when I proposed to Kyla—"

"Which time?" laughed Lee Clark, Ciel's stocky fireplug of a husband.

"Each time," Zweli chuckled. "I knew that I was doing the right thing. I knew from the first moment I saw her that I wanted to be with her for the rest of my life."

"Perhaps it's different for John," Dr. Keren Bailey considered. Cady's husband looked perfectly comfortable in a thickly cabled rust-colored sweater. "John and Chiara have been together for so long, they're practically common law. Maybe they don't feel the need to get married the way we all did."

"Hold on a minute," Lee said, his tail up. "I can tell you right now, there's no way Abby Winters is going to let her baby girl shack up with any man, not even John Mahoney."

"What's that supposed to mean?" John asked.

"Abby thinks the world of you, you know that," Lee said. "She would have orchestrated an arranged marriage for you and Chiara if—" He abruptly went silent and took a sip of his beer.

"If what?" Zweli asked.

It occurred to John that Zweli, the newest addition to the Winters family, probably wasn't fully aware of the Mahoney-Winters feud.

"If Almadine," Christopher said, his blue eyes dimming in the faint porch light.

"Good ol' Almadine." Lee raised his beer in a mocking salute.

"Don't invoke her name," Keren said. "Sorry, John."

"It's cool," John said. "She is what she is. And you all know what she is."

"I don't," Zweli said. "What, does she not like Chiara?"

"She hates her," John said.

"She hates the whole family," Lee added. "Always has."

"Why?" Zweli asked.

"Because…" John struggled for the simplest way to explain his mother's feelings for the Winters family. "She thinks they're not as good as she is," he shrugged. "My mother is a snob."

"How did you turn out to be so decent?" Zweli asked.

John smiled. "I spent as much time as I could here at Chiara's house. The decency rubbed off."

"I hear that," Lee agreed. "So when are we going to get the chance to officially welcome you to the family?"

"Cady figured you'd have asked for Chiara a long time ago," Keren said. "Either that, or you'd have moved on to someone else."

John looked at Keren as though he'd suddenly sprouted antlers and a shiny red nose. "Moved on?"

"Fallen in love with someone else," Keren clarified.

John laughed out loud. "I wouldn't even know how to go about it. I can't remember a time when I didn't love—" A blush rose in his cheeks, and it was strong enough to chase away his shivers. Too late he realized that he'd said too much.

"Oh, you better propose to her now, before she flies off to Timbuktu, or wherever it is that company of yours plans to send her," Lee advised. "You gotta catch Chiara between flights, you know."

"I'm not too sure about that," Christopher said, fastening the top button of his plaid flannel shirt against the chill. "Chiara might have her own plans for her future. They might not even include John."

Horror danced in the eyes of the other husbands.

"What I mean is this," Christopher began in the voice that he once used during his long-ago days as a physics professor. "Chiara has always done her own thing. What we took as spontaneity was simply her reluctance to give advance notice of her plans. She's never felt the need to share her feelings with her sisters, or even her mother. Of course, being the youngest of five probably has a lot to do with that. Chiara has her own life now, and she probably wants to keep it that way. By marrying John, one of her family's oldest friends, she'll be pulled back into the Winters collective." Christopher pushed at his imaginary glasses. "It's like the Borg, on *Star Trek: The Next Generation*. There's no true individuality—"

"Do you feel a chill?" Lee interrupted, asking no one in particular as he briskly rubbed his arm. "I feel a chill. I think it's time for me to go back inside and see what Abby's got going for dessert."

"Me, too," Zweli said. "I want a piece of that raspberry-peach cheesecake before my nieces eat it all up."

"I just don't want hear about the Borg," Keren chuckled. "See you inside, man," he said to Christopher before strolling back into the house with Lee and Zweli.

After a moment of silence, John looked at Christopher and said, "I always liked *Star Trek: TNG*. I wrote a paper about it in high school comparing Jean-Luc Picard, the pragmatist, to James T. Kirk, the crusader. I got an A on it."

"I only brought up *Star Trek* because I couldn't think of a better way to get the other guys to give us some privacy," Christopher said. "I wanted to ask you about Chiara."

"I know," John groaned. "That's all anyone wants to ask me about."

"I don't mean about marriage. Something's wrong."

John dropped his eyes to the beer in his hand.

"Clara mentioned it when I got here with Troy and C.J. this morning, and throughout the day I've noticed that Chiara seems preoccupied. Not in a good way. Is everything okay, John?"

He kept his tongue until he could work out an answer that wouldn't betray Chiara in any way. "She's having a rough time at work."

"I suppose it might just be the loss of her partner, but it seems like there's more to it." Christopher sighed and ran his fingers through the silver-streaked red at his right temple. "She seemed tired today. And anxious. Let her know that Clara and I are here for her, will you?"

"Of course," John nodded. "She knows that."

"And you, too," Christopher added. "We're all here for you, too, John."

❧

Christopher was one of the reasons Almadine Mahoney despised the Winters family. As John stood alone, his cold hands gripping the frozen railing of the back patio, he heard again his mother's angry voice in his head.

"That Abigail Winters is going to allow her daughter to marry a *white* man!" Almadine had hissed

upon John's news that he'd been invited to the
wedding as Chiara's guest. "She's actually going to do
it! That family has no shame, no pride! There are
plenty of good strong black men out there that need
wives. Clara Winters could have picked one of them!"

"You said Clara was a plain-faced bookworm,"
ten-year-old John had reminded his mother. "You said
she was going to end up a spinster married to her
work if she didn't pull her face out of a book and start
looking for a husband."

"I know what I said!" Almadine had snapped
shrilly. "And if you think you're going to that
wedding, you got yourself another think coming!"

It was Christopher who had enabled John's participation in his wedding. Christopher, who had just
finished up graduate school, had dug into his own
pocket to pay for John's rented tux. Almadine had
refused to attend the service or the reception, but had
demanded copies of the photos that John was in.
She'd also bullied him into bringing her a plate of
food from the reception.

John gripped the railing a little harder, until he felt
his blunt fingernails digging crescents into the weath-
ered wood. Christopher had always been there for
him, more of a big brother than a friend. John had
never viewed Christopher as his mother had, as the
"white husband." Christopher was simply a member
of the family John himself had always longed to
belong to.

Ciel's marriage to Lee had created even more chaos in the Mahoney household. "The Clarks have lost their minds!" Almadine had raved. "Letting that handsome boy marry Ciel Winters. What kind of name is 'Ciel?' Abigail Winters has all the nerve in the world putting her girl up to marry into the Clark family. They'll find out, though. The Winters are trash and the Clarks will have the good sense to put the trash out in the morning."

"I guess you don't want to go to the wedding, then," twelve-year-old John had asked his mother, fully expecting her resounding no.

"Oh, I'm going to this one," Almadine had declared viciously. "I want to see with my own eyes if Ciel Winters has the nerve to wear white. I know she's already spread her legs for that boy. That's the only way she could have got him to marry her!"

John angrily tore himself from the railing. He was accustomed to his mother's insults about the Winters daughters, but he'd never found a way to dull their sting. Cady and Kyla had invited John to their weddings, but had felt no obligation whatsoever to invite Almadine, a fact that still bit at his mother.

"That Cady was always too wild," Almadine had stated upon learning of Cady's impending nuptials with Keren Bailey. "Figures she'd go out and find a man nobody knows anything about. He's probably some kind of molester or criminal."

"He's a doctor, Mother," twenty-five-year-old John had told her. "He's the head of oncology at Raines-

Hartley Hospital. He's rich, too. His parents were awarded millions in some kind of cancer lawsuit settlement before they died."

"That's probably why she wants to marry him," Almadine had snorted. "Lord knows those Winters never had two nickels to rub together. Where's the wedding and what time are we supposed to be there?"

"Cady invited *me*," John had told his mother, secretly delighting in his news. "Just me."

"Well, ain't that a blip," Almadine had gasped, thoroughly taken aback. "That little bitch calls herself snubbing me?"

And a few years later, when Kyla married Zweli, Almadine considered herself snubbed once more. "I didn't want to go to that Hollywood heifer's wedding anyway," Almadine had announced. "Who does she think she is, Angela Bassett? You won't catch Angela Bassett running around on television in nothing but a see-through bathing suit."

John leaned back on the railing and loosely crossed his arms over his chest. Through the windows over the sink, he saw that the brightly lit kitchen was filled, this time with an army of people helping Abby put away food, scrape and pack dishes into the dishwasher, and generally restore order to the house. It was dark and most of the merriment of the holiday had been spent, yet laughter and frivolity ruled in Abby's kitchen.

Clarence chased his little sister Ella around the prep island with his favorite new toy, a plastic automatic weapon that shot a gooey slime-like substance instead of water. Danielle, carrying a half-eaten sweet potato pie into the kitchen, chatted with Tiffani McCousy, Troy's buxom girlfriend. Tiffani, whose request to be called Tiff had led inevitably to another one of Cady's nicknames, seemed like a pleasant person, but John knew Troy well enough to agree with Chiara's first impression. Tiffani had beautiful cinnamon skin and luxurious black hair, but Troy surely liked Tiff because of her outrageously oversized bosom.

John shook his head and chuckled to himself. The kids were growing up so fast, and it didn't seem so long ago that he and Chiara had been considered "the kids."

No one was more in tune with the fact that he and Chiara were no longer children than John. His childhood had been spent with Chiara, and he hadn't been exaggerating when it almost slipped out that he couldn't remember a time when he hadn't been in love with her.

It had never occurred to him to invite any other girl to the sixth grade Fiesta formal, or to the junior high dances. Throughout high school, no other girl had appealed to him as Chiara had, and he'd never asked another girl to a movie or to a sporting event. It was Chiara's praise he'd sought after he'd done his best in a game or a track event, and she was the first person he'd gone to after getting his acceptance to George Washington University. Chiara had been more than a friend through the years, more than a lover. She'd been his inspiration to be the best man he possibly could, to transcend the harshness of his upbringing to be the kind of person he wanted to be, rather than the creature his mother had tried to engineer with belts and switches.

Chiara's friendship had been the one thing he'd been able to rely on throughout his life. So many times, she had brought light into his darkness, saving him with a smile, a hug, a kiss, or the power of her silence. Zhou had placed Chiara in a situation that had stolen the light from her, and John resolved to do whatever he could to restore it. As his frozen legs carried him to the back door, John realized that he owed nothing less to the woman to whom he was matched for life.

CHAPTER SIX

Almadine Mahoney wore her holiday best, a holly-green tweed suit she'd ordered from a Christian shopping catalog. Her thin arms crossed tightly and her skinny legs scissoring rapidly to keep up with John's long strides, Almadine followed her son from the front door to the family room, sniping all the way.

"This is Christmas," she hissed. "You should have spent the day with your family! We waited all day for you."

John glanced into the dining room. The second catered dinner in two days sat on the table, which had been draped with Almadine's heirloom linen tablecloth. The thick white carpeting revealed the truth of his mother's "we." John could make out only two sets of footprints in the tattletale carpeting, a tiny set belonging to his mother and a much larger trail that had to be his father's.

Upon entering the family room, John encountered a big leather recliner stuffed full of his father. Two plates were stacked on the blond ash end table next to the chair, each bearing the evidence of Bartholomew Mahoney's first and second dinners.

"Merry Christmas, Dad." John bent over to give his father a brief hug. "Did you have a good day?"

Bartholomew, who'd been drowsing off before a pre-recorded boxing match on the wide-screen television mounted on the wall before him, fully awakened with a snort. "Oh, it was all right," he yawned. "We beat our sales goal from last year, so I can't complain. I moved three Hummers. Merry Christmas to me," he chuckled.

Transfixed, John watched the rolls of his father's stomach bounce with his laughter.

"Did George make it over?" John asked, seating himself on a dark leather ottoman near his father's chair.

"For a little while, then it was just me and *her*." Bartholomew threw a fat thumb in the direction of the wide archway, where Almadine leaned stiffly against the wide wooden frame. "Did you make it over to your little girlfriend's house today?"

"Chiara's not little anymore, Dad. I can't really call her my girlfriend, either. She's—"

"Well, that's the best news I've heard all year," Almadine piped in. She squinted, which made the lines in her ebony skin appear even darker and more severe. "Did you go by her house today?"

"Yes." John marveled at his mother's resemblance to a praying mantis. "I had some gifts to deliver."

"Boy, you need to save your money to buy a house," Almadine interjected. "There's a pretty little three-bedroom on the market right around the corner, over on Heger Court. There's an open house next week. We can go and see what's wrong with it, and make an offer, and—"

"I'm not interested in any houses on Heger Court," John interrupted. "And my finances are in order for buying a house. Lee Clark has managed my portfolio for the past seven years, and I won't have any trouble with a down payment." He deliberately failed to mention that Chiara figured prominently in his plans to purchase a house.

"How're Abby and the girls?" Bartholomew asked. "Doing good?"

Almadine's lips tightened into a fist-like configuration as John said, "Everybody's doing really well. Kyla's book is selling well, and she's finishing up her first movie. Cady's book won another award and her publisher just signed her to a three-book deal. Clara's just won a five-million dollar research contract, and Ciel's been nominated for a state assistant district attorney position."

"Well, that sounds all right," Bartholomew said with a nod of appreciation. "Abby did a good job with her girls."

"She would've done better if she could've kept her man around," Almadine snapped. "Happy men don't go running around the world writing useless stories when they have five children and a wife at home."

John changed the subject. "Did Granddaddy come by today, Dad?"

"He was over last night, so he spent today with your Uncle Otha," Bartholomew grunted as he reached across his body for the remote control. "Otha invited us over, too, but your mother had already planned to have the caterers come and whatnot, so we stayed here in case any of the other folks she invited came over."

John spent a moment studying his hands. He knew that Almadine had invited a lot of church friends and distant relatives to Christmas dinner, totally ignoring the fact that most of those people would want to spend the holiday with their own families. Her own father hadn't shown up, opting instead to spend the day with his son.

"Me, I'm glad nobody came," Bartholomew laughed. "I didn't have to talk to nobody and I didn't have to give up my favorite chair to nobody."

"How was the food?" John asked, glancing at his father's dirty plates.

"You know I don't much care for all that fancy stuff your mama likes." Bartholomew belched. "But I managed to put down a good plate or two. Why don't you get yourself something to eat?"

"I'm not hungry, Dad, but thanks," John said.

"Oh, you ate at the Winters house," Almadine accused. "My food isn't good enough for you now?"

John used his thumb and middle finger to vigorously massage his temples. "I don't have anything against your food, Mother. I was at Chiara's house, there was food there, and I ate some of it." *And it*

*was a thousand times better than anything you could
have ordered from a caterer,* John bit back.

"George came early this morning," Almadine
threw out. "Even though he was in the middle of
studying for his finals, he took time out to come be
with his mother and father."

John so wanted to tell his mother that George
was full of it, that finals took place *before* Christmas
break, not during, and that George showed up on
Christmas morning for one reason only—to collect
presents. But instead he said, "I actually have to be
at work tomorrow, Mother. I should be getting up to
bed."

"Ten minutes? That's all we get out of you for
Christmas?" Almadine asked angrily. "You ran out of
here last night, and you're running away now. Look
at your father, he's all upset now."

Bartholomew pleasantly snored, his large head
tipped forward onto his chest.

John surrendered. "Fine. I'll stay up and visit
awhile."

"Don't do me any favors," Almadine said with a
dismissive wave of her hand. "I'm only your
mother."

❧

John laid his clothes neatly over the back of his
mother's desk chair before climbing into the day bed
and pulling the horrible cotton-candy sheets over his
nude body. An entire day spent with Chiara's large,

energetic family hadn't been as exhausting as two hours with his mother. As he stared at the ceiling, John's heart felt as heavy as it ever had when he was a child.

Almadine no longer hit him physically, but her verbal blows still hurt, and because of them John hated being at home. He hated feeling out of place, unloved, empty, as if his heart were encased in the same plastic that covered Almadine's expensive living room furniture. Home wasn't supposed to make you feel like that. It was supposed to feel the way he felt at Chiara's house.

Abby had used a few choice words when Cady's twins used their new bath crayons to tag the foyer walls, but she hadn't rushed to the site with a bucket of hot water, sponges and industrial cleaning solutions. She'd kept the drawings and hadn't bothered to mask her pride when she showed them to her arriving guests. That was the difference between the Winters and Mahoney residences: Abby had built a home where each member of her family was valued. Almadine had nothing more than a house filled with pricey furnishings and meaningless objects, her two sons foremost among them.

John tried to work up a head of steam over how easily George extracted himself from family gatherings with lukewarm lies, but he couldn't begrudge his little brother his freedom. George might not have been on the receiving end of Almadine's wrath as often, but he'd suffered, too, having been forced to witness his big brother's punishments.

Old guilt stabbed at John when he recalled all the times he would sneak away to play at Chiara's, leaving a whining, sometimes sobbing George at home alone with Almadine. Part of the abandonment was because George was so much younger, seven years and eight months exactly. The other part, the part that disturbed him most, was the real reason he'd left George behind: because he wanted to keep the Winters family all to himself.

Chiara's house was filled with people who cared about him, who actually wanted him around. They treated him as though he belonged. They loved him, and he didn't want to have to share it with anyone, not even George.

He knew that Abby loved him. She'd said so. John couldn't recall a single time Almadine had claimed to love him, other than after a whipping when she'd say, "I wouldn't do this if I didn't love you."

Abby's love had been expressed with suffocating hugs, a handful of change to take to the neighborhood confectionary with Chiara, a dozen warm cookies with a tall glass of milk, and more than once, cotton balls dipped in witch hazel swiped over his injured skin.

Claire Winters, Chiara's grandmother, hadn't been as demonstrative, but she'd loved him, too. She'd had words with his mother at least once that he

knew of regarding the way Almadine treated him.
The one time he'd overheard his mother and
Grandma Claire arguing had been when he was
almost thirteen years old. He'd spent a Monday
afternoon at Chiara's, and Claire had noticed an
open welt on the back of his neck. Chiara had made
an offhand comment about Almadine's belt getting
away from her.

Claire had plainly asked if Almadine had beat
him, and John's answering silence had been answer
enough. Claire had turned off the fire under the
dinner she'd been preparing, and she'd walked John
home. To Almadine's face, right there on her front
doorstep, Claire had promised to call the St. Louis
Child Protective Services if she ever saw another
mark on John. Not only that, she'd get her grand-
daughter Ciel, the new lawyer, to help her get
custody of John and George while Almadine sat "her
scrawny butt in the Missouri Correctional Institute
for Women."

Almadine had never raised a hand to him again.
She'd claimed that it was because John had gotten
too big to whip. But John knew that it had been
Claire's threat that had ended Almadine's whippings.
John's only regret had been that Claire hadn't threat-
ened his mother with CPS sooner.

John hugged his thin pillow to his chest and
squirmed, trying to get comfortable. The sharp
creases in the new sheet were still evident, and they
bit into his skin. He smiled, thinking of the connip-

tion Almadine would surely have if she knew he was sleeping naked under her roof. He'd given up pajamas years ago, when he'd gotten his first apartment. In defiance of his mother, he spread out as much as he could on the small bed. He was a grown man and would sleep buck-ass naked if he wanted to.

His large frame filled the bed, but it still seemed too empty without Chiara beside him. They'd maintained separate apartments in Chicago but lived less than two blocks apart. Having grown up with so many people in her house, Chiara had become addicted to her privacy and independence. USITI discouraged office romances, so separate addresses were necessary in that regard as well. For John's part, it would have killed his mother to know that he was "shacking up" with Chiara.

John's favorite thing in the world was sleeping with Chiara. Not sex, although that was wonderful too, but actually sleeping. He loved the way she snuggled up to him as she slept, the way her body moved, the soft touches she gave him in slumber.

Thinking so hard about her must have conjured her, because there she was on the other side of the window, carefully pushing aside Cecile Brunner's blunted bare vines. John had left the window unlocked from the night before, and Chiara swung it open. Wrapped in her white fox fur coat and mukluks, she entered the room on a silent blast of cold air and a rush of crystalline snowflakes that glittered in the street light.

She slipped off her boots at the foot of the bed, and John sat up. "I really wish you wouldn't keep risking a fall by—" He smelled the cold on her coat as she untied the belt closing it. "I wish..." The coat slipped from her shoulders to reveal flawless bare skin. "I-I..." he stammered, finishing on a pained groan as Chiara let her coat pool at her feet. She untucked the covers from the foot of the bed, and like an odalisque approaching her sultan, she crawled into the bed and up the length of John's body. Her loose, luxurious hair stroked him, her bare skin warmed as it generated delicious friction against his. She stopped halfway, her small, strong hands gripping his thighs, parting his legs. She slithered between them to nest at the juncture of his thighs. His flesh instantly responded to the caress of her warm breath, rising to fill the heat of her mouth as her cool lips gripped him.

There was nothing subservient about Chiara's seduction—her beauty and confidence, and the power she drew from them, were the headiest aphrodisiacs John had ever experienced. She knew what he liked, and what she herself liked, and she was excellent at combining the two.

John's fists clutched handfuls of the bed sheets. His neck arched, forcing his head into his pillow. He cringed against the sheer pleasure of Chiara's lips and tongue working in concert with light strokes of her fingertips. When he couldn't stand it for one more second, he gripped her shoulders and tugged her atop him. Breathing hard, she straddled him and guided him inside in one mighty, welcoming thrust of her hips. She bowed her head and John raised his, their teeth clacking as they mated their mouths, matching each deep thrust of their bodies.

Chiara shifted position, planting her right foot flat on the bed and bringing her center even more into contact with John's. When she stretched her left leg alongside his outer thigh, John groaned out loud and fastened his hands at her hips to push himself deeper. In the farthest recesses of his mind, he realized that she was imitating a position they'd seen in a painting in Japan. The old bed responded to her new position with a loud creak that sounded like a gunshot.

Ten seconds later, the doorknob rattled. "John," Almadine called. "Are you all right in there?"

"F-Fine," he managed, struggling to keep his voice even with Chiara suckling his earlobe. "I'm fine."

"Are you playing games on my computer?" Almadine asked sharply.

"No, Mother." He winced in sweet, silent delight as Chiara leaned farther forward to tempt him with the tip of her breast.

"I don't want you burning my electricity all night," Almadine complained from the corridor. "Go to bed!"

His mouth occupied with the silken sweetness of Chiara's flesh, John was unable to answer his mother. He moved Chiara slightly so he could roll on top of her without separating from her. He took her breast and lightly flicked his tongue over the tip of it before tasting it fully, drawing on it in long, gentle tugs that complemented the slow, deep rhythm of his hips. Chiara, her eyes closed, bit her lip to stifle her noises of pleasure as her body clenched around John, forcing him to smother his own cries against her breast.

"Do you hear me, John?" Almadine nearly shrieked.

"Yes!" he groaned, pulsing into Chiara with the force of his climax.

"All right then," Almadine responded. "Good night."

John shuddered in Chiara's embrace and held her tightly in his arms. He planted noiseless kisses in the sheen of perspiration covering her shoulder and collarbone. Then, as quietly as he could, he eased onto his side, fitting Chiara between himself and the back of the day bed. It was a tight squeeze, but he liked it.

She pillowed her head on his right arm and smiled serenely as she used her fingertip to wipe away a bead of sweat from his forehead. John cupped her breast, admiring its new fullness. Chiara pushed one of her legs between his, pressing her abdomen fully against him.

"What are you doing here?" John whispered so softly he practically mouthed the words.

"You came to me last night when I needed you," she said just as quietly.

"How did you know I'd need you tonight?"

Her soft hand came to lightly rest on his cheek. "Because I know you."

"I saw a house I think you'd like," he told her. "It's in Kirkwood."

Her gaze went to his throat. "Mmm."

"You don't want to move back to Missouri, do you?"

"Not especially."

"I know," he sighed. "You don't want to live too close to your family."

She still refused to meet his eyes. "We've talked about this."

John was forced to recall all the late night talks they'd shared in this very bed. They had outgrown the awkward, inexperienced fumbling of their adolescence, but one thing hadn't changed. Chiara still longed to live her life far from the watchful eyes and uninvited opinions of her mother and sisters.

"We almost got caught tonight," she giggled quietly. "It's a good thing you locked the door."

John smiled and passed a hand over her upper arm. "Remember the last time she almost walked in on us?"

The sparkle in Chiara's eyes was answer enough, even though she said, "Do you really think that I could forget?"

Staring deep into her eyes, John could almost see her as she'd been twelve years ago, on the night of their senior prom. For once, Bartholomew had intervened on John's behalf and forced Almadine to allow him to attend prom, but Almadine had forbidden him to attend any of the after parties. That hadn't been much of a hardship for him, considering that he hadn't been invited to any. But Chiara, his date, had been on the A-list for every party.

He'd taken Chiara home after their magical night aboard a Mississippi River paddleboat, and then he'd gone home himself, sulking the whole way. He'd barely gotten out of his tux before Chiara appeared at his window in the jeans, T-shirt and sneakers she'd thrown on.

John had welcomed her with open arms, and without words, without really expecting to, they had ended up on his cozy little bed as they had many times before. But this time, they hadn't stopped at kissing and snuggling. Chiara had pulled away from him, and standing before him like a gift from God, she had removed her clothing. She'd silently watched as John had taken off his. They'd never seen each other nude; in fact, neither had either of them ever seen a live member of the opposite sex nude. Their explorations had begun innocently. But when Chiara had lightly gripped him between his legs, right then and there John surrendered ownership of himself to her.

He'd watched her face as he'd touched her in kind, and he thought he'd never seen anything as beautiful as her closed eyes, her parted lips and the slim column of her neck as her head fell back in response to his touch.

In retrospect, their first coupling had been unimaginative, but the logical extension of promises they'd made one month earlier during their senior trip to San Francisco. There had been a little pain at first, for both of them, but that brief discomfort had given way to an uncharted universe of unbelievable sensation.

Slightly tender and definitely exhausted, John had kissed Chiara farewell at the window just before dawn. Their exertions had left Chiara more jubilant than tired, and after climbing down Cecile Brunner, Chiara had stood on the ground beneath John's window and shouted, "I love you!" before sprinting out of sight.

John, naked and thoroughly spent, was closing the window just as Almadine burst into his room. He never knew what had roused his mother and sent her into his room. She probably had forgotten herself, once she saw her oldest son standing fully naked in front of an open window at five A.M.

Almadine's wrath had been loud and swift, and had ended with her banning him from the use of a car, phone and computer for a month. But John hadn't cared, not with Chiara coming to him under the cloak of night to share intimate moments in the bed where they had given each other their virginity. In the tiny bed they had grown more intimate emotionally as well as physically, and after their interludes, when they quietly mapped their futures by the light of the moon and stars, neither of them could imagine a life without the other. Nor could they imagine living within the ready grasp of either family.

"John?"

Her utterance of his name brought him back. "I'm sorry. I was thinking about prom night."

She grinned. "I made you mine that night."

He took her hand and kissed her fingertips. "I was yours long before then."

Moisture welled in her eyes, and hung on her lower lashes before trickling over her cheeks. "I'm sorry," she whispered. "Everything makes me cry these days."

He took her chin and kissed her. "It's okay. I want you to stop worrying, though, about everything. I figured out what to do about the master chip."

She wiped her eyes and looked at him expectantly.

"I have to go to Chicago on Monday to see Mr. Grayson. I'll take the chip with me, and I'll tell him that Zhou sent it to me by accident or something. No harm done."

"He'll never believe you."

"I'll make him believe me."

"John, he can smell a lie. Remember what he did to Laura Van Oker?"

"I'm tougher than Laura Van Oker," he smiled.

"But John, I—"

He caught her words on his lips. He kissed her, and his hands moved over her, until she relaxed against him. When she sighed his name and clasped his buttocks, he brought her right leg up and over his left and pushed into her. He loved her, driving thoughts of the master chip, Laura Van Oker and Emmitt Grayson's suspicious mind cleanly out of her head.

CHAPTER SEVEN

Chiara quickly but carefully rifled through the neat stacks of bills, envelopes, notes and papers on Almadine's desk while John yanked the covers from the daybed. The desktop thoroughly searched, Chiara focused on the drawers, pulling each one out and rummaging through it. Through her mounting panic, she was careful to replace the items as close to their original positions as possible.

"It wouldn't be in there," John whispered loudly. "I left it right here on the lamp table. It can't have crossed the room by itself and jumped into a drawer."

"Do you think your mother came in and cleaned up while you were at my house yesterday?" Chiara whispered back.

"My mother would have been too busy watching the front door to clean." John lifted the mattress so Chiara could peek under it.

On another day, under different circumstances, they might have laughed at the idea of searching a room in the early morning light in their birthday suits, but with each passing moment, their panic grew. The master chip that John had left on the lamp table had disappeared.

"It's gotta be here somewhere." John settled the mattress back on the bed frame and dropped to his hands and knees to help Chiara look under the bed.

"This is just perfect," Chiara said between gritted teeth. Terror flashed in her eyes and she took John's arm in a death grip. "Do you think someone came in and took it?"

"I doubt Mr. Grayson sent someone to search my childhood bedroom, if that's what you're thinking. There's no reason anyone would suspect that I have the chip, or that it was here at my parents' house," he assured her.

Chiara swallowed hard. *He watches…* "Did you bring it to the hotel with you the other night?" She had a hard time keeping her budding hysteria from affecting the volume of her voice. "You might have left it there. Oh God, if someone found it, or even worse, threw it away…"

"I left it right there." John pointed to the lamp table. "I should have put it in my wallet, but I figured it would be safe here." He ran a hand over his head in frustration. "I'll admit this is odd, though. My father never comes in here and my mother is usually pretty good about keeping her hands off things I leave in the open. It's the hidden stuff that she's always trying to get into."

Chiara barely heard a word. She paced the floor, anxiously worrying one hand over the other. "Mr. Grayson has surveillance everywhere at USITI. He monitors our e-mail and our phone calls. I'm sure he has ways of keeping tabs on us on the road. You head the information systems department, John. You know better than I do how Mr. Grayson spies on us."

John sat on the edge of the daybed and pulled Chiara down onto his lap. "That's work-related, not personal. USITI's got the right to protect its interests."

"Yes, but how far do you think Mr. Grayson will go to do that?" She shuddered and drew closer to him. "Remember when Laura Van Oker lost a set of R-GS chips? Mr. Grayson interrogated her in security for two straight days. He threatened to charge her with grand larceny, and then he put her on in-house suspension for six months, even after the chips were found right there in the building. She'd set the kit down in the coffee room and a maintenance person accidentally threw it away. She made an honest mistake and Mr. Grayson treated her like a felon."

"It was more than that, Chi." John wrapped his arms around her and locked his fingers together. "Laura wasn't cut out for sales. Not many people are. You and Zhou were the exception to the rule. But in the end, you're just as expendable as anyone else."

Chiara had no argument. Technical sales had the highest employee turnover rate of any department at USITI. The travel and separation from friends and family made the job difficult, but the continual whispers around USITI blamed Emmitt Grayson for the short careers of his technical sales representatives. The pressure to sell was subtle, passive, like the movement of a glacier. It had crushed a lot of capable employees. But Chiara thrived in that environment. She and Zhou had earned kudos for their sales numbers and longevity in the department. The average tour of duty in sales was twenty-two months, and Chiara and Zhou had logged five years and landed some of USITI's biggest accounts. Their recent acquisition, Siyuri Robotics in Tokyo, had been their most lucrative contract, and the last client she would ever snare with Zhou.

"Zhou and I brought in almost half a billion in contracts to USITI," Chiara said, not nearly as proud of the statistic as she'd once been. "Mr. Grayson wouldn't have wanted to lose us."

"He might. If one of you took something that belonged to him."

"Do you think that chip is worth killing for?"

"I've been in information systems for seven years, Chi, and I've never seen anything like it. You said yourself that you submit them directly to Mr. Grayson. They must contain information that's useful only to him."

"Do you think Zhou corrupted it somehow?" Her forehead wrinkled in thought. "Could that be why you couldn't read it? When we were in Tokyo, Zhou didn't have any trouble programming the sales codes and data onto it."

"It's got one-way loading, so to speak," John explained. "Anybody can put data onto it, but you need a key to unlock it, to retrieve data."

"What kind of key?"

He shrugged. "A password, most likely. Or it could have a timer that would disable the security programming at a certain time for a specific length of time."

"You info systems people figure out passwords all the time," Chiara said, recalling the days early in her USITI career when she shared a desk in that department with John.

He gave her a wary glance. "We don't try to figure out Emmitt Grayson's. He's got fences around the walls around the vault that stores his passwords."

"How do you know?"

"I helped him build the security system on his personal computer. I hate to brag, but Mr. Grayson is the only one who knows more about his systems and products than I do." John abruptly stood, standing Chiara on her feet as well.

"What is it?" she asked, her eyes wide in alarm.

"There's one person who might know as much about as USITI's system as I do." John grabbed Chiara's coat and helped her into it.

"Who?" Chiara asked as John tugged on his black sports briefs.

John's mouth became a severe line. "The same person who took the master chip."

❦

John used his fist to bang on the hollow steel door. "I know you're in there, George," he called, not caring if he awakened the entire fourth floor of the dorm. "Open the damn door. It's John and Chiara."

Chiara listened closely at the door. "He's not there. It's too quiet."

John banged even harder. "That's how I know he's in there." He maintained the banging until the door flew open and he was face to face with his little brother.

George Mahoney looked as though he'd just been freshly rolled in a downtown gutter. His yellow T-shirt, emblazoned with black letters spelling BYTE ME, was stained under the armpits and had been splattered with what looked and smelled like two-day old taco sauce. Underneath his uncombed ten-inch afro he wore glasses with thick black frames, and behind them, purple-black circles hung under his chocolate eyes. George had his mother's stick-like build, and his legs looked like kindling in the red and white horizontally striped sports briefs he wore. He scrubbed his long, bony fingers over the stubble covering the lower half of his face as he greeted his visitors with a pleasant, "Wha's up?"

John recoiled from the stench of his brother's breath. "What the hell have you been eating?" he asked as he barged past George and into the oddly lit room.

Chiara followed, but drew up short when the smell hit her, too. "Decomposition, and I think I just stepped in the body." She scraped her shoe on a bare patch of carpet.

"Happy holidays to you, too." George indignantly shut the door, closing out the light from the corridor and plummeting his room into eerie blue-white light.

Once John's eyes adjusted, he realized that the only illumination in the room came from George's giant pair of flat-panel computer monitors. "I want it back, George. Now."

"Want what back?" George asked far too innocently.

"Let in some light, man," John said. He tripped over clothes, books and an inflatable chair on his way to the window. He snapped the shade and it wildly rolled up, flooding the room with bright light that made George wince sharply and cover his eyes with his splayed fingers.

"Easy on the UV, bro," he pleaded. He rushed to the window and drew down the shade. "What day is it?"

"The day after Christmas." John shook his head.

"Really?" George took off his glasses and cleaned them with a corner of his shirt. When he replaced them on his face, Chiara saw that they were actually dirtier than they'd been before.

"I should probably go to the cafeteria and get some food," George said.

"And some water," Chiara added. "To bathe in."

John picked his way through a minefield of George's junk to get to his brother's computer station. Two computer processing units fed information to two flat-panel quad screen displays, but George had a separate table loaded with disembodied circuit boards and a Frankensteinian assortment of items he'd rigged from parts he'd ordered from computer catalogs, purchased at Radio Shack, inherited from John, or salvaged from the dumpster behind his dorm.

An empty clear plastic card sat propped on one of George's keyboards, and the item John and Chiara had come to retrieve, the missing master chip, was snugly installed in one of the circuit boards.

John was all set to really chew out his thieving brother when something on one of the monitors redirected his attention. "No," John gasped, his eyes wide.

"What is it?" Chiara rushed to his side, nearly tripping into his arms over a half-empty two-liter bottle of Jolt cola.

John, his face washed blue in the cold light of his monitors, stared at George. "You figured out the password?"

George smiled proudly and squeezed between Chiara and John to sit in his swivel chair. "I hit it a few hours ago. It took forever."

"Or since yesterday when you left the house," John said, stunned.

Chiara peered closer at the screens. A different website was displayed on each quarter. She recognized all of them. Their sales data was programmed onto the master chip.

George pointed to his left hand monitor. "This screen shows Asia-based pharmaceutical companies. The right screen's domestic, all U.S. biotech firms."

Chiara cleared off a folding chair full of empty Mountain Dew bottles and Fritos bags. She sat down, her eyes dancing from screen to screen. "I know these companies. They're USITI clients. Zhou and I sold to them. These look like secure pages."

"Look at this." George grinned in delight. He double-clicked his wireless mouse, bringing one company to full view on screen. "ChemoTech has a new arthritis drug coming out in a few months. The Food and Drug Administration just approved it so the company's ready to go public. I'm going to borrow some money from Dad and buy a few hundred shares of stock."

John spent another long moment staring at the screen before he turned his worried gaze to Chiara.

"R-GS," she said, understanding dawning. "*Argus*. The monster from Greek mythology who had a hundred eyes."

"Turn it off, George," John commanded.

George was too excited about his discoveries to heed his brother's order. "I've got the inside scoop on every company on this chip." He greedily rubbed his hands together. "This is only the tip of the iceberg. There's at least fifty corporations—"

"Get out of it, George!" John shouted. He squatted and reached under the table to yank the power cord from its dust-covered surge protector.

"Hey!" George cried as John crudely plucked the master chip from George's motherboard.

"This thing might have gotten a man killed," John said gravely. "What can you tell me about it other than what we just saw?"

❧

George agreed to share his findings under two conditions: that they treat him to breakfast and that Chiara sit next to him in the cafeteria. The cafeteria was sparsely populated since most of the students were away for the holiday break, but there were enough foreign students milling about to suit George's purpose. Whenever he saw someone he knew, he'd scoot closer to Chiara or put his skinny arm around her shoulders.

Chiara was too concerned about the master chip to object to George's using her to impress his chums.

"Now that all your little schoolmates have seen you cuddling up to Chiara, are you finished collecting your cool points?" John asked him over their now cold breakfast plates.

George hunkered over a plate heaped high with eggs, bacon, ham, pork sausage, home fries, and flap-jacks. As he began to speak, he dressed his food from small dishes of applesauce, butter, whipped cream and maple syrup. "That chip is a thing of beauty," he started, "a real masterpiece."

"Could you lower your voice?" John suggested. There weren't many students around, but George seemed to know enough of them to want to show Chiara off. George only knew fellow computer nuts, and the last thing John wanted was for his brother to leak the existence of the chip to hackers who were as obsessed as George.

George bowed low over his food and leaned farther over the table. Very quietly he said, "That chip is nothing but a big ol' catalog of rootkits."

Chiara's eyebrows drew together in thought as she searched her memory. Much of what she'd learned in her early days in information systems had been forgotten or was now obsolete, and she wasn't as up-to-date on current security information as she could have been. But then it came to her.

"Rootkits." She swallowed hard. "That's hidden software. It can be used for—"

"Spying," George said through a mouthful of eggs and syrup. "Duh."

"Rootkits are practically undetectable," John said. "USITI implants them in all of the R-GS chips as part of its digital rights management technology. It's supposed to prevent unauthorized users from gaining access to a company's computer system. It's a security feature that USITI has perfected, and why the R-GS system is so popular. In five years, no system USITI has sold to has reported any hacking troubles."

"Well, your boy Emmitt Grayson has perfected his system," George said. "Chiara, you said that you and Zhou Chen programmed sales data onto the master after you sold the R-GS chips? Well, the location and access information for each R-GS chip is encoded in what looks like inventory control numbers. As soon as an R-GS chip is used, the rootkit installs itself auto-matically, usually in the most basic level of the oper-ating system. The files it contains are impossible to delete, and they're invisible. I went through the secure files of at least twenty companies before you guys broke down my door, and not one of them sent up flags, closed me out or blocked my access. I read the private e-mails of the president of BioGenesis, one of the biggest medical research facilities in Asia." George stared dreamily into space as he said, "Emmitt Grayson created a ghost, man. It's the perfect spy tool."

"If someone has the master chip, he has complete, undetectable access to whatever system uses the R-GS chips," John said. He pushed away his lukewarm cup of coffee. "He can go in whenever he wants, and no one knows he's there."

"Can't antivirus software detect the rootkits?" Chiara asked.

"Antivirus software hasn't been invented yet that can detect Grayson's bad boys," George said, his respect for the technology evident.

Chiara breathed hard through her nose. "Investment whiz, my ass," she sneered.

"Huh?" George grunted.

"A story ran on Emmitt Grayson in *American Investor* magazine a few months or so ago," Chiara seethed. She nearly shook with anger. "Grayson had the thing blown up and framed and hung it in USITI's lobby. It talks about his great investing instincts, and how he's made such savvy choices for the past five years. He's made millions in the stock market on top of the millions he makes peddling his spyware. He's a thief, and a liar, and he's made me a party to it!"

"Chi, calm down." John reached across the table and took her trembling hands.

"He killed Zhou over this," she whispered.

"Do you think your friend knew how the master chip worked?" George asked. "Maybe he wanted to keep it for himself. I would."

"Zhou wasn't like that," Chiara said. "He was one of the most honorable men I ever knew. If he'd known how the master chip functioned, he would have—" Suddenly something clicked. "He would have confronted Grayson. He would have quit the job." Her lower lip quivered, but she held back her tears. "He told me, John. Zhou told me what Grayson was up to. I just didn't get it."

John gripped her hands tighter without meaning to. "There's one thing I still need to figure out."

"Just one?" Chiara chuckled somberly. "There are about a dozen things I have to puzzle through, and I have to do it before I go back to work next week. What's your thing?"

John held her gaze. "How did Zhou find out how the master chip worked?"

Chiara, in a gesture of thanks for his help, allowed George to hold her hand as they walked him back to his dormitory. She didn't know George very well, despite the fact that he was John's brother. The two Mahoneys couldn't have been more different, and those differences were glaring in the sunlight.

John's full, sensuous mouth was perfectly balanced by the strength of his jaw and the shape of his cheekbones. The same set of lips in George's much narrower, longer face became cartoonish when they parted to reveal his big white teeth, although there was a certain sexiness to the younger Mahoney's goofy smile.

John kept his hair short, neat, professional. George, perhaps in response to the numerous scalpings his mother had given him as a boy, grew his hair as long as he could. He was four inches shorter than John, but with his hair combed out as it was now, he was six inches taller than John. George's afro was so big that when he turned his head, his hair seemed to lag a second or two behind.

His tight-fitting Royal Navy sweater emphasized the scrawniness of his arms, and as Chiara hooked her arm through his, she felt as though she were hanging onto a coat rack. John had inherited his father's meaty build with none of the predisposition toward obesity. John worked out regularly to maintain his chiseled physique. George worked out, too, but managed only to become sinewy, like his mother.

And John wasn't the only Mahoney in love with a Winters woman. Though George hadn't mentioned her, Clara was the woman of his dreams. Despite the darkness of George's room, Chiara had noticed the poster he'd tacked to the ceiling above his saggy, cluttered bed. The poster, signed by Clara Winters Holtz, announced a lecture on bioentanglement physics she'd delivered at Washington University two years ago. According to John, George had been infatuated with Clara ever since.

"So, uh, Chiara," George said at the entrance to his dorm, clearly reading Chiara's mind. "How's your sister?"

"Still married and still twenty years older than you."

"Never give up on a good thing, that's what I always say," George smiled.

John snorted. Clara and Chiara were the first and last of the Winters sisters. Though they were twelve years apart in age, they both had the same big, pretty, molasses-dark eyes, full-lipped, bow-shaped mouths and dimples in their cheeks and chin. They bore such a strong resemblance to each other that Cady, with her annoying habit of furnishing nicknames, had labeled them Pete and Repeat. John wondered if George was attracted to Clara because she looked like Chiara, a woman he could never have. Not that he could ever have Clara, either.

"Do you think you could take some time away from studying for finals to help us out?" John asked with a sarcastic twitch of an eyebrow.

George cast a guilty smile toward the sidewalk. "Man, you know I had finals last week, before break. I only told Moms that so I could make a quick getaway."

"How do you think you did?" John asked, dreading the answer. George was one of the smartest people he knew, but one of the least self-directed.

"I've got my computer classes in the bag but I let some of my electives slide a little."

"How little?" John asked.

" 'Bout halfway down the alphabet," George grinned.

"Mother will kill you if you bring home anything less than a B, you know," John warned.

George laughed. "I've been changing my transcripts since the ninth grade. I haven't met a computer system I couldn't hack into."

"I'll keep that in mind," John muttered.

"Who needs good grades anyway?" George wondered aloud. "It's talent that matters. I've already turned down a job offer from some software outfit in Massachusetts. I'm holding out for a West Coast firm. That way I can pursue a part-time career in the film industry."

"You want to be an actor?" Chiara said.

"Not just any actor." George flexed his tiny muscles in a variety of poses.

John cracked his first smile of the day. "You're not still stuck on becoming—"

"Buck Hardrive," George announced, striking a Superman pose, "computer software designer by day, porn superstar by night." He strutted toward the dorm entrance, imitating an electric guitar riff he'd heard in one of his favorite dirty movies.

"He can help us," John said to Chiara as they waved goodbye to him.

"Do you think it's wise to let him keep the chip?"

"We don't have much of a choice. George is the only person I trust enough to hide it."

"I'm afraid he'll do something outlandish," Chiara fretted, "like take two million dollars from Siyuri Robotics and donate it to his high school computer club."

"He won't do that." John took her in a one armed hug and kissed the top of her head. "He knows how serious this is."

Chiara didn't know whether to laugh or cry at the thought that her salvation rested on the narrow shoulders of Buck Hardrive.

CHAPTER EIGHT

Chiara's early Friday morning flight to Chicago was right on schedule, which gave her enough time to retrieve her car from long-term parking and drive to USITI with only minutes to spare before her eight-thirty A.M. appointment with Emmitt Grayson. The new year was barely two days old, and Chiara was already dreading what it held in store.

There was no ladies' lounge on the top floor of the building, only Grayson's office and a spacious lobby for his receptionist, secretary and visitors. Chiara spent a moment in the ladies' room on her own floor, the seventh, to check her appearance.

Full-length mirrors lined the shorter wall facing the door, which had always bothered Chiara. Visitors to the building were always caught off guard when they first entered the restroom and encountered their own reflections walking toward them. Chiara fixed her eyes on her reflection as she entered the lavatory, and she tried to see herself as Grayson would.

She wore white, the best choice for her coloring and one of her favorite colors. White represented purity and innocence, and in Asian cultures, mourning. She wanted to communicate all three when she sat down with Grayson. She'd combed her hair into a sleek chignon, careful not to make it too severe. Her makeup had been applied with a light hand, but she wore no color on her lips. Her only jewelry was a pair of brilliant, Cartier diamond earrings that John had given her for Christmas.

She studied her reflection closer and admitted that her honey complexion looked a bit wan. She tried to convince herself that the mild nausea swirling in her belly was a remnant of her bumpy flight, but she knew better. It was due to a couple of things, the least of which being her impending face-to-face with Emmitt Grayson.

"Face to frost," Chiara mumbled to herself.

Emmitt Grayson had never been an easy person for her to get a handle on. Everything about him was cold and distant. When she tried to imagine him alone with Zhou, carrying out a murder, she couldn't see it. Murder would have required a certain amount of passion and feeling, two things she was certain Grayson lacked.

But then maybe that's why they call murder cold-blooded, she reasoned. In which case, she had no trouble imagining Grayson slipping Zhou enough medication to put him out of commission forever.

Chiara smoothed the front of her slim, snug-fitting skirt. She turned slightly sideways and pressed her tailored jacket front over her abdomen. The wool Anna Sui design was alluring yet professional, and the right shade of white for January. Dressed to take on the world—or at least Emmitt Grayson—Chiara exited the ladies' and took the elevator to the office in the clouds.

❦

While Chiara had headed directly to the technical sales and public relations department, John had gone to his old digs in information systems. He'd only been gone three months, but his former officemates greeted him as though he'd been gone years. They filled him in on all the USITI goings-on, the feature story being that of the recent suicide of sales rep Chen Zhou. John knew that his co-workers were fishing for any inside information he could provide. They knew of his long history with Chiara and itched to know what she might have told him.

John kept his comments bland and noninformative to the point of total boredom. When talk turned to promotions, firings and general gossip, John couldn't stop his thoughts from wandering ten floors up, where Chiara was probably just sitting down to her meeting with Grayson.

Once George had uncovered the master chip's capabilities, John had realized that he couldn't go through with his original plan to return the chip to Grayson under the guise of a misdelivered package. Grayson would never believe it, and he would surely have assumed that Chiara had had something to do with the chip's disappearance.

Chiara had come up with her own stopgap: to tender her resignation.

John planned to do the same, after a decent interval in which he would seek new employment. He couldn't afford to just up and quit, despite his contempt for Emmitt Grayson and his devious software. He had practical considerations, such as a house to buy and the family he hoped to soon put in it.

Emmitt Grayson himself, as part of his determination to diversify his rapidly growing corporation, had recruited both him and Chiara straight out of George Washington University. Their starting salaries had been ridiculously high, the benefits amazing—what company offered four weeks of paid vacation, matching 401Ks and pension eligibility from day one?

The job had seemed too good to be true, and after they started working in the Chicago headquarters they started seeing things that, in hindsight, should have tipped them off as to the true character of their employer.

The ceilings were speckled with small black domes that concealed surveillance cameras, and those were the ones in plain sight. As Chiara had pointed out, John's work in information systems made him a party to other forms of surveillance, such as the flagging of suspicious e-mails. There was a separate communications department devoted solely to monitoring phone calls. The party line was that calls were monitored to ensure customer satisfaction, but John was certain that all calls, not just those to customers, were monitored.

Too many USITI employees had become former employees after making the mistake of using their office computers to work on their resumés, or speaking to prospective new employers by phone from USITI.

While John regretted the way Chiara's USITI career was ending, he was relieved that she was leaving. She loved traveling and introducing USITI's products to new clients, but she'd always hated the office part of the job, where she was tied to her desk handling questions from the field and researching the potential new clients Grayson handpicked. Her departure would free her to move to St. Louis, something she'd seriously considered in light of John's transfer.

Armed with the status report on the St. Louis office, John went into a meeting of his own with his Chicago counterpart. The work John had been so proud of suddenly meant nothing as he discussed it, knowing that far above his head Chiara was facing a situation that would change her life.

Grayson spent a long moment studying his clasped hands, which rested on his desk, before he turned his expressionless gaze on Chiara, who sat directly in front of him in one of his uncomfortable leather and chrome chairs. She met his eyes and held them, but to her shame she looked away first.

She softly cleared her throat. "It's all there in my resignation letter, Mr. Grayson," she began, her voice the only sound in the cavernous office. "But I thought I owed it to you to tell you in person. It's time for me to move on. I've been planning to return to St. Louis, and—"

"Perfect," he snapped. "As you know, we're establishing a new base there, our first operation west of the Mississippi. It would be an excellent fit for you and extremely beneficial to USITI as well."

She held his gaze and said, "I don't want to work for USITI."

She replayed her words in her mind and was satisfied that she'd spoken plainly, emotionlessly. There was nothing Grayson could read into her delivery, yet she was still alarmed by the intensity of the silence rising between them. To her relief, Grayson looked away first this time.

Chiara continued. "My employment contract—"

"Remains in effect for six more months," Grayson spoke over her.

Chiara sat even straighter in her chair. "According to section seven, paragraph three, article nine, I can terminate my employment without thirty days' notice if an extenuating circumstance, whether medical, physical or emotional, prevents me from being able to perform the duties to which I'm assigned." *It's good to have a sister who's a lawyer,* Chiara thought smugly as Grayson's nostrils flared.

He drew several long, deep breaths, his eyes slightly narrowing at Chiara. "And what might your extenuating circumstance be?"

"I'd rather not disclose it at this time."

Grayson blinked in shock or surprise. "Then, pursuant to section seven, paragraph six, article two of your contract, I won't allow you to leave USITI without suffering the consequences."

Is that what happened to Zhou? Chiara was tempted to ask. Instead she said, "I'm well aware of the consequences. I'll forfeit my pension, severance pay, accrued sick and vacation pay, as well as any bonuses I've earned up to this point."

"You've been with me for a long time, Chiara. Are you willing to lose thousands of dollars to prematurely depart USITI without even providing me with your reason for doing so?"

"Money isn't the most important thing in the world to me," she said.

"I see."

"I don't think you do."

Grayson's pale eyes suddenly seemed as dark and cold as the waters of the great lake behind him.

"What I mean is that you don't know me well enough to know what's important to me," Chiara explained. "Our relationship has been strictly business and strictly professional."

"When do you plan to leave?"

"In two weeks. I've scheduled some vacation time, so I won't be in the office. I thought a clean break would be best."

"Two weeks," he echoed, stretching the 's' into a long, sibilant syllable. "Perhaps in that time I can persuade you to reconsider your resignation."

"I won't." She uncrossed her legs in preparation to stand.

"Of course you realize, Chiara, that your sudden departure casts suspicion in your direction regarding my missing master chip. USITI has done everything possible to recover the chip, to no avail. We're left with one conclusion: that Chen Zhou lost it, destroyed it…or gave it to someone else."

Chiara settled back into her seat. *This is it,* she told herself. *Here we go.* "Are you accusing me of stealing your chip, Mr. Grayson?"

"I'm simply recommending that you remain at USITI until the unpleasantness surrounding Chen's death and the mystery of the missing chip is resolved," he said smoothly. "Otherwise, USITI has no choice but to pursue it as a criminal matter, a case of corporate embezzlement."

"I didn't steal your chip!" Chiara said, too forcefully.

"Can you prove that you didn't?"

"Can you prove that I did? I believe the burden of proof is on the accuser, not the accused."

"Indeed you're right," Grayson grinned. "And to that end, USITI is handling this situation internally.

The last thing I want is for our clients to learn that we've had a severe breach of security. I'll find that chip, and when I do, the guilty party will be punished to the furthest extent of the law." He reached under his desk, his sudden movement startling Chiara's heart into her throat. He withdrew a white business card from an unseen compartment and slid it across his mirrored desktop. "There's a car waiting for you downstairs, Chiara. You'll be taken to USITI Security. Give this card to the receptionist. She'll direct you from there."

Her fingers trembled as she picked up the card and looked at it. It bore a single sequence of numbers. "What is this?"

"A mere formality." Grayson smiled, but it had no warmth and it failed to reach his eyes.

A separate building twenty minutes away from USITI headquarters housed security. A wide, semicircular driveway allowed access to the ten-story structure, which was square and all glass on the outside. It appeared as though one could see all that went on inside from the outside, but Chiara knew otherwise. There was nothing open about USITI Security, and what went on there was a mystery to all but the few who worked there.

Chiara's driver had kept his silence through the drive to security, and he maintained it even as he opened her door for her and escorted her to the reception desk in the glassed-in lobby. He didn't leave her side until the receptionist had taken Chiara's card, studied it, and directed her to an elevator that would take her to the sixth floor.

The doors opened onto a floor decorated all in white and chrome. It was fashionably sterile, empty and impersonal, like a laboratory. Chiara had little chance to really look around because a second receptionist rounded a desk and approached her. The woman wore a white lab coat, a mid-length black skirt and sensible black pumps. She looked more like some sort of medical assistant rather than a receptionist, and Chiara's heart began to jump when the woman peeled her white wool coat from her shoulders and took her handbag. She quickly stowed them behind the reception desk and then returned to Chiara.

Though the woman smiled, it seemed like a mask, and Chiara recoiled when she attempted to take her arm.

"Follow me, then, right to this room here," she said briskly. "Just go in and have a seat. The examiner will be right with you."

"Examiner?" Chiara said.

The woman gave her a tiny shove into a small gray room and shut the door. "Someone will be right with you, Miss Winters," came the woman's voice through a speaker system set somewhere in the walls. "Please have a seat."

Chiara eyed a squarish, gunmetal gray table and matching metal chair. She turned around and reached for the doorknob only to find that there wasn't one. "You have got to be kidding me," she murmured.

She wanted to kick herself for allowing the woman to take her handbag because her cell phone was in it. But after looking around the room and finding the surveillance camera mounted in one corner of the high ceiling, it occurred to her that she probably wouldn't have been able to get a signal to call out anyway.

Besides, who would she call? The police? And tell them what? That she was being held against her will at work?

She managed to calm herself a little, but her nerves prickled sharply once again when the door opened and a man entered. With his broad chest, big belly, and bushy mustache, he looked like a bulldog ambling on its back legs. He didn't look at Chiara as he toddled into the room, followed by another man in a white lab coat who pushed in a cushioned leather swivel chair on casters.

The man in the lab coat parked the swivel chair on the other side of the table. "Miss?" he prompted, escorting Chiara to the metal chair and encouraging her to sit with a less than gentle push to her shoulders. The bulky man plopped onto the cushioned chair, and he used a yellowing handkerchief to mop the sweat from his balding pink pate.

Yet another man in a lab coat entered the room carrying a notebook computer with a collection of thin cables and tubes attached to it. Once he'd set the equipment on the table and neatly arranged the parts, Chiara recognized what the kit was. She'd never seen one in real life before, but she'd seen one pictured in one of her sister Cady's freelance newspaper articles, "Going on the Box."

"Mr. Grayson sent me here for a lie detector test?" She almost laughed. "All because I want to quit working for him?"

"Would you mind removing your jacket, miss?" the bulky man asked.

She finally noticed the pale hand of one of the other men. He stood just behind her left shoulder, awaiting her jacket.

Chiara angrily undid her jacket and took it off. She slung it over the man's arm, and he vanished with it. The other man approached her and began hooking her up to the lie detector. The bulky man watched as a blood pressure cuff was fastened around Chiara's right arm, just above her elbow. "I'm sure you recognize that," the examiner said, opening the notebook computer and squaring it to face the monitor screen away from Chiara. "It's a standard blood pressure cuff, which will send changes in your blood pressure and heart rate to my computer here. The two fingerplates now being attached to the index and ring fingers of your left hand are called galvanometers, and they'll measure electro-dermal activity."

"You mean how much my fingers sweat if I lie," Chiara said primly.

The examiner answered with a warm chuckle. "To call this appliance a lie detector is a misnomer, Miss Winters. No machine can detect a lie, and in all the years I've been administering these exams, I've yet to discover what an actual lie looks like. This box measures physiology—changes in blood pressure, breathing and perspiration rate."

"Lots of things can trigger those changes," Chiara said. "The anxiety produced by having to take a damn *lie detector test* can make it look like someone's lying."

"No one is making you take this test, Miss Winters," he said, even as his assistant strapped a thin rubber tube around Chiara's chest. "The Employee Polygraph Protection Act of 1988 allows a business, in this case United States IntelTech, to request the exam, but no one can force you to take it."

The assistant stood at Chiara's side, a rubber tube lax in his hand.

"According to the EPPA, an employee cannot be disciplined in any way or discharged based on refusal to take the test," the examiner said.

"Then I refuse to take it," Chiara stated flatly.

"However," the examiner continued, "the EPPA does not apply to businesses under contract with the federal government." The beady black eyes wedged in his chubby face stared hard at Chiara. "And as you know, USITI has several federal contracts, one of which you yourself engineered."

Chiara surrendered. "I guess I'm taking your little test then."

The assistant leaned over to fasten his remaining tube around her waist. When he moved it too close to her abdomen, she balked and shoved his hands away. "Is this safe?"

The examiner's gaze sharpened. "None of this equipment is invasive. It won't leave any marks." His cheeks bulged in a smile. "It won't even wrinkle your pretty white blouse. That's a pneumograph tube. It's filled with air, and it'll measure the expansion of your chest and diaphragm. It's harmless, Miss Winters."

She allowed the placement of the last tube, and the assistant started for the door. Once they were alone, the examiner said, "A very serious crime has occurred in your workplace. I'm not here looking for a deceptive person. I'm looking for the innocent one. When I take this chair and face you in that one, I'm totally objective. The instant I determine that your results show no deception, I take your side. I become your champion."

Chiara knew that this was the point where she was supposed to thank him, to show gratitude for his potential faith in her. But she'd read Cady's article thoroughly. She knew that the examiner was only trying to gain her trust, to make her feel as though he were her only ally. "How long will this take?" she asked blandly.

Three and a half hours later, Chiara, again in the company of the robotic driver who'd delivered her to

USITI Security, emerged into a frigid January afternoon. She was glad for the cold because it masked the
trembling that had resulted from her testing ordeal.

The examiner had been professional, as far as she
could tell, and Chiara had answered his questions
honestly. Well…as honestly as she could.

The examiner had explained his procedure in full
and had reviewed his questions with her before
starting the test. And just as Cady had written in her
article, the questions were an odd assortment of
inquiries relevant to the missing master chip, questions designed to catch her in ordinary white lies, and
questions to which lies would make no sense. And
they'd come in random order, a tactic designed to
illicit measurable responses.

"Are you 30 years old?" he'd deadpanned in a tone
completely devoid of the animation he'd shown
earlier.

"Yes," Chiara had responded.

"Have you ever stolen anything in your life?"

"Yes," Chiara had answered. Who hadn't? She'd
tasted grapes before buying them at the market, and
that was a form of stealing. She'd used pens at her
doctor's office and forgotten to return them, and that
was a form of stealing, too. And she'd purloined a veri-
table pirate's treasure in loose change in the years she'd
spent taking her church offering to 7-Eleven on
Sundays.

"Have you ever told a lie?"

"Oh, for Heaven's sake," she'd groaned in frustration. "Of course I have. I lied two minutes ago when you asked me if I was comfortable."

"Please answer the questions with a yes or no, Miss Winters," he'd instructed in his peculiar wooden voice. "Have you recently traveled to Malaysia?"

"Yes," Chiara sighed.

"Have you recently traveled to Japan?"

And on and on it went, with innocuous questions, such as "Were you born in St. Louis, Missouri?" sprinkled among weightier ones, such as "Do you have knowledge of the missing master chip?"

Sitting in the back of the hired car, Chiara wanted to kick something in frustration over that particular question. *Of course I have knowledge of it,* she inwardly seethed. *Grayson himself provided me with it when he told me about Zhou's death.*

Her driver slipped behind the wheel and started the engine. Chiara was so flustered she almost didn't notice a second understated black Town Car facing the opposite direction in the curved driveway. Her own driver spent a moment fiddling with his headset phone and Chiara watched as the other driver exited his vehicle and opened the back door.

John, resplendent in a long black coat over his dark gray wool suit, exited the car. His expression tense and possibly annoyed, he glanced in her direction, but gave no outward sign that he'd seen her. Chiara sat forward to get a better look at him, but noticing her driver's flinty eyes in the rearview mirror, she muted her reaction. She sat back in her seat and her driver put the car in gear, angling it away from USITI Security.

Just relax, she thought hard, telegraphing the two words to John as her driver took her farther and farther away from him. *All you have to do is relax...*

CHAPTER NINE

Chiara spent the next few hours at her desk buried in long-neglected paperwork. She went about the business of writing letters to clients she'd initiated contact with, informing them of her imminent departure from USITI, and she started a list of existing clients to whom she and Zhou had sold R-GS chips. She compiled the list by hand, on lined paper. She wanted as few of her activities conducted on her office computer as possible, knowing that Grayson was monitoring every move she made.

She kept to herself, and her officemates seemed to respect her desire to be alone. Chele Brewster, one of the few women employed in technical sales, approached Chiara close to the end of the day.

Chiara couldn't help smiling when Chele knocked on her open door and hesitantly entered. The two saw each other primarily at staff meetings and in passing between sales junkets. Chele, a native of New Orleans, had the café au lait coloring of her Creole ancestors but the patrician features of her English father. Her fluency in French, German, Dutch and Hungarian, along with her intelligence, perfect figure and exuberant sense of humor made her ideally suited for the European markets she covered for USITI.

"Is this a bad time?" Chele asked, her hands clasped at her back.

"No, it's fine." Chiara beckoned her into a chair. "I meant to thank you for the card you sent to me in St. Louis. I'm sorry I didn't do it sooner. I've had some things on my mind."

"I'll bet." Chele leaned forward to rest her crossed arms on her knees. "Zhou was a great guy. It's a shame you have to deal with the fallout over that chip."

"So it's common knowledge?"

"Not really," Chele said, lightly running her fingers over the red silk of her skirt. "Mr. Grayson called a few of us into his office and told us that Zhou had misplaced a master. He wanted to know if Zhou had talked to any of us about it. You know," she shrugged a shoulder, "the standard reconnaissance."

Chiara nodded.

"Hey, I was thinking we could grab a cocktail or something after work," Chele said. "If you want to talk or something."

"I appreciate the offer, but I haven't been home in a week and a half," Chiara said. "I spent the holidays with my family in St. Louis, and I came here straight from O'Hare this morning. I'm looking forward to just being by myself for a while. Could I take a rain check?"

"Sure. But you'll have to redeem it after the eigh-teenth. Geoff Mathis and I are leaving for Zurich

tomorrow afternoon. Mr. Grayson finally won over
that Swiss plastics manufacturer that he's been wooing
for the past two years. They just installed a complete
R-GS system, and Geoff and I are going to be
spending two weeks training and troubleshooting.
Should be fun."

"Uh huh," Chiara said absently.

"Are you sure you're okay?" Chele asked, standing
to get a better look at Chiara.

"I'm fine," Chiara said. "I just need to get home
and get some rest."

Chele looked at the delicate Rolex circling her
wrist. "Five o'clock," she said. "Time to clock out."

A loud knock sounded on Chiara's door, startling
both women. "Not quite," said Emmitt Grayson, who
stood in Chiara's doorway. "I need to see you in my
office, Chiara. Now." Without waiting for a response,
he turned and vanished into the corridor.

"Guess you're staying after class today, Chiara,"
Chele teased.

"I guess I am," she managed, her hands suddenly
clammy with sweat.

◈◈◈

Chiara stared hard at Grayson, her mood darkening to match the purple twilight settling over Lake
Michigan. John, who'd already been seated in front of
Grayson's desk when Chiara arrived, leaned back in
his chair with his left ankle propped upon his right
knee. He could have been sitting on Abby's back

porch, shooting the breeze with Lee, Keren, Zweli and Christopher for all the concern he showed at being subjected to Grayson's silence for five minutes.

Chiara fought her natural tendency toward fidgeting and instead kept her energy and concentration on Grayson, who continued to peruse the papers and charts neatly arranged on his desk. Chiara wished that she could read Grayson's thoughts and know what fresh headache he planned to lay on her now.

When he looked up at her, the intensity of his gaze replaced Chiara's annoyed impatience with a new brand of fear. Grayson scowled, which made his face look as though it had been carved from granite. His hands were so tightly clenched upon his papers that his knuckles whitened. For a long moment, he stared between Chiara and John, his thin lips pursed to the point of invisibility.

Here it comes, Chiara thought dismally. *Whatever he did to Zhou, he's about to do to John and me.*

She frantically thought back on key questions. "Do you have knowledge regarding the whereabouts of the missing master chip?" "Do you know who has possession of the missing master chip?" "Are you concealing information regarding the missing master chip?"

With thoughts of the ruins in her head and of the time she and John had shared their first sloppy, giggly kiss beneath the biggest willow, Chiara had answered "No" to each, hoping that her happy memory would mask her lies. Convinced that her falsehoods were about to be flung in her face, she clenched her right fist within her left hand and locked her jaw.

"I owe you both an apology," Grayson finally said.

Chiara almost choked on the breath she was holding. John placed his left foot on the floor, and only then did Chiara notice how tightly his hands gripped his knees. She lowered her eyes to her hands as a wave of guilt crested within her. John hadn't asked for any of this—to be treated like a criminal, to be spied on and subjected to Grayson's mistrust and possible wrath. She hadn't asked for it either, but if she'd kept her mouth shut about the hidey hole, Zhou would never have been able to involve John.

Whatever happened to John from here on out would be her fault, and the thought made Chiara sick.

"Are you all right, Chiara?" Grayson asked, no real concern in his voice.

She pressed her fingers to her forehead. "I'm fine. Just tired."

"I understand, given today's events," Grayson said. "And again, in light of the results of your polygraph exams, I extend my most sincere apologies for subjecting you to the ordeal. Your results certainly clear up the matter regarding the master chip. Unfortunately, evidence of a separate deception was brought to light."

John stared somewhere beyond Grayson's head. Chiara kept her eyes on her boss.

"Would either of you care to divulge any information regarding this matter?"

"I have no idea what this 'matter' concerns," John stated.

"Is this something that involves John or just me?" Chiara asked, earning a short, stunned glance from John.

His cold glare on Chiara, Grayson said, "It involves both of you." He turned to John. "Your polygraph shows a probable deception in answer to question forty-three."

"You'll have to be more specific," John said coolly. "I don't remember the numbers of every single question. That could have been 'Do you like ham?' and my answer could have registered as untrue. In general, I don't care for ham at all, but over the holidays I had a ham with a cherry-apricot glaze that was simply delicious. Do I like ham? No. Did I like that particular ham? Yes."

Grayson sighed heavily through his nose. "You're hiding something, Mr. Mahoney. Your results show that you have no knowledge of my chip but they also show that you are, and I quote, 'concealing information vital to your performance at USITI.' As for you, Chiara, your answer to question fifty-five raised a red flag. 'Are you withholding information that may affect your work?' " Grayson flattened his hands on the desk and hungrily leaned forward. "Would either of you care to explain yourselves?"

"I have nothing to say about the results of my polygraph, other than that I've done nothing to compromise USITI or my employment here," John calmly stated.

"Very well then, Mr. Mahoney. You leave me with few options. Chiara, you're too valuable an employee to let go over the mere suspicion of wrongdoing, particularly given your stellar performance in technical sales and public relations. Mr. Mahoney, although you have been an exemplary employee as well, I can't risk keeping you in a sensitive position such as director of St. Louis information systems. Chen Zhou made a very brief visit to St. Louis within twenty-four hours of his return from Tokyo, the same time frame during which I believe he absconded with my master chip. While I have no evidence that Chen Zhou made contact with you while he was in St. Louis, I cannot overlook such an alarming coincidence. Mr. Mahoney, your employment here at USITI is terminated as of—"

"I'm pregnant," Chiara said over him. "John is the father. That's the secret we've been keeping."

Grayson's eyelids fluttered in shock. His mouth dropped open slightly before he regained his composure. "Mr. Mahoney, is this true?"

John, as wide-eyed and stunned as Grayson had been, stared at Chiara. "Yes."

"And this is what you two are hiding?" Mr. Grayson asked.

"We haven't been hiding it," Chiara said. "We just didn't feel the need to share our private, personal business with anyone outside the two of us at this point in time. Office romances aren't forbidden, but they're certainly discouraged here at USITI. But with John in information systems and me halfway across the globe on sales trips twice a month, we never felt that our relationship compromised our work. My pregnancy hasn't affected either of our job performances, but as your polygraph shows, I knew that it would eventually."

"This child," Grayson began, "is it the reason you planned to leave USITI?"

"Yes," she answered truthfully, though it wasn't the reason she wanted out so suddenly.

"Was Chen Zhou aware of your condition?" Grayson asked.

"No. John and I haven't told anyone, not even our families."

"May I ask why not?"

"It's too soon. I wanted to wait until I was further along."

Grayson tapped his left thumb on his desk. "And here I am, ruining your surprise. I do apologize, Chiara, John. Congratulations."

"Am I allowed to go back to work now, or am I still terminated as of…" John held his hands wide, waiting for Mr. Grayson's response.

He prefaced his answer with a crocodilian grin. "You have a child to support, Mr. Mahoney. By all means, return to St. Louis and continue your fine work for USITI. I hope you bear no hard feelings for the time you've spent in the hot seat, as it were. Just as you'll do everything within your power to ensure the better welfare of your child, you have to understand my desire to preserve the security and interests of USITI."

John stood and adjusted the front of his jacket. "It's all crystal clear, Mr. Grayson." He glanced at the dark sky and then took a quick peek at his watch. "My flight back to St. Louis leaves in an hour. I might just be able to make it to Midway. If we're finished here, I'd like to prevail upon Chiara for a ride."

"I'll need another word with her," Grayson said. "Have my assistant arrange a car for you. Thank you, Mr. Mahoney."

"Certainly." John knew a dismissal when he heard one. He nodded his head and left.

Grayson waited a long moment after John had closed the door behind him before he said, "John Mahoney appears to be quite a remarkable man."

"He is," Chiara agreed.

"You've known him for a number of years, yes?"

"Since we were eight years old." She chewed the inside of her lower lip, thinking of the anguish John had endured to be her friend. Hundreds of Sundays and hundreds of beatings, and he'd just taken one more for her.

"It would seem that your fortunes are inextricably bound," Grayson said.

"I suppose they are, especially now."

"Do you love him?"

Chiara flinched. She was totally taken aback, not by the question itself, but by who was asking it. Grayson was single, and as far as Chiara knew, he'd never been romantically linked to anyone. Grayson knew more than Bill Gates about the intricacies of computer technology, but when it came to interpersonal relationships, he seemed completely clueless. In answering him, Chiara chose words that condensed her long, sometimes complicated history with John. "Yes. I always have."

"Do you plan to marry him?"

Chiara's older relatives had bedeviled her and John with that very question on Christmas day, and just as it had then, it brought a devilish smile to her face. "We have some things to settle first."

"Such as, if I may ask?"

"My career goals."

"I can help with that, Chiara. Would you change your mind about resigning if John Mahoney were to be named your new partner?"

She shifted uncomfortably in her chair. "I don't see how that would benefit us, especially once our baby arrives."

"Your child could travel with you," Grayson suggested. "USITI could provide a childcare allowance to hire a nanny who would go wherever you did. A family traveling for business would be above reproach, unimpeachable. Who wouldn't trust a handsome family in any business deal?"

Grayson's face broke in a toothy smile that made Chiara draw back against her chair. "After my father died, I hardly ever saw my mother," she said after regaining her composure. "She taught high school by day and worked as a cashier at a supermarket by night to support me and my sisters. My grandmother raised me. I want to raise my child myself. I won't ever pick USITI or any other company over my child."

Grayson's smile melted away. "That's a noble ambition, Chiara, if impractical. You make a good living, one that enables you to easily support a child. It would be a shame for you to give up your career in your prime. Your potential here at USITI is infinite. I'd really like you to think about what it would mean for your future to remain at USITI."

Chiara stood, ending the meeting whether Grayson was finished with her or not. "That's all I've been thinking about for the past two weeks, Mr. Grayson. I'm going home now, sir."

❧

Chiara didn't start running until she exited the elevator that had taken her to the underground parking garage. Her arms and legs felt weak and shaky as she ran to her bright red Mitsubishi Eclipse, which sat isolated in its assigned parking spot. She spent a moment sitting in the idling car, tightly gripping the steering wheel, taking deep breaths to send fresh, clean air to her brain.

"That was close," she whispered. "That was so, so close." She pressed one hand to her abdomen as if embracing the new life sheltered there. "You just saved our lives, baby." *And I'm going to do everything I can to make sure they stay saved.*

She gunned the engine and raced to the exit, barely stopping to swipe her keycard to activate the mechanical arm barring her way. Her tires squealed as she pulled into traffic on North Michigan Avenue, and zoomed away from USITI, hopefully for the last time.

She reached her apartment building in no time at all and found a good spot on the street. Her doorman greeted her warmly and hurried to retrieve her mail, which he'd collected for her during her absence.

Chiara thanked him with a huge tip, and rather than wait for one of the two elevators to crawl down to the lobby from one of the higher floors, she swept into the stairwell, working her cell phone out of her handbag as she started up the stairs.

She dialed John, hoping to catch him before he boarded his plane and had to turn off his cell. She'd reached the third floor before he finally answered.

"Hey." She almost moaned at the sound of his voice.

"Hey, baby," he said. "Are you all right?"

"I had to tell him," she panted. "He would have fired you and ruined your whole career."

"There are other jobs. I'm going to start looking for one as soon as I get back to St. Louis." He quieted for a moment. "Why are you breathing hard?"

"I'm walking up the stairs to my apartment." She reached her floor and threw open the heavy fire door to her corridor. "I finally made it."

"Are the elevators busted?"

"No, but they're slow as cold molasses, and I want to get home and take a long, hot bath."

"You live on the eighth floor," John scolded. "You know you shouldn't be exerting yourself like that."

"I'm allowed to exercise, John," she chuckled.

"It's good to hear you laugh."

She reached her front door and slipped her key into the knob lock and then the deadbolt. "I finally feel like we have a chance to walk away from all this." She pushed her door open and instinctively put her hand out to flip the light switch on the wall just inside the door. "We just have to figure out what to do about…that's funny."

"What?"

"It's dark in here." Keeping her door open with her foot to allow in the light from the corridor, she flipped the hall switch once more, and still nothing happened.

"Then turn on a light."

"That's just it," she said. "I'm trying to. Plus I left my living room and bedroom lights on a timer. They should have come on already."

"You set the timer, but you probably forgot to plug your lamps into it," John said. "You've been on the forgetful side ever since you found out you were pregnant."

Chiara let the door close behind her and walked deeper into her apartment, toward the dark living room. "You're probably right." She slipped off her coat. She held the phone to her right ear with her shoulder as she groped inside the kitchen to turn on that light with her right hand while she used her left to toss her coat at a chair in the dining room.

The kitchen fluorescents quivered on, washing everything in a flat white light, including the hooded figure in black that lunged at her. The stranger tore the phone from her grip as his hand went to her throat. He forced her through the doorway and slammed her against the wall of her corridor, closing her throat with his vise-like hold.

Her attacker held her phone to her head with his free hand and John's voice filled her ear. "Chiara? Baby, are you still there?"

Her fingernails raked at the gloved hand denying her air. She brought her knees up to try to push him away, but he used his taller, wider frame to immobilize her.

"Baby?" John said once more, his voice rising.

The word triggered Chiara's most basic survival instincts.

Rather than clawing at the gloves protecting his hands, she brought her manicured thumbnails to the one vulnerable spot she could still make out through her blurring vision: the eyeholes of his black hood. She dug her thumbs in down to the knuckle, and her attacker growled in pain. He dropped her phone and released her neck. Drawing in long, noisy breaths of air that rasped against her raw windpipe, Chiara bolted for the door. Her shoes weren't made for speed and she stumbled over her own feet.

The man in black tackled her at the door, throwing her against it as he wrestled her wrists into his hands.

"You've got something I want." His voice was calm, low, almost conversational. Tears of blood dripped from his eyes and onto Chiara's white jacket. "I don't want to hurt you to get it. But I will."

"M-My wallet's in my h-hand-handbag," Chiara almost sobbed. "Take it. It's right by the door."

He clamped both her wrists in one hand, and when he shifted to reach for her purse, Chiara took that opportunity to throw him further off balance. She twisted her hands out of his grasp, locked her fingers in a double fist and drove it down hard, toward his crotch. She caught him high on his thigh but well off the mark, enraging rather than crippling him. He grabbed a handful of her hair with one fist and pounded the other one into her, his first blow catching her on her collarbone. She curled up on her side, her arms folded over her torso, taking the blows to her shoulders and face.

The man wrenched her head back and forced her knees from her chest as she continued to scream for help. He climbed over her, positioning his knees on her upper arms to hold her down. His gloved left hand clamped over her mouth, stifling her and forcing her to fight for every breath.

"One more sound…" He finished his warning by showing her his right hand, which was curled into a fist the approximate size of a small canned ham. "Now let's try this again."

Chiara cried out in pain when he shifted his weight to reach past her head for her bag. He emptied the contents onto her chest and took up her wallet. After swiping a smear of blood from his eyes, he removed all of her credit cards, business cards, cash and receipts, letting them rain down on her before he sat back on his knees and shook his head.

"It's not in the apartment, it's not in the purse," he muttered, thinking aloud. "It's a needle in a damn haystack."

Chiara vigorously shook her head. "I don't know what you're talking about," she cried. "I don't know what you want!"

He hooked his fingers inside the lapels of her blouse, taking hold of it along with her jacket. "I think you know perfectly well what I want," he sneered, and with one fierce tug he ripped open her clothing.

"Help me!" Chiara shrieked as his hands moved roughly under the silk of her white bra. "Somebody help!"

She tried to buck him off, screaming as loud as she could all the while. The man sitting astride her drew back his right fist. It was the last thing Chiara saw before she felt an explosion of pain that ended in silent blackness.

CHAPTER TEN

The glow of clean, bright light from the kitchen was the first thing Chiara saw when her eyes dragged open. Her neck and lower back throbbed in pain, but it was no match for the stinging, swelling sensation burning the entire right side of her face. She brought a shaky hand to her right eye, fearful that she'd find it popping from the socket because of the pressure behind it.

Whimpering, she frantically scrambled backwards, terrified that her attacker was still near. Realizing that she was backed up against her front door, she whirled around and pulled the door open, crawling on her hands and knees into the corridor.

"Help!" she screamed, finding her feet and launching herself at her nearest neighbor's door. "Please, somebody, help!"

Three doors down, the elderly Jefferson Petrie, a retired University of Chicago African-American Studies professor, stepped halfway into the corridor. "Good Lord," he gasped, clutching his quilted smoking jacket closer about him.

"Please," Chiara sobbed. "Someone was in my apartment!"

"Dear girl," Mr. Petrie called to her, catching her as she stumbled into his arms. "Are they gone? Have you called the police?"

"No, I…" Chiara let Mr. Petrie pull her into his apartment. He slammed the door behind them and bolted it, and then took Chiara by her shoulders. "I need to call the police. I-I need…a phone…"

"That, and a shot of brandy." Mr. Petrie guided her through the foyer, into his living room, and into a short, squatty, overstuffed leather wing chair. Chiara sat stiffly in the chair while Mr. Petrie fussed over her. No matter how hard she hugged herself, she couldn't stop herself from shaking. Mr. Petrie vanished for a moment but returned with his cordless phone in one hand and a short snifter of brandy in the other.

"Yes, The Sovereign, on West Farwell Avenue," he said haughtily. "A woman has been attacked in her own home. She's sheltered here with me, in apartment 814."

He offered her the brandy, but she declined, softly saying, "I'm pregnant."

Mr. Petrie's eyes became dark brown circles of surprise. He tossed back the brandy himself before speaking once more into the phone. "Please, send someone immediately." He hung up on the 911 dispatcher and sat on an ottoman. He took Chiara's hand. She gave him credit for not cringing at the blood caked in her nail beds. "Is there anyone else I can call for you, Miss Winters?"

John, she wanted to cry out. But she couldn't force herself to speak his name. She wouldn't let herself drag him into this fresh mess. "I just need the police."

"You're covered in blood," Mr. Petrie said. "Would you like to lie down?"

"It's not mine," she told him. "It's his."

Mr. Petrie gave her hand a comforting squeeze. "Good for you, darling. I'll run along and get you a fresh shirt just the same."

Chiara was suddenly aware of her now buttonless jacket and torn blouse. She ran her hands over her body, taking personal inventory. Her skirt was missing its hook and eye closure, her pockets had been turned out, and the zipper had been ripped open right down into the seam. Her skin still bore the memory of her attacker's touch, but he hadn't raped her. She pulled her torn blouse together to cover herself. A fresh fall of tears flooded from her eyes as she thanked heaven for that singular blessing.

Mr. Petrie returned with a folded French blue button-down, breaking the dry cleaner's tape on it as he neared her. He helped her out of her bloody jacket and into the shirt, buttoning it for her when her hands proved too unsteady.

"Tell me about your latest business trip," Mr. Petrie said brightly. "You were in Japan, weren't you?"

Her head bobbed up and down in a nod as she wiped her cheeks dry. "You don't have to try to distract me, Mr. Petrie. I appreciate it, though."

"You've been such a wonderful neighbor, Miss Winters," he told her, resuming his seat on the ottoman. "When I think of all the times you've helped me with my confounded computer or taken my trash out for me, it sickens me that I can't do more for you now. One of the reasons I've enjoyed residing here at The Sovereign is because of its thick, sturdy walls. If the walls were thinner, and if I were twenty-five years younger, perhaps I could have stopped this from happening to you before it got good and started."

"You're helping me now, Mr. Petrie," she said through a weak smile. "This is what matters now."

He lightly touched the injured side of her face. "I hope they catch the bastard who did this to you." He braced his hands on his knees to help push himself up. "I must have a steak or something for that eye."

Loud, rapid knocking on his door nearly startled Chiara out of her chair. Mr. Petrie veered away from the kitchen and hurried into the foyer. "Who is it?" Chiara heard him call through the door.

"Chicago Police," came the voice on the other side.

"Please display your badge before the peephole," Mr. Petrie said.

Mr. Petrie was apparently satisfied because Chiara heard him fiddling with his locks and chains. "She's right over here in the living room," he said, directing the pair of officers. "She's been injured, I'm not sure how badly. She's quite shaken up."

Chiara looked up at the officers, both of whom seemed to tower over her. Before they could speak one word to her, a shorter man in a blue polyester suit butted in front of them.

"In my twelve years as manager of The Sovereign, I've never had a tenant attacked in my building," ranted Louis Hopkins, the man who had been almost sickening in his fawning over Chiara when he signed her to a lease seven years ago. "The officers here will be conducting a full investigation of what happened tonight, Miss Winters, and I assure you, they'll discover where lies the liability for your unfortunate experience this evening. Is there anything you'd like to tell me now, regarding this incident, that might sway my opinion as to whether I allow you to serve out the remainder of your lease?"

"I can enlighten you, Mr. Hopkins," Mr. Petrie said, thrusting out his barrel chest and standing at his full five and a half feet.

Mr. Hopkins shot Chiara a look of disgust before turning an ingratiating grin on Mr. Petrie. "Yes, Mr. Petrie. What is it?

"Well, if I were Miss Winters, I'd certainly have the officers here investigate how a decent, law-abiding tenant could have been attacked, possibly even killed, in her own apartment. I'd also hire an attorney to represent my interests regarding the remainder of my lease. Miss Winters is the one who should be asking questions of *you* where building security is concerned. I've been a tenant here for twenty-two years, and I'd say that ever since you took over its management, security has been lax, if not downright crappy."

"Chiara!"

John had begun calling her name the moment the elevator opened on the eighth floor of The Sovereign. He sprinted down the hall to her apartment, his black coat flapping behind him. Fear clawed at his gut when he saw the light of a flash camera bleeding into the corridor through her open front door.

He burst into the apartment to find at least four policemen and five other men, two in suits and one in a smoking jacket. One of the officers used a double-handled camera with a huge flash attachment to take photos of Chiara's living room. Another man was in the kitchen using a big floppy brush to sweep dark powder on the doorframe. One of the men in suits, his gold badge clipped to his waist, stopped John as he tried to move deeper into the apartment.

"This is a crime scene, sir," he said, the words issuing from beneath a neat black mustache. He flashed his detective's badge at John, who barely noticed it. "I'll have to ask you for some ID. Now what brings you here tonight?"

"I called you." John fished out his wallet and shoved it into the detective's hand. His heart jumped into the back of his throat at the sight of Chiara's apartment. The place looked like Hurricane Katrina had hit it. Her dining room table was a flat disc of blond maple, its legs sawed off and scattered. Her maple bookcases were flat on the floor, her books strewn about with pages littering the floor. The ceiling light fixtures she'd chosen with such care upon moving into the place were broken, the bare bulbs dangling like lost stars. Every drawer had been removed, every piece of furniture overturned. John's favorite chair, a custom-built recliner, had been flipped over and ripped apart.

"Mr. Mahoney," the detective said. "Are you a friend of the victim?"

"He's her boyfriend," said the man in the smoking jacket, who John vaguely recognized as one of Chiara's neighbors. "Or her fiancé or something."

John tore his eyes from the destruction and fixed them on the swarthy detective. "Where is she? Is she all right?" He forced his way past the detective, who followed close on his heels.

"She's fine," the detective tried to assure John, who stepped over the wreckage of Chiara's belongings to reach the living room. "She's being treated, and then we're going to collect her statement."

"Chiara," John almost moaned upon seeing her in the dining room. She was standing with a paramedic in the one bare patch of hardwood. Mindless of the paramedic applying a cold pack to her face, John took her in his arms. "Baby," he sighed. "My baby, my baby."

"Miss Winters was attacked here earlier this evening, Mr. Mahoney," the detective said.

"I heard her scream when we were on the phone," John said, his eyes never leaving Chiara's face. "When I lost the call, I phoned the police from Midway." He cradled Chiara's face in his hands. "I got here as fast as I could. I should have stayed with you tonight."

"You should have gotten on that plane and gone back to St. Louis," Chiara told him. She clamped her jaw to stave off new tears. "You shouldn't be here. I don't want you here."

"Ma'am, we really should get you in the wagon and take you to a hospital," the young paramedic said.

John turned to him. "She's pregnant. Did she tell you?"

"That's why I think she should go to the hospital," the paramedic responded. "She should be checked out in the ER tonight and then see her regular OB/GYN as soon as possible."

John turned back to Chiara. He reached for her face, but didn't touch it.

Chiara wanted to look away. John's eyes told her what his mouth hadn't, that whatever pain she felt was nothing compared to how he felt at knowing that she'd been assaulted. "I don't need you here, John," she insisted in a broken whisper.

"Just like I didn't need you every time I took a beating," he murmured near her ear.

"It's not the same." Her arms went around him, despite her desire to see him go. "You're not safe around me."

"Let me worry about me." *Let me worry about all of us.*

❧

John was asked to step outside Chiara's trauma room while a doctor gave her a cursory physical exam and a nurse took scrapings from her fingernails and swabbed her cheeks, chin, forehead and chest. A female crime scene investigator appeared to collect Chiara's clothing, including Mr. Petrie's shirt. She then asked Chiara to strip out of her hospital gown and stand on a square of sticky white paper. Chiara's hair was combed straight down and her entire body was brushed.

"I know this isn't the most pleasant experience," the investigator said, "but there's a good chance that the man who attacked you left evidence of himself behind. You can hide your face and fingerprints, but it's virtually impossible to hide your DNA. If he has a record, his DNA profile is probably in the system. Finding him will just be a matter of time."

"I understand," Chiara said.

"If you'll just carefully step off the paper now." The investigator held the paper in place as Chiara peeled her bare feet from it. The waiting nurse helped her back into her gown.

"I'm taking you up to obstetrics now, Miss Winters," the friendly nurse said. "A technician is waiting to conduct an ultrasound."

"I want John to come with me," Chiara said, gingerly seating herself in the wheelchair the nurse held for her.

"Absolutely," the nurse smiled.

John took over the wheelchair and let the nurse lead him to the elevators. She chattered amiably about the unseasonably cold start to the new year, the renovations the hospital was making to its maternity and oncology wards, the new menu in the cafeteria—whatever popped into her mind to fill the silence.

Chiara knew that the nurse was trying to put her at ease and keep her comfortable, but the harder she tried to be nice, the greater Chiara's worry grew.

The rest of her injuries had been dressed and treated, and the ultrasound was the last thing left to do. It was the most important thing, and the one that scared her most.

"Here you are, Miss Winters," the nurse said, ushering her and John into a dimly lit exam room and the waiting hands of an ultrasound technician. "Good luck to you."

Chiara's lips formed the words "Thank you," but her mouth had become so dry that no sound came out. John, his jaw tense, took off his coat and jacket before helping her onto the exam bed. He held one of her hands in both of his.

"How far along are you, Miss Winters?" the technician asked as he rolled up Chiara's gown.

"About twelve weeks or so," she answered, keeping her eyes on the speckled ceiling tile.

"Then you've had at least one of these already."

Chiara flinched when a squirt of warm transducing gel landed on her abdomen. "I had one at eight weeks, to confirm the pregnancy and make sure everything was where it was supposed to be."

"Well, this one will be just like that one," the technician said. He used a remote to completely douse the lights.

Chiara fixed her gaze on John, who stared, unblinking, at the ultrasound's viewing monitor.

"Okay," the technician said, moving the transducer over Chiara's lower belly as he watched the black-and-white pie-shaped image on the viewing monitor. "Let me find where your little angel is hiding in there…"

Chiara closed her eyes. It seemed to take forever to search the universe inside her. She'd been so nervous about her meeting with Grayson that she hadn't been able to eat anything for breakfast. The polygraph had literally eaten her lunch hour, and any dinner plans she might have had had been canceled by her assault. There was nothing in her stomach or bladder to aid the discovery of anything residing in her uterus. She was about to ask John to get her a bottle of water, when the technician smiled.

"Eureka," he said. Chiara's head whipped toward the monitor. Using his keyboard controls, the technician used little white crosses to point out specific areas on the sonogram to John and Chiara. "This is the gestational sac, and right here you can clearly see your baby. That flutter there, that's the heartbeat."

The technician moved his highlighting crosses all over the baby, taking measurements and readings from all angles. Chiara's muscles stiff from holding John's hand so tightly, and just when she thought she couldn't stand one more second of silence, the technician said, "Everything looks really good."

Chiara let out a long, loud sigh of relief. John scrubbed his free hand over his face, letting it rest over his mouth, his eyes closed. By the light of the sonogram, Chiara studied his face, and through a haze of her own tears, she caught the telltale quiver in his chin. He composed himself quickly and brought her hand to his lips, kissing it warmly.

"Here's a photo or two." The technician tore off a long strip of black and white photos of the baby and handed them to John.

"Can you tell if it's a boy or a girl?" he asked.

The technician grinned. "Ordinarily, I'd say it's too early, but your babe's giving me a clear view of the goods. If you really want to know, I can tell you."

John, his eyelashes moist with unshed tears, looked down at Chiara. "I'd like to know. I can't have this guy know and me not know."

"It's a boy," Chiara said.

"You saw that on the sonogram?" John wrinkled his nose. "The baby's got my father's big ol' Charlie Brown head and I recognize an arm, but I didn't see anything that would indicate that this baby is a boy."

"I just know it's a boy," Chiara said.

John looked at the technician. "Well, is she right?"

"Always trust the mother's instincts," he said. He set the transducer in its cradle and used a handful of paper toweling to clean Chiara's belly. "Congratulations, you two. I'm going to go over these pictures with the OB on call, but she'll probably want to keep you overnight just as a precaution. She'll be in soon to talk to you," he said before excusing himself from the room.

John helped Chiara sit up. She finally relaxed her cramped fingers and saw that she'd been holding John's hand so tightly her nails had cut into his skin, drawing crescents of blood. "I'm so sorry," she said, dabbing at the tiny spots with the hem of her gown. "I guess I don't know my own strength."

"I know it," he said tenderly. "I've relied on it for most of my life."

Her voice broke as she said, "I don't feel very strong right now."

"Here." He gathered her into his arms. "Take some of mine. Take all you need. If you're not up to it tonight, I can tell Detective Vincent that you'll give him his statement tomorrow."

"I want to do it tonight, get it over with," she said into his chest. "I'm not even sure what I can tell him. It all happened so fast. I unlocked the door, everything was dark, I went into the kitchen, and some guy grabbed me. He choked me."

"Was he white or black?" John asked.

"I don't know. He wore a hood."

"Did you see his eyes?"

"Not well, but well enough to gouge them." She enjoyed a flash of satisfaction, remembering how he'd cried out. "His eyes were blue," she recalled. After a long moment of thought, she said, "I saw a little bit of his skin in the eyeholes. He was white."

"See, you remember more than you think. The more you can tell the police, the better the chances are of catching him before he does this to someone else."

"He won't." She pulled out of John's embrace to look into his face. "I was attacked because of that chip."

John said nothing. He used both hands to smooth her hair from her face. "You're on vacation now, right?"

She nodded.

"I think I'll take some time, too," John said. "It's gonna take a few days to get your place cleaned up and packed and to figure out what was stolen."

"Nothing was stolen," she said.

"How do you know?"

"Because *I* was attacked."

"I don't understand."

"Ordinary burglars don't completely disembowel sofas. They don't gut chairs and mattresses and saw the legs off tables and chairs." She lowered her voice, even though they were still alone. "He was looking for the *chip*. He went through everything in my apartment. I was gone for nine days. He had plenty of time to do it. He didn't ransack the place in one night. He was there tonight looking for me because he didn't find what he was looking for in my apartment." She clutched John's shirtfront, her hands trembling. "He searched *me* for it."

John stubbornly clung to his disbelief. "Chiara, look—"

She searched his eyes for a flicker of agreement. "Someone sent that man after me. You know that, don't you? I had four hundred dollars in my wallet, and he left it there on the floor," she insisted. "He ignored the Cartier earrings you gave me. This was no ordinary robbery. That man walked away from four hundred dollars and diamond earrings because he was looking for something even more valuable. If he'd found it, he could have had four hundred thousand dollars by the end of the day. You know why I was attacked. And you have to know that you're not safe, either."

John offered no argument, not when what she said was exactly what he was now thinking. "We're packing you up and getting the hell out of Chicago," he resolved.

Chiara gave her statement to the detective, and John was impressed with her skill at answering questions without actually answering them.

"Can you think of anyone who would attack you, Miss Winters?" the detective asked.

"No one I can name," Chiara replied, staring him dead in the eye.

The detective didn't press her, though his eyebrow twitched at her response. He thanked her for her time and gave her his card, in the event that she thought of something he hadn't covered during his exhaustive questioning. When he left, John closed the door behind him and felt as weary as Chiara looked.

With all their official business taken care of for the time being, John took over Chiara's care. He'd arranged for her to have a private room in the hospital, one of the luxury rooms typically reserved for ailing celebrities and politicians. With its television console, walk-in closet and full-sized bed, it was more like a hotel room than a hospital room, though it still contained all the standard medical equipment.

Eager to finally take a shower, Chiara did so while John ordered dinner from a service that handled deliveries from area restaurants. He turned down her bed and fluffed her pillows before knocking on the bathroom door.

"Baby, can I wash your back for you?" he called through the door.

"Please," Chiara said, the drumming of the water almost drowning out her voice.

When John entered the steam-filled chamber, his shirt instantly adhered to him. He quickly removed his clothing and joined her in the shower stall. Too late he tried to mask his horror at the sight of her water slickened body. An ugly, purplish-blue blotch was blooming above her buttocks, and smaller versions were taking shape on her hips and upper thighs. Her upper arms bore deep finger marks, and horrible blotchy bruises marred her forearms and shoulders. The fresh red bruises on her throat made John clamp his jaw in anger.

"Son-of-a-bitch," he spat.

"It's that bad?" she asked him.

John felt more helpless than he had as a kid when he'd been the one on the receiving end of a beating. "I should have—"

"Don't say it," she ordered. "If you'd been there, he might have done worse. He might have been armed. He would have used a weapon on you."

"Emmitt Grayson is going to pay for this," John promised. He took the soap from her and briskly lathered his hands. Gently, he slicked the lather over Chiara's body, careful not to cause her any more pain.

"It's been a day, huh?" Chiara turned to face him.

John's hands moved over her upper arms. "It's been a day, baby." She pressed her body into his, and he was able to shove his anger far enough away to devote the proper attention to Chiara. She allowed him to wash and rinse her from head to toe, and then bundle her into a thick white towel. She was so tired, so bone weary from living through the longest day of her life, she fell asleep in John's arms as he carried her to the bed.

John tucked her under the covers and watched her as she slept. "I love you," he whispered. "And I'll kill the next man who tries to lay a hand on you."

CHAPTER ELEVEN

"Do you remember the first time you married me?" John asked.

Chiara, propped up on a nest of pillows with the white sheets pulled up to her underarms, toyed with a plump strawberry tomato she'd plucked from the salad that had arrived late the night before, when she was asleep. "I remember how the gold band you gave me turned my finger green."

"Come on," John pleaded, smiling softly as he tucked his right arm under his pillow and turned onto his back to look up at her. "What did you expect? I was on a fixed income back then."

Chiara touched the tomato to her lip, though she had no appetite for it. She gazed at the man lying beside her. The bed sheet only half covered him, leaving him exposed from the waist up. She knew his beautiful brown body perhaps better than she knew her own. She had studied the patterns of the crisp, dark hair arranged on him, had traced each cut of muscle and followed tendons and veins. She knew every secret of his man's body, which was probably why it was so easy for her to see through him, to the rail-thin third-grader he'd been the first time she'd agreed to be his wife.

On one of the brightest, hottest Sundays, they'd skipped church, as usual, to go to the ruins and 7-Eleven. John had spent six quarters on the gumball machines outside the store, hoping to get a plastic capsule containing a tiny yo-yo. He'd received five gumballs, all yellow, and a gold-plated tin ring with a glittery white plastic stone.

John had shared his gum with her, and as they'd walked back to the ruins, Chiara had blown a bubble bigger than her head. John had popped it, leaving her with a full beard and mustache made of gum. He'd stood there, holding the ring out to Chiara on the palm of his hand, and he'd said, "Do you want to get married to me?"

At nine years old, Chiara hadn't had anything better to do. "Okay." She'd shrugged indifferently. She'd slipped the ring onto her index finger and tightened it by pinching the rounded ends together.

They'd run back to the ruins to ask Cady, who'd been reading a Kitty Kincaid romance novel under a tree, to perform the ceremony. As she thought back on it, Chiara realized that she should have been suspicious of Cady's instant agreement. Cady was sixteen, and her eager participation in their games had never bided well before.

After delivering a speech that left Chiara and John squirming in the hot sun, their tightly clasped palms adhering with sweat, Cady had pronounced them husband and wife. John had balked at Cady's directive to kiss the bride. Cady, reenacting the plot of the romance novel she was reading, assigned Kyla the task of kidnapping the new bride.

Kyla swooped down, grabbed Chiara by the waist and carried her off to the highest platform of the tallest slide. John revealed a side of himself that the Winters girls had never seen. Standing on the steep, wrought iron steps of the slide, he literally fought an uphill battle to rescue his little wife—no small feat with Cady acting as guard. John had gotten so angry and so upset by his inability to rescue Chiara that Cady and Kyla had taken pity on him and freed her of their own accord.

Chiara had consoled her husband and later, exacted her own revenge by gluing together the last twenty pages of several of Cady's unread romance novels.

"Cady still complains about the books I ruined," Chiara said. "But at least she never tortured my husband again."

"Torture," John scoffed. "That defines the nature of the second time we were married."

"Excuse me?" Chiara said, taking offense.

"It wasn't torture being married to you." He laid a warm hand on her abdomen. "It was torture for my mother."

"She was ridiculous," Chiara recalled. "It was a tenth-grade sociology project, and she acted like we were being told to worship Satan."

John rolled onto his back and stared at the ceiling. Sociology had been one of his least favorite classes during his sophomore year of high school, but it had satisfied one of his elective requirements, and Chiara had been in the class, too. When Mr. Collins had begun a segment on marriage and family, the boys in the class had almost openly rebelled at the thought of being assigned a wife, occupation, economic and education level, and worst of all—a baby.

Mr. Collins had pulled names from two hats to pair up the couples. He'd groaned out loud along with the rest of the class when he'd randomly matched Chiara Winters to John Mahoney. "I guess this is meant to be," he'd laughed as he'd given them cards bearing their vital information: John, a college-educated accountant, would be married to Chiara, a college-educated, stay-at-home mother of one.

Chiara had sulked at her so-called occupation.

"You don't have to do anything," John had told her. "I'm the man. I do all the work."

"Stay-at-home mothers do everything!" Chiara had railed right there in class. "They do all the cooking, the housekeeping, the laundry and the grocery shopping. They have to go to the post office and the bank, and they have to take the kids to the doctor and the dentist. Stay-at-home moms don't get to do anything fun!"

"You've given this quite a bit of thought, Chiara," Mr. Collins had said. "Some of the finer points of this assignment won't be lost on you."

"I wouldn't be a stay-at-home mother if you paid me," Chiara had said. "Actually, I'd only do it *if* you paid me, and even then, you'd better be paying me a lot."

"John?" Mr. Collins had said. "It appears that you and your new wife are already having your first major conflict. She wants a career. She doesn't want to take care of the home and family. How would you go about resolving this?"

John had been at a complete loss. "I could mow the lawn," he'd offered.

For Chiara, the assignment had quickly worsened when she and John received their baby. The doll was computerized and programmed to be fed, changed, to cry inconsolably and laugh, all unpredictably. As the stay-at-home half of the assignment, Chiara had been responsible for most of the baby's care. When she met John at school the morning after her first night with the baby, John had considered divorce proceedings.

Chiara's hair, a wavy fall of black normally kept in a neat ponytail, looked as though she'd combed it with her feet. The big, wide eyes that had always sparkled with mischief were heavy-lidded, with dark circles beneath them. She'd never been a fancy dresser, but she'd always looked nice, but as she handed the baby over to John, he saw that she was wearing sweat-pants and an old T-shirt with one black sock and one blue one.

"This thing cried all night," she'd told him. "When it finished crying, it started peeing, and when it finished peeing, it started pooping. Have you ever tried to change electronic poop?" she'd demanded. "The computer times you. If you don't change the diaper fast enough, the crying just gets louder and louder."

"It can't have been that bad," John had said, trying not to laugh at her. "It's just a robot." Then he'd made the biggest mistake of all in trying to give the baby back to her. "I have P.E. first period," he'd said. "I can't take the baby with me."

"I'M TAKING THE DAY OFF!" Chiara had hollered through clenched teeth. "I don't want to see you or your baby until tomorrow morning!"

And with that, John had become a single father.

Chiara had taken pity on him through the day, helping him in spite of herself with an electronic diaper change during lunch and a feeding during eighth period homeroom. But she'd flat out refused to take the baby home with her that night.

"I have a science test tomorrow, and I need to study," she'd said.

So John had taken the baby home. He'd immediately smuggled the baby up to his room. Everything had gone fine until midnight, when the baby began to cry. John had tried feeding it, burping it, changing it and reprogramming it, all to no avail. As the baby's pre-programmed distress grew, so did its volume. Almadine, her black hair tightly rolled in tiny pink curlers that matched her Pepto-Bismol pink pajamas, had burst into John's bedroom to find him pacing with the baby on his shoulder, religiously counting off the number of gentle pats to the baby's sensory pad needed to quiet it.

Sensory pads were located all over the baby to monitor the frequency and intensity of the contact it received. When Almadine got over her initial shock and discovered that the baby was fake, she grabbed its ankles and tore it from John's shoulder. The next morning, she'd taken the baby to school to confront Mr. Collins about his "reckless" assignment, which she believed would only encourage teenagers to engage in premarital sex.

Almadine had refused to believe Mr. Collin's contention that the computer baby was the surest deterrent to teen pregnancy he'd ever encountered, and that his assignment was meant to teach his students lessons in compromise and problem solving.

In the end, John had been able to carry on with the assignment because Chiara had agreed to be the full-time evening caregiver for the baby, which Mr. Collins determined showed signs of abuse equal to two fractured hip sockets—damage John knew had been caused by his mother's rough handling.

Now, as John took her barely touched salad from her lap and set it on her bed table, Chiara looked him in the eye and said, "I'm sorry I wasn't more flexible during our second marriage."

"You know what they say," John smiled. "The third time's the charm."

"Oh, you think so?" Chiara grinned.

"I know so." John might have elaborated had a soft knock not sounded on the door.

He hopped out of bed and into his trousers. Even though it was six in the morning, a member of the hospital staff would have just entered after knocking. The fact that the visitor remained out in the corridor gave John cause for concern.

"Who is it?" he called, pitching his voice lower and adding a touch of menace.

"It's me," came a muffled voice that made Chiara's heart leap. "Now open the frickin' door, Mahofro."

John was still buttoning his shirt when Cady Winters-Bailey entered the room. With a practiced flourish she swept off her wool cape, tossed it toward John—who caught it with his face—and went directly to Chiara's bedside. Chiara pulled the sheets up higher as Cady sat down and lightly embraced her. When she pulled away, she said nothing as she studied Chiara's face. Chiara grew increasingly uncomfortable. It was never a good thing to be under Cady's laser-like scrutiny.

"Nice digs," Cady finally said, shifting her eyes to take in the room.

"You'd be amazed at how the doors just fly open here when you mention Dr. Keren Bailey," John said, seating himself on Chiara's opposite side.

"That was mighty impressive at the door," Cady told John. "You sounded just like Samuel L. Jackson."

Chiara ignored her sister's jibe. "Keren got this room for me?"

"Keren donated a lot of money to this hospital when they started renovating the pediatric oncology ward six months ago," John said. "The admitting department became very accommodating when I told them that you were Dr. Bailey's sister-in-law."

"How did you know about Keren's donation?" Chiara asked.

"Cady told me at Niema's christening in July."

Chiara dropped her gaze to the control panel on the inside of her bed rail. "Oh."

"You were in South Korea," John said gently. "That deal took twice as long as you expected it to, remember?"

"Yeah," Chiara sighed. "Right." If she weren't already sore enough, she might have kicked herself. John had attended more of her family's functions and special events than she had, and the weight of her neglect started her eyes watering. "I'm the worst sister in the world." The words quivered from her lips as tears rolled over her lashes. "I've missed all the kids' christenings, most of their birthdays—"

"You give really good gifts, though," Cady said. "The twins love the Malaysian moon kites you gave them for Christmas."

Grinding tears from her uninjured eye with the heel of her hand, Chiara went on as if she hadn't been interrupted. "—I've missed all the big holidays—"

Cady took her hand and gave it a sisterly squeeze. "It gives us a chance to talk about you behind your back."

Chiara sobbed openly, the heat of her tears making the battered side of her face ache. "I get beat up and you abandon your children to fly here to be with me at a moment's notice. I don't deserve your generosity, Cady."

"First of all, I didn't abandon my children." Cady's big ponytail of curls bounced as she crossed her arms over the chest of her baggy black sweater. "They're with their father, thank you. Besides, I didn't come all the way to Chicago to see you. When John told me that someone attacked you, I came up to make sure that you didn't kill the other guy."

Chiara chuckled in spite of her misery.

"You're a scrapper, you always have been," Cady said. "Whoever jumped you is lucky he caught you off guard." She took Chiara's chin and tilted her face toward the recessed light mounted above the headboard. "Remember the time Randy Cates said that you and John were like 'Rudy' and 'Buuud' from *The Cosby Show*? The bus driver had to pull over to get you off him. You tore him up."

"I guess I'm not as tough now as I was when I was ten," Chiara sniffled.

"You're still plenty tough," Cady assured her. "Pregnancy can make you feel vulnerable, at least in the early stages. How far along are you?"

Chiara's eyes went wide and her mouth dropped open. She whirled on John. "You told her?"

"I haven't told anyone," John protested. "You're the one who's been telling everybody. First Emmitt Grayson—"

"To save our jobs!"

"—and then Mr. Petrie," John finished.

"It slipped out!"

"No one told me," Cady said, settling the argument before it got much louder. "I figured it out on my own. It's pretty obvious, actually. You're about three months or so?"

Chiara threw her hands up in surrender. "How the hell could you tell? Did you read my chart or something before you came in?"

Cady pinched back a self-satisfied grin. "I read *you*."

"How's that?"

"You were very quiet and withdrawn at Christmas, and I assumed that it was because of Zhou. But then I noticed that that you were acting like a big ol' crybaby. You cried when you saw Claire Elizabeth kiss the stuffed doll you gave her, you cried when you saw Tits McFloozie kiss Troy under the mistletoe—"

"Tits McFloozie?" Chiara cut in.

"Tiff McCousy," John clarified. "Troy's woman."

"You even cried when John gave you those fat diamond earrings, and normally you would have played it off or punched him in the head," Cady finished. "You never used to be such a wet end, so I started thinking there must be a hormonal reason behind the excessive waterworks. The shirt you were wearing when you first came home gave you away, too."

"In what way?"

"You looked like Tits McFloozie in it. Your boobs aren't usually so…noticeable. And now, your face confirms my suspicion."

"My face looks like road kill."

"Exactly. I'd think that most people who are attacked try to protect their faces." Cady demonstrated, slightly curling forward with her hands and forearms shielding her head and face. "Your face is a mess. You were curled up," Cady moved her arms to her midsection, "but you were protecting something else. *Someone* else. Since you're not showing yet, I figure you at about three months."

"Three and a half," Chiara said. "Damn it. You better not tell Mama, or Clara, or Ciel, and especially not Kyla."

"I won't tell." Cady plucked at a worn patch on the knee of her jeans.

"I mean it, Cady."

Her eyebrows shot up. "I won't."

"You let things slip in a way that seems like you're not spilling a secret, when that's all you're doing. You can't tell anyone. Not yet. Especially not now."

"I can keep a secret," Cady said.

"You're a reporter," Chiara scoffed. "You're genetically predisposed to reveal secrets."

"I'm a freelancer, so I get to pick and choose the secrets I reveal, and I'm a woman of my word. I won't tell anyone."

"Promise," Chiara challenged.

"Look, I didn't tell anyone that you and John got married, did I?" Cady threw out in her defense.

Chiara looked at John and saw her own shock mirrored.

"Of course, it's not legal, since I was the one who performed the ceremony when you were ten," Cady laughed.

"Nine," John and Chiara corrected, both of them smiling in relief.

Cady couldn't stop laughing. "Man, you should have seen your faces when I said that. Are you guys really that scared to get married?"

☙❧

After final examinations from an obstetrician, a plastic surgeon and a physician's assistant, Chiara was released with a prescription for acetaminophen and an outpatient treatment plan that called for ice packs, rest, and as little stress as possible.

Standing outside her apartment with Cady while John took a quick walk-through, Chiara doubted that she could manage the stress-free part of her doctor's orders.

"It's fine," John said, coming out and taking Chiara's hand. "Well…you know."

Chiara had looked forward to showering in her own bathroom and getting out of the green scrubs she'd been given to wear home. But seeing all of her belongings destroyed or strewn around the apartment made her want to run back to the hospital. The wreckage in the light of day was bad enough, but watching Cady's reaction made her feel even worse.

Chiara started at her big sister's expression of horror. "I know it looks bad, Cady, but—"

"Burglars?" she shrieked at John. "You told me that Chiara walked in on a burglary. This is more than just a burglary!" She encompassed the clutter and debris in the living and dining rooms with a wide sweep of her arms. "Have the police scoured the place?"

"Yes," Chiara said.

Cady went back to the front door and opened it. She squinted at the two lock plates on the outer side. "There are tool marks on your locks. They were picked. Did the police talk to your neighbors, ask if anyone heard anything?"

"They said they would," John responded as Cady reentered the apartment and locked the door.

"Do they know when the break-in occurred?" Cady moved farther into the apartment. She stepped over a shredded sofa cushion to get into the kitchen.

"They aren't sure," Chiara said. She felt a little weak and leaned on John for support.

"This happened on Christmas Day, Chiara," Cady said, disgust in her voice. "The day right after you left for St. Louis."

"How can you tell?" Chiara was almost as impressed as she was afraid of her sister's high-powered observation skills.

A small white object came flying out of the kitchen. John caught it, and he and Chiara looked at it. It was the analog timer from Chiara's stove. Chiara almost smiled. Zhou had given her the complicated little kitchen gadget as a housewarming present. It showed the date and time, recommended cooking times for boiled eggs, frozen vegetables and such, and it had a space in back to store matches for igniting pilot lights.

Cady leaned against the doorframe of the kitchen. "Was that thing working when you left for St. Louis?"

"Yes," Chiara said.

"Then the break-in occurred at one a.m. or one p.m. on December 25, according to when that timer got broken," John observed.

"I can't imagine anyone breaking in at one in the afternoon," Chiara said.

John pulled his cell phone from the inner breast pocket of his jacket. "I'm calling Detective Vincent. He would have had this bagged as evidence if he'd seen it. He said that narrowing the time down would help a lot."

"When you get the detective on the line, tell him to interview the lady in apartment 816," Cady said. "I'll bet she heard something."

"Mrs. Mayo?" Chiara said. "She's a hundred and ten years old. She's deaf as a doorknob. All she does is watch television twenty-four hours a day. She's also the meanest woman in the building."

"Whatever," Cady said with a lift of a finely arched eyebrow. "All I know is that when we passed her unit, I smelled White Diamonds."

"Mrs. Mayo bathes in the stuff," Chiara said.

"I smelled it at your door, too, before we came in. She came nosying around here recently. And if she's so deaf, how did she know we were coming down the corridor? It's not like we were beating drums or making a lot of noise. I saw the shadow of her feet at her door as we passed. She probably just pretends to be hard of hearing so people don't pester her with idle chatter. She was probably watching us through her peephole. And if she watches TV twenty-four hours a day, she was probably awake when your place got hit. She saw or heard something," Cady said confidently. "Every building has a Mrs. Mayo."

"I'll mention her to Detective Vincent," John said. Stepping carefully, he made his way into Chiara's bedroom so he could have some privacy for his call.

"What kind of trouble are you in?" Cady asked.

Chiara wanted to sit, but all of her furniture was in pieces. "It's nothing John and I can't handle."

Cady kicked aside everything in her path to get to the remnants of the sofa cushions. She stacked them in a chair-shaped pile and helped Chiara sit on them. She then sat cross-legged on the floor in front of her. "Is this part of your handling it? Who did this?"

"I don't know."

Chiara bowed her face to stop Cady's eyes from boring into hers. It was far easier to confound a poly-graph machine than it was to get one over on Cady.

"This doesn't look random," Cady persisted.

"I'm sure it wasn't." Chiara laughed nervously. "I'm a woman living alone who travels a lot. Whoever was watching me probably thought it would be easy to come in and rob me."

Cady anxiously rubbed her hands along her thighs. "You were being watched?"

"I didn't mean…Cady…I just want to start packing the place up," Chiara finished when all other possible explanations failed her.

"Packing? Don't you mean cleaning? There's nothing her to salvage. Even the lining of your drapes has been ripped out. Who does that?"

Chiara squirmed in her makeshift chair as she watched Cady's face tense in thought. Once Cady put her mind to work on a problem, it was only a matter of time before she found the answers she sought. The most worrisome thing about her was that she never needed much to work with. When they were kids, Abby used to give them 50,000-piece puzzles to keep them busy on rainy Saturdays. Cady had a canny knack for puzzling together pieces of sky, empty ocean or barren desert. The ripped draperies were just another piece to go along with what Cady already had at her disposal: Zhou's death, the trashed apartment and the physical assault. If Cady found out about her sudden resignation from USITI, Chiara was sure that her sister would piece it all together.

And then there would be yet another person placed in the line of Emmitt Grayson's fire.

"The only piece that doesn't fit is the baby," Cady muttered.

"Cady, please. Stay out of it," Chiara said.

Cady narrowed her amber eyes. "Stay out of what?"

"Stay out of my business!" Chiara snapped. "I don't need you snooping around, sticking your fingers in pies that have nothing to do with you. Respect my privacy, if you don't mind too damn much."

"All right, this is enough, Chiara," Cady said. "You and John have always been this satellite partnership orbiting the rest of us. Until I met Keren, I envied you. I didn't have anyone who understood me without me having to explain everything. I didn't have anyone with whom I could share all of myself, and not just the good parts."

Chiara let Cady take her hands.

"You two take it to an extreme," Cady went on. "All you seem to need is each other, and that's not always a good thing. Now seems to be one of those times. Whatever's wrong, you have to know that you've got family that can help. Don't forget that."

Chiara uneasily pulled her hands free of Cady's. "I won't forget."

"I want to help," Cady said.

"Good." Chiara deliberately misinterpreted her meaning. "We can start packing today."

"What was stolen?"

Chiara held her tongue.

"What were they looking for?"

"We're taking care of it," Chiara said with deadly calm.

"Who's we?"

"Me, John and George."

Cady's spine stiffened. "George who?" Her lips parted with a tiny pip of understanding. "Not George…" She turned a wary eye on Chiara. "Good Lord, Chiara, how much trouble are you in?"

CHAPTER TWELVE

"I called the right sister," John said. He and Chiara stood in Chiara's living room, which was now empty except for an air mattress pushed to one corner. "Detective Vincent just finished talking to Mrs. Mayo. She recalled seeing three strangers in the corridor around one A.M. on Christmas morning. She said that she'd 'bet dollars to donuts that they weren't Santa's elves making a delivery.' Once he had Mrs. Mayo's statement, Detective Vincent re-interviewed the doorman, and forced him to revise his first statement. He admitted that he let in three men claiming to be here for a party on another floor. He lied originally because he didn't want to get fired."

"Cady doesn't mess around," Chiara remarked.

"The disposal crew is giving her a hard time," John said, lightly stroking Chiara's upper arms. "I'm going down to the lobby for a minute to remind them of the price they quoted before they started the job."

"You'd better hurry," Chiara smile weakly. "Before Cady pulls out her lawyer card."

"You mean Ciel?"

Chiara nodded.

"Will you be okay for a few minutes?"

"I'll lock the doors and keep my cell phone in my hand the whole time," Chiara promised.

He kissed the end of her nose, exited the apartment and waited in the corridor until she'd locked and latched her door behind him.

She shook her head in amazement as she strolled the perimeter of her living room. Shortly after her arrival from the hospital, Mr. Petrie had rung her bell, offering the use of an air bed if she chose to stay in her apartment rather than check into a hotel. Sick of hotels and hospitals, Chiara had readily accepted Mr. Petrie's offer. Cady had made the bed with the sheets Mr. Petrie had included—Chiara's bed linen hadn't been damaged, but she couldn't bring herself to sleep on anything her intruders had touched—and Chiara had fallen upon the bouncy bed and slept for hours.

When she awakened, she saw how productive Cady and John had been. John had changed into a pair of jeans and a sweater after the airline had shipped his overnighter back to him. Cady had called in a waste removal crew that had bagged, boxed and carried out everything that had been ruined while John helped Cady salvage whatever could be saved, primarily Chiara's bed and bath linen, clothes and books.

No evidence remained of the broken picture frames, torn photo albums, smashed television and sound system and ripped drapes. Aside from black plastic bags filled with the items she was keeping, the apartment almost looked as it had when she'd first viewed it, when she'd first fallen in love with the building and had decided to move in.

Of course, back then there hadn't been holes in the walls or sections of molding ripped out where the vandals had likely been looking for a concealed safe, according to Detective Vincent. And the built-in shelving in the living and dining rooms hadn't been smashed.

The vaulted, multi-colored marble ceilings, original to the building and prime examples of the coolly sophisticated ornamentation popular in Chicago architecture during the late 1800s, were still intact.

Now that the rooms were empty, Chiara saw that her hardwood floors still gleamed like warm toffee despite their fresh nicks and gouges. She'd kept them protected by gorgeous rugs she'd sent home from the Far East, but those rugs were now rolled up and slumped in a closet.

The bathroom had been left relatively unscathed, suffering only the removal of the medicine cabinet from the wall and the overturning of the small shelving unit Chiara had used to store towels. The elegance of the bathroom made up for its smallish size. Although it held a basin, toilet, shower and tub, the high ceilings made the room seem less confining. Tiny wall tile imported from Morocco formed lovely mosaics while the floor was a single slab of Carrera marble from Italy. The fixtures were original to the building, and Chiara had always liked the whimsy of faucets curved like an elephant's trunk and hot and cold water knobs shaped like stylized pineapples.

Her bedroom faced north, which was perfect because the sunrise left her alone. Her queen-sized bed, which had filled the floor space, had been crudely battered apart and the mattress slashed. The matching bureau had been scrapped, along with the bed, since so many of its drawers had been destroyed.

Cady had repeatedly assured her that her renter's insurance would cover her belongings and even much of the damage to the apartment. But no amount of money could ease the pain of leaving, of knowing that she'd been driven out of the home she'd loved so well for so long. She'd been scared out, and now she was planning to go back home to start all over again.

She'd made a conscious effort to curb her newborn crybaby side, and she hadn't shed a tear as the disposal team carried out the last of the furniture she'd chosen so carefully. But as she stood at her bare living room windows, staring east toward the darkness of Lake Michigan far in the distance, she couldn't fight the combined power of hormones and grief. She mourned her old life even as she embraced the potentials of her new one. It was the transition that was so hard because of how it had been brought about.

"Someone attacked me in my own home because of that stupid…" She pressed her fingers to her mouth. Because of Zhou, who put the master chip in her possession? Because of Grayson, who'd created it? Because of George, who'd uncovered its use?

Or because of herself, for being so damned naïve.

Her whole body hurt, and now her soul ached too at the thought of the number of people she'd unknowingly helped deceive in her service to USITI. She wrapped her arms around herself and slid down the wall, her tears bursting forth. She had no idea how long she'd been weeping when John found her and enveloped her in his warmth.

"Shh, shh," he soothed, pressing her head to his chest. "It's okay."

"I don't want to leave this way," she sobbed. "I loved it here, John. We made a good life here. I didn't want my last memories of this place to be awful."

"They won't be," he said earnestly. "I won't let them."

❧❧❧

Cady and Chiara spent the night on the air bed while John slept on a pallet made of bath towels and blankets. Cady began her second morning in Chicago by venturing out for breakfast for the three of them, while Chiara went about completing her exit plans for USITI.

"I called Chele Brewster," Chiara told John after he'd taken a quick shower. "She always works on Sundays, and she's agreed to seal the boxes I left in my office Friday morning. She's having a courier deliver them to me tomorrow."

John peered at Chiara, his eyes moving over her face. She'd pulled her hair into a ponytail, and in her simple black tunic, form-fitting black pants and soft-soled boots, she looked like a college student rather than a technical sales rep. The swelling on the right side of her face had lessened to the point where she could fully open her right eye, but the coloration was vividly grotesque. The ER doctor had told them that the bruising would look worse before it got better, and at the moment, Chiara's face looked as if it had been painted in psychedelic shades of yellow, purple and black.

John's intense stare made her bring her right hand to the injury site. "I know how it looks. That's why I didn't want to go into the office myself."

Holding a towel about his lean hips, John went into the bedroom. "Did you tell Chele what happened?"

"No. She's a good person, but we don't call her the town crier of technical sales for no reason."

John put on a fresh pair of black sports briefs, but he had to wear the same jeans he'd worn the day before. "Would you mind if I went and picked up your boxes myself when Cady gets back? There won't be a full staff at the office since it's Sunday."

"No," she said. "But why?"

John poked his head and arms through a long-sleeved T-shirt, one he'd left at Chiara's before he'd moved back to St. Louis. "I need to send an e-mail."

"To who?"

"To my team in St. Louis."

"You can send it from here," Chiara said. "My Internet cable is still operable, and you have your laptop."

"I need to send this e-mail from USITI." He tugged on some socks, laced on his sneakers.

Chiara worked one hand over the other as she followed him into the dining room, where his briefcase, laptop and wallet sat on the counter separating the dining room from the kitchen. "Please don't do anything foolish, John. Don't do anything that will rouse more suspicion than we're already under."

"I won't."

"I've been thinking," she said.

"I know. I heard you tossing and turning on the mattress all night. I don't know how Cady slept through it."

"Maybe we should go to the state attorney," she said quietly. "Maybe we should have done that in the first place. Just turn the chip and the information about it over to the authorities."

John leaned back against the counter, crossing one ankle over the other. "I thought about that, too. And then I thought about Zhou. If he knew what the chip did, why didn't *he* take it to the proper authorities? Why did he put it in our hands? Maybe he thought he was protecting himself against Grayson, by using the chip as leverage."

He scrubbed both hands over his face in renewed frustration. "Zhou obviously underestimated Grayson. We can't afford to do the same thing. We need security. Leverage. I don't think we can get that by just turning over the chip to the state attorney's office. Grayson would be arrested, probably indicted, and what then? He's already proven that he's willing to kill over this chip. All he has to do is make a phone call, and the same psychos who came here and trashed your apartment will find us and take us out. We either spend the rest of our lives running, with our baby, or we end up like Zhou."

"Okay," she responded. "I had the same feeling, for the most part. I'm just so scared. I just want this to be over."

John crossed his arms and looked at her for a very long time. When he spoke, his words hurt Chiara almost as much as her attacker's fist had. "I'm disappointed in you," he said.

"Wh-What?" she gasped. All the air seemed to have been sucked from her lungs.

"You've never let me, your family, or anyone else dictate how much control you have over your life," he said. "You've always been the fierce one. The fighter. You're letting Emmitt Grayson get the better of you."

"I didn't *let* anyone destroy my apartment," she argued, the heat of her rising anger evaporating the tears she might have shed. "I didn't *let* a man blitz me and beat me unconscious. I'm lost here, John. I don't know what to do from one moment to the next! I've never had to fight my way out of something like this before. Do you think I'm enjoying this? Do you think I like feeling helpless and used and…and…weak? I was helpless last night, and Grayson used me, but I'm not weak! Don't you dare accuse me of not being able or willing to fight!"

The pretty brown eyes that had seemed too big for her face when she was a kid blazed with fury, and a tiny smile came to John's face. "That's all I wanted to see, baby. I needed to see that you still had your fire." *We're going to need it, before this is over.*

❧

"Who is it?" Cady asked sweetly, even though peering through the peephole she saw perfectly well who it was.

"It's John," John grunted. "Open the door, please."

"John?" Cady repeated. "John who? I know no John."

"Quit messing around, Cady." Chiara tried to work her way around Cady, who used her body to block access to the doorknob and locks.

"I'm sorry, sir, but you can't come in without properly identifying yourself," Cady giggled.

"Still sixteen inside that thirty-seven-year-old body," John complained.

"The body's only thirty-six, boy," Cady said. "Now do you want to come in and dump those boxes or not? They sure look heavy."

"It's Mahofro," John grudgingly said. "Now open the damn door, please."

"That's not funny, Cady," Chiara said, nudging her sister out of the way to open the door for John. "It wasn't funny when we were kids and it's less funny now."

Cady shrugged. "It's funny to me."

"Thanks, baby." John, carrying two sealed file boxes, gave Chiara a kiss on the cheek as he passed her to set the boxes in the living room.

"What's this?" Cady asked.

Without meeting her sister's eyes, Chiara said, "I resigned from USITI last week."

Cady's left eyebrow shot up. "Oh really? Just like that? You upped and left your job?"

"Actually, I've been thinking about moving back to St. Louis for a while now," Chiara said, kneeling over her boxes to strip away the sealing tape while John set up his laptop on the kitchen counter. "It's something that's been on my mind since John's transfer, but I hadn't decided one way or the other for certain."

"Seems to me as though you'd move for John, even if you wouldn't do it just to be with your own family," Cady remarked.

"As goes his nation, so goes mine, is that what you think?"

"Well…"

"Contrary to what you and everybody might believe, John and I are separate people with our own lives and responsibilities. It was his choice to move to St. Louis and I supported it, same as he supported my choice to stay up here in Chicago."

"Never mind that you're hardly ever in North America, let alone Chicago, and that John is up here with you every weekend when you are in town," Cady said. "Hardly anything changed when he moved."

"Our arrangement works well for us." Chiara rooted through her boxes, making sure that everything she'd packed the day before was still there. "It always has."

"Since you're going to have all this free time now, maybe you should think about planning a wedding," Cady suggested.

"Or about getting another job." Chiara took inventory of the framed photos of her nieces and nephews.

"You're pregnant, kiddo," Cady reminded her. "It won't be so easy getting another sales rep job. You'll have to tell your employer that you'll be having a baby in six months."

Chiara was a little too forceful in replacing her framed photos in the box. "I don't want to work in sales ever again, and especially not for another software company."

"That's another piece of the puzzle, isn't it?" Cady said. "You're having some kind of serious trouble at USITI."

After exchanging a look with John, Chiara made a quick-fire decision to handle Cady the same way she had handled Grayson. She called upon the diversionary tactic of using one truth to avoid revealing another. "My boss made me take a polygraph test yesterday."

"Why?" Cady looked alarmed. "Because your sales partner committed suicide?"

"Zhou was under suspicion for stealing." Chiara hated saying the words, even if they were true. "Mr. Grayson wanted to see if I knew anything about it, and apparently my word wasn't good enough for him."

"Did you fail it?"

"I passed. I remembered the article you wrote on the dubious reliability of polygraph tests," Chiara said. "I remembered Aldrich Ames."

"Aldrich Ames was a fat liar, though," Cady said. "He passed two polygraph exams when he was spying on the U.S. for Russia. When he told his Russian handlers that he had to take a polygraph exam, they told him that the best way to pass it was to just relax. If you didn't have anything to hide, why would you need tips from Aldrich Ames?"

"I passed the test where the theft was concerned, but it registered a deception on something else. I hadn't told anyone about the baby. I had to tell Mr. Grayson after that."

"So is that why you quit? Because Mr. Grayson forced you to reveal your pregnancy?"

"I don't like other people getting in my personal business." Chiara went back to her box.

"You've been there for almost eight years." Cady shook her head. "It seems like a lot to throw away for something he would have found out eventually."

"Like I said," Chiara sighed, squatting at her boxes. "I was planning to leave anyway. This just moved the date up sooner." She picked up a thick white envelope sitting atop the second box. "John? Was this with the rest of my stuff?"

He peered over the kitchen counter. "No, Chele gave that to me before I left. She said it was on your desk when she took care of your boxes. It had your name on it, so I brought it along."

Chiara used her thumbnail to open the envelope. She shook the contents, a thick vellum folder with the USITI logo in burgundy against the cream cover, into her hand. "It's a dossier." She opened it and scanned the first page before snapping it shut. "He's got to be kidding," she muttered under her breath.

"What is it?" John asked, concerned.

"Work," she said, slapping the folder on top of her box just as a knock sounded on her door.

❧

"Chiara."

Emmitt Grayson filled her doorway. He was so out of context standing at her door on a Sunday afternoon, Chiara could only stare at him.

"May I come in?" he asked.

"Uh…um…of course, certainly," she managed through her shock.

Grayson, his long, tall form wrapped in a black Burberry coat, brought a whiff of winter in with him. He peeled off his black gloves and shoved them into his coat pocket. "I realize I should have called first, but my manners deserted me when I heard what happened to you."

Chiara aimed a sharp look at John, one he translated to mean, "What the hell have you done?"

"Chele Brewster brought your attack to my attention today," Mr. Grayson said. "Inadvertently, of course, so don't be too cross with her. I happened to be nearby when she was ordering flowers for you." His hands danced awkwardly in the air before finally lighting on her upper arms. "My God, Chiara," he muttered, his frosty blue eyes scouring her face. "You might have been killed. And your baby…" He took a step away from her, his fist to his mouth. "The authorities are handling this to your satisfaction?" he asked firmly.

"Yes," Chiara answered, startled by his unexpected display of emotion.

"Your medical needs are covered?"

"Yes."

With one fist on his hip, Grayson paced in a wide circle, the emptiness of the room allowing his long strides. He muttered softly to himself, seemingly oblivious to John and Chiara, who caught a snippet of his conversation with himself. "First Chen Zhou, now Chiara…What's going on here?" He whipped around, turning his attention back to Chiara. "Miss Brewster informed me that you'd lost many of your possessions, but I never imagined the loss to be total. I'm sickened at the thought of you having been alone here, at the mercy of that maniac. Perhaps you'll allow me to hire a personal security team for you, Chiara, at least until—"

"That won't be necessary, sir," Chiara said. "I've got John and my sister here. I'll be fine. I'm leaving for St. Louis in the morning."

Grayson flinched, noticing Cady and John for the first time. "Hello," Cady said, offering her hand. "I'm Cady Winters-Bailey. Pleased to meet you."

"I assure you, the pleasure is all mine," Grayson said, taking Cady's hand in both of his. He nodded toward John. "I hope all is well, Mr. Mahoney."

"It will be," John said. "Just as soon as I get Chiara home with me."

"Very well, then." Grayson spent another long moment looking at Chiara, as though the answer to his earlier conundrum were written in the bruises on her face. "If there's anything I can do, anything at all...please don't hesitate to ask. You've been..." He suddenly looked uncomfortable and cleared his throat as he plucked his gloves from his pocket. "You've been a valuable part of USITI, Chiara, and I want you to know that you can always turn to me for help."

"Thank you, Mr. Grayson," Chiara said. "I...I'll keep that in mind."

He finished putting on his gloves before he took Chiara's face with his fingertips. His eyes seemed to record every detail of her face before he met her gaze directly. Chiara couldn't tell if the warmth she saw in his eyes was the reflection of her own emotion, or something organic to Grayson. But as quickly as the emotion appeared, it disappeared when Grayson let go of her face and started for the door.

"My driver is waiting for me, and I have urgent business to take care of at USITI," he said, opening the door. "Please make sure you update me with your new phone numbers and address, Chiara. I've got you for two more weeks, and it is my sincere hope to keep you around longer." He glanced over his shoulder, and he almost looked tender. "I don't want to lose you, Chiara."

CHAPTER THIRTEEN

Chiara and John had an early dinner with Cady before seeing her off in a taxi for a flight to St. Louis out of Midway. At Chiara's insistence, Cady had agreed to fly home instead of spending one more night on the air mattress and then climbing into Chiara's Mitsubishi and riding with her and John to St. Louis.

After dinner, John had suggested dessert at the Park Grill Restaurant, which was housed in the McCormick Tribune Plaza and Ice Skating Rink in Millennium Park, one of their favorite parts of the city. Bundled in a thick, voluminous wool cape she'd picked up in Japan, she'd held John's hand as they'd strolled around the rink after dessert, watching the skaters. "Feel like taking a spin on the ice?" John asked.

"It's on my personal list of no-nos until after the baby is born," Chiara said.

"Add climbing Cecile Brunner to that list, would you?"

"I wish it were summer," Chiara said. "We could stay for a concert at the Pritzker Pavilion, or go to Navy Pier for fireworks."

"You sound like you don't want to go home tonight." John put an arm over her shoulders and pulled her closer.

"I don't. I feel safer out here in the moonlight than I do under my own roof. What used to be my roof."

"I'm surprised Mr. Hopkins let you out of your lease so easily."

"I'm not," Chiara laughed dryly. "Once his doorman went on the record saying that he let in strange men in the middle of the night, Mr. Hopkins was agreeable to anything I asked of him. He's not even holding me liable for the physical damage to the apartment, not that he could anyway. None of it was my fault."

"It's not, you know," John said. "None of it."

They walked back to Chiara's car passing Cloud Gate, Anish Kapoor's dazzling, stainless steel "Bean." The 110-ton elliptical sculpture looked like a gigantic drop of mercury, and it reflected Chicago's skyline and Millennium Park. It was Chiara's favorite element in the park, along with the brushed stainless steel ribbons that made up the headdress topping Pritzker Pavilion. As she and John walked away from it, Chiara imagined what it would be like to watch her child's face the first time he saw the Bean for himself.

At the car, John took the wheel. "Could you take the scenic route?" Chiara asked him.

He obliged, driving past many of Chiara's favorite sites, places she and John had shared. He took her south, to Buckingham Fountain in Grant Park, before doubling back north. The fountain was off for the season, but Chiara had no trouble picturing the fountain in its summer glory, when its center jet, surrounded by over one hundred smaller jets, shot a pillar of water 150 feet into the air. As lovely as the fountain was by day, it was positively breathtaking at night when its lights were lit.

John took South Lake Shore Drive to East Balbo to get to North Streeter Drive so he could drive her through Navy Pier. They had patronized every restaurant and shop there during their years in Chicago, and had taken many twilight walks along the Pier's East End, which offered perhaps the city's best view of the Chicago skyline and Lake Michigan. "I can't wait to bring the baby back here in a few years," Chiara said, her eyes glued to her window.

"He won't be a baby in a few years," John chuckled. "He'll be a little boy."

"I can't wait to take him on the ferris wheel and to the Crystal Gardens." Chiara had enjoyed Navy Pier so much as an adult that she was sure that she'd love sharing it with her child even more. "We'll be able to do the things we never did before, like go to the Children's Museum and ride the carousel."

"I'm looking forward to taking him to the Skyline for his first reggae concert," John said. "And miniature golf. We can't deny the child the singular delight of miniature golf at Navy Pier."

Chiara's heart sank a little when John had finished circling the Pier and steered them north, toward home. She leaned her head against the window and stared up at the pearl moon hanging in its blue velvet home. *At least the moon will be the same,* she told herself. *Whether it's shining on me here or in St. Louis.*

The drive to St. Louis wouldn't be so bad; she'd done it numerous times before. But actually crossing the river from Illinois to St. Louis would be the hard part. Driving to St. Louis from Chicago, she'd always felt as though she were literally crossing from one world to another through the wide, welcoming legs of the Gateway Arch. Behind her was the civilized hustle and bustle of Chi-town, while before her lay the staid stillness of St. Louis. The city was boring in that regard, but having traveled the world, Chiara had a keener sense of something she was sure that John now felt, too—that even quiet little dead zones like St. Louis held many dangers, some of which were smaller than a postage stamp.

John used Chiara's keys to unlock her door. Even though common sense told her that she had nothing to fear as John opened the door and walked into the apartment, she clutched at the back of his heavy coat.

"Everything's fine," he said, flipping on the freshly replaced foyer light. "We're the only ones here." He took her cape and ushered her into the living room where she suddenly stiffened and sucked in a sharp breath of air. "It's okay," he assured her. "This is my work."

Chiara swallowed nervously at the sight before her. Roses, hundreds of roses in every shade of red, filled her living room. The windowsills, the kitchen counter, the floor space surrounding the air mattress—everywhere, roses. And the air mattress itself was covered in a layer of petals so thick they looked like a textured blanket.

John stepped around her. He took off his coat and hung it with hers in the foyer closet. "Mr. Petrie helped me out with this," he said. "He likes you a lot. I think he's really going to miss you." John moved about the room, using wooden matches he'd picked up at the restaurant to light candles Chiara was only now noticing. "I think he got Mrs. Mayo to help him. She gave him most of these candles."

Chiara covered her mouth with her hands. The golden light of dozens of flickering candles warmed the room. Standing amid the bouquets of roses, John turned to her and offered his hand. Chiara went to him as though magnetized. "I wanted your last memory here to be a good one," he said.

"When did you do all this?" She smiled in amazement.

"I picked up a few things when I went for your boxes. I ordered the roses online and Mr. Petrie agreed to accept delivery while we were out. He offered to come in and arrange them, too. He's a good guy."

"What else did you pick up?"

John bent down and retrieved a small, dark brown bottle from the side of the air mattress. "This is arnica oil. I got it at that naturopathic skin care boutique near Loyola. It's supposed to relieve pain and muscle soreness. It's also good for reducing swelling and discoloration."

Chiara took the bottle, opened it and sniffed at the cap. "It's nice. Since when did you become a mystical medicine man?"

"I read about arnica in Kyla's book," he said.

"I thought her book was just recipes."

"You haven't read it?"

Chiara guiltily dropped her eyes. "I haven't gotten around to it."

"It's more than just a cookbook. Your sister gives a lot of tips on using healthy, natural things to promote good health. In her section about sunflowers she wrote about the pain relieving properties of arnica oil."

"Am I supposed to drink it?"

John smiled and took the bottom of her tunic. "Nope." He eased the garment over her head and cast it aside. Chiara's skin pleasantly prickled when his hands went to the front closure of her silky black bra. He stripped it off her and went to work on the side zipper of her pants. They, and her black bikini briefs, joined the rest of her clothes on the floor. John took the oil from her and guided her onto her belly on the air mattress. The cool, velvety rose petals delighted her skin as she stretched out atop them.

John knelt beside her and poured a small measure of the oil into the palm of his hand. He rubbed his hands together, warming it, before he applied it to her bruised shoulder blades. Ever so gently, his hands glided over her, working the oil into her skin without causing her further discomfort. He stood on his knees to reach every part of her back and shoulders, and Chiara moaned into the pillow of her arms.

John's therapeutic touch left no part of her neglected. From her neck to her ankles, he eased her aches in ways her prescription medication couldn't. When she rolled onto her back, inviting him to expand his treatment, she wasn't prepared for his serious expression.

"It helps," she told him. "It's probably you more than the oil, but it hardly hurts anymore."

She could only imagine how the colors of her bruised chest and thighs clashed with the beauty of the rose petals. "I'm so ugly now." She crossed one arm over her chest, the other over her midsection, and she brought her left leg up over her right.

John tenderly pulled her arms apart. "No," he said firmly. "I don't think I've ever seen you look more beautiful."

She reached up and took his face, drawing his mouth to hers. She kissed him, leaving no doubt in his mind that despite how her body looked, she was ready and eager to share it with him. John handled her more tenderly than he ever had, and that care stimulated Chiara even more. She hugged his head to her as he kissed her throat and collarbone, took the hardening tips of her breasts between his lips. His hands tightened at her waist before he moved lower, tasting the oil on her skin on his way to the welcoming heat between her legs.

Cradling her buttocks in his hands he held her to his mouth, first delicately sampling her, then nibbling with an aching tenderness that made her wrap her legs about his head and shoulders. His hunger seemed insatiable, relentless in its gentleness as he worked his tongue against the hard nub hidden within her soft petals. When he took it lightly in his teeth and flicked his tongue over it, she cried out, her noises of pleasure echoing in the near empty apartment. Her kissed her there as deeply and fully as he'd ever kissed her mouth, and her legs fell wide apart, offering him everything she had.

John tore away from her to tug off his sweater. Sitting up slightly, Chiara grabbed his face and roughly kissed him, tasting herself on him. John's desire for her was so great his hands trembled as he unfastened his jeans and struggled out of them, Chiara making his work harder by suckling his nipples and taking his growing thickness in her hand.

He kicked off his sneakers and socks and spread himself over her, careful not to put too much of his weight on her. Chiara took his hand and slipped it between her legs, guiding his fingers in the way that most pleased her while using her other hand to bring him to his fullest. John moved lower, oiling his body with the residue from hers, and kissed her breasts. Chiara guided his longest finger into the slick heat of her body and John took a long, easy draw on her nipple. Her hand tensed around him, almost painfully, before it began moving in firm, steady strokes that matched those of his finger.

John's muscles strained from the effort of holding back, of letting Chiara determine the pace of their coupling. Blinded, deafened by his need to plunge deep inside her, John became a creature of primal instinct, using his mouth at her breasts to bring her to the same place of senseless want that she had taken him.

A guttural groan crawled out of her throat as she tossed her head back, her hips driving into John's hand. She pulled at his wrist, removing his hand, and then grabbed his hip and urged him atop her. She guided him into her heat, thrusting upward as he trembled downward, catching his mouth in a deep, satisfying kiss. She hooked her arms around his shoulders, and on shivering arms he supported his weight, his head thrown back. Against the background of roses painted in candlelight, John was a thing of beauty that made Chiara's heart surge.

Digging her fingertips into his hard biceps, she raised herself to suckle his earlobe. He wrapped his arms tight about her shoulders and waist, the slow, deep movement of his hips driving her with exquisite tenderness into the mattress. Sweat from his brow dripped onto the rose petals, which adhered to their skin and gave up their heady perfume as John and

Chiara became one more completely than they'd ever thought possible.

Cocooned in his embrace, her legs tight about him, Chiara had never felt safer. Or more powerful. His love was a tangible thing that pulsated through her veins, replacing pain with pleasure, leaving strength in place of fear. He was her friend, her lover, the other half that made her complete. His gentle passion was strong enough to transport her to a world immune from harm, and Chiara lost herself within the sanctuary of John's loving. She cried out loud when he shuddered upon her, his love exploding within her to ignite dizzying pulses of pure sensation from the place where they were joined. Chiara voiced the pleasure of each one of them, until John covered her mouth with his and kissed her back to their bed of roses. Chiara lay on her back, wonderfully weak, with John's weight and warmth half cloaking her. As John gazed down at her, working his fingers through her hair, Chiara wondered if her body had ever been treated so well.

"What do you think about having a real wedding in the near future?" John asked her.

If John hadn't proposed so many times before, Chiara might have reacted with more excitement and less practicality. "I think we need to wait until it's safe."

"Going about our ordinary lives would go a long way toward convincing Emmitt Grayson that we don't know anything about his chip."

"But we do know about it." She touched the tip of her index finger to his lower lip and traced its fullness. "And we have to do something about it. We can't just forget about it and act like it's no big deal."

"I know," he sighed. "But we can't let it rule us, either." He leaned over her to grab something from the floor. It was a tiny black velvet pouch. "If your finger turns green this time, someone at Jeweler's Row will have some serious explaining to do."

John upended the pouch and a ring dropped into his palm. He took Chiara's left hand, slipped it onto her finger and pressed her hand to his heart. He didn't have to say he loved her, or that he wanted to spend the rest of his life with her. He'd never loved anyone else, never even had a chance to, not when Chiara had come into his life so early that he could scarcely remember her not being a part of it.

Chiara took John's hand and placed it on her abdomen. "I never needed a ring. And now I have something so much better."

"I love you," he said simply. "I always have."

"I know," she smiled. "I planned it that way."

Laughing, John pulled her even closer. She rested her head on his shoulder and raised her arm, displaying her ring for both of them. It wasn't just beautiful with its unusual, intricate pattern that looked like burled wood. It was evidence of John's good taste and his knowledge of Chiara's. "It's *mokume gane*," Chiara said, moving her hand to make the ring look as though its ripples were in motion. "You remembered."

"Well, you talked about it enough when you discovered it during your last trip to Tokyo," John remarked. "I remembered the '*gane*', and fortunately the jeweler knew what I was talking about. I forgot all about the '*moku*' part."

"*Moku* means wood, *me* is eye and *gane* is metal," Chiara said. "It's a technique that was used by metal-smiths to decorate samurai swords. It's where you layer combinations of gold, silver, copper or platinum, and then use heat and pressure to fuse the metals without melting them. You can take the patterned sheet of metal and carve it into whatever design you want, and roll it into whatever thickness you want. Like for this ring, for instance. John, it's beautiful. I love it."

"You can give me mine at our wedding," he said.

"And I'll be hiding mine until then," Chiara said. "If Mama sees this on my finger tomorrow, there'll be a whole lot of questions I really don't want to have to answer."

❧

"Look at all the cars," Chiara said. John had parked the Eclipse a few houses away, the closest he could get to Abby's driveway, which was stacked with cars. "It's not a holiday. Why are there always so many people at my mother's house?"

"That might not be a bad thing," John said, unlocking the doors. "The more people around you, the better. It'll be harder for another one of Grayson's bruisers to get to you."

Chiara turned in the passenger seat of her tiny car to face John. "I don't think he did it. Grayson didn't send that man after me."

"Come on, Chiara." John shook his head and uttered a laugh of disbelief. "Who else could it have been?"

"You saw him at my apartment. He seemed genuinely concerned that I'd been attacked."

"I made sure that he knew about it, even if he didn't orchestrate the attack himself. I told Chele Brewster and enough people in information systems to make sure that everyone in that building knew what happened to you."

"If Grayson sent someone after me, why would he come to the scene of the crime? That's sick."

"He had Zhou killed." John's grip tightened on the steering wheel. "You think he'd bat an eye at having you beat down? If he didn't arrange it, who did?"

"He was worried, John. He seemed scared. He knows something's going on, but I don't think he's behind what happened to Zhou and me. He's a thief and a sneak, but I can't make myself believe that he had me hurt. Maybe he has some idea of who did do it, though. I've never seen him look so lost and confused."

"I think you're giving him too much credit."

"That dossier came from him. There's a research company in Maryland that he wants me to read up on. He's keeping me domestic, to keep an eye on me probably, but there's no way he would kill me. I'm as big a part of his scams as the master chip. The masters are useless without me to sell the R-GS systems that go with them." Her voice took on a brittleness that made her words sound somewhat desperate. "I'm number one, remember? I'm the one who always makes the sale."

"You're on vacation, Chi. You don't have to do anything for that company ever again, and Grayson can't do a thing about it."

"But I have to do something about it, John!" The image of his handsome face blurred as tears rose in her eyes. "I know what he's doing! Grayson sees faceless companies and maybe that makes it easier for him to steal their secrets and profit from them. I meet the people behind the corporate banner. I get to know them. They talk to me about their employees, their families, their lives. Grayson's isn't a victimless crime. He's stealing from people who trusted me to sell them a product that would make their information systems secure, not vulnerable to a predator like Grayson."

"What can you possibly do to fix what he's done?"

"I can go to that company in Maryland." Her throat was tight with tears. "And I can convince them not to buy the R-GS chips. That's one less company Grayson can steal from."

"Grayson would know that you mucked it up on purpose."

"Probably." Chiara chuckled bitterly. "I'm his pet, and everyone knows it. I'm his perfectly trained, pedigreed sales dog. No one sells better than me. I can sell styling gel to Mr. Clean."

"I know," John said gently. "When we were in the sixth grade, Sybille Hasse threw away an old pencil case and you sold it back to her for a dollar."

"Grayson knows how good I am. He values my salesmanship, and he's relied on it for five years to get his R-GS chips into position. He wouldn't risk getting me killed, not until he finds someone who does the job better than I do."

"And then what happens? He lets you walk away, free and clear, never knowing for sure if you knew anything about his missing master?"

She nervously chewed the edge of her right thumbnail. "I don't know anymore. All I know…" She sat forward to avoid looking into his eyes. "All I know is that I don't want you involved in this anymore."

John exited the car and went to Chiara's side of it. He opened her door and squatted before her. "I'm involved and you know it. Zhou got both of us into this mess, not you. I won't abandon you to handle this alone."

Chiara nodded through a fall of tears. It had always been the two of them. John had always been there to defend her, to support her. He'd paid for his love for her, with no less than his flesh.

She laid a hand on John's cheek. "I've been to the other side of the world, and I've always come back for one reason. For one person."

Smiling devilishly, John said, "Who?"

"You," she whispered, smiling through her tears. "Always, always you."

A dozen voices greeted Chiara at once when she entered the house. John closed the door behind them and held back as Chiara's family swallowed her up in hugs and loud, cheerful greetings, and bustled her from the foyer and into the living room. Abby, who had opened the door for them before they'd even had a chance to ring the doorbell, was first in line. She alternated between hugging Chiara and pulling away to look at her youngest daughter's bruised face. Tears welled in her eyes, and John would have bet money that they were tears of mingled happiness and sadness.

"Welcome home, Aunt Chiara," Danielle said, squeezing between Chiara and Abby. Abigail, adjusting her new glasses, popped up too, along with Ella, whose blue-black braids swung merrily about her head.

"Why aren't you guys in school?" Chiara asked. "You get Mondays off now?"

"It's a staff development day," Danielle said. "We got out at noon."

"Welcome home, Chi," Clara said. Her eyes moved over her face. "When Mama told me that you'd been hurt, I didn't think…" Her words caught in her throat and she abruptly caught Chiara up in a hug. She rubbed her hands over Chiara's back the way she always had when they were younger, and Chiara needed comforting after a spill on her bike.

"I'm okay." Chiara wriggled out of Clara's grasp only to be caught up in Kyla's, who held Niema at the same time.

"I'm so sorry for fighting with you at Christmas," Kyla said earnestly, her chin pressed into Chiara's shoulder. "I'm so sorry you were hurt. You're home now, kiddo. You're safe."

Chiara hugged Kyla back, remembering the incident two years ago when Kyla had been the victim of a home invasion. She'd known her attacker, her ex-manager, who had forced himself into her apartment. He'd hit her and might have done worse if Cady hadn't been there with Kyla's baseball bat.

"Where are the boys?" Chiara asked her sister Ciel, who stood patiently in line to greet her.

"Christopher is delivering an end table he made for one of the St. Louis Cardinals, Zweli's picking up one of Mama's friends, and Lee's in New York City meeting with one of his investment clients," Ciel said.

"I didn't mean the married boys," Chiara clarified.

"Troy and C.J. are around here somewhere, and Clarence is looking for his lizard." Her expression serious, Ciel used her right hand to brush a lock of hair from the right side of Chiara's face. "He lost it here on Christmas."

"That little monster has been running free in my house for two weeks," Abby scowled.

"Clarence?" Chiara said, pulling her hair back in place to conceal as much of her bruising as she could.

"The lizard, smartie," Ciel grinned. "If you haven't contacted an attorney in Chicago, I can recommend someone."

"An attorney? For what?"

"For your negligence suit against The Sovereign, to start with," Ciel said. "When you sign a lease, you're entitled to a reasonable expectation of security and safety, especially when you're living in a building that charges fifteen hundred a month for rent on a one-bedroom apartment."

"I'm not suing anyone, Ciel."

"It's like *Wild Kingdom* in here!" Abby shouted when Clarence zoomed by, hunched over, chasing something with sharp claws that skittered across the bare sections of the hardwood floor.

"John, catch him, he's running right for you!" Clarence laughed. "Hi, Aunt Chiara!" he called as he disappeared into the dining room.

"Keep that thing out of my kitchen!" Abby hollered. "I don't want any salmonella near my pies!" Sweetening her voice, Abby turned back to Chiara. "I made your favorite, cherry, and banana crème for John, and—"

"Mama, you didn't have to go to any trouble," Chiara insisted. "I'm a little tired from the drive, and I have a headache. I'm not in the mood for a party."

"This isn't a party, honey," Abby said. "It's just the family." She turned toward the foyer, and cupped her hand over her mouth to bellow toward the basement. "Troy! C.J.! Come on up and say hello to your aunty!"

The sound of heavy footsteps came thundering from the stairwell that opened into the kitchen, along with the voices of Chiara's half-grown nephews. Troy entered the room first and gave Chiara a hug and peck on the cheek. C.J., who at sixteen was the same size as his big brother, was making his way to Chiara when he was bumped aside by a pair of gigantic breasts.

"I'm so glad you're here, Aunt Chiara!" squealed a voice issuing from behind the breasts, whose arms grabbed Chiara in a bear hold. Chiara stared wide-eyed at Clara, who sat across the room on the arm of the flowered sofa. The breasts freed Chiara when John entered the archway between the living room and foyer.

"You must be John Mahoney," the breasts said, opening their arms to him.

"Yeah, this is Mahofro," Cady said smoothly, inserting herself between John and the breasts. "But you can call him Mr. Mahoney."

The toothy smile behind the breasts shrank. "I feel like I know everybody else so well," she said, turning back to Chiara. "I can't wait to get to know you better, too."

Cady swooped upon the breasts and clamped an arm around their owner's shoulders, guiding them to sit on the loveseat with Chiara. "This is Tiff McCousy, Troy's little friend," Cady said to Chiara. "And I just know you two are going to be best friends!" she teased, pitching her voice higher and speaking too fast. "You can have sleepovers and do each other's hair, and paint your nails, and call boys and practice kissing on your hands."

Chiara squirmed out of Cady's embrace. "Sounds like real fun," she said, hanging out her tongue.

Kyla, trying not to laugh, almost jiggled Niema out of her arms as she tried to nurse her in the comfy armchair opposite the loveseat.

Tiff crossed her arms petulantly and stood up. With a silent, cross look at Cady, she started from the room, halting beside Troy. "Your aunt is so mean to me, Troy," she said before giving him a pointed look and leaving in a huff.

"Get the hell outta here," Cady said under her breath. "Fraud."

Troy scratched the back of his head and took a few steps toward Cady. "You don't have to be so mean to her, Aunt Cady."

"See what a snitch she is?" Cady said to the room in general. And to Troy, she added, "You'd better step off before you get cussed out, kid."

"Why don't you go check on Tits—er, *Tiff*," John advised. "Sorry, man. Just a slip of the tongue."

"It's Aunt Cady's bad influence is what it is," Troy said as he left to find Tiffani.

"He really likes her," Clara said, shaking her head.

"I like her, too." C.J. grinned lasciviously, his raisin eyes glittering as a blush rose to deepen his terra cotta complexion.

"You can go back downstairs, too," Clara admonished. "Grandma put in a pool table, a dart board and a television specifically so you children would have something better to do than eavesdrop on adults." She waited for C.J. to lope off before she said, "That means you, too, DNN!"

"How did she know I was here?" Danielle whined from the other side of the archway, where she'd been pressing herself to the wall.

In a much lower voice, Clara said, "Cady, it really hurts Troy's feelings that you don't like Tiffani."

"None of us like her," Cady said stubbornly, throwing one leg over the other and making a fuss of smoothing her wool skirt over her knees.

"Yes, but you're the only one who openly shows it," Clara pointed out.

"Niema shows it," Cady argued. "She cries every time Tits tries to hold her."

"Niema is a baby," Clara said. "You're an adult, supposedly. We hold you to a certain standard of maturity."

"How am I immature?" Cady asked, flattening her hand on her chest.

"Tits," Clara said.

"Mahofro," Chiara chimed in.

"Those are just affectionate nicknames," Cady protested.

"They're disrespectful," Ciel put in from her position near the fireplace.

"And annoying," Chiara said.

"Oh, shut up, Repeat," Cady grumbled.

"See what we mean?" Chiara said. "Just because I look like Clara, you call us 'Pete' and 'Repeat.' That one's not even original."

"You're right," Cady agreed with an empty smile. "I think I'll call you Ditto from now on. Or how about Li'l Clara?"

Abby reached across Chiara to pat Cady's knee. "Don't get your back up, honey. But for Troy's sake, you really should be a little nicer to Tits. *Tiff!* Lord, now you've got me started."

Chiara laughed in spite of herself, and would have taken that moment to excuse herself if the doorbell hadn't chimed.

"That must be Zweli with Miss Etheline." Abby started for the door. "I was wondering what was taking them so long."

Chiara, poised to bolt from the room, would have made it if Cady hadn't grabbed the back of her top. The loosely woven knit garment, which Chiara had purchased from a street vendor in China, gave Cady great fingerholds. "Uh uh," Cady said. "If we have to sit through an afternoon with Miss *Evil*ine, then so do you. You're the only reason she's here. Mama talked to her on the phone this morning and made the mistake of mentioning that you were moving home today. She invited herself over, and you know Mama."

Chiara looked for rescue in the archway, where John had been chatting with Keren, who'd been holding Virginia. Both men had disappeared with the baby in a flash of corduroy and wool the moment the front door began to open and Miss E.'s loud, deep voice rolled into the foyer.

"Praise Jesus, we got here in one piece!" When Miss Etheline Simpson stamped her feet on the braided welcome mat, it sounded like an angry bull about to charge. "Dr. Zweli, you drive as if Satan and all his soldiers are trying to bring you back home."

"I made a point to drive the speed limit, Miss Etheline," came Zweli's weary voice. "After you expressed your concerns about my driving the last time I picked you up."

"Well, it's a good thing I sat in the back seat all the same," Miss Etheline said with a breathy sigh.

"Poor Zweli always gets stuck driving Miss Crazy," Cady whispered to Kyla.

"It comes with the territory," Chiara replied, remembering Lee's joy when Cady and Keren got married. As the newest son-in-law, Keren had inherited Lee's agonizing chore of chauffeuring Miss Etheline to and from select Winters family functions, a task Lee had inherited from a much-relieved Christopher. *That's why my beloved brothers-in-law keep trying to prod me into a wedding,* Chiara thought, pinching her lips together. *Miss E. is a human chain letter, and they want to pass her off once and for all.*

Miss Etheline remained in the foyer, bossing Zweli around as though she'd bought him at auction. "Help me out of this coat, child, I'm burning up in here. Abby keeps it hotter than the devil's kitchen in this house. Wish I had money to burn on heating oil like some folks do."

Carrying a heap of red wool blend that Chiara assumed was Miss Etheline's coat, Zweli grimaced into the living room as he passed the archway on his way to the closet under the stairwell.

"Say hello to Miss Etheline, everyone," Abby directed uncomfortably as she returned to the living room.

"Hello, Miss Etheline," the Winters sisters chorused flatly.

With her fists resting on her waistline, which appeared to be directly under her armpits, Miss Etheline's large physique seemed to fill the archway with only a few inches to spare on each side. She wore a two-piece jacket dress in a purple-and-pomegranate woven polyester print that seemed to shift about her bulk with a life of its own. The thick soles of the black orthopedic shoes laced tightly to her big, square feet easily brought her up to a good six feet. Her thinning gray hair was pulled back in a tight bun that had been supplemented with fake hair the color of burnt chestnut. She stood silent for a moment—the only respite from her voice the household was likely to enjoy until Zweli took her back home—and peered over the tops of her big, thick, window-like glasses, studying each person in the living room.

When she started for the biggest, most comfortable armchair where Kyla was nursing Niema, Chiara realized that Miss Etheline had zoomed in on her target. And that she was sitting directly in the center of the crosshairs.

CHAPTER FOURTEEN

Removed to another chair, Kyla rested Niema over her shoulder and gave her a gentle burping. Niema's soft coos were the only sounds in the room as everyone grew silent, eager to see the imminent show-down between Miss Etheline and Chiara. Neither Almadine Mahoney nor Emmitt Grayson had been Chiara's first nemesis. It was Miss Etheline Simpson, a friend of Abby Winters for almost fifty years. The two women had met in college. Abby had been a student working on her degree in education and Etheline had been employed in the cafeteria, working the breakfast and lunch shifts.

Chiara never knew how her mother and Miss Etheline had become friends, never mind stayed friends, considering Etheline's bossy, condescending ways. The only reason she could think of to explain the endurance of the friendship was that Abby knew that Miss Etheline had no other family or friends, which guaranteed that Abby would never turn her back on her.

Cady had long ago proposed that the reason Miss Etheline had no children was because, like a piranha, she had eaten them. Nothing Chiara had seen of the woman in the ensuing years had disavowed her of that notion.

From the age of five on, Chiara hadn't known a moment's ease in Miss Etheline's presence. The woman picked on everything, especially things that couldn't be helped, and therefore left Chiara in a position she couldn't possibly defend. She'd sent Chiara running outside crying one Thanksgiving when she'd pointed out that one of Chiara's ears appeared to be higher than the other. And worse had been Abby's attempt to console her: "Miss Etheline doesn't mean anything by it, baby," she'd said. "It doesn't matter how your ears are attached since they both work, right?"

Long gone, though, were the days when Miss Etheline could reduce her to tears with one of her snide observations. For one, Chiara had stayed out of her sight even on her few previous visits home. Secondly, Chiara wasn't a little girl anymore. And third, Miss Etheline had picked the wrong damn week to pick a fight with Chiara Winters.

Even Niema quieted when Miss Etheline fixed her rheumy eyes on Chiara and drawled, "So the prodigal one has returned at last." She tapped one of her thick, blunt fingers on the arm of the chair.

"Yep," Chiara responded.

"I bet your mama was glad to see you."

"Forget the fatted calf," Chiara said. "Mama would have killed and spit-roasted one of my sisters if I'd asked her to."

"Yes, your mama sets quite a store by her girls. Even the ones that break her heart." Miss Etheline's cheeks bulged in a tiny smile. She took a long sip of the iced root beer she'd requested from Abby, and the dark beverage clung to her upper lip, making her light mustache even more pronounced.

"That's not fair and you know it, Ethel," Abby broke in. "I let my girls live their own lives."

"Doing God knows what with God knows who in God knows where," she trumpeted.

"God knows it's my life and my business," Chiara said sweetly.

"I know that John Mahoney's around here some-where," Miss Etheline said, craning her neck as though he were hiding behind her chair. "I had me a dog once who was like him. Always followed me around. Little fellow did everything I told him to."

Chiara's nostrils flared, but she held her tongue.

"I was just talking to Almadine the other day," Miss Etheline went on. "We were talking about what a shame it is that John is wasting his life worrying after somebody who ain't never gonna settle down and marry him."

"I'm sorry to hear that you and Mrs. Mahoney don't have anything better to do than talk about John's love life," Chiara said stiffly.

Miss Etheline belched out a chuckle. "Love?" She laughed out loud. "Love ain't got nothin' to do with it. If it did, you would've married that boy by now and pumped out a few of his babies."

"Ethel, why don't you come into the kitchen and help me put out lunch," Abby offered, reaching for Miss Etheline's hand.

Miss Etheline sat still. "I didn't come here to work, and I'm fine right here." She narrowed her eyes at Chiara, her glasses making them appear even larger and more sinister. "When are you going to make your mama happy and marry that boy?"

Chiara took a deep breath through her nose and nearly gagged on the scent of overripe cabbage that always seemed to emanate from Miss Etheline. "The last thing I would ever do is get married for the sake of making someone else happy," Chiara said.

"You really are a selfish little girl."

Chiara's fingers burrowed into the cushion she was sitting on. "You're a mean old lady."

Cady bit down on her lips. Clara's wide, pretty eyes became even wider. Kyla smothered a laugh in Niema's shoulder, and Abby frantically gripped handfuls of her apron. "Please," Abby started. "This is supposed to be a nice afternoon. I don't want any fighting."

Chiara wasn't sure whom her mother was appealing to, but she doubted it was Miss Etheline. "I'm just defending myself, Mama. After all these years, I certainly don't expect you to do it."

Miss Etheline abruptly sat up, the chair creaking under her weight. "Don't you talk to your mama like that in front of me!"

"You're the reason I spoke to her like that!" Chiara fired back. "If you don't want to hear it, you can go home."

"Chiara, I won't have you being rude to Miss Etheline," Abby said, showing her spine to the one combatant she could. "Apologize."

Miss Etheline sat back, smiling smugly. Chiara stared at her mother, her face burning with fury. Before she could work out a suitably vicious response, Ciel's voice broke the uncomfortable silence.

"Clarence!" she called sharply. "Would you come in here?"

A few seconds later, Clarence, followed by Abigail and Ella, ran into the room. "What is it, Mama?" he asked breathlessly.

Ciel tipped her head toward Miss Etheline.

His shoulders slumped, Clarence dragged his feet over to the armchair. "Hello, Miss Etheline," he dead-panned.

"Look at you," she said. "Your mama lets you run around looking like you ain't got a home to go to. Let me see your teeth."

Clarence whipped his head toward his mother, his young face wrinkled in curiosity.

"Don't go looking at your mama," Miss Etheline snapped. She clutched Clarence's shoulder and dragged him to her, bouncing his slight body off her gigantic bosom. "Let's see them teeth."

Clarence bared his choppers.

Peering down her nose, Miss Etheline said, "I knew it. I bet your mama and daddy let you eat sugar for dinner and more sugar for dessert."

"We had chicken last night," Clarence said.

"Don't talk back. Hand me my purse, boy," she commanded.

Miss Etheline's purse, a big black thing that could have doubled as a weekend tote, sat beside the chair. She could have grabbed it herself merely by hanging her arm over the arm of the chair, but she seemed to take more pleasure in watching Clarence heave the heavy thing onto her widespread knees.

As Miss Etheline rooted through her purse, Abigail and Ella, clutching each other's arms, tried to back out of the living room. "Where do you two think you're going?" Miss Etheline snapped. "You just come on over here."

Ella, the more sensitive of the two sisters, held onto Abigail even tighter as her chin began to tremble.

Miss Etheline withdrew her coin purse and unsnapped the latch. She spent a long moment shuffling her fingers through the coins before she pulled out a quarter and offered it to Clarence.

"What's that for?" he asked.

"It's for you," she barked, forcing the coin into his palm.

Clarence stared dully at the quarter. "Thank you, Miss Etheline."

"You're welcome. Girls, come on over here. I want to look at you."

Ella began crying in earnest, and Abigail couldn't seem to make her feet move. Troy, Tiffani and C.J. provided a much-needed distraction when they entered the room. "Mom, I need to run Tiffani down to the drugstore," Troy said. "We'll be back—"

"Oh, you don't see me, do you?" Miss Etheline broke in.

"Miss Etheline," Troy said, his face breaking into a fearful smile as he approached her. He was careful to remain out of arm's reach. "Good to see you, ma'am."

She peered around Troy. "Who's she?"

Tiffani pushed her way forward to take Miss Etheline's hand. "I'm Tiffani McCousy." She pasted on her biggest beauty contestant smile and tilted her head, flipping her chemically straightened black hair over one shoulder. "I'm Troy's girlfriend. We've been together for two months." She giggled, her big white teeth reflecting in Miss Etheline's glasses.

Miss Etheline gave her a wide, bright smile that Tiffani clearly mistook for friendliness. "How old are you, baby?" she asked pleasantly.

"Eighteen, same as Troy." She kneeled, since Miss Etheline seemed to have no intention of turning loose her hand.

Miss Etheline's eyes settled on the front of Tiffani's tight black knit top. "You're Troy's girlfriend, you say?"

"That's right." Tiffani's smile wilted a bit, and she looked down at her hand. Chiara thought she heard Tiffani's delicate bones grinding together under the pressure of Miss Etheline's grip, which Chiara knew from experience to be strong enough to buckle unopened beer cans.

"I just bet you're quite the handful, Miss Tiffani," Miss Etheline said. "You better keep an eye on these two, Clara, before you end up a grandma before you're ready. I can just guess what you're heading down to the drugstore to buy."

Tiffani snatched her hand away, and Chiara actually felt a little sorry for her.

"Don't act all offended with me, Miss Tiffani," Miss Etheline said. "I know what you young people are all about, especially a fast little thing like you."

"Ethel!" Abby snapped.

"Mama, we're not—Tiff and I aren't—we don't—" Troy stammered, his face reddening as his aunts and cousins looked at him.

"I can tell just by looking at her that Miss Tiffani likes to throw her weight around, if you get me," Miss Etheline cackled.

"That doesn't mean I'm catching it!" Troy nearly shouted.

"Ethel, really," Abby intervened as John and Keren dared to peep into the living room from the foyer. "I'm not going to have you here anymore if you keep upsetting everybody."

"If the truth is upsetting, ain't nothin' I can do about that."

Abby stood her ground. "I won't have you imposing your 'truth' on my family anymore. Did you even look at Chiara before you started in on her? She's had a hard week."

"Every day of my life is hard," Miss Etheline grumbled. "You don't hear me complaining about it."

"No, you just take your misery out on my children and my grandchildren." Abby crossed her arms over her chest.

Chiara almost smiled. It had been long in coming, but finally, Abby was defending her family against the mighty Miss Etheline.

"What you goin' to the drugstore for if it ain't to buy rubbers?" Miss Etheline bellowed at Troy. "That's the only thing young peoples go to the drugstore for these days, rubbers and birth control pills."

"What the hell have we missed?" John said, appearing with Keren.

C.J., who was standing nearby, colored deeply. "Miss Lethaline," he started, implementing yet another of Cady's nicknames, "thinks Troy and Tiffani are running off to knock boots. Grandma got mad and now they're fighting."

"I really wish you wouldn't speak like this in front of the children," Abby directed at Miss Etheline.

"I didn't call them in here," Miss Etheline said defensively.

"I called Clarence in here because there's something I need him to do," Ciel explained in cool, precise tones.

"What?" Miss Etheline scoffed.

"Clarence." Ciel pointed to Miss Etheline's chair.

"I have to show her my teeth again?" he whined.

"No. But I'd be extremely appreciative if you removed your Christmas present from Miss Etheline's root beer."

Clarence's eyes brightened as he smiled. "You found him!"

Miss Etheline's heavy eyebrows drew closer. "Him?"

Clarence reached for his lost gift, the eight-inch bearded dragon perched on the highly polished side table next to Miss Etheline's chair.

"What the—" was all Miss Etheline managed before Clarence's grasping hands sent the chubby, reddish-orange lizard scurrying up Miss Etheline's arm, its filed-down claws catching in the garish fabric of her top.

Miss Etheline threw her arms up and hollered, the sound not totally unlike that made by a wounded draught cow Chiara had seen put down in a Malaysian village. The lizard, perhaps more frightened by Miss Etheline than she was by it, sought refuge on her shoulder, which drove her to her feet. Beating at herself with her oven-mitt sized hands, Miss Etheline became a purple-and-pomegranate tornado as she spun in frantic circles, screaming, knocking over her chair, the side table, and everything else in her path.

Niema, ordinarily a quiet and good-natured baby, opened her sweet little mouth and added her terrified screams to Miss Etheline's. The baby's cries awakened

Sammy and Claire Elizabeth, who'd been napping upstairs.

The lizard, apparently enjoying the ride, climbed higher atop Mount Etheline, cresting the summit of her fake bun to display the rough orange ridges and scales under its chin, the beard for which its species had been named.

Keren handed Virginia off to Cady. "Hold still, Miss Etheline, and we'll get it!" he said, reaching for her head.

"Bearded lizards are very gentle," Danielle called, finally entering the living room from her eavesdropping perch in the foyer. "He's just playing with you!"

"Don't hurt him!" Clarence pleaded, getting in Keren's way.

Kyla, using Niema to stifle her giggles, huddled with Clara and Ciel, who shook with silent laughter. Cradling a now-sobbing Virginia to her chest, Cady watched her husband's attempts to subdue Miss Etheline and her passenger, a delighted smile on her face. Troy and C.J. joined Keren in trying to remove the lizard from Miss Etheline's hair while Tiffani leaned against the archway, covering her mouth with her hands to capture her amusement. Abigail and Ella fell into each other's arms, laughing, and Abby shunted them out of the room, chastising them through her own wheezy snickers.

Through the chaos of collapsing furniture and bodies leaping clear of Miss Etheline's erratic path, John sought out Chiara. She wasn't laughing, and at the sight of her, his own merriment vanished. No one other than John noticed Chiara slump sideways and fall face first to the loveseat.

❧❧❧

John carried Chiara up to one of Abby's guest rooms. "Would you get the door?" he asked Keren, who'd readily abandoned his zookeeping duties when John called to him after failing to rouse Chiara.

Keren closed the door just before Abby and the rest of her daughters would have entered the room. For good measure, he locked it, which earned an outcry of protest from Abby.

"One minute she was sitting there, the next..." John was at a loss.

Keren sat beside her and pressed two fingers to her neck, searching for her pulse. He next parted her eyelids and examined her pupils. He lifted one of her hands and gave her inner wrist a series of light slaps that roused her.

"I feel dizzy," Chiara moaned, trying and failing to raise herself to a sitting position.

"Keep her there," Keren said softly. "I'm going to get my bag."

Chiara pressed a shaky hand to her clammy forehead. "I can't stay here, John," she pleaded softly. "I've been here for an hour and I've already had enough of these people."

"Those people are your family," he told her gently, kneeling beside her. "I think—"

Her cross expression cut him off. She already knew what he thought: that her family was wonderful. John always greeted Abby with long, tight hugs, the kind he would have reserved for his own mother if Almadine were the hugging type. Abby was matronly but elegant and sophisticated at the same time. Each of her daughters, save Chiara, stood a few inches over her, but still they looked up to their mother. Abby's waist had thickened a little since she'd retired from teaching over the summer, but that was likely due to the elaborate dinners she prepared for her huge brood. Abby had a beautiful head of silvery-grey hair that complemented her cocoa skin, and her full, cheerful face remained unlined but for a gentle fan of wrinkles that appeared near her eyes when she laughed, which was often.

John had a son's love for Abby's face, which was soft and kind, unlike the hard angles of his own mother's. Almadine was ten years younger than Abby, but had deep lines etched around her mouth that made her look twenty years older. Almadine's breathing always became heavier and her ebony skin seemed to darken when she engaged in one of her tirades, which had inspired George to follow Cady's example and give his mother a nickname: Darth Vader.

The Mahoney home was well ordered, both on the surface and behind closed doors. But John had always thrived on the "cacophony of chaos" that prevailed in Abby's home. When Zachary Winters was killed in the Mideast, Claire and Hank Winters had stepped in to help care for Chiara and her sisters. They had been the grandparents John never had, gifting him with the hugs, sweets and kind words that his own Baptist preacher grandfather withheld, convinced that too much affection would undo the work of his daughter's rod.

John knew that it was easier for Chiara to take her family for granted than it was for him. They belonged to her and always would, no matter what. It was easy to toss aside what you could never actually throw away.

"You're safer here, you know that," John said, trying a different tack. "And it won't be forever."

She squinted her eyes and covered them with both hands. "It's too much, John. The kids were running all over the place, Niema and Virginia were trying to compete for America's Screamiest Baby, Miss Etheline was stampeding around the place like a mad elephant, Danielle can't stop eavesdropping for five seconds, Cady keeps looking at me like she knows what's going on, Clarence's lizard is running free, Mama, Clara and Ciel treat me like I'm five years old, Kyla treats me like I'm an idiot, and underneath all of that, I have to live here knowing that I might be endangering every single person in this house." She took a few tear-filled breaths. "I can't live with that, John. If anything happens to Mama, or the babies, or—"

"Nothing will happen." He took her hands and removed them from her face. He held them atop her abdomen.

"How can you know that?"

"I don't," he answered honestly. "I just think there's safety in numbers."

Chiara softly wept and John folded her into his arms. "I want to go home," she murmured into his chest.

"You are home," he chuckled lightly.

"Not this home. Our home. Chicago."

He held her by her shoulders. "You just fainted. I think you should stay here and rest."

Chiara snorted. "Like I can rest here. These people suck the energy right out of me."

"I wish I had so many people who cared about me," he told her, his eyes searching hers.

"They care about you, John, and you know it. They like you more than they like me."

"You're going to have to tell them to give you some space."

She laughed and leaned back against the head-board. "Have you met my family? Have you ever known any of them to do anything I ask them to?"

John was spared an answer when Keren returned, slipping through the smallest possible gap in the door and closing it quickly behind him.

"That's my baby in there!" came Abby's cross voice, along with a good deal of banging on the locked door. "Keren! How dare you lock me out of one of my own bedrooms! Keren! What are you doing in there?"

"I'm removing Chiara's appendix," Keren called in a rare flash of humor.

Abby's voice became only so much background noise as Chiara eyed the dark leather medical bag clutched in Keren's hand. "What are you really doing?"

"I'm going to check you over. Fainting can be symptomatic of a number of serious ailments."

"That's not necessary," Chiara insisted, even as Keren nudged John aside to get next to her. "I'm tired, and I've been under a lot of stress that I haven't been handling very well, and…there was the attack…and…"

"You're pregnant," Keren said very quietly as he put on his stethoscope.

"Big-mouthed Cady," Chiara sneered.

"Shh…" Keren placed the chest piece of his stethoscope over Chiara's heart and listened. "Sounds good." He hung the stethoscope over his neck. "Strong and steady. Don't be mad at Cady." He glanced at John. "She didn't tell me about your condition."

Chiara frowned at John.

"I had to tell him," John said. "You passed out."

Keren examined Chiara's nail beds. She was embarrassed at how she'd nibbled her usually mani-cured nails down to the quick during the drive to St. Louis. Keren didn't comment on the ragged state of her nails, declaring them a nice healthy pink before he placed a blood pressure cuff on her and repositioned his stethoscope. "I can't know for certain without running tests at the hospital, but I'd say that you just had an anxiety attack. Is there something going on, other than…you know." He nodded toward her midsection.

Chiara chewed her lower lip while Keren checked her blood pressure. When he was done, he pronounced that stat okay as well. "John, would you mind getting her some juice? You might have fainted because your blood sugar is low," he told Chiara.

"Sure thing," John said. He listened at the door until, satisfied the coast was clear, he cautiously opened it.

Alone with Keren, Chiara found herself close to tears again.

"I know you the least of all my sisters-in-law, but you've always been my favorite," he said. "There's something so mysterious and intriguing about you. And I've always admired your independence and how you live your life the way you want to, not how your mother or your sisters recommend." He laughed softly. "They're all very smart women, but they have a tendency to prescribe what's best for *them*, not necessarily what's best for the person they're bossing around."

"So you have been paying attention," Chiara said dryly.

"You're safe here," Keren said.

Chiara choked back a laugh. She hadn't felt safe since she last spoke with Zhou in Tokyo.

"You're not alone, either," Keren told her.

"I know." Chiara wiped her nose with the cuff of her sleeve.

"If you need help with something, you know Cady and I—"

"I know," she sniffled. "All I have to do is ask."

"Do you want to talk about what happened in Chicago?"

She shook her head. "I just want to go to sleep." *For about two weeks,* she added to herself.

"Okay." Keren patted her shin before standing. "If you change your mind…"

"Thanks, Keren, but…"

He looked down at her, his concern plain in his dark eyes. She also saw that the fact that he had married into her family made him no less devoted to her than Cady, or Abby, or any one of her blood relatives. "Just being here is enough," she said. "For right now. Thank you."

CHAPTER FIFTEEN

"Are you alone?"

Chiara thought it prudent to establish Tiffani's whereabouts before she allowed Troy to open the trapdoor. She had relocated to the attic, at Cady's insistence, and was unpacking her garment bag when Troy paid her a visit.

"I took Tiff home a little while ago," Troy said, the trapdoor muffling his voice. "Can I come up?"

If you must, Chiara thought. But what she said was, "Sure."

Chiara had to smile at the sight of her nephew climbing the stairs into the attic. All she had to do was blink to see him at six, gamboling around the dusty clutter that had occupied the attic before Abby's renovation. He had his father's height now, and at six feet tall he had to stay near the center beam to keep from banging his head on the lower, sloping sides of the roof.

When he sat in the overstuffed suede armchair near the foot of the bed, Chiara was sure that he wasn't going to talk to her about his favorite TV show or how his favorite baseball team had fared lately. One look in his eyes told her that her nearly adult nephew had more adult concerns on his mind.

"What's up, kiddo?" Chiara asked as she shook out a white knit dress before slipping it onto a padded hanger.

"Do you like Tiffani?" he asked.

Chiara shrugged a shoulder. "I don't know her. She seems…um…"

"Just say it. Your opinion matters a lot to me."

"She seems really into you," Chiara finished. "Us, too. I thought I was going to be buried alive in her breasts."

"I know." Troy smiled wistfully.

"You'd better be careful with her," Chiara warned. "She knows you're off to Stanford in August, right?"

"Yeah."

"Well, she looks at you like she wants to swallow you in one bite." Chiara went to the empty armoire and opened the doors, filling the attic with the scent of new cedar.

"She does," Troy smiled shyly, "but…"

Chiara hung up her dress and the rest of the items in her garment bag. "But what?"

"I want to wait."

"For what?"

"Until we're married," Troy said as he rubbed his knuckles along the soft denim covering his thighs.

Chiara paused in her unpacking to sit at the head of the bed. "Your senior spring trip isn't to San Francisco, is it?"

"No," he said. "Why?"

"No reason." She turned back to her unpacking.

"I don't want to do it with Tiffani just because all the other guys are doing it all over the place," Troy went on. "I want it to be real. Like with you and Mahofro. My mother says that you guys have been together since you were little."

"Don't call him that," Chiara requested softly.

"That's what Aunt Cady calls him."

"Aunt Cady refuses to see that John is a grown man and not some curly-haired kid who used to hang around all the time. John deserves your respect. He's a part of this family, not one of your little playfriends."

"He's not really a part of the family," Troy argued weakly. "He's just your boyfriend."

"That shows what you know," Chiara said. "You've known John all your life, so give him credit for that at least."

"You know what I mean, Aunt Chiara," Troy said.

"No, actually, I don't." She set her feet hard on the floor and grabbed at her suitcase.

"I think I'll just shut up now," Troy said.

"Good idea." Chiara struggled to get the heavy case onto the bed, and Troy got up to lift it for her.

"I didn't mean to hurt your feelings," he told her.

Without thanking or looking at him, she unzipped the big black case and began taking stacks of folded shirts and trousers from her suitcase. "You didn't."

"Seems like I did." Troy took a step away from her, his hands forlornly in his pockets.

Chiara went to the cherry bureau that had once belonged to her Grandma Claire and slapped a stack of shirts into the deep, bottommost drawer. "I don't like people undervaluing my relationship with John just because we don't wave a marriage certificate around. I love John, more than anyone could possibly understand."

."But we do," Troy said, holding his hands wide. "We see it. That's why we can't figure out why you won't get married. It seems like you are already in a lot of ways, but no one can understand why you won't just—"

"I don't like doing something because everyone wants or expects me to." She approached her nephew, her socks moving her soundlessly across the polished hardwood floor. "All those women downstairs spent most of my life telling me what to do. How to dress, what to eat and when to eat it, who to be friends with, even what to watch on television. One of the main reasons I went to George Washington University was because it was at the other end of the country! I had to get away. John is the only thing in my life that has always been truly mine. He's the only thing they haven't tampered or interfered with. There's no way I was going to let marriage be something they decided for me, too."

Troy's forehead wrinkled in curiosity. "What do you mean 'was?' "

"Troy!" Clara's voice at the bottom of the attic startled Troy and Chiara. "I'd like a word with you about Miss Tiffani!"

"Uh oh." Panic flashed in Troy's eyes.

"Good luck, kiddo." Chiara gave him a light shove toward the trapdoor, where Clara's voice met him.

"That girlfriend of yours told Danielle all about her first kiss," Clara ranted, her words drawing Troy down the stairs and out of sight. "And apparently it took place with an eighteen-year-old junior counselor on a seventh-grade school camping trip. You and I need to have a chat about that fast little…"

Clara's words trailed off as she and Troy moved farther from the stairs. The quiet solitude of the attic didn't last long as Abby and Cady made their way up the stairs, Abby leading the way with a cloth-covered tray.

The tray reminded Chiara that she hadn't eaten since lunch almost nine hours ago, and even then she'd had only a few french fries.

"I thought you might be hungry, baby," Abby said. "I made your favorites."

"Thanks, Mama." Chiara sat at a lovely cherry-wood table with an intricate ebony inlay, one of Christopher's handmade originals.

Abby set the tray before Chiara and uncovered it with a flourish. Chiara's stomach rumbled its gratitude, even though her anticipation dropped a bit when she saw what her mother had brought her: macaroni and cheese, spaghetti and meatballs, corn muffins, miniature corndogs and salami and cheese rolls fastened with toothpicks. They were her favorite foods, all right. From when she was in grade school.

"I know it's a lot, but I figured you could use a little fattening up," Abby smiled, lovingly cupping Chiara's chin.

"Oh, that's nothing for Chiara," Cady said. "She can eat for two these days."

Chiara shot her sister a withering look.

Abby ignored the exchange and took the empty chair opposite Chiara. "Reverend Kurl is stopping by for lunch tomorrow," she began carefully. "He wants to talk to you."

Chiara swallowed a bite of macaroni and cheese that suddenly lodged deep in her esophagus. "What for?"

"Well, I just figured that since you moved back home, you and John would want to get things rolling."

"I can't *conceive* of a better idea, Mama," Cady said, her smile overbright with mischief.

"Things like what?" Chiara asked in a low voice.

Abby patted her head, avoiding Chiara's gaze as she hummed "The Wedding March."

Chiara's temper flared, and it felt like flames licking at her face and hands. "Maybe Almadine would rather have her father marry us," she said coolly.

Abby's eyes widened in shock. "Almadine almost had a fit when I ran into her at the market and told her that John was moving you back here. She probably won't want to have anything to do with your wedding, God willing. And why would her daddy marry you? You're not Baptist."

"Then why'd you send us to his church when I was little?" Chiara countered angrily.

"It was the closest church to the house," Abby said, leaning over the table. "And you never went anyway. Maybe if you'd done like you were supposed to, John wouldn't have had such a hard row to hoe at home with Almadine."

Chiara's wrath drained away, replaced by a mixture of shock and guilt so profound, it took her a moment to find her tongue. "You think I don't know it was my fault that he took all those whippings?" Her voice had no strength in it, even though she wanted to yell in her mother's face.

"Mama," Cady began, her expression grave, "that wasn't fair. I'm the one who took Chiara to the park every Sunday. We hated that church. I was fifteen years old and I was having nightmares about going to hell and having devils burn my skin with hot pitchforks. Almadine's father put the fear of Satan in you without bothering to balance it with the comfort of God's love and mercy."

"I didn't mean it the way it sounded," Abby tried to explain. "All I meant was that—"

"I know *exactly* what you meant, Mama." Chiara struck away the tears of anger that had sprung to her eyes. Her appetite vanished, she left the table, curled up on the bed with her back to her mother and sister and quietly wept into her pillow.

"Chiara, you know I didn't mean it that way," Abby persisted. Chiara heard her mother's chair scoot away from the table, but then her movement stopped.

"Leave her alone, Mama," Cady said. "Let her get some rest. You guys can talk in the morning. Chi's had a long day."

Chiara wasn't sure how long she lay there, her heart so heavy that it hurt with every breath. She was so deep in her misery that she almost didn't hear the soft tapping at the window.

"Chi, open up."

She raised her head to see John perched on the roof outside the casement windows Abby had installed as part of her renovation. She eased off the bed and dragged herself to the window. John's smile faded as he watched her unlatch it and crank it open barely enough to accommodate the width of his face.

"I wanted to say goodnight," he told her, searching her eyes. He reached in an cupped her face. "You've been crying."

"I cry all the time," she sniffled. "You know that."

"No." His eyes bored into hers, and he was alarmed that, for once, he couldn't clearly read them. "This is different."

Chiara dropped her gaze to the window latch. "I'm tired," she croaked. "That's all."

"Well, I only came to say goodnight," he said.

With his fingertip balanced under her chin, he raised her face and touched his lips to hers. Chiara closed her eyes and her knees weakened under the power wielded by that lone, sweet kiss.

"Goodnight," she whispered into his lips before drawing away and closing the window. John touched the glass, but stopped short of calling her back as she returned to the bed and lay down, fully dressed. As stealthily as he could, John moved back across the pitched roof and dropped down to the tiny balcony situated outside one of the second floor bedrooms. He climbed over the railing, and stepping between the balusters, he eased his way over to the corner where he used the ridges between the red bricks of the house to climb down to the side porch.

Only when he was safely on the sidewalk and looking up at the dim glow of golden light from the attic casements did he stop to wonder why Chiara's kiss goodnight had felt so much like goodbye.

❧

"Glad you could meet me," John said as George took a seat on the opposite side of the wooden booth.

"I don't have classes on Tuesdays. You're paying for this, right?" George grinned.

John rolled his eyes. He'd never known his little brother to pony up for anything other than computer equipment, most of which he bought under the table or out of a trunk.

"Is this a safe place to talk?" George asked in a lowered voice.

"Depends on what we talk about." John raised a hand to signal their pierced and tattooed waitress, whose waist and wrist chains jingled as she brought them a pair of menus. "This place should be pretty safe."

John had thought Blueberry Hill on Delmar was probably the best place for him and George to discuss their business. The restaurant wasn't so full that other patrons surrounded them, but it wasn't so empty that the nearest diners could overhear them. The restaurant's motif was music, and the walls of the piano room, where John and George had seated themselves, were covered with rock and roll and rhythm and blues memorabilia among other oddities, such as animal heads, vintage comic books and dozens upon dozens of photos of the restaurant's proprietor with the celebrities who had visited the place. The jukebox featured a wide assortment of swing, blues, be-bop, jazz and soul selections. Right now a doleful Muddy Waters track played softly in the background. John was confident that he and his brother would enjoy the solitude they wanted amidst the chaotic décor. Plus the burgers were the best in town.

"Are you guys brothers?" the waitress asked, the gold stud in her tongue clacking against her teeth as she spoke.

John chuckled. "How could you tell?"

"I couldn't, at first," she laughed lightly. "What can I get you guys to drink?"

"I'll have the Brussels Black Ale," John said.

"Woodchuck Cider for me," George said.

"Apple or pear?" asked the waitress.

"Pear," George responded.

"I'll be right back, fellas." Tucking her order pad into her back pocket, the waitress left them.

"I must be slipping," John said.

"How so?" George wondered.

"She knew we were related." John couldn't have resembled George less as he sat there in his worsted wool business suit, an almost new pair of Cole Haans on his feet. His subtly patterned, dark Borrelli tie alone had likely cost more than George's whole ensemble, which consisted of black Converse high tops, a pair of bright green track pants, a black ribbed turtleneck that looked awfully familiar and a piece of stretchy black fabric George was using as a headband to restrain his wild afro. "Is that my shirt?"

"Looks good on me, doesn't it?" George plucked at it. "Mom gave it to me."

"It's not her shirt to give away," John said pointedly.

"She said you abandoned it."

"I had to go to USITI in Chicago." John took off his jacket and neatly laid it across the seat beside him. "She knew I was coming back."

"She was expecting you Friday night. You didn't get back until yesterday, and by then she'd done your laundry and had her own little eviction ceremony. She was just mad because you spent the weekend in Chicago with Chiara." George smoothed his hands over his chest. "She gave me first pick of your stuff."

"That explains why half my laundry was gone when I got home last night." John scrubbed a hand over his head in frustration. "Your mother really is unbelievable."

"You should have called her and told her that you'd be coming home later," George said.

"I'm a grown-ass man, G. I shouldn't have to report to her."

"Then you probably should have gotten your own apartment instead of staying at her house until you found a place of your own. It's been three months, man. The longer you stay, the harder she's going to fight to keep you under her thumb."

"I didn't want to sign a lease because I figured on finding a house once Chiara moved here, at least that was the plan," John said. "I figured staying at home wouldn't be so bad, since I'm hardly ever there."

"Well, Chiara's here now." George looked up to see the waitress returning with their drinks. She set them on the table and told them that she'd be right back for their orders. "You guys can start moving forward with your plans."

"Our plans have been circumvented somewhat." John turned his glass in circles, staring at the black brew. "You know that."

George sighed heavily. "Yep."

"She was attacked in her apartment on Friday. She wasn't hurt seriously, but whoever did it tore the place to bits looking for—" He grew silent when the waitress came back for their orders. John asked for the seven-ounce hamburger with mushrooms and grilled onions and a house salad.

"You're buying, right?" George asked again, to make sure.

John rolled his eyes.

Without looking at the menu, George cleared his throat and said, "I'd like a side of toasted ravioli, onion rings, and fried mushrooms, the hickory burger—"

"Five ounce or seven ounce?" asked the waitress.

"Seven. Could I also have that with bacon and cheddar cheese? Extra bacon, if you don't mind." George winked at John.

"Will that be all?" the waitress asked.

"Uh…could you also get me a couple of tamales with a side order of chili, but that'll be to go."

"Gotcha," said the waitress.

John leaned an elbow on the table. "You forgot dessert," he offered wryly.

George snapped his fingers. "Oh yeah. Could I get a couple of slices of blueberry pie?"

"Sure thing," the waitress smiled.

"I don't want dessert," John said.

"Oh, I didn't order it for you," George said.

Giggling, the waitress left to place the order.

"Man, how do you stay so damn skinny eating like that?" John asked in amazement.

"I'm like a camel." George stretched out in the booth, his feet bumping John's out of his way. "When I get the chance, I load the hump. Otherwise, I'm mostly on the Ramen noodles and HoHos diet."

"If you need money, all you have to do is ask," John said.

"Mom's tight, and you know it," George said. "Dad'll slide me some here and there, but Mom keeps an eagle eye on the checkbook."

"Ask *me*," John said. "I haven't asked Mom for money since I was ten. She's worse than a loan shark."

"She makes you pay her back?"

"Not in money, but she finds ways to collect. I asked for fifteen dollars for a school field trip to Six Flags in the fifth grade, and she gave it to me easily enough. But then I had to spend six Saturdays in a row cutting back Cecile Brunner. She said it was the way of the world, that no one gets anything for nothing."

"So what's this lavish lunch actually going to cost me?" George asked, only half joking.

"Just some information." John took a long drink of his beer before he said, "Chiara doesn't think that Emmitt Grayson was behind the attack on her, or even Zhou's death. I'm not sure I agree with her, but it would be nice if we could find out more about…other candidates."

George leaned forward, resting both forearms on the table. "Like who?"

"Maybe it was someone from a company Grayson's been spying on, someone who found out what he's been doing," John threw out.

"Maybe...but the R-GS rootkit is so sublime. You wouldn't know you were being spied on unless you'd been told."

"Grayson might have a partner we don't know about, someone who's up to something. He looked very concerned when he saw Chiara's face after the attack."

"She's okay, isn't she?"

"She's healing well. But her nerves are getting the better of her. This is a lot for her to take on top of being pregnant."

George's eyes slowly widened to the point where John thought they might just drop right out of his head. "Chiara's going to have a baby?"

John gave him a tiny smile of pride. "That's what being pregnant means."

"And the baby's yours?"

"Boy, I will smack you—"

George shook his head and raised a hand in supplication. "Man, I'm sorry, I'm just...damn. You and Chiara are having a baby."

"Don't tell Mom and Dad."

George made a sputtering noise. "Don't worry. I like living too much. Moms is gonna shit when you tell her, and then she's gonna kill you. Then she's gonna shit *again*."

"You know," John said as the waitress brought their food, "that's an image I could have lived the rest of my life without imagining."

It took the girl a moment to unload her tray with George's complete order, including the bagged tamales and chili. The brothers delved into the food, John helping himself to a big onion ring before they continued their conversation.

"When's the baby due?" George asked around a bulging cheekful of his hamburger.

"July." John set down his burger and wiped his hands on a paper napkin. "Want to see a picture?"

George, his mouth too full to answer, shrugged his shoulder, which John eagerly took as a yes. He pulled out his wallet and carefully slipped out two squares of flimsy plastic-like photo paper. "This is at eight weeks, and this one is the most recent photo, at twelve weeks."

John set them on a napkin to protect them from moisture and oil residues on the table, and slid them before George, whose face crumpled in confusion. "It's all head," George said.

"And body. But everything will catch up to everything else, in time."

"It's got Dad's head," George said.

"It's not an 'it,' George, it's a he."

George peered closer at the photos. "I can't even tell that it's human. How can you tell that it's a boy?"

"Chiara says he's a boy. Stop calling your nephew 'it.' "

George slowly set down the fried mushroom he was about to eat. "My nephew?" His lips slowly curled into a wide smile of goofy pride. "Uncle George...I like that." He reached a hand across the table and gave his brother a congratulatory handshake. "I can't wait to teach him how to defrag a CPU." He chuckled. "It'll be funny watching Mom babysit."

"Uh uh." John took his pictures back and tucked them safely in his wallet. "Grandma Almadine is never going to be left alone with my baby."

"You're thinking about the number she pulled on RoboBaby, aren't you?" George said. "You know she wouldn't treat a real baby, her own grandson, like that."

There was too much doubt in John's heart and George's voice for him to give his honest response. "She's not good with babies. Real or computerized."

"Well, on the topic of computers," George said, "who else is on your short list of suspects for what's been going on with you and Chiara?"

"The only other possibility I can think of is a rival software company," John said. "The R-GS is one of the bestselling security systems out there, and it's the dominant system overseas. Someone might be willing to go to any length to discover the secret of the chip's success, and getting their hands on a master would certainly help them reach that goal."

"Could it be someone inside USITI?" George suggested. "When I read that *American Investors* article on Emmitt Grayson, I was like, 'Damn, if I worked for him, I'd want a bigger slice of the pie.' The article declared his net worth—*net*, man—at three billion dollars, and a lot of it comes from his own personal investing, not from company profits and income."

"Of course, now we know how he got to be such a good investor," John said scornfully. "You've studied the chip, right?"

George nodded, once again unable to speak as he shoved a toasted ravioli dripping with marinara sauce into his already full mouth.

"Is there a way of exposing the coding for the rootkit? Can you isolate it, and create counteractive programming that would expose it, or even disable it, once the chip is installed and activated? More simply put, can you design an alarm that alerts the user when the master is coming through the back door?"

"Yeah." George quietly burped. "A rebound chip."

"Never heard of it."

"I haven't finished inventing it yet." George took three long gulps of his fruity beer and then used his sleeve—John's wool cashmere sleeve—to wipe his mouth. "I have to clone the master chip I already have, decode and map it, then design the counterprogramming. The alarm, so to speak."

John spent a moment in deep thought. "How long will that take?"

George licked ravioli crumbs from his fingers. "Hard to say. Two, maybe three days, if I burn two-four-seven. But cloning it isn't the problem. Finding a way to test it is."

CHAPTER SIXTEEN

John invited George back to his office, presumably to tour USITI's new St. Louis facility. John introduced his kid brother to his co-workers and the director of human resources, explaining to all that George would be graduating from college in six months and was considering applying for a job at USITI.

John's true intent in bringing George to USITI was to give him a chance to try to infiltrate the computer system, but no opportunities presented themselves where George could get on a terminal without being seen.

"It's okay," John said, more to himself than to George as they exited the elevator that opened into the basement level of the parking garage attached to USITI's downtown office building. "We can try again some other time. Early on a weekend might be best, but I was hoping to have you here in plain sight. Folks would be less likely to think that you were up to something."

John aimed his remote car alarm at the Nissan Z parked in one of the premium reserved spots near the elevator doors. George hurried ahead to the passenger side of the shiny, silver coupe and kissed the door-frame. "This is the sweetest ride, J." He stroked his hand over the sleek line of the aerodynamically designed roof. "Can I have it when you're done?"

John opened his door and tossed his briefcase in the backseat. "I'm glad I left it at Lambert when I flew to Chicago, or else our mother probably would have given it to you, along with my clothes."

At the mention of clothes, George's hands flew to his chest. "Man, I left my parka upstairs." He jogged off toward the elevator. "I'll be right back."

John started to get into the car, but the scent of George's bagged tamales on the floor of the front seat drove him back out. "That smell will never come out of the carpeting," John complained under his breath. He was starting around to the passenger side of the car to get the bag when a shadow fell over him. Before he could turn on his own, he felt hands on him, clutching at the black wool of his Chesterfield. He was spun and thrown against the side of his car, a pair of pale, hairy hands tightly holding onto his lapels, a black-hooded face only inches away from his.

"You and your pretty girlfriend are playing with the wrong person," John's assailant growled, using his larger, wider body to hold John against the car. "You tell me where the master chip is, and I'll make sure that you leave this little meeting with your face intact."

But for his hands, the man making the threats was dressed in black from head to toe. John's gaze locked on his blue eyes and the deep red gouges carved beneath them. John suppressed a satisfied smile at the sight of the bright red, ruptured blood vessels in the inner corners of the whites of the man's eyes. "She got you pretty good, didn't she?" John said calmly.

His attacker's eyes darkened in the dimly lit recesses of the parking garage. "Not as good as I got her." He gave John another hard shove. "Not as good as I'll give her the next time I see her."

A strange feeling of calm moved through John. It was akin to the acute relaxation he'd felt after taking exotic exercise classes in Singapore, a combination of yoga and martial arts. A regimen he and Chiara had maintained off and on once they'd returned to Chicago.

Ever so slightly, John smiled.

His attacker's eyes narrowed.

John clutched the man's wrists, keeping them in place on his coat front as he gave the man a vicious head butt. The man's feet weakened and his hold loosened as he staggered back, but John held onto him, keeping him on his feet. John, that queer sense of peace flowing even stronger within him, drove the flat of his foot into his assailant's left shin, driving a cry of pain from the man before doing the same to his right shin, bringing him to his knees.

John pried the man's fingers from his coat, keeping a hold on his right hand. He bent it at a sharp angle that forced the man's upper body to awkwardly follow the movement of his hand. "Who sent you to

Chiara?" John shouted in his face, his calm falling away to expose the fury that had been fueling it. "Who sent you here?"

The man used his free hand to swing at John, who smoothly blocked the blow with his forearm before smashing his fist into the center of the man's hood. Blood gushed through the hood, wetting John's coat front and leaving a fine red spray on his tie.

"Who sent you?" John shouted again.

His assailant, grunting against the pain, lunged at John, catching him about his waist and bringing him down to the asphalt clear of John's car and the neighboring vehicle. He scrambled on top of John, trying to twist his hand free and bite John through his hood. John bucked the man off and used his knees to slam him into a car. Even though his heavy coat encumbered him, John was nimble and fast enough to pin the man to the ground with a knee to his chest.

"This is your last chance!" John warned through gritted teeth, his hands at the man's collar. "Who sent you?"

The man's blue eyes defiantly stared at John as he breathed heavily through his hood. John's assailant was now at his mercy, and John had none for him. John encouraged him to respond by giving him two jaw-cracking blows to his face. When that failed to loosen his tongue, John turned to a move he'd learned from his own mother. Using the hood to give himself a good grip, he grabbed the man's ear and yanked it.

The man screamed but not before John heard the sound of tearing flesh. John was aware of people gathering around him before he realized that the man's agonized screaming actually formed words.

"Carlton?" John repeated, lifting the man by his ear and walking him to the wall, blocking him in between two parked cars so he couldn't escape. He let go of the man's ear and yanked off the hood. He was unfazed by the sight of the blood smeared all over the man's face.

"Carlton Puel!" the man said more clearly.

"All right, stop right there, boy!" hollered a voice from behind John. "Put your hands where I can see them and turn around."

"It's not what you think," John said. He turned, expecting to see one of the usual garage rent-a-cops. Instead he faced one of St. Louis's finest crouching in the middle of the driving lane, his gun aimed squarely at John's gut. The officer leaned to one side. "You, too, back there," he instructed.

John raised his hands. "This was an attempted mugging, officer. I was attacked."

The officer's tiny blue eyes peered at John, then at the man staggering forward behind him. "Yeah. Right."

"John!"

The startled officer whipped his head in the direction of George, his gun hand following. George's whole body flinched as though trying to outmaneuver a bullet.

"Don't!" John said, addressing both George and the officer.

Sweat ran in rivulets down the officer's bright pink jowls as he unclipped a radio from his belt and spoke into it. "I need backup at Lucas and 14th, basement level of the parking garage. I caught a two-forty in progress, I have both parties under control, and I'm taking them in."

"John, what—" George started, thoroughly confused.

"I dropped my keys," John said, his mind spinning with the name he'd been given. "Get them and follow me."

"But John, what the hell happened, man?" George persisted.

"Shut up and go about your business, boy," the officer snarled at George.

"Just do what I say," John told his brother. "And don't take any more of my clothes. I might be gone awhile."

❧

Despite having his hands cuffed to the back rungs of the hard chair he'd been shoved into two hours ago, John sat up tall and straight. While his attacker sat nearby on a wooden bench, his right hand cuffed to a chain connected to a metal ring in the floor, John had received the seat of honor right at the scuffed metal desk where his arresting officer, Conroy Jerkins, hunkered over an old keyboard. His hooked index fingers ploddingly hopped over the scrambled alphabet, pecking out the letters that spelled the words John had used to answer his questions.

John had never been arrested before, and he might have been more troubled by the experience had he not been thinking so hard on the name his assailant had given him. He stared beyond the cluttered, dingy precinct room and into the rapidly darkening sky beyond the grate-covered windows. The sky seemed too deep and too dark because of the full storm clouds that had rolled in. Deep in his own thoughts, John didn't notice the tall, dark-skinned man in the brown suit who had appeared at the desk.

"What've we got here?" the man asked, snapping John out of his reverie. The man put his hands loosely on his hips, and John noticed the gold badge clipped to his belt. One word gave John a tiny bit of hope: CAPTAIN.

"This guy beat the hell outta that guy, Cap." Officer Jerkins threw his thumb in the direction of John's attacker. "I'm just finishing up my arrest report."

The captain looked John up and down, taking in John's elegant but understated suit. Even though it was now rumpled and spattered with dried blood, it still proved a better tailored cut than the captain's. The captain eyed John's tie before moving down to his Cole Haans. His gaze then shifted to John's personal effects, which sat in a plastic bin on Jerkins's desk.

As the captain studied the contents of the box, John took yet another silent inventory of the items that had been removed from him upon his arrest. The contents of his wallet: driver's license, American Express Gold, VISA Signature, BP gas, USITI identification, AAA membership and auto insurance cards, a photo of him and Chiara taken on a beach in St. Kitts, two sonogram images and one-hundred and eleven dollars in cash. Additionally, there were the assorted things from his pockets: forty-seven cents in loose change, an opened tin of Altoids and a silver Cross ballpoint pen that Abby Winters had given him upon his graduation from GW.

The captain, wearing a scowl as heavy as his thick mustache, turned to John's assailant. John hoped the captain saw what he did: a burly man in black jeans, a black long-sleeved T-shirt and worn leather jacket with dried blood crusted in the creases of his face, beneath his purpling eye sockets and along the edge of his torn right ear.

The captain stepped over to him. "Where's your ID?"

Pressing his head to the wall behind him, the man just stared at him.

"What's your name?" the captain said more loudly, a crack of thunder punctuating his command.

The bloodstained man snorted and hawked a blood clot at the captain's feet.

"Have it your way, John," the captain said.

"Pardon me?" John replied.

"Not you." The captain went back to John and picked up one of the sonogram photos from the evidence box. "I meant John Doe over there, who won't tell us who he is."

"It's 'cause he's probably got a rap sheet long as my arm," Jerkins predicted.

The captain didn't look up from the photo. "What about him?" He used the photo to point at John.

"I'd rather you didn't handle my personal effects, sir," John said. Of all the humiliation he had endured so far, he refused to add the mauling of his baby's picture to it all.

"No record," Jerkins said. "Mahoney's clean."

"Have you finished Mr. Mahoney's statement?" The captain stared at the photo a moment longer.

Jerkins pressed a button and closed his document. "Yeah. It's banked."

"Give me the rundown," the captain told him.

Officer Jerkins leaned heavily on the desk, the lower two buttons of his uniform shirt threatening to give way under the stress of his shifting bulk. "During my patrol of the parking garage at Lucas and 14th at approximately 5:45 P.M., I came upon these two guys going at it."

" 'Going at it?' " the captain repeated. "What the hell does that mean, Jerkins?"

"Mahoney here says that John Doe over there attacked him and he was defending himself, but…" Jerkins shook his big round head skeptically. "Something's hinky."

"Something like what?" the captain asked. "You can't believe that this man," he indicated John Doe with a sweep of his open hand, "who has no ID, no wallet, and who won't provide us with his name possibly attacked Mr. Mahoney, who has a clean record, clear ties to the community and a United States IntelTech identification card that establishes his reason for being in that garage? What does this look like to you, Jerkins? I'm dying to know."

"It looks like what it usually is." Jerkins sat back in his swivel chair, which creaked in protest. "A drug buy gone wrong."

"For God's sake," John murmured disdainfully.

"Look at him, Captain," Jerkins said, pointing at John Doe's face. "He's a mess, and *this* guy wants to say that John Doe attacked *him?*"

The captain spent a moment staring up at the water-stained ceiling tiles. The sky outside seemed to grow angrier along with the captain, whose nostrils flared. "Did you ever consider that John Doe picked the wrong man to target today, Jerkins? Somebody always comes off the worse in a fight, and from the looks of it, today's not the first time John Doe got his face handed to him on a platter." The captain used his universal key to unfasten John's handcuffs. "Return Mr. Mahoney's personal items and take John Doe to booking. We'll get an ID once we take his picture and run his prints. I can't imagine that he's not in the system already."

"Right, Captain," Jerkins said.

"And one more thing," the captain added. "Apologize to Mr. Mahoney for wasting his time."

John rubbed his wrists where the handcuffs had gouged his skin. Grudgingly, he said, "That isn't necessary, sir. I'm sure Officer Jerkins was just doing his job."

Officer Jerkins's pink face reddened as the captain said, "Trust me, Mr. Mahoney. What Jerkins did to you was not a part of his job. You're free to go, with the apologies of this department. If you'd like to press charges against John Doe there, I'll take your statement and file the complaint myself."

༺ঞ্জ༻

John was halfway down the wide steps leading to the lobby of the police station when he spied George, Chiara and Cady in a huddle at the information desk. George saw him first and called the entire station's attention to him when he shouted, "John! Man, I thought you were being sweated in a little room under a bare light bulb."

Chiara met him at the bottom of the stairs. Her face was so taut with worry and concern, John feared it would crack if she spoke. "You're drenched," he commented after embracing her.

She tensed in his arms. "It's storming outside," she said in a strange, brittle voice.

"When George called, I went right to my mother's to get Chiara," Cady said. "She was so worried about you, she was waiting for me at the curb when I picked her up. She got soaked."

John held Chiara's shoulders and stared into her eyes. "I'm all right," he said firmly, determined to put her mind at ease. "I didn't need you to come down here."

"I called Cady," George confessed.

John looked at him, confused.

"I wanted to come straight here," George said. "I thought I should tell Chiara, but I didn't want her to come racing down here in a panic. So I called Cady first, and she picked up Chiara and brought her down here."

"I wish you'd have just done what I asked, and taken my car back to your dorm," John grumbled.

"I thought you might need bail," George explained. "Would you rather I called Mom and Dad?"

John gave him a look that clearly said, "Don't be stupid," before he turned back to Chiara. He took off his Chesterfield and started to drape it around her.

"I'm fine," she said, scooting from under the heavy black coat. "I just came down to make sure—" She choked on a sob. "To make sure that you were all right."

She flinched a little when John took her damp shoulders. "He's in custody," he told her.

"So it was the same man?"

Cady stepped closer, her delicate eyebrows drawn at severe angles. "The man who attacked Chiara in

Chicago?" she asked. "He's the same man who mugged you?"

"It seems so," John said.

"What's his name?" Cady demanded. "Why is he targeting the two of you?"

George, John noticed, was easing farther away.

"Cady, I need to go home," Chiara implored.

"George, give me my keys," John called to him.

"I need a lift back to the dorms, too," he said, tossing John his car keys.

"I'll take George," Cady offered. "He's on my way." She pinned John and Chiara with an incisive stare. "We'll be talking about your mugger when I get back to Mama's house."

Chiara took Cady's sleeve. "I want *you* to take me to Mama's. Please. Let's go."

"Chiara, I can take you," John said. "It's no problem."

She kept her eyes on the floor. "I don't want you to."

"You take George," Cady advised gently. "I'll take my sister home. I have to pick the twins and Virginia up from Mama's anyway."

"I'll drop by after I get George to the dorm," John said.

"Don't," Chiara said. "I don't…you shouldn't…"

John seemed to be the only one who understood her halting request. "Why not?"

She wrung her hands in anxiety. "I just don't want you to!" she blurted. "Cady, let's go." She started away, pulling her bewildered sister after her.

John began to follow her. "Chiara, don't walk away like this!"

"Leave me alone!" Chiara whirled on him, her flared knit skirt swirling around her ankles. Her voice was close to a shriek as she pleaded with him. "Stay away from me, John, please."

Several police officers looked up from what they were doing. John decided it was probably best not to press Chiara further, given her emotional state and the fact that he'd just been released from police custody.

Cady intervened. "Let me get her home and into some dry clothes. You can talk more later."

"I won't want to talk later," Chiara said grimly. "Come on, Cady."

❧

Cady's Honda Pilot had barely come to a stop at the curb before Chiara shoved open the passenger door, sprinted up the stairs in front of Abby's house and bolted into the house.

"Chi, is everything okay?" was all Abby got out before Chiara ran up the two flights of stairs to the attic, threw open the trapdoor, and locked it shut behind her. The thick weave of her long-sleeved top and skirt seemed to weigh on her petite frame as she paced the rug floor in her soft-soled boots.

Her mother's words echoed in her head, the one place where she couldn't close them out no matter how hard she tried. *Maybe if you'd done like you were supposed to, John wouldn't have had such a hard row to hoe.*

Chiara tortured herself, wondering how much more John's love for her would cost him. She went to the tall windows, pressing her hands against them. Rather than feeling sheltered from the storm that continued to rage outside, she felt trapped. Home was supposedly the safest place for her right now, but just as she'd placed John in danger, her presence now endangered her whole family.

She peered at the cars parked on both sides of the street, wondering if one of them contained yet another man in black who watched Abby's house, carefully choosing his next victim. She perched on the wide windowsill, shivering in her damp clothes, and she watched the street, a silent sentinel determined to protect those she loved, even if it meant leaving them.

CHAPTER SEVENTEEN

Chiara stared, unblinking. Ribbons of raindrops striped the long windows, almost mirroring the teardrops trailing over Chiara's cheeks. Her eyes were raw from using the cuff of her sleeve as a handkerchief, so she no longer bothered to wipe the tears away. She really was a crybaby, and she refused to blame it on hormones and stress. Each tear was a symbol of renewed mourning, this time for John.

She sat on the windowsill, her shoulder pressed to the glass. The double panes were supposed to keep the cold out and the warmth in, but a chill still permeated Chiara's damp sweater. She hugged her knees to her chest and rested her forehead on them. She sobbed a bit harder, her shoulders shaking, missing John so much already even though she hadn't yet told him what she'd decided to do.

It was hard enough admitting it to herself, even as she forced herself to plot out her plan.

She was leaving St. Louis, first and foremost, and she would have to get the master chip from George and take it with her. The farther she got from her family and John and George, the safer they would be. Fear jabbed at her heart at the thought of packing her bags and heading to some unknown, unfamiliar destination.

"You can't have it both ways, you idiot," she softly berated herself. *At best I'm a hypocrite, staying in Mama's house, hating every second of it, all the while endangering everyone here. And at worst, I end up being cruel if I move to a new city and have John's baby on my own.*

John had been her touchstone over the past three weeks, but now it was time for her to solve the problem of the master chip on her own. It was time to put John out of it, once and for all, before he really got hurt. Or worse.

Chiara sobbed in earnest, shaking from the force of her tears. Gone was her promise to John to stay strong and fight. She felt more alone, afraid and helpless than ever, and she hated it. She might have sat there all night, until her unfamiliar emotions condensed into nothing more than self-pity, if not for the dark shadow on the other side of the window.

Startled, she hopped off the windowsill and backed away from the glass. She'd reached the night table and the phone sitting on it before a flash of lightening illuminated the large figure who had tapped the glass.

"Chiara, open up," John said, hooding his eyes with his hand to keep the hard, steady rain out of them.

"Go home, John," she yelled, approaching the windows. "I told you not to come here!"

John's hair and the shoulders of his coat glistened with rain, which as the evening wore on had become more like sleet. The shingles beneath his feet looked plenty slippery, and in his Chesterfield, suit and Cole Haans, John wasn't dressed for climbing even under less icy conditions. "Let me in!" he directed more forcefully, hauling himself over the railing in front of the windows. "I almost slipped twice just getting up here. I need to talk to you."

"There's nothing to talk about, and I don't want you here!" Chiara shrieked, her arms stiff and her fingers splayed. *"Don't ever come back here!"*

John stood there, the wrath of nature beating upon his head and shoulders and Chiara glowering before him. His heartbeat seemed to grow louder in his ears as he contemplated his next move. After the afternoon he'd had, he was in no mood to be rejected. For the second time that day, John did something totally out of character. Without thinking, he gripped the railing behind him for support and kicked the center support of the window frame. The locking mechanism flew into the room, along with a chunk of the wood it had been built into. Both windows crashed open, and John swooped into the room on a rush of freezing rain and bitter wind. As John strode toward Chiara, the crystal droplets dotting his coat and hair disappeared, melting in the heat of the room or from the heat of his temper.

John was furious, but this anger was different from the cool, killing rage that had fueled him in the parking garage. Fear flavored his fury as he made his way to Chiara, who stood her ground, looking at him with raw, wounded eyes. She'd tried to send him away before, but he'd worn her down. This time, she seemed willing to maintain her resolve, willing to kick him right out of her life under some misguided attempt to be noble.

He struggled to remain calm, so he could speak to her without frightening her. But one way or the other, he'd make her know that he wasn't about to leave her, especially not over something neither of them had control over. The one thing he'd learned today was that he'd kill before he let anyone harm Chiara again. His consternation grew as he wrestled with his own desires and those he saw in the troubled depths of her eyes. What she wanted, what she demanded of him, was the one thing he couldn't make himself do.

John stood before her, the cold wetness of his coat further chilling her still-damp clothes. His shoulders rose and fell heavily, his chest heaved, and his hands clenched and unclenched. She had seen so many sides of him, but never this one, this hulking, larger-than-life figure who seemed capable of anything. Despite his fearsomeness, Chiara wasn't afraid. This god of fury before her was still her John, the man she'd loved for so long that the love was a vital part of her, like her brain or her heart. His love had sustained her, had shaped life within her. He was incapable of hurting her. She didn't shy away from the heat of his stare as he pinned her in place with his gaze.

"Do you want me to leave you?" He blanched as he asked the question.

The stiffness of his face and the finality of his tone told Chiara that he wasn't asking about just tonight.

When she answered, her words trembled from her lips as hot tears spilled from her eyes. "I've caused you so much pain. I thought it was all over once your mother stopped using her switch, but it's starting again and—"

He took her by her shoulders and raised her heels from the floor. "You gave me freedom! Can you imagine what it was like for me to sit there in my grandfather's church, listening to him shout and spit about punishment and hell? My mother spent all day in prayer clusters and my father was always at work, so I had to sit there in the pews all alone." He eased his grip, setting her flat on her feet but not releasing her. "Then came a Sunday when we were running late, and as we drove into the church parking lot, I saw you running across the street between Cady and Kyla, and you vanished into the park."

John could see the image in his mind perfectly, and as with all fond memories, he relived it more vividly than he had when the memory was first forged. He could smell his mother's overpowering lavender perfume and feel her iron-like grasp cutting off the circulation to his hand as she'd dragged him into the church. He'd pulled away from her slightly, straining to see Chiara. But she'd been so short, he'd lost sight of her and had tracked her big sisters instead, right into the park. He'd felt the sudden absence of the bright sun once he'd been pulled into the dark interior of the church and shoved into an aisle seat in a front pew. As his portly grandfather had preached, working up a sweat, John had stared at the seam of daylight peeking from beneath a cracked window.

Outside the church was where he'd find comfort. He'd known that instinctively, and the following Sunday, after Almadine had sat him in the front pew, he'd bounced right back up and followed her down the aisle. Outside the nave, she'd turned right and gone downstairs for six hours of devout prayer with her cronies. John had kept walking straight, right through the doors and into the clear spring day.

It was his first taste of total freedom and open rebellion, and it was delicious. He'd wasted no time in crossing the street into Tower Grove Park, and he'd found Chiara and her sisters.

Standing now in the darkened room with Chiara, with January's frigid breath blustering around him, John made his confession to Chiara. "I found peace, faith, comfort, friendship and devotion when I went to the park with you. All the things I'd never found at my grandfather's church, I found in you. You didn't make me leave church every Sunday. I made that choice. Stop blaming yourself for all the punishments I got. It was a fair tradeoff for all the happiness you've given me."

"You could have been killed this afternoon," she wept.

"I wasn't," he stated firmly, reinforcing the obvious.

"He might come after you again. If you're not involved with me, it might keep you safe," she implored.

"He won't."

"You sound so sure. But I can't take any chances. Not with you."

He tightened his grip and gave her a hard little shake that made her head bobble. "Tell me what you want then, Chiara, once and for all! And you'd better mean it, or I'll make the decision for you. I'm sick of you trying to push me away. Do you honestly want me to go?"

"No," she whispered miserably.

"What?" he demanded.

"No," she said a little more loudly.

"Then tell me what you want." His eyes burned into hers, daring her to say anything other than what he needed to hear.

Chiara studied his face, unable to identify all the emotions shaping his features but fully understanding the impact they had on him. She knew him so well, loved him so well, that she could diffuse them if she were willing to answer him truthfully. She couldn't make her mouth say the words she needed to, the ones that would send him away, hopefully to safety.

"You," she finally said through a fresh fall of stinging tears. "I want *you*, safe and whole and—"

John ground his mouth to hers, pulling her to him. Chiara held his face, kissing him deeply, sharing the only warmth she could with the winter storm brushing her damp clothing with cold. John's breathing came deeper and harder as his own heat mounted within him. Without separating his mouth from Chiara's, he shrugged out of his Chesterfield and jacket, letting the heavy garments drop to the carpet. Chiara's small, soft hands lightly came to rest upon his before guiding them to her breasts. John framed their firm fullness, stroking them, the dampness of Chiara's sweater readily conducting the heat of John's hands to her flesh. He trailed kisses along her chin and throat, supporting her with a hand at the small of her back when she hung her head back and pressed her hips into the hardness fighting the confines of his pants.

John's seeking lips parted to allow his tongue to dip into the hollow of her throat before his head moved farther down, to suckle the tiny tents his hand raised at her breasts. Chiara's soft moans encouraged him, and he delighted each breast in turn, drawing her nipples into rock-hard points hungry for more direct contact.

He lifted her sweater and pulled the garment over her head. Her slender arms came down to cradle his head to her bare breasts. He tasted the most sensitive parts of them, tracking them with his tongue before pulling on them, creating a delicious tug that reached deep into Chiara's core. John's hands moved up her sides and along her back, the heat of his palms raising goosebumps where the cold air had kissed her.

Chiara slipped her left hand between them and tugged John's shirt from the waistband of his pleated trousers. John returned his lips to hers, to free his hands to remove his shirt and unfasten his pants. They didn't bother to make the short trip to the bed. Gently sucking the plumpest part of John's lower lip, Chiara sank to the floor, pulling John's weight half atop her. He supported himself on one elbow so he could look at her, and he felt every part of himself grow at the sight of her. Chilly air temporarily cooled the heat of the attic. It goosepimpled Chiara's skin and kept her brown sugar nipples as taut as John's touch had. Her hair was a dark cloud of silk framing her head. Her parted lips, slightly swollen and moist from his kisses, trembled a little as she stared up at him.

Through touch and the somberness of his eyes, John tried to tell Chiara what his words hadn't. His body shook with suffering as much as passionate need. Someone had come after him as a way to get to Chiara, and while he hadn't lost control, he'd come close. He would honestly have left John Doe's brains splattered on the asphalt, and that scared him almost as much as wondering what would happen next. There was nothing more important to him than Chiara and the baby sheltered within her.

With a warm, strong hand planted firmly over her abdomen, John tried to transfer that message to her.

She understood him clearly, and when he lowered his head to kiss the space between her breasts, Chiara invited him to take his solace freely. She raised one knee and hooked her toes into John's waistband. She used her foot to shove down both his pants and his boxers. Kissing his way down to her navel, John put his hand under her skirt. He drew his fingertips lightly over her calf, the sensitive hollow behind her knee and her thigh before coming to rest at the humid heat between her legs. Her legs widened to better accommodate his hand and the long finger he used to trace the wet cleft covered by her panties.

The storm had done its job well, and the damp cotton stubbornly clung to her skin as he tried to lower her panties. One quick tug at the gusset tore the seam, snapping the piece in two and granting him unobstructed access to her slick sweetness. Chiara's back arched and her eyes closed as her hips rose to meet the deliberate, skilled movement of John's fingers. She clasped the sides of his head and brought his mouth to hers. Her tongue dipped in and out of his mouth, copying the movement of his finger, further stoking the fire in his loins.

John used both hands to free her from the wet weight of her skirt before wriggling the rest of the way out of his pants and boxers. He covered her with his body, the promise of peace and fulfillment moving through him as Chiara wrapped her legs about him and angled her hips upward, to welcome him. John forced himself to ease into her, savoring every grasping second of her body's acceptance of him. Chiara showed none of his restraint, and she brought her legs higher, allowing him to completely entomb himself. He hunched over her, taking one of her dark peaks gently between his teeth, alternately nibbling and flicking his tongue over the pair of them until Chiara gasped his name and clutched his buttocks.

His hips moved, his abdominal muscles bunching and hardening in the rhythm Chiara set with her hands at his backside. He framed her head with his elbows, bearing most of his weight as he increased his speed and his depth, forging the deepest possible bond between them. Her fingers lightly stroked the supersensitive area just below his buttocks, then glided along his back and over his shoulders to his chest, where she dug her fingers into his hard pectoral muscles and brought her lips to the flat disc of flesh capping it. She scraped her teeth across it, then suckled and nibbled it, forcing a groan and a grimace of blinding pleasure from him. He rose on his hands and his arms shook as he stiffened upon her and erupted deep inside her. Chiara's hips took over the movement his had temporarily abandoned, and once he was able to move, John came to rest on one elbow again. He used his other hand to separate their sweat-slickened abdomens, to give his thumb access to the hard kernel tucked within Chiara's swollen folds.

John matched the motion of his hips to that of his thumb. First slow and deep, then shallow and quick until Chiara was biting the heel of one hand to stifle her cries. When John once again brought his mouth to her breasts, her release came quick and hard. Her body responded so powerfully, she nearly forced him out. They embraced and rode out the crest of her climax, their bodies still sealed.

In their all-too-brief moment of pure oneness, Chiara knew that she and John were exactly where they belonged, in that place neither of their families, friends—and now enemies—had the power to reach. It was the place where John found relief from every blow he'd ever taken, every drop of blood he'd shed. They floated back down and became once again aware of the time and space around them. John dragged his coat over them, shielding them from the cold that now felt more refreshing than brutal. John held Chiara tightly, his limbs wrapped around hers, all the while thinking that the woman molded to him was more than a part of his life.

Throughout high school and college, John's friends had taunted him about being sprung because of his refusal to ever flirt with other women. John knew their teasing came from a place of envy, because they were never more obnoxious than when he saw them watching Chiara with longing and hunger in their greedy eyes.

John used to wonder if he were indeed some sort of freak—was it normal to want one woman as much as he wanted Chiara?

Normal or not, he wasn't unique. All of Chiara's brothers-in-law looked at their wives with the same adoring possessiveness he felt toward Chiara. He loved her more than his own life. She was his life.

And Carlton Puel would pay for turning it upside down.

❧

"George said you could have killed that man."

Chiara's soft voice issued from the warm cocoon she and John had formed inside his coat. As she tipped her head up on his crooked arm to look at his face, the movement of the satin lining and Chiara's silken skin against him kindled the embers that never fully died between them. "Does that scare you?" John stared past her, fixing his eyes on the stubby legs of the cherry wood armoire to avoid seeing any disappointment in Chiara's face.

She used a finger to drop his chin and guide his gaze to hers. "No," she assured him. "It makes me feel safe."

"Just as much as I wanted to kill him for going after you, I wanted to hurt him for trying to hurt me," John said, a trace of the injured boy he'd once been creeping into his man's voice. "I've taken enough beatings to last me the rest of my life. I wasn't about to take another one."

"My mother thinks it's my fault that Almadine whipped you so much," Chiara said.

"No," John uttered in disbelief. "That doesn't sound like Abby. It doesn't matter what she thinks, anyway."

"But she's right," Chiara admitted softly. "Even after I knew what Almadine was doing to you, I kept hoping you'd come to the park, just to spite her. If I'd just gone to church like I was supposed to—"

"I'd have still gone to the park," John said. "I hated church. I wish I'd thought of sneaking off on my own sooner."

"Wherever the blame falls, I'm not sorry." Chiara nuzzled his nose with hers. "Those Sundays in the park with you were heaven."

John held her even closer. "No, this is heaven. Right now. And I think things are going to change for the better fairly quickly."

"How so?"

"He gave me a name."

Chiara's mouth dropped open. "John Doe told you who he was?"

"I made him tell me who sent him after us."

Chiara didn't want to know what John had done to convince John Doe to reveal the name of the person who'd hired him. All she wanted was the name.

"Carlton Puel," John said. "He's the founder of Vulcan Semiconducter in Phoenix. He's one of USITI's manufacturers."

Chiara sat up, dragging the coat with her. John gave in to an involuntary shiver. Wearing only his socks, he scurried to the windows and closed them. He grabbed one of Chiara's ponytail holders to loop the crank handles together to keep the windows from flying open again, since he'd broken the lock and support beam.

Chiara stood up, holding the coat tight around her. "Zhou and I met him in Kuala Lumpur in September, at the ACM Expo & Forum. It's the biggest convention and trade fair in our industry. Grayson sent all of his overseas technical sales reps to it, and Carlton Puel arranged a sightseeing day for us. He took us all out to dinner that night, too."

John, shivering from the cold still permeating the room, climbed into the bed and pulled the covers up to his chest. "And you haven't seen Puel since?"

Chiara slowly lowered her weight to the edge of the bed, her forehead wrinkled in thought. "I haven't. But Zhou might have." She turned to face John. "When we arrived in Tokyo last month, for that sales trip to Siyuri Robotics, he checked his e-mail on the plane. I didn't see the message, but he deleted one of them and said it was from 'that pesky chip man.' "

"Puel's company makes microchips," John said.

"And he's a real noodge, too. When we were at dinner in Malaysia, he couldn't take no for an answer."

John abruptly sat up. "He hit on you?"

"He followed me around, buying drinks for me, talking about how he wanted to expand his company into programming and design, and how he was looking for experienced sales reps to add to his team. It was the usual song and dance we got from a lot of the companies there. USITI has a solid reputation, and most industry people know that Zhou and I are the best at what we do. *Were* the best," she corrected. "Zhou was fine until our last day in Tokyo, John. The only time we weren't together was right after we made our pitch to Siyuri. I went shopping and Zhou went back to the hotel. Or so he said. That's the only time he could have met with Puel, or anyone else, without my knowledge."

"You think Puel is the one who sent Zhou over the edge?"

"Him or someone working for him," Chiara said. She chewed the already ragged edge of her thumbnail. "He and Grayson have been business associates since Grayson founded USITI. If Puel found out how the R-GS system works—"

"And how lucrative it can be," John said.

"He might have gotten in touch with Zhou. To get a master chip of his own."

"Do you think he's the one who killed Zhou?"

"Unless a likelier candidate comes along, yes," Chiara said. "It's Puel or someone he sent after Zhou when he didn't get the master chip."

"He just makes microchips," John said. "He had no control over what USITI puts on them. How would he even know what the master chips do?"

"I don't know. Maybe Grayson told him. There's so much we still don't know."

"Not for long," John said confidently.

"Why?"

"We've got our own techno ferret on Carlton Puel's case right now. I gave George the name when I took him home from the police station tonight."

"Do you think George knows what he's doing?" Chiara felt a fresh surge of guilt regarding George's involvement. "He won't get caught?"

Loud banging on the trapdoor startled them and cut off John's response.

"She can't have heard us," Chiara whispered. "The floors and ceilings are really thick." Drowning in John's coat, she shuffled over to speak through the closed trapdoor. "What is it, Mama?"

"I need to talk to you."

Chiara turned a baffled eye on John. She'd never heard her mother sound so severe. "Can it wait?"

"No."

"Well, what's it about?"

The unlocked trapdoor flew open, brushing Chiara onto her bottom to avoid being smacked in the head. A small brown cylinder with a white cap, a prescription pill bottle, arced into the door space and landed on the carpet. It rolled a few times, finally coming to a stop near the leg of a squatty, cushioned armchair. Chiara picked up the bottle and read the label as her mother's footsteps on the staircase faded.

"What's the matter?" John whispered.

Chiara displayed the bottle for him. "Mama found my prenatal vitamins."

CHAPTER EIGHTEEN

Abby sat at the dining room table, absently smoothing her hands over the crisply ironed linen tablecloth. Chiara, hastily dressed in a pair of old jeans and a loose-fitting pashmina sweater, took a seat opposite her mother and watched the hypnotic movement of Abby's hands over the pristine white cloth.

Abby wore a plain white shirt that buttoned in the front, a short strand of seed pearls and navy blue corduroy pants. This, minus her ever-present cooking apron, was her typical post-retirement uniform. The rigidity of Abby's face made Chiara uncomfortable. She wasn't used to seeing her mother's gentle features hardened into an unreadable mask.

Chiara opened her mouth to speak just as Abby's hands ceased their rhythmic motion over the table. "I wasn't going through your things," Abby began with forced calm, her gaze fixed downward. "I was cleaning your bathroom and I accidentally knocked over the toiletry bag you had sitting on the edge of the sink. That pill bottle rolled out with everything else." Abby finally looked up and turned the full measure of her confusion and dismay on Chiara. "Why, Chiara? Just tell me why?"

"Why what?" Chiara leaned her right elbow on the table and cupped her hand under her chin. She had to sit on her left hand and tightly cross her ankles to keep from squirming in her chair.

Propping her elbows on the table, Abby covered her face with her hands. "Why would you want to go and…and…*humiliate* me like this?" she said through her hands.

"It's not like you found a controlled substance, Mama," Chiara said. "They're vitamins."

"*Baby* vitamins!" Abby hissed through her hands.

"Actually, they're for adults," Chiara pointed out flippantly.

Abby's hands came slamming down on the table. "Oh, you think you're such an adult now, do you?"

Chiara forced her voice to remain light. "I don't see what the big deal is, Mama."

Abby launched herself onto her feet, sending her chair crashing into her beloved black Victorian pine buffet. "Wh-What's the…Like you don't…Are you tryin' to mess with…*YOU KNOW DAMN WELL WHAT THE BIG DEAL IS, GIRLIE!*" Abby fired off, the cords in her delicate neck standing out like telephone cables.

Chiara, blown back by the force of her mother's voice, held onto the table with both hands. The fine hairs on her arms and at the back of her neck stood on end, and sudden terror like none she'd known so far flooded her chest cavity. Abby's scorching words washed over her like a heat wave, and Chiara heard nothing familiar in her mother's words or voice. "I'm your *mother*, and you've got the high nerve to come into *my* house and *not* tell me that you're pregnant?" Abby raged, as if possessed by whatever god ruled offended mothers. "Is this how I raised you? Is this—"

"Reared."

Caught mid-word, Abby's mouth hung open but no sound came out. "What?"

"Animals are raised," Chiara said. "People are reared. You corrected that on a paper I wrote in ninth grade, where I said that I was raised by a single mother and my grandpar—"

"Are you trying to make me go off on you?" Abby threatened loudly.

"I'm having a hard time appreciating your feelings, Mother," Chiara started boldly, "because quite frankly, I'm the one who should have her back up. You had no right to go through my private things."

"I didn't exactly 'go through' anything!" Abby shouted. "Don't leave your 'private things' lying around in *my* bathroom if you don't want me to see them."

"Why do you keep yelling at me?" Chiara asked.

"I don't know what else to do!" Abby shouted.

Chiara had a suggestion. "You could calm down, and we could talk about this like grown women."

Chiara's advice seemed to further inflame Abby. "Calm down, calm down," she repeated, more to herself than to Chiara. "I find out that despite my best efforts to raise my baby girl, all I raised is a baby mama!"

At those words, John made his presence known. "Mrs. Winters," he said, stepping into the dining room from the foyer, "that's not exactly fair to—"

Abby stopped him with an angrily wielded finger and another booming explosion. "Where did you come from?" Before giving John a chance to work out an answer, a more pressing inquiry came to mind. "Are you the daddy? *YOU BETTER BE THE DADDY!*"

John had come down hoping to diffuse the fiery emotion of the situation between mother and daughter, not add his own butt to the burner. He took a seat on Chiara's side of the table, a symbolic move as well as a sensible one—the table was too wide for Abby to easily go for his throat. "The baby is mine, Mrs. Winters," he said. "Chiara and I planned to tell everyone, but we wanted to wait until the time was right."

Abby tossed her hands in the air and John and Chiara flinched. She shook her head and patted the top of it with one hand in one of her more characteristic signs of agitation. "And when would that be? When you send us a postcard inviting us to your baby's fifth birthday party?"

"I wanted to wait until at least twelve weeks," Chiara said. "Anything could happen, Mama. This is my first baby, and I've needed some time to get used to the idea myself." She cast a covert glance at John, and squeezed his knee under the table. "We didn't plan this."

Abby stubbornly propped her fists on her hips. "So what you're trying to tell me is that you and John just happened to find yourselves buck-ass naked—"

"Mama, please." Chiara cringed, flames of mortification igniting in her face.

"—and things just happened to stumble into the perfect position to make a…" Abby gasped sharply and her hands went to her mouth. "Baby!" Tears flooded away her wrath and she rounded the table to throw her arms around Chiara. "My baby's having a baby!"

Chiara allowed her mother to sob on her shoulder for as long as she could with Abby's weight bowing her back in the chair. Chiara silently pleaded with John for help, and he took Abby by the shoulders and guided her into his freshly unoccupied chair.

"I wanted to tell you as soon as we knew," John said.

Chiara's mouth flew open in indignation. Even though it was true, he didn't have to tell Abby.

"This is Chiara's first baby, and she wanted to keep it to herself for a while before she told everyone," John went on. "So many things are happening all at once. My transfer to St. Louis, Chen Zhou's death, Chiara's resignation from USITI…" He took a short step toward the side table near the archway and grabbed a wooden tissue box. He set it before Abby after plucking out a few tissues, which she gratefully accepted. "Chiara didn't want to add to the chaos the news of the baby."

Abby turned red, offended eyes on John. "You're confusing chaos with joy, John Mahoney. I've seen all my girls through the births of my grandchildren, and it hasn't been the least bit chaotic." Abby touched the seat of her chair and then John's shirt. "Why are you all wet?"

"There were thirty-six people in the waiting room when Cady's twins were born," Chiara reminded her mother, and in so doing, effectively brought her mother's attention back to the matter at hand. "Cady's delivery was more like a block party than a delivery."

"It *was* a party!" Abby declared. "We were happy for Cady and Keren, same as your family deserves the chance to be happy for you."

"I don't want a million people breathing down my neck every step of this pregnancy," Chiara said. "I'm not like Cady. I don't crave attention."

As Chiara expected, Abby rushed to her third child's defense. "Cady doesn't crave attention, it just naturally comes to her."

"Kyla's worse," Chiara said.

"That's not fair, and you know it." Abby caught a sniffle in her handful of crumpled tissue. "She's an actress. People are interested in her. The attention is part of her job, and when she was pregnant—"

"She was offered twenty-thousand dollars to have her labor and delivery broadcast on the Internet," Chiara interrupted.

"But she didn't accept it, did she?" Abby pointed out. "Kyla knew that her baby was something to share with her family, not the World Wide Web."

"Look, Ma—"

"Here we go with the 'Ma.' "

Chiara held her face in her hands. "Look, *Mother*, this is my pregnancy and I'm delivering the news on a need-to-know basis. When I have the baby, it'll be the same way. I want to do this *my* way, from beginning to end. Everybody always thinks they know what's best for me, when they don't even really know me. When I told Mr. Grayson—"

Chiara realized her mistake three seconds after Abby whirled on her, her face crumpled against a fresh flood of tears.

"You told your boss and you didn't tell me?" Abby sobbed. "Oh, Chi!" She pressed her tissues to her eyes with both hands. John hugged her as her shoulders shook with the force of her tears.

"We didn't tell him because we wanted to," John said over Abby's mournful wailing.

"I had to tell him, Ma," Chiara said. "This baby saved our lives," she added without thinking.

Fortunately, Abby had ears only for her own misery. "Who else knows? Your dry cleaner? Your parking garage attendant?"

"Cady knows," Chiara started, "but...she...uh..." Her words withered in the heat of Abby's treacherous stare.

"We didn't tell her!" Chiara held up her hands as if to ward off her mother. "She figured it out on her own. You know how she is, Mama. Cady can look at you for two minutes and then tell you the one secret you've been hiding."

Abby stood and started for the kitchen. "Cady's on my list now, too, because she could have told me."

Abby's hand thumped loudly on the swinging door as she opened it and blew into the kitchen. A short moment later, Chiara and John heard her say, "Why didn't you tell me that Chiara was pregnant?"

They raced into the kitchen to find Abby standing over the little telephone table between the back and basement doors. Her hands on her hips, she loomed over the phone to aim her words directly at the speaker. "After all these years and everything I've done for you girls, you pay me back in secrets and subterfuge! What else are you girls hiding from me?"

"I'm not hiding anything," came Cady's voice through the speaker.

Chiara could have choked her for the extra emphasis she placed on her first word because it made Abby slowly turn and again fix her suspicious scowl on her and John.

"Well?" shot from Abby's lips with the force of a sniper's bullet.

Chiara couldn't bring herself to lie to her mother's face, but she didn't dare tell her about the master chip. John, as usual, came to her rescue.

"We haven't told Almadine yet," he said.

Muscle by muscle, nerve by nerve, Abby's face relaxed until it almost totally slackened. It reshaped itself into a slowly blooming smile that filled the kitchen with its usual warm, merry glow. The news of Almadine's ignorance had a narcotic effect on Abby, calming her to the point where she cheerfully bid Cady goodnight and retrieved a fresh apple cobbler from the pie keeper at the end of the sink counter.

"Almadine honestly doesn't know, John?" Abby sniffed delicately as she took three dessert plates from a cabinet over the counter.

"She honestly doesn't know." John opened the cutlery drawer in the prep island and collected three forks and a pie cutter.

Abby almost skipped into the dining room with the pie and plates, and John and Chiara followed her. "When do you plan to tell her?" Abby asked. She sat the pie on the table and spooned three fat servings from it, carefully setting each one on a plate.

"I don't know." John took a plate of the cinnamon-scented dessert and resumed his damp chair. "I'm leaving it up to Chiara."

Abby slid a plate to Chiara. "Well, when are you going to tell her, Chi?"

She shrugged. "I don't know. Do we really have to tell her at all?"

"How about two days after the baby is born?" Abby laughed.

"Mrs. Winters," John gently chastised.

"All right, all right," Abby said, her laughter easing up. "You really ought to tell her soon though, or else she'll act out a storm about the wedding."

Chiara slowly stopped chewing. John turned and looked at her, his expression unreadable. "What wedding?" Chiara said.

Abby chuckled. "Yours and John's, of course. Whose do you think? The sooner we get to it, the better, while you're still small enough to fit into a pretty dress. Rev. Kurl could perform the ceremony, and you could have the reception at Kyla and Zweli's. Their backyard is beautiful, and can accommodate at least two hundred guests. And the lake in the background would be so lovely for your pictures." Abby stopped to take a breath, but Chiara still couldn't get a word in. "I'm sure Cady knows a good caterer. She's always planning events for Keren's department, and the food is always delicious. Ciel could point you to a good florist, and you know she's the one to take with you when you're negotiating all your service contracts. It's a good thing you're leaving USITI, Chiara. You've got your work cut out for you."

"I can't waste time on a wedding right now," Chiara said in a rush before Abby could start in on other possible contributors to her most precious day. "It's not a good time."

"Good or not, time is something you don't have," Abby told her. "That baby will be here before you know it, and it's going to need a daddy."

"Excuse me, Mrs. Winters," John rested his fork on the edge of his empty plate, "but my child has a father. I was there when he was conceived and I'll be there to greet him when he comes into this world."

"That's what they all say," Abby scoffed. "It's easier to leave when you don't have a ring to remind you of where you belong."

John's jaw tightened. "I don't need a ring to know that I belong with Chiara."

"Have you met John Mahoney?" Chiara asked sardonically. "This man has been a part of my life, a part of our family, for more than twenty years. You think the responsibilities of fatherhood will drive him away?"

Abby refused to meet their eyes directly as she said, "You never know what a man will do after a child arrives."

"If anything drives him away, it'll be a bossy, dictatorial mother-in-law," Chiara said.

Abby stood and gathered their empty plates. "Maybe if I'd been *more* bossy and *more* dictatorial when you were little, you'd have better sense than to settle for being some man's baby mama!"

Chiara caught the fiery look in John's eyes before he launched to his feet, but she wasn't quick enough to take his arm and stem the tide of his words.

"That's the second time you've called Chiara a baby mama, and I resent it," John boomed in a voice that made Chiara's hands slide from his arm and Abby pause in the doorway between the kitchen and dining room. "There are worse things than Chiara being pregnant. You seem to be more concerned about how her pregnancy reflects on you than the fact that she could have lost the baby as a result of the attack in her apartment last week. You're more worried about what people like Rev. Kurl and Etheline Simpson will think about this pregnancy than you are about what it must be like for

Chiara right now, to be pregnant and completely stressed out by—" He caught himself as Chiara tugged on his arm to shut him up. "Other things," he finished. "I love you, Mrs. Winters, and I love your daughter. Perhaps it's best that I just come out and tell you right now that I'm not just 'some man,' and Chiara is not my baby mama. I'm her husband. She's my wife."

❧

"Did you have to tell her like that?" Chiara snapped at John as they kneeled over Abby, who'd collapsed in a dead faint.

"I was only trying to put her mind at ease about the baby," John said. He grunted as he scooped Abby up and carried her into the living room where he gently deposited her on the sofa.

"You were mad at her and wanted to shut her up," Chiara accused. "I can't believe you told her. When she comes to, you better pretend like she hallucinated it."

"No." John crossed his arms over his chest.

Chiara tucked a pillow under her mother's knees to elevate them. "If I'd wanted her to know, I'd have told her already!" she whispered sharply before turning to Abby. "Mama?" she said loudly. "Mama, wake up!"

"Wha…" Abby muttered drowsily. "What happened?"

"You could have given her a heart attack," Chiara hissed at John.

He leaned back against the mantel of the fireplace. "I can't wait to see how *my* mother reacts when we tell her."

"About the baby or the…" She darted her head twice toward Abby, who finally opened her eyes and tried to sit up.

"Both," John said.

"Are you okay, Mama?" Chiara asked. "You fainted." She pressed her hand to Abby's forehead, and she was slightly concerned by the clamminess of it. "Should I call Keren or Zweli, Mama? You took a real good spin on the floor."

"I don't know what happened," Abby said, patting her hair back in place. "One minute we were talking, and the next…" Her chin quivered and her eyes filled. "Are you really married?"

Chiara's answer caught in her throat, which suddenly felt very tight. For the first time in her life, she actually felt guilty about her desperate need to keep her life compartmentalized.

"Are you going to faint again?" Chiara asked.

"No, baby," Abby said softly through her tears. "I just want to know what's going on."

Chiara looked at John, who came and knelt at her side. He took her hand and gave it a supportive squeeze.

"When the time's right, Mama, I'll tell you ev—"

"*AREYOUMARRIEDORNOT?*" Abby hollered, the whole sofa shaking from the force of her eruption.

"Yes," Chiara and John said together.

CHAPTER NINETEEN

It was close to midnight by the time Abby had amassed her army: daughters one through four, her sons-in-law and her grandchildren. Abby had called Cady first, to make sure that she hadn't known of Chiara and John's marriage, and from there Cady had placed the next call, to Kyla, in the Winters family phone tree.

Chiara's comings and goings had always fascinated the rest of the family, and even though it was a week-night, Abby's house once again looked like family was gathering for a holiday, National Pajama Party Day, once the whole gang descended.

Ciel, a little bleary-eyed from having been awak-ened from a sound sleep only an hour earlier, sat in a position of power at the head of the dining room table. Abby had called upon her to preside over a very special ceremony: the verification of the marriage certificate Chiara had reluctantly provided.

While Ciel perused the document with the assis-tance of her laptop computer to resource reference material, the rest of the family passed around the one photo that documented the marriage.

"Can I see it now?" asked Danielle, who still wore her winter coat over her nightgown.

"I agreed to let you come as long as you sat in the living room and kept quiet," Clara told her youngest child. "Keep rocking the baby."

Danielle scowled, but continued the gentle rocking movement of the baby carrier containing a lightly snoring Niema. She matched the pace Abigail and Ella had set with Virginia, who was tucked into her own baby carrier.

"You look so young," Troy said to John as he peeped over his mother's shoulder to look at the photo.

"They *were* young," Clara said. "When was this again?"

"Yes, Chiara," Abby said stiffly. "When was it you decided to run off and get married?"

Chiara and John sat hip to hip at the dining table as though they were double defendants in a criminal trial. Chiara's sisters and their husbands and their older children were arranged around the room opposite them, like a jury allowed to wear flannel pajamas, slippers and soft, fat rollers. Since they were all assembled, Chiara figured this would be as good a time as any other to tell them about her marriage to John.

"Well," she began on a deep sigh, "we didn't run off."

"We did it during our senior trip to San Francisco," John added.

"Oh, my Lord," Abby gasped, settling heavily into a chair. "You got married on your high school trip?"

Chiara nodded, bowing her head to hide her smile.

"Cool," Troy said, earning a lethal glance from his mother.

"We had a free day on Friday, our last full day there," John said. He rested his forearms on the table and gazed at his clasped hands. "We decided to do something really special."

"You couldn't go to Fisherman's Wharf or Ghirardelli Square, like every other tourist?" Kyla suggested dryly.

"It was a spur of the moment thing," John said. "We knew we would get married someday, and it just felt right at that time."

"That's why I hate those senior trips, and prom, and all that other nonsense where children," Abby glared at Troy and C.J., "yes, *children*," she repeated angrily, "get to pretend to be adults."

"It's not like that," Troy interjected. "We'll have adult chaperones for our senior trip to Hawaii this spring."

"Just so you know, Clara," Ciel said through a yawn, "Hawaii's marriage requirements are the same as California's in that there's no waiting period between the application for a marriage license and its issuance, and you can marry immediately once the license is issued. No blood tests are required, either."

Clara's face darkened. "You ain't goin' to no Hawaii."

"Tiffani is a junior," Troy said calmly. "She won't be going on the trip."

Clara brightened. "Then you can go to Hawaii."

"How many chaperones will be on your trip?" Abby asked.

Troy shrugged. "I don't know. Two or three."

"For a class of one hundred students?" Abby asked, horrified.

"I'll volunteer to be a chaperone," Christopher said.

"Me, too," Lee laughed.

"Want to go to Hawaii, Ky?" Zweli asked. "We can all chaperone."

Abby went on the attack. "You all think this is a joke, don't you? Have you seen what these kids do just for prom? When I was still teaching, I used to chaperone the proms, and it would make your head spin to know what these young people get up to these days."

"It's just for fun, Grandma," Troy nearly whined.

Talk of prom was too much for Danielle, and she zipped into the dining room, leaving Abigail and Ella in charge of Niema and a freshly awakened Virginia. "I can't wait until I get to go to my prom!" she gushed, her hands clasped under the soft point of her chin. "Remember Aaliyah, that singer who died when I was little? She wore a dress in one of her videos that I just loved and I want to wear one just like it when I go to the prom, only I want mine in red. My boyfriend will pick me up in a lime green stretch limousine, the kind with the lights that change colors on the ceiling—"

Christopher used a freckled hand to rub his temple, which suddenly seemed to sport more gray hairs than red. "My little girl wants to go to the prom with a pimp," he fretted.

"—he'll be wearing a red tux to match my dress, but with a white vest and a white bow tie," Danielle went on as if her father hadn't spoken. "After the prom we're going to go to a hotel suite with all our friends, and—"

"See what I mean?" Abby cut in. "This girl isn't even in high school yet, and she's already planning her practice honeymoon. That's all the prom is these days. I used to see young men planning the most elaborate ways to ask a girl to the prom. One of the students I tutored got his parents to hire a skywriter to present the invitation. If the boy's parents had had as much sense as they had money to burn, he wouldn't have needed tutoring to pass remedial English."

Danielle gleefully hopped up and down. "Ooh, I'd love to have my boyfriend hire a skywriter for me!"

"Go down to the basement and help C.J. amuse Clarence and the twins," Clara ordered her.

Danielle, sulking, skulked off, leading with her lower lip while her Aunt Cady said, "John, how did you propose to Chiara?"

But for the corner containing Abby, the overall mood in the room lightened with Cady's question.

"We were on the chartered bus, driving across the Golden Gate Bridge on Saturday, our first full day in California," John recalled. "Chiara was taking pictures of the Bay and Alcatraz. She was standing out of her seat and she was wearing a pair of blue jeans, this funny white sweater—"

"The one with the knobby bits of yarn on it," Chiara said, lacing her fingers through John's.

"And her hair was down, but it was a lot shorter than it is now," John went on, looking at Chiara as though seeing her as she'd been that day on the bus. "San Francisco Bay is supposedly one of the most beautiful places on the west coast, but I didn't see anything that day more beautiful than Chiara. She turned her camera on me and took my photo just as I said, 'Let's get married.' "

"I laughed and said okay, but I thought he was kidding," Chiara said. "But over the next few days, he seemed too happy and too quiet. When we got our free day on Friday, a lot of the kids wanted to go to Fisherman's Wharf, but John told our chaperone that we wanted to go to the Civic Center, to take photos of city hall."

"I'd buy that," Kyla said. "I shot a TV movie in San Francisco a few years ago, and the city hall really is a gorgeous building. It's one of the best examples of Beaux Arts architecture in the world. Its dome is fourteen inches taller at the spire than the one on the Capitol in Washington, D.C., and the inside has the most beautiful California marble, Indiana sandstone and Manchurian oak."

"Thank you for that lovely commercial interruption," Cady said, tucking her hands into the pockets of the coat she wore over her robe. "Chiara, you were saying?"

"Well, Mr. Collins, our chaperone, was also our sociology teacher, and he thought John was so mature to want to go to the Civic Center. He figured he could trust us on our own, and he went with everyone else to the Wharf."

Abby harrumphed. Loudly.

"Mr. Collins is the one who married us the second time," Chiara chuckled.

Cady raised her hand. "Don't forget me. I married you the first time."

"Does any of this make sense to anyone other than Cady, Chiara and John?" Abby asked the room.

"It makes sense in a Winters family kind of way," Lee said. "In that it doesn't have to make sense to the rest of us, only to the folks directly involved."

"Thank you, Lee," Abby said snidely, "now shut up."

"When we got to city hall, I told Chiara what I really wanted to do," John said. He smiled at the tabletop as he said, "I told her that we could get married, right then and there, since we were both eighteen." He looked up and took in everyone in the room, not really focusing on any individual person. "We must have stood outside city hall for ten minutes, looking at the building that looked just like a cathedral."

"It took me only two minutes to agree to your plan," Chiara said. "I was annoyed that my hair was a mess."

"It was windswept," John said. "Very sexy."

Abby scowled.

John cleared his throat. "I'd already made the appointment for a confidential marriage license."

"What's that?" Zweli asked.

"You don't need witnesses for the ceremony, and the license itself won't be made public," Ciel volunteered as she looked at her monitor, the words on screen reflected in her glasses. Her delicate eyebrows moved a bit closer together. "There's something else about it, though," she started.

"We had to wait about thirty minutes for the license," John said. "And then we were able to go right into the private ceremony room and exchange our vows."

"It was perfect," Chiara said, wondering if anyone else could feel the radiant heat of her blush. "Just me and John and the officer of the court."

"She did a cartwheel on the plaza as soon as we left the building," John said. "I don't think my feet touched the ground once when we were leaving."

"So did you get any pictures of city hall?" Keren asked, earning a light pop on the arm from Cady.

"We got a tourist to take our photo in front of the building," John said. "That's it right there." With a tip of his head, he indicated the photo that had been circulating, which Abby then chucked onto the table.

Chiara picked it up and held it where she and John could look at it together. Other than their marriage certificate, this photo was the only evidence in existence of their third wedding day. The bride wore a black denim skirt and leather coat, and the groom wore a cable-knit sweater and khaki trousers. Thinking about her own baby growing under her heart made Chiara see how truly young she and John had been when they'd legally sealed their lives together. It had seemed like the most natural thing in the world to do, the perfect finish to high school. It had been a pact of the mind and heart more so than the body, because they'd waited another month, for prom night, before consummating the marriage.

As if picking up the thread of Chiara's thoughts, Abby boldly asked, "So after you got married, while everybody else was running around Fisherman's Wharf, you two went back to your hotel and…and…"

"Bumped uglies?" Lee said.

"We caught up with everyone else at the Wharf, actually," Chiara said primly. "John and I didn't get married just to have sex."

Zweli and Lee giggled like a pair of schoolboys. "Already doin' it to it," Zweli mumbled.

"No, we weren't," Chiara said. "And if you keep it up, I might be so bold as to speculate that I'm the only one of Abby Winters's daughters who didn't have premarital sex with the man she married."

Lee, Zweli, Keren and Christopher all shifted from foot to foot or glanced up at the ceiling. "Good heavens, look at the time," Lee said. "Ciel, honey, I think I'll go check on Clarence and the girls, see if they're asleep on their feet."

"I think I'll chase down the twins," Keren said, making his escape with Lee.

Abby covered her ears with her hands. "No more," she said, shaking her head. "I don't want to hear another word unless it comes from Ciel."

"Huh?" Ciel grunted, popping from behind her laptop monitor. "What are we talking about?"

"Premarital sex," Cady said.

"We were not!" Abby said through clenched teeth. Turning on Ciel, she said, "Have you verified that marriage certificate? Is it legal?"

John took Chiara's hand under the table and rested it on his thigh, squeezing it. Chiara breathed a little heavier and bit her lower lip as she awaited Ciel's verdict.

Ciel took off her glasses and set them carefully on the table. "I'm sorry, Mama," she sighed heavily, casting a quick glance at Chiara and John, "but everything appears to be in order. John and Chiara have been legally married for the past eleven and a half years."

For a second, it looked as though Abby would faint again. She seemed to gain strength by saying,

"Why didn't you tell me? Why do you hide so much all the time, Chiara?"

"I don't know how you managed to keep it a secret for twelve years," Cady said. "I'm impressed."

"I always wondered how you could wait so long for Chiara," Abby said to John, earning a look of indignation from Chiara. "I don't mean it that way, Chi, you're worth waiting for. But John is so handsome and so sweet, and he's got a good job and a good head on his shoulders. I always wondered why he never gave in to any of the women who threw themselves at him."

"Of course, Mama, this also explains why Chiara never fell for any of the men who chased after *her*," Cady said. "It's not like she didn't have her share of admirers. Remember that guy in Taiwan who sent six dozen roses to the house for her? And that other one in Chicago, who used to send her baskets of breads from his bakery?"

"John's the only man I ever let in my heart," Chiara told her family. "There's never been anyone else because there was never room for anyone else."

"I loved Chiara before I even knew what love was," John said simply.

"All this time, you guys have been married," Christopher said, pushing at his imaginary spectacles. "Why didn't you ever live together?"

If looks were daggers, Abby would have pinned Christopher to the wall like a bug in a specimen tray.

"Sorry, Mom," Christopher said.

"I thought we were too young to set up house-keeping," Chiara said. "I didn't want to have to make dinner and do laundry for two people while going to college. It was enough work to take care of just myself."

"Chiara likes having her own space," John said. "And I've always respected that."

"I don't get it." Abby ground the flats of her fists into the sides of her head. "Why get married and then go your separate ways?"

"We wanted to be married, Mama," Chiara insisted. "It was our way of being together without...being together."

"I still don't understand why, in all these years, you never told anyone that you were married," Abby said.

Christopher cleared his throat, to capture everyone's attention. "I'd imagine that their elope-ment was a covert act of rebellion. It was John's way of striking a blow for independence from his controlling, domineering, overly strict mother, and it was Chiara's first adult decision free of the interfering opinions of her mother and older sisters."

Clara, Ciel and Kyla accosted him all at once, denying any undue influence or pressure they might have subjected Chiara to over the years. Christopher, his shoulders hunched against the attack, looked to Zweli for help. But Zweli had slipped into the kitchen.

"Forgive me, Christopher," Abby said above everyone else, "but you're completely off the mark.

There's no logical explanation for what John and Chiara did, none at all."

"I have one," Cady said quietly. "It feels good to have something that's all your own, something you don't have to justify or explain to anyone else. I can't think of anything more precious than true love. When you find it, you want to cherish it and hoard it and keep it all to yourself, like some kind of priceless treasure. You don't lose anything by sharing it with other people, but other people do have a way of gettin' all up in your business, as though your happiness belongs to them somehow, too." Cady gazed at Chiara, and there was no mistaking the envy in her eyes. "Chiara had twelve years of glorying in her secret, with no interference from anyone else. It's a testament to the incredible bond that she and John have always had."

Cady's words left the room spellbound. Until Abby broke it.

"Well, I want me a wedding," she said saucily. "And with that baby on the way, you two had best be getting on with it."

The room went totally silent. No one moved, other than to shift his or her wide eyes to Chiara.

"Baby?" Clara repeated, gawking at Chiara. "You're having a baby?"

"*We're* having a baby," John said proudly.

Clara pressed her fingers to her forehead. "Oh God," she moaned, her eyes darting wildly from person to person. "Our baby sister is having a baby. I remember when I used to change her diaper, and wipe applesauce from her chin. Dear Lord, I feel as if *I'm* going to be a grandmother."

❧

Lee was carrying a sleeping Ella's dead weight to his car when Ciel cornered John and Chiara in the foyer. "Mama's in the kitchen with Clara—" she started.

"Commiserating or celebrating?" Chiara asked.

"I can't tell, but look, there's something I didn't tell everyone about your marriage documentation," Ciel said as quietly as possible.

"Yeah," John said, scuffing the toe of his shoe against the fringe of Abby's Persian runner. "I thought you might catch that."

"The marriage is still legal," Chiara said. "Isn't it?"

Ciel held her baby sister's intent gaze. "Would it make a difference if it weren't?"

The early days of their marriage had been fun for Chiara, if for no other reason than the one Cady had stated so plainly: Chiara had enjoyed having a secret from her mother, sisters and Grandma Claire. It wasn't until years later, after Almadine had visited John for the first time in Chicago, that Chiara had the slightest twinge of doubt regarding her future with John.

Almadine had done all but have Chiara kidnapped and buried in a shallow grave to keep her and John apart through high school, and college had been a welcome respite from Almadine's meddling. Getting recruited together to work at USITI had been a godsend as well, because it had meant that they could stay together. But when Almadine came to Chicago for the first time to visit John, she'd been so unpleasant that Chiara had considered leaving USITI to put some distance between herself and John. The transfer to sales and public relations had come along then, and instead of quitting, Chiara had simply switched departments. And that too, had turned out to be a good move for her and John.

Chiara had invited John on a number of her sales trips, and with absence making the heart grow fonder, each exotic locale they'd visited together had been like a mini honeymoon. Bangkok, Seoul, Jakarta, Hong Kong and Kuala Lumpur had been just a few of the cities they'd enjoyed, but Singapore had been their favorite.

Each trip had given their relationship an element of fantasy, a way of stepping out of their individual lives and uniting in very special, very unique ways. They had ridden elephants in Jakarta, had learned self-defense in Thailand, had learned to catch and clean squid in Kuala Lumpur…the world had offered them so much, and they had taken advantage of it far from Almadine's disapproval and well-intentioned meddling from the Winters camp.

Their latest trip to Singapore in October had been so beautiful and wondrous that they'd let themselves be swept up entirely in its romance. Far from USITI,

Almadine and the Winters clan, Chiara and John had created the most tangible proof of their love, a baby, which had united them more strongly than marriage ever could. Even as she retrieved the marriage certificate from her private files for Ciel's perusal, Chiara had been unconcerned as to what the verdict would be. No matter the validity of the paper in her hand, no one could ever convince her that she and John weren't married.

"No," Chiara said. "It wouldn't matter to me if the certificate isn't legal, but for Mama's sake I hope it passes muster. Does it?"

"I guess so, even though you lied on one of your documents," Ciel told them. "To get a confidential marriage license in California, you have to sign a statement declaring that you've been living together as husband and wife," Ciel said. "The law doesn't state the amount of time you have to be cohabitating, but I can't help wondering how you two pulled that off. Your driver's licenses would have had separate addresses on them."

"We used our school address as our residence," Chiara said. "We were at school together more than we were in our separate houses anyway. When we got back to St. Louis, we filled out a change of address form so that the marriage certificate would be forwarded to a P.O. box we rented for three months."

Ciel smiled. "It's ingenious, I have to give you that. I owe you much belated congratulations." She wrapped an arm around John and Chiara each and pulled them in for a hug. "You are going to have a real wedding now, though, aren't you? Mama will go nuts if you don't."

Chiara cringed. "I really, really hate doing things that I hate just to make other people happy. I don't like going to weddings, never mind having to throw one of my own. Yours and Clara's were okay because I was a kid and got to drink punch and eat crap all day, but now I've got something to live up to. Cady's was pure madness, with that carnival she had for her reception, and Kyla's was crazy too, with all the paparazzi coming out to crash it. I didn't realize what a popular personality she was until Zweli had to tackle that tabloid reporter who tried to take Kyla's picture when she was in the bathroom at her reception. My problem is more specific to the family. I'm the last daughter. Mama knows this is her last wedding, and I know she's going to try to steamroll me."

"Think of it this way," Ciel said. "You had the marriage you wanted. Just make sure that you have the wedding you want, too."

A short, choppy laugh escaped Chiara. "You guys have never let me do anything the way I wanted to."

"Everything's negotiable, Chi." Ciel winked on her way out. "Never forget that."

CHAPTER TWENTY

Four days after his baby and his marriage were outed at Abby's house, John was back there again to pick up Chiara to take her to George's with him. The two of them had been trying to reach him for days, with no response by phone or e-mail. They'd been so worried about him that when he finally called to arrange a meeting, John and Chiara were more than ready to kill him.

"Where've you been?" John demanded angrily by way of greeting when George opened his dorm room door for them.

"On a job interview," George said. He stood aside to let them enter.

John blinked in surprise. "Really? Wow…" He calmed a little, and Chiara put her hand over her heart in relief.

"We thought you'd been abducted and tortured, or worse," she said. "Don't disappear like that again, George."

"Your timing's a little strange, but it's good to see that you're thinking about life after graduation," John said. "I was worried that you'd be one of those ten-year undergrads, or end up graduating and going to work at Starbucks."

"Oh, I didn't want the job," George smiled. He removed the wide yellow clip-on tie he'd been wearing with his black button-down shirt. "I just wanted to get into the company to plant a file on one of the company hard drives. I just got back from the airport, actually, and—"

"Exactly where did you interview?" John said over his brother.

"In Phoenix, Arizona. With Vulcan Semiconducter," George said.

John covered his mouth with his hand and stared at Chiara in disbelief.

"That's Carlton Puel's company." She sank into George's squeaky swivel chair. "George, you're crazy."

"The man himself interviewed me," George said proudly, completely ignorant of John and Chiara's distress. "He offered me a job in his fledgling programming department. Seems Mr. Puel is looking to diversify, specifically to expand into software security and encryption. He's looking for a few good designers to create new junk for him."

John couldn't speak for a long moment. Chiara felt sick to her stomach. "For someone so smart," John began, "you are incredibly stupid! Do you think Carlton Puel can't add two and two? He sent someone after me. Do you honestly believe that he'll think it's a coincidence that he interviewed a Mahoney a week after he sent someone to assault a Mahoney?"

"He offered me seventy-thousand to start, plus incentives, bonuses, full benefits and use of the company ranch," George said pitifully.

John threw off his Chesterfield and paced in what little floor space was free of George's refuse and discarded clothing. "I don't care if he offered you ten million dollars and Clara Winters in a mesh bodysuit, you never should have gone to Arizona! How did you even pay for your airfare?"

"I didn't have to pay for it." George dropped his eyes to his bright white sneakers. "It's not unheard of for companies to foot the bill for travel expenses for people they're very interested in hiring. Besides, I didn't accept the position."

"Oh, well that's a relief," John said sarcastically.

"Puel wanted me to cut my hair," George said. "There's a dress code, too. I can't hang without my hair and my duds."

John's mouth hung open in disbelief. "Those are the only reasons you didn't take the job?"

"Those, and because I'd go to jail for fraud if I was hired with the resumé I submitted." George went to his desk. He lifted an empty can of Mountain Dew and grabbed four sheets of paper. He gave two each to John and Chiara.

"Scott Turner?" Chiara said, reading the name at the top of the first paper out loud.

"It's my cover," George said with a lopsided smile. He opened his wallet and pulled out an Ohio state identification card, a Social Security Card, and a student ID—with George's picture on it—from Ohio State University.

"How did you get these?" Chiara gasped. "This is totally illegal," she added, conveniently forgetting her own experience in fraudulent documentation.

John looked up from the second of the two sheets of paper George had given him. "This transcript says that Scott Turner is a straight-A student at the Russ College of Engineering and Technology at Ohio State University."

Chiara studied her own copy. "He's fluent in Spanish, Japanese and Xhosa?" She looked at George in curiosity. "Xhosa?"

"It's a Bantu language," George grinned. "I figured it would make Scott more cosmopolitan, more well rounded."

"Borrowing his identity could get him hurt, or even killed," John said stridently. "Carlton Puel is a dangerous man."

"Scott Turner is me, John," George explained. "He's totally made up. If you search for him on the Internet, you'll see this resumé posted with online job sites, but that's the only evidence of this Scott Turner you'll find." He pointed to his fake driver's license. "Scott Turner isn't as common a name as John Smith, but it's common enough to confound anyone who might try to search for more background online."

"All Vulcan has to do is contact Ohio State to find out if Scott Turner is a student there," John argued.

"He is," George chuckled. "I hacked into admissions and enrolled him. It only took about ten minutes to get in."

"Chess Club, Biology Club, Cross Country Team, *Computer Science Review* editor," Chiara said, reading off Turner's list of school activities. "He keeps busy."

"Plus he's got a 3.7 GPA," George said. "Puel's human resources manager e-mailed me the same day I posted the resumé online."

"Your phone number is a 314 exchange," John said. "That might have tipped someone off that you didn't come from Ohio."

"Scott Turner has his own toll-free number specifically to field calls from potential employers. He's taking his post-graduation job search very seriously. He's very professional."

Chiara left the chair to give George a peck on the lips. "He's very clever, too."

"Don't praise him," John chastised. "George, did you actually plant a file at Vulcan?"

"Yep." George went to his computer and called up the file he'd programmed specially for Vulcan. "I did it before I even got there. I overnighted a disc with the Scott Turner resumé and references files on it. The references file is the one I needed Vulcan to download. As soon as human resources opened it, I was in. All I have to do now is wait."

"For what?" George asked.

"For the file to open a backdoor into Vulcan's e-mail system. It should happen soon, if not already."

"What activates the back door?" Chiara asked him.

"Human resources has to log on to its e-mail account and forward twenty of its messages to Carlton Puel. The Scott Turner resumé was obviously forwarded, so that started the countdown. After number twenty, I should be able to hack into Puel's e-mail. I'll be able to find out who he's communicating with and what he talks about."

Even though Chiara was impressed with George's abilities, one question still bothered her. "Why did you go there in person? The Scott Turner files did all the work for you."

George's satisfied smile melted. For the first time, Chiara saw him as an adult, and not the laidback, silly student he usually was. "I wanted to see the man who hurt you," he said, encompassing Chiara and John in his gaze. "I wanted to see the bastard we're going to put in jail."

❧❧❧

For the next week, Chiara anxiously awaited news of George's success or possible discovery. Though she felt safer knowing that John Doe wasn't likely to come after her again following his arrest, she wasn't so sure that Puel wouldn't send someone else, so she remained at home behind closed doors unless her mother or one of her sisters could accompany her where she wanted to go. Even as she valued the safety in numbers her sisters offered, she hated that old familiar feeling of being babysat.

When Cady invited her to go shopping in The Loop early Saturday, Chiara accepted if for no other reason than to take her mind off the wait for George's plan to take effect. Clara, Danielle, Ciel, Abigail, Ella and Kyla were already piled in the black Honda Pilot when Cady pulled the roomy vehicle up to the curb in front of Abby's house. Once Chiara climbed in, bundling her brushed Alpaca bat-wing cape around her, Cady sped off, barely giving Chiara time to close the door.

"Thanks," Chiara said, turning to see if Abby was on her heels. "Mama's gone crazy lately. Every time I turn around, she's shoving a bridal or baby magazine under my nose. She wanted to buy me this horrible wedding dress she saw in *Modern Bride*. It was a floor-length, peau de soie monstrosity with skinny straps and no back. The skirt flared about a mile and had two big pleats in the front. The worst part was this big old pink bow in the back with tails as long as the train."

"It actually sounds kind of pretty," Ciel said.

"Mama's just excited," Clara said, turning in the front passenger seat to look at Chiara. "She always makes a fuss over you."

"You're the baby," Kyla teased with a roll of her dark eyes. "You give Mama all of her lasts, so she takes more of an interest in them."

"I give her all of her what?" Chiara asked.

"You were her last baby," Clara said.

"Yours was her last high school graduation," Ciel added.

"Yours was her last college graduation," Kyla threw in.

"And yours was supposed to be her last walk down the aisle to hand you off to John Mahoney," Cady said. "You stole that from her."

"The only thing I stole was my free will," Chiara said. She propped her elbow against the window and slumped in her seat. "If anything, I stole it back."

"I get to give you all your firsts, right, Mom?" Danielle asked, tearing her attention from the hand-held video game with which her cousins entertained themselves. "Your first baby, your first diaper changes, your first potty-training, your first teaching the baby how to walk…" Danielle's long, brown sugar tresses swayed from side to side as she swung her head with her litany of firsts.

"Actually," Clara began, "Chiara gave me all my firsts. I was in the sixth grade when she came along, and your grandpa had just died. I was Grandma Abby's big helper."

"Like Troy was when I was a baby?" Danielle asked.

"Oh, hell no," Clara laughed, her raisin eyes sparkling. "Troy was no kind of help when you were born. Every time I had to change your diaper, he disappeared. One time, I asked him to bring me a onesie for you, and he went to my purse and brought me a dollar bill."

"Boys are useless when it comes to babies," Abigail muttered from the farthest back seat without looking up from her game.

"I changed Chiara's diapers and gave her bottles when Mama was at work," Clara recalled.

"Which was all the time," Cady said. "Clara was a good big sister, Danielle. She practically had four little girls of her own by the time she was twelve."

"It got a lot easier when your Great-Grandma Claire and Great-Grandpa Hank came to live with us," Clara said.

"Nana Claire was the best," Danielle said fondly, tears shining in her eyes. Five years after Claire's death, and Chiara was amazed at how sharp and fresh the pain of loss still was for all of them.

"I think you need to make a left turn here to get off Skinker," Ciel said, gracefully changing the subject. "Forest Park Parkway is closed off at the intersection."

Chiara sat up straighter to see orange pylons blocking part of the intersection. "How long has the parkway been closed?"

"Too long." Cady made the turn, but then suddenly veered right, circumventing the pylons and making her own shortcut to continue along Skinker.

The construction on Forest Park Parkway was just about the only thing that had changed about St. Louis. When she was younger, Chiara had derived a certain comfort in the unrelenting sameness of the city. She could go away for a year and come back to find everything exactly as she'd left it. But after discovering so much more about other parts of the world, coming back to St. Louis made her feel as though she were being kenneled while the rest of the world moved on without her.

Common sense told her that the situation wasn't permanent, that her options would broaden once she'd dealt with Emmitt Grayson. She didn't think it would take much convincing to get John to pursue employment outside St. Louis, possibly even outside the United States. And she had no qualms about rearing her child elsewhere.

She smiled to herself as they neared the corner of Delmar and Skinker, and Cady flashed her left turn signal. *Maybe I should tell Mama that we're going to move,* she thought. *It would certainly distract her from pestering me about a wedding.*

All Cady's years of Boston living went into action once more as she zipped across the path of an oncoming Ford Excursion to make her left. "Too slow, Romeo!" she called happily, cruising along Delmar.

Chiara was pleasantly surprised to see that even though some of the stores she'd always liked in he Loop were gone, they had been replaced by boutiques that looked just as eclectic and unique as the old ones. "Can we stop there?" Chiara asked, noticing a colorfully wild storefront display filled with Afrocentric clothing.

"Soul Hippi?" Danielle said, smiling. "That's a funny name."

"Soul Hippi," Ella echoed from the seat beside Abigail. "Sooouul Hippi."

"Knock it off, Ella," Ciel warned. "Don't start."

"Don't start what?" Cady asked as she attempted to reverse parallel park her car between an old VW Bug and a glitzy black Porsche Cayman.

"Ella will latch onto some word and repeat it until we're all ready to choke her," Ciel said. "Yesterday it was 'coconut.'"

"She said coconut for about a hundred hours yesterday," Abigail complained as she locked her game in its boxy little case. "Dad asked her what she wanted to wear, and she goes, 'Coconut, coconut, coconut,' like that makes any kind of sense."

"Is that true, Ella?" Chiara asked, grinning.

"Soul Hippi, Soul Hippi," Ella answered merrily.

"Girl…" Ciel warned.

"Soul Hippi," Ella mouthed.

"Cady," Kyla said warily, "you might want to drive around and find another parking spot. I don't think you have room here."

"I have room," Cady insisted, turning in her seat to better aim the car. "This is the zen of parking. If I believe I'll fit, I'll fit."

"Well, let me explain the reality of parking," Kyla said. "That Cayman costs about fifty grand. Do you want to pay for denting it with this big ol' barge of yours?"

"How do you know how much that car costs?" Clara asked.

"Zweli took a spin in one a while back, when we were in California doing post production on my film."

"When will it finally be finished?" Danielle asked, bouncing in excitement.

"It's scheduled for release next fall," Kyla said. "I'm looking forward to it."

"Me, too!" Danielle clapped her hands under her chin. "All my friends are going to be so jealous when they see me on *E!* at a real Hollywood premiere!"

"What's the title of the movie again, Ky?" Clara asked.

"*Catching the Moon*," she said.

"I like that," Chiara said, lurching forward as Cady finally brought the car to a stop. "There's a romance to it. It's inspiring."

"That's the whole point." Kyla, looking like a movie star in a red, fitted wool coat and big pair of chic Chanel sunglasses, opened her door, pulled her seat forward and helped Ella and Abigail out of the rear-most seat.

Everyone else spilled from the car, and Cady spent a moment admiring her parking job.

"Hold my hand to cross the street, Ella?" Chiara offered.

"Soul Hipp-pip-pippi!" the little girl responded as she slipped her hand into Chiara's.

Chiara and her sisters browsed through the racks of clothing artfully scattered throughout the small boutique while Danielle, Abigail and Ella amused themselves by trying on accessories handed to them by a very patient sales clerk.

"This has me all over it," Kyla sighed lustily as she held up a two-piece summer ensemble with a criss-cross halter top and long, flowing skirt in a brilliant green, orange and yellow print. "Can't you see me wearing this to the beach with Zweli and the baby? Once I lose the last fifteen pounds of my baby weight, of course."

Chiara grunted her approval, although the outfit Kyla was admiring was a radical departure from her current Jackie Onassis costume.

"I'm getting this," Cady said, showing them a free flowing, floor-length dress in muted shades of teal, green and ocean blue. "It'll grow with me until the baby's born, and I can still wear it afterward as a wrap or a cover up."

"What will you need to cover up?" Ciel asked as she sorted through a rack of snazzy patchwork skirts. "You bounce right back to a size five after each of your pregnancies."

Abigail scurried over to Ciel carrying a white dress on a hanger. "Can I have this, Mama, please, please, please?"

Chiara looked at the garment and fell in love with the simple straight sleeveless dress. It would have looked like any other spring dress but for the single braid of fabric along the back, which gave it both orig-inality and sweetness perfect for a girl Abigail's age. Chiara tried to picture her niece in the dress, running around Abby's back yard at the Fourth of July barbeque, her hair, as thick and dark as molasses, gleaming as it streamed behind her in a silken banner.

The only image that came to her mind, though, was that of a little girl of her own dashing about with her cousins in the darling summer dress.

She shook the picture out of her head. "Let me buy that for her, Ciel," Chiara said. "I really want to."

"Sure," Ciel agreed.

"Thank you, Aunt Chiara," Abigail said, crushing Chiara's legs in a hug.

Ella appeared with an embroidered black Kofi hat sized perfectly for her head. "Soul Hippi?"

"Soul Hippi," Chiara said, taking the hat from Ella and adding it to her "to buy" pile.

"This is you, Chi." Cady stepped up to her and held a long white dress up to her shoulders.

Chiara fell instantly in love and took the garment to one of the tri-fold mirrors staged near the fitting rooms. The crisp white halter dress was made of silk jersey that moved like air. The alluring, low-cut bodice complemented the plunging back. Chiara knew just by looking at it that the floor-length skirt would be just right for for her petite frame. The dress was so simple in its silhouette and execution, but so well made that it rivaled many of the garments she'd purchased from well-known designers overseas. Just as she'd been able to envision her own little girl someday prancing about in a Soul Hippi sundress, she easily pictured John's face looking upon her in this white dress as they stood together, hand in hand, before their families and God on a beach someplace far away.

"Would you like to try that on?" the smiling sales clerk asked.

"I don't need to," Chiara replied. "I'm taking it."

"Special occasion?" the salesgirl asked, her smile widening.

Chiara shyly suppressed a grin. Without realizing it, she had just chosen the dress for the wedding that, up until that moment, she hadn't wanted to have. "Yes," she told the salesgirl. "It's for a very special occasion."

"Let me take those things up to the counter for you," the woman offered.

Chiara thanked her and piled Abigail's dress, Ella's hat, two other skirts and two tops she'd selected into the woman's arms. She was adding her white dress to the pile when her cell phone began to ring.

Certain that it was John, she quickly began rooting through her handbag for her phone. It stopped ringing before she found it, but the moment she fixed her eyes on the Caller ID window and saw George's phone number, another cell phone rang. Nearby, Cady dug her phone from her pocket. She didn't answer it, but merely read the message in her text box.

"Uh, we have to go," Cady announced. "I have someplace to be."

"Me, too," Chiara said as she made her way to the cashier's stand.

No one heard Clara's cell phone ring, but she was reading the message box as she joined her sisters at the checkout. "I've gotta run, too," Clara said.

"What are the odds of all three of you being called to the Bat Cave at the same time?" Kyla asked.

Chiara, Cady and Clara all looked at her suspiciously.

"What?" Kyla asked, totally ignorant of the impact her words had on her sisters. She set her purchases on the counter and waited her turn to check out. "I just think it's weird that you all get called at the same time. Unless it's Mama, and then I have to wonder why she didn't call me and Ciel, too."

And then, as if on cue, Ciel's phone rang. She looked at her Caller ID, and then glanced at Cady and Chiara, uttering one word. "George?"

Chiara nodded. Her stomach dropped to her knees when Cady and Clara nodded, too.

CHAPTER TWENTY-ONE

"You have five seconds to explain this before I knock you out," John told George once he was able to speak.

George had called his cell phone, and John had rushed to the dorm to find Chiara and her sisters crammed into his brother's messy little single. At first, he'd thought that Chiara had told her sisters everything. But when he'd entered the room to see George cowering behind Clara, he'd known immediately whose lips had gone loose.

"It's all *her* fault." George pointed an accusing finger at Cady. "She made me tell her what was going on."

Hands low on the hips of his jeans, John slowly shook his head. "How the hell did Cady make you do anything?"

"She came over here and practically kicked down my door," George said in a nervous, high-pitched voice. "After she visited you guys in Chicago. She made me tell her everything."

John continued to scowl.

"She said she was going to tell the registrar that I've been changing my grades!"

Clara turned and looked at George. "You change your grades?"

"Yes, ma'am," he said meekly.

"All the best geeks tamper with their grades," Cady said. "It was a guess that paid off."

John stood before Cady. "Chiara asked you," he started. "No. She *begged* you not to get involved in this."

"That was awfully hard for me to do after I saw her face smashed," Cady said. "What's done is done. I got involved, and before you light into George again, you should know that I'm the one who recruited Clara and Ciel to help."

"Why didn't you call me?" Kyla whined petulantly. "I could have helped, too. What are we talking about anyway?"

"May as well tell her." John threw up his hands. "The rest of the world knows."

"No, it doesn't," Cady snapped impatiently. "But it will soon, if everything works out the way we've planned."

Chiara shook in confusion and annoyance. "I still don't get this. Who's 'we?' What plan? John and I have been proceeding with the utmost caution. After what happened to Zhou, we didn't want to involve any more people in this than we had to. The only reason we brought George in is because he's freakishly savvy with computers, and we needed someone who could dissect a microchip. Even after I was attacked, I didn't want to move back home because I didn't want to put any of you in the line of fire." Tears shining in her eyes, she turned on Cady. "And now you've gone and dragged the whole damn family into my mess!"

Cady stepped over George's plaid comforter, which lay half on and half off his bed, to get to Chiara. She cupped her sister's face and struck two tears away with her thumbs. "Your mess is our mess. There's no way I was going to let anyone get away with hurting you. If you hadn't mentioned George, I never would have gotten to the root of the problem. I knew I wouldn't get a thing out of you or John. But George sang like a canary with the right incentive."

"Incentive?" George burst out. "You put me in a headlock and started pulling out my nose hairs!"

"She's always been a dirty fighter," Kyla said.

"Yeah, well," George sulked. "She's lucky she's pregnant, or I would've given her such a roughneck-style thump."

"Oh really?" Clara said.

George humbly dropped his head. "No, ma'am."

"So why'd you call us here, George?" John asked.

"He didn't call me." Offended, Kyla crossed her arms over her chest. "I'm not a member of the secret club."

"You have a tiny baby to worry with," Cady said. "I figured you had enough on your plate."

"Well, could you at least tell me what's going on?"

Chiara sat Kyla down on an overturned milk carton George used as a laundry hamper and filled her in on everything that had happened from the time she'd spoken with a drunken Zhou in the Seiyo lounge in Tokyo to the moment George had summoned them all by cell phone at Soul Hippi. From there, she required a few answers herself, and she looked to George to provide them.

George found the courage to step away from Clara, but he didn't stray far, not with John staring at him with menace in his eyes. "Cady started looking into Emmitt Grayson and USITI's sales reports to see what companies had purchased R-GS systems in the past five years," George said. "When we came across the *American Investors* article detailing Grayson's amazing success at playing the stock market, we had to get Ciel involved. She got Lee to provide us with information about Grayson's investment portfolio."

"Great," Chiara said dismally. "Now Lee's breaking privacy laws."

"No, everything he gave us was publicly accessible," Cady said. "George and I did the less-than-legal part."

"I did a little creative hacking, and we found out that Grayson's biggest investment successes came from buying and selling the stock of companies he'd previously sold R-GS systems to," George said. "Once we had the skinny on Grayson's finances, I started working on a way to combat the master chip."

"That's where Clara came in," Cady said. "She has access to secure computer systems that enabled George to work on the chip without triggering any of USITI's built-in self-destructs or security measures."

"Clara helped me fine-tune my rebound chip, too," George said. "We're a really good team."

"Geeks of a feather," Clara sang airily.

"Does the rebound chip work?" John asked, perking in excitement.

"Don't know," George said. "We need to install it in a system that uses R-GS chips."

"I can try it at work," John offered.

"It can't be an internal USITI system," George told him. "The rebound chip will let the computer user know when there's an interloper, but it's specific to the USITI master. So any USITI system would be immune to the rebound effect."

"The rebound chip can't tell on itself," Clara explained simply.

"I am so totally confused," Kyla said. "I hate computers, and this is why."

"The rebound chip uses the same programming and pathways as the master, only in reverse," Clara explained. "It's really quite brilliant."

George blushed furiously under Clara's praise.

"The master chip opens a backdoor to Grayson, at USITI. The rebound trip is designed to send an intruder alert to the violated computer, not USITI. If you were to install a rebound at USITI, you'd get a message saying that a USITI user is on your computer. It cancels itself out, since obviously a USITI user would be using a USITI computer."

"I'll take your word for it," Kyla sighed, giving up any effort to figure out the master-rebound chip conundrum.

"What about Carlton Puel?" John asked. "Did you get anything on him?"

George hurried to his desk and rifled through several untidy stacks of papers. "I accessed his personal e-mail this morning and found six e-mails from Emmitt Grayson delivered on January 4."

"The day Grayson came to see me at home," Chiara said.

Holding several sheets of paper, George began to read. " 'If you touch her again, I'll see to it that you pay personally.' Grayson sent that to Puel. Here's Puel's response: 'All I want is my fair share.' Then Grayson replies, 'Until my personal property finds its way home, our agreement remains as it stands.' "

"George helped me do some digging on InfoSysTech, the database newspapers use to collect information on people," Cady said. "It might not mean anything, but Emmitt Grayson and Carlton Puel were college roommates. They've known each other for quite a long time. Maybe Grayson confided in him about how the R-GS and master chips function."

"What about Puel's finances?" John asked. "Is he doing as well as Grayson?"

"Not by a long shot," George said. "He pulled $505,000 in net income last year with two million in bonuses compared to Grayson's $1.85 million net take with over eight million in bonuses."

"No wonder he wants a master chip," Chiara said. "He provides the chips for Grayson to program, yet he rakes in less than half of what Grayson makes using the chips."

"Puel is obviously convinced that the chip is in your possession, guys," Cady said to Chiara and John. "He's the one who sent Anthony Taylor."

Chiara's forehead wrinkled. "Who?"

"John Doe. The man who attacked you in Chicago and jumped John in the parking garage."

Chiara was amazed. "How did you get his real name?"

"I went back to the police station the day after you were released," Cady said. "The cops ran John Doe's prints but he wasn't in the system, and he still refused to give them his name. I asked the precinct captain if I could have a word with him, and I convinced John Doe to give me his name."

"Did you put him in a headlock?" George asked.

"Didn't have to." Cady's lips pulled into an enigmatic smile. "I gave him a candy bar."

"You scared him with a Snickers?" John asked skeptically.

"I put his discarded wrapper in an evidence bag and told him that I'd give it to the police," Cady said. "A candy wrapper with his prints on it could be placed at the scene of any unsolved crime between here and Chicago, and since he'd been arrested, his prints are in the system now."

"God, Cady, you threatened him with blackmail?" Ciel asked, aghast.

"It was only a threat. I threw the wrapper away once he gave me his name."

"We searched Anthony Taylor on InfoSysTech," George said. "He's a resident of Phoenix. When I cross-referenced him with Carlton Puel and Vulcan Semiconductor, I got a hit on the Vulcan combination. Puel used his in-house travel department to book Taylor's flights from Arizona to Chicago and St. Louis. I also found travel records for Puel that put him in Malaysia and Tokyo at the same time Chiara and Chen Zhou were there."

"We're close to nailing both of them, Chiara," Cady said. "It's almost over."

Chiara's knees weakened. She took a few deep breaths and her hands restlessly fidgeted with the cuffs of her sleeves. Her jaw tensed as she approached Cady. "My whole life, I've had the four of you bossing me around and always trying to do what you think is best for me." Her voice shook, and it was difficult for her to force words past the thick lump plugging her windpipe. "I begged you to stay out of this, Cady, but as usual, you went ahead and just did what you wanted without giving a single thought to what repercussions your actions would have on me. Or John, or George…" She stood face to face with Cady for a moment, but then she suddenly threw her arms around her big sister. "Thank you," she whispered. "Thank you for not listening to me."

John maneuvered around more of George's land mines of clutter and filth to gently rub Chiara's shoulders. "So what's next?" he asked, directing the question to his fresh allies.

"We have to test the rebound chip," Clara said.

Chiara pulled away from Cady, but continued to hold her hand. "How do we do that?"

"You have to make one more sale for USITI," George said.

❦

Three hundred miles stood between Chiara and Emmitt Grayson, yet she still felt the familiar chill of his unblinking eyes on her as she spoke to him by means of a conference line in John's office at USITI-St. Louis.

Sundays were full-fledged workdays at the St. Louis office, with the information systems department handling technical and operating questions from computer users all over the world as part of USITI's 24-hour/7 days a week customer service policies. USITI employees, John's employees, sat in well-ordered, spacious cubicles speaking pleasantly into headset telephones on the other side of John's office door, while inside the office, Chiara grated her sweaty palms along the knees of her jeans.

She'd hoped to get away with leaving a message for Grayson, one to which he could later respond with a simple yes or no. But as was his habit, Grayson was in his office on Sunday, surfing the Internet. In retrospect,

Chiara had come to believe that Grayson's Sunday surfing shifts were devoted to accessing the waves of confidential and lucrative information made available to him by the master chips.

Whatever he was doing, Chiara had hoped to be received by his voicemail, not Grayson himself, when she called his office line at nine A.M. Sunday morning.

"I've been reading the dossier you sent to me right before I left for St. Louis," Chiara started abruptly. "Westcott Technologies sounds really exciting. I was…uh…well, I was curious as to whether you'd assigned another team to pursue an R-GS sale to Westcott. If not, I'd like to take a run at it."

Grayson was so silent for so long, Chiara thought the call might have been disconnected.

"May I ask why?" he said eventually, "given that your resignation from USITI is effective as of tomorrow?"

Chiara slumped in relief. She had him now, and she knew it. Her stomach still turned tiny somersaults, but her voice gained strength. "I've been living with my mother here in St. Louis, and…well…it's not quite as exciting as flying off to Tokyo or Kuala Lumpur."

"I can't imagine that Baltimore is any more exciting," Grayson said.

"If you'd rather I not accept the assignment, then by all means, I'll return the dossier and—"

"Please don't misunderstand me, Chiara," Grayson hastily cut in. "I'd be extremely grateful if you were to visit Westcott Technologies. I've been trying to acquire that account for some time now, and quite frankly, I can't think of a better person for the sale than you."

"I appreciate your faith in me, Mr. Grayson," Chiara said. And then she went for the money question, that one that would help decide the success or failure of her plan. "How long will it take you to select a partner for me?"

Leaving Chiara sitting stiffly and holding her breath, Grayson thought about it. "I'm confident that you can handle Westcott on your own. It's a small, family-operated organization. A single sales representative of your caliber and qualifications will be far more effective than a team. I believe the more personal we make our pitch, the greater the likelihood of success."

Chiara released a long, silent sigh of relief. "Thank you for that vote of confidence, Mr. Grayson." *Even though it's totally misplaced,* she thought.

"How soon would you like to go to Baltimore?" Grayson asked. "I'd like to put the wheels in motion as soon as possible."

Chiara glanced up at John, George and Cady, who stood in a huddle far from the telephone. His eyebrows raised, John exchanged meaningful glances with George and Cady, and then gave Chiara a thumb's up.

"As soon as possible fits my timeline perfectly," Chiara said.

"Is your mother coming?" Chiara asked as she and John stood in Abby's tiny library, peering through the sheer curtains. "I don't see her car."

"My father might be bringing her, or she might walk," John said. "George could be giving her a ride."

Chiara smiled. "You invited George?"

John lifted one shoulder in a small shrug. "I figured it was time to stop keeping all of you to myself, considering how much help he's been in the past couple of weeks."

"That's mighty generous of you, John," Chiara allowed. "Although I'm not sure a baby shower will be his cup of tea."

"A houseful of women not George's cup of tea?" John scoffed. "Please. That kid'll have Miss Etheline eating out of the palm of his hand and your mother showering him with kisses."

"While she tries to talk him into getting a haircut," Chiara said knowingly. "Miss Etheline isn't coming, by the way. She told Mama that she won't ever come back here again until I apologize for being so 'smart' with her."

"Are you going to?"

"Mama said that wouldn't be a very smart thing for me to do." Chiara took one more look through the ecru sheers covering Abby's windows. "I think she's glad that I managed to do in one afternoon what she couldn't do in fifty years. Get rid of Etheline Simpson."

John took Chiara's hand and set a kiss on the back of it. "Ready to face them?"

"Ready or not, let's get it over with," she sighed.

Practically overnight, Abby had organized a baby shower for Chiara and John. The guest list included all of the Winters sisters, their families, and all of Abby's friends. John and Chiara had no friends in St. Louis to invite, and none from Chicago who could come on such short notice. The Mahoneys had all been invited, which was the only reason Chiara and John had agreed to the event. Because there would be so many people in the house, many of whom were mutual friends with Almadine, the shower was the perfect opportunity to give Almadine the two pieces of news they'd been concealing for so long.

A tidal wave of happy greetings, whistles, cheers and general noise greeted John and Chiara when they emerged into the overcrowded dining room. The surfaces of the black Victorian pine buffet and dining table were covered in food, thanks to Abby's idea of making the event a potluck supper, and gift boxes and bags were stacked waist high in the living room. There were so many presents wrapped in pastel papers or covered in frolicking giraffes, kittens or cherubs. Big ticket items—a bassinet, a high chair and a complicated contraption called a Whisper Soft Swing guaranteed to keep baby asleep and nestled in cloud-like comfort—spilled into the foyer and lined wall all the way to the front door.

Chiara gripped John's hand a little harder. Her sisters, aunts and her mother's friends had gone well above the call of duty for her baby, and Chiara felt a hitch of shame at having hoarded her secret for so long.

"Just wait until the wedding," Zweli said close to John's ear as he handed him a dark brown bottle of beer. "They like weddings just as much as they like babies."

"We're already married," Chiara told her brother-in-law. "We don't need to have a big wedding."

"What you need and what you're gonna have are two different things, Chi," Zweli chuckled. "Do you really think you can deprive these ladies of the chance to see you and John...renew your vows?"

"Hey, I like that." John sipped his beer. " 'Renew our vows.' It sounds better than getting married again."

"We'll have to see," Chiara agreed diplomatically. "Right now, let's just get through this baby thing."

The floral-printed loveseat had been reserved as the place of honor for Chiara and John, and he seated her before he joined her.

"Oh, it's so nice to see a young man with manners," one of Abby's teacher friends commented as she beamed at John over the tops of her half-spectacles.

"John used to mow my lawn for me, before he started high school," an older neighbor lady, Mrs. Vida Kinloch, said. "I never knew such a nice, quiet boy. Never talked back and he was always on time." She lowered her voice, but not so much that she couldn't be heard. "Now that Chiara, she's a whole other story. She used to ride her bike up and down the street while John was workin', tryin' to get him to skip off with her. Abby should've put her to work, too, 'stead of letting her run 'round doing what-all she wanted."

Chiara chomped the inside of her lower lip, biting back the caustic response she wanted to deliver. John took Chiara's hand in both of his, mutely telling her what she already knew: that Chiara's company was the only reason John had mowed Mrs. Kinloch's lawn. She lived a few doors down from Chiara, and the lawn mowing job had given him a reason to be on Chiara's street, if only for a few hours on Saturday morning.

John's attention to Chiara's right hand seemed to bring attention to her left, and one of the sharp-eyed guests spoke up. "Is that your wedding band, Chiara?"

She resisted the urge to curl up her hand and sit on it, instead, raising it, back out, to display her ring. Her eyes met John's, and she smiled, proud to wear her ring out in the open.

Her smile faded when she heard, "It's so plain," from somewhere in the back of the room.

"It's still real pretty," another older woman said a little too insistently.

"Well, I ain't never seen a wedding band that look like that," another voice declared, not bothering to mask its disapproval.

"They're young and just starting out," someone else said. "They can put some diamonds in it later, when they're in a better position."

"How much did the ring cost?" Ciel asked pleasantly from her position near the fireplace, as if she and Chiara were alone in the room.

John handled that one. "I don't see why the cost of the ring should matter."

"It does to these people," Chiara hissed softly through a petrified smile.

"How much was it?" Ciel persisted. "You can tell us. You're among friends."

A hearty chorus of agreement met Ciel's words, and John suddenly felt trapped. Thankful that his mother wasn't there, he gave his rapt audience the purchase price of the ring, including the shipping expenses from Japan for good measure.

Every eye in the room seemed to bulge from its home for a second, but every tongue remained silent.

"It's made of three layers of metal," John went on to break the silence. "Platinum, titanium and white gold. It's an original piece I commissioned from one of Japan's most respected metalsmiths. Chiara likes Japanese art, and I thought this ring would be a unique way to represent my love for her."

John realized what Chiara and Ciel already knew, that his heartfelt explanation was wasted on most of the shower guests when one of the woman said, "Ooh, Lordy! All that money on a wedding band!"

"It may not have the sparkle and shine, but Chiara definitely got herself a piece of the rock!" laughed someone else.

"I think we should move on to opening the gifts," Abby announced. "If we don't get started now, we'll be here all night."

Cady, Kyla, Ciel and Clara took the role of attendants to the mother-to-be. Cady sat at on the arm of the loveseat with pad and paper, recording what gift came from whom for the thank you notes to come later so that Chiara and John had only unwrapping to worry about.

With the orderly precision of the National Guard, Kyla, Ciel and Clara set unopened packages before Chiara and John, discarded the used wrappings, and then stacked the gifts in another corner of the living room.

A set of three crocheted baby blankets in white, yellow and green inspired a loud round of oohs and aahs. "They're so soft," Chiara remarked, rubbing one of them against her cheek. "Are they handmade?"

"Yes," the gift-giver, another one of Abby's teacher friends, said, "but not by my hands!"

A sterling silver Tiffany & Co. bunny bank from Ciel and Lee left onlookers capable only of subdued whispers. "When the baby's born we can have his or her initials engraved on it," Ciel said.

"It's so heavy." Chiara had to use both hands to hold the tiny bank.

"Lee filled it with Sacajawea dollars," Ciel explained with a wink.

"Why those?" John asked.

"When Clarence lost his first tooth, the only money I happened to have in my wallet smaller than a five dollar bill was some loose change and a Sacajawea dollar I'd gotten for change at stamp vending machine,"

Ciel began. "I put the Sacajawea dollar under his pillow with a note from the tooth fairy reminding him to take care of the teeth he had left. The next morning he woke up, all excited. He thought that the image of Sacajawea on the coin was the tooth fairy, that she'd given him her own money."

"Like Queen Elizabeth," Kyla laughed.

"We leave Sacajawea dollars for our kids every time they lose a tooth," Ciel said. "I wanted to pass that tradition on to you and your children."

John tested the weight of the gleaming bunny. "We'll have to have ten kids to use up all this tooth fairy money."

"Okay," Chiara whispered as she kissed his cheek.

"Our gift sort of goes with Ciel's," Kyla said, setting a distinctive pale seafoam box tied with white ribbon in Chiara's hands.

Chiara opened it and withdrew a pair of sterling silver Tiffany photo frames embossed with bunnies sniffing at daisies. "These can be engraved, too," Kyla said. "Once the baby has a name."

Cady's gift was next, and Chiara thought it perfectly represented her big sister's tendencies toward practicality and excess. Cady hadn't wrapped the stylish Briggs & Riley diaper bag which looked more like a traditional backpack than baby gear. She'd stuffed the bag to the point of overflowing, giving everything inside a cursory wrapping in pastel tissue paper. Chiara pulled out short-sleeved kimono tops, leggings, onesies, bodysuits, soft-knit hats, socks, tiny mitts, bibs, adorable bear-, pig-, cow- and penguin-shaped cloth rattles, a fleece receiving blanket, cloth diapers for burping and wiping up throw-up, baby wipes, infant gas drops, Balmex, infant nail clippers, Calendula baby wash, wash cloths and hooded towels and lavender massage oil.

"There's a case of diapers and baby wipes, too, but they wouldn't fit in the bag," Cady said.

"There's nothing left for us to buy," Chiara said to John with a soft chuckle.

The whole room erupted in laughter.

"That's what you think!" someone called.

"I know these things won't last forever, but when the baby first gets here…we're all set, and then some." Chiara unsuccessfully fought to hold back tears. "Seeing all this, and all of you here, it really shows me how much a baby needs, both in everyday equipment and attention and love." She picked up the brightly colored patchwork stuffed giraffe someone had given her and gave it an offhand hug. "This baby will come into the world receiving so much, and I'm so grateful to all of you. Thank you."

"There's still tons more to go, Chi," Cady said.

"You haven't opened our gift yet." The low, cold voice was accompanied by a flat, slim box that whizzed through the air and landed on the floral rug at Chiara's feet.

"Mother," John said, working out the only word that came into his mind at seeing Almadine standing in the archway. She still wore her black coat and hat. John moved to greet her and his father and brother, who stood behind her.

"Almadine, it's so good you could come," Abby said graciously, holding out her arms.

Almadine, scowling, took off her coat and thrust it at Abby. "My husband and sons insisted," she said, using jerky, angry motions to straighten the tight-fitting jacket of her black suit. "Although I don't see why we were invited here for your daughter's baby shower. Your Cady pushes 'em out faster than I can count, and what's more—"

Almadine's black eyes darted around the living room. They landed on Chiara, the gifts at her feet, and then the women crowded into the living room.

"Mother," John started, all too familiar with the bright shine of panicked rage rising in Almadine's eyes. "We should have told you that this shower isn't for Cady, but I was afraid that you wouldn't come."

Almadine's mouth worked furiously, but her tight lips produced no words. Her hands fisted, her shoulders swallowed her neck, and her whole body seemed to shake.

"Lord, here it go," muttered a wary voice from the living room.

And then it did.

Almadine's stiff arm lifted to aim a deadly pointed finger at Chiara as one word exploded from her. "Jezebel!"

CHAPTER TWENTY-TWO

Abby threw Almadine's coat to the floor and stepped over it to confront the skinnier, wrathful woman. "Don't you come into my house and start calling my baby girl names!" Abby breathed heavily, her shoulders dramatically rising and falling.

Almadine stepped past Abby and gave John a push to remove him from her path. "Seductress!" she hissed, moving ever nearer to Chiara, who stood to face her. "It took you twenty years, but you did it. You turned my boy from the Lord and you corrupted his flesh and led him into sin!"

"Mother, stop it!" John shouted, taking her by the arm.

"Almadine, that's enough," Bartholomew sighed heavily. "We knew you were gonna act out, that's why we didn't want to tell you why we were coming."

Almadine's eyes rolled wildly around to pin Bartholomew in his tracks. "You knew this hussy was pregnant?"

Abby pushed up the sleeves of her prim white blouse. "I am gonna whip that woman's ass once and for—"

"John told us a few days ago," Bartholomew admitted, placing his big bulk between Abby and his wife. "And I'd appreciate it if you wouldn't call my daughter-in-law a hussy."

"Daugh…wha…" Almadine stared at John. Then she stared at Chiara. "You married my boy?"

"He's not a boy," Chiara said as gently as she could. "And I'm not a Jezebel or a hussy. I'm the mother of your grandchild."

Almadine's facial muscles seemed to wilt. Despair and confusion took turns canceling out her wrath, and she suddenly seemed to be fully aware of all the eyes fixed on her. She turned and started back into the foyer. Bartholomew, George, Abby, John and dozens of gifts blocked her path to the front door, so she went the other way and fled through the dining room and into the kitchen.

Abby started after her, but John caught her shoulder. "Maybe I should talk to her," he said. The last thing he wanted was a physical altercation between his mother and Abby in front of so many people.

"Let me go," Chiara volunteered, to her own amazement as much as anyone else's.

"You don't want to do that," George warned through an apprehensive smile. "When she gets like this…well, I've never seen her as angry as this. I don't know what she'll do."

"Look," Chiara started, rapidly becoming thoroughly annoyed. "She's going to have to deal with me sooner or later, and it might as well be now."

Chiara took deep breaths to steady her nerves as she made her way to the kitchen. She opened the swinging door cautiously, half expecting one of the new Wusthof chef's knives Abby had received for Christmas to come flying at her. To her surprise and relief, Almadine was standing near the back door, her right elbow cupped in her left hand, her right hand clutching a wad of paper toweling to her eyes.

Chiara moved soundlessly to the sink. She grabbed a few tissues from the box beside the dish drying rack and brought them to Almadine. "Those paper towels are scratchy," she said.

Without looking at Chiara or thanking her, Almadine snatched the tissues from her hand. She turned her back to Chiara and blew her nose. Chiara couldn't remember the last time she'd been under the same roof with Almadine, never mind the same room. Even when Almadine had visited John in Chicago, Chiara had kept her distance from John's apartment until Almadine and all traces of her had vacated the premises.

This close to her for the first time in years, Chiara saw that time had wrought its own punishment on Almadine. Deep lines creased the ebony skin of her face, and her thin hands looked more like talons. Her hair, a flat, dimensionless shade of black, was obviously dyed. For the first time Chiara could recall, she saw something other than meanness, hatred, anger and envy in Almadine's face.

Almadine looked old, which softened Chiara's heart.

But only a little.

"Does it even matter to you that I love him?" she asked.

Almadine didn't turn, made no effort to respond. She only hunched her shoulders tighter, practically folding in on herself.

Chiara walked around Almadine, forcing a confrontation. "Does it matter to you that he loves me?"

"No!" Almadine snapped. "John was a good boy before he fell in with you. He was my boy!"

"He's still yours," Chiara said, surprising herself with her ability to remain calm in the face of the spitting harpy before her. "He'll always be yours. In spite of everything."

"Is everything all right in here?" Abby asked, entering the kitchen from the hallway with John close on her heels.

"Everything's fine, Mama," Chiara said impatiently. "Mrs. Mahoney and I were just trying to talk."

"Talk?" Almadine spat. "I don't have one damn thing to say to you, not now, not ever!"

"You're going to have to let go of all this hate and anger some time, Mother," John said. "You may as well try to start now."

"Don't think I'm going to forgive you for this ambush," Almadine threatened, jabbing a finger toward John. "You and your father and your brother are all in this together. I hope you're all having a fine time making a fool out of me, because I promise you, it won't ever happen again!"

"No one's trying to make a fool out of you," John said wearily. "I wanted you to come here and be a part of my happiness."

A high-pitched, scratchy laugh crawled out of Almadine's throat. "You got a baby in that little Jezebel, ran off and married her, and you expect me to sit around and be happy about it? Is this how I raised you? To be a fornicator, and a sinner, and—"

"Mrs. Mahoney," Chiara tried to cut in.

Almadine's arms went stiff at her sides and she seemed to swell with rage. "You led my boy away from the church!" she blasted at Chiara.

"You drove me from the church!" John fired right back, his voice shaking the rafters of Abby's house. For the first time Chiara saw the resemblance between mother and son. Pain and anger shaped John's face into a near mirror image of his mother's as he untethered everything he'd ever wanted to say to her. "Every time I did something you didn't approve of, you'd start muttering 'spare the rod, spoil the child,' like it was some kind of magic solution to your complete lack of parenting skills. You blistered me with that damned rod for five straight years!"

Almadine's narrow chest swelled as she drew a long, deep   breath. " 'He that spareth his rod hateth his son!' "

" 'But he that loveth him chasteneth him betimes,' " John countered furiously. "I know Proverbs, too, Mother. Just because I didn't sit in church having the Bible fed to me doesn't mean that I haven't read it in an attempt to understand you. To find a justification for you."

"The justification comes from Solomon," Almadine said through gritted teeth.

"Solomon?" John laughed bitterly. "The same Solomon who was such a shitty father that his own son Rehoboam grew up to be a tyrant who barely escaped being stoned to death for his cruelty? Nowhere else in the Bible is there a call for corporal punishment. Jesus taught mercy, forgiveness, humility…Jesus saw children as being close to God. In the book of Kings, it says that Solomon displeased God. In Matthew, God says, 'This is my son, with whom I am well pleased. Listen to him.' God never says listen to Solomon." John, although not calmed, lowered his voice. "When my child is born, I will not spoil him with anything other than under-standing, encouragement, devotion and love. I will never raise a rod to him."

"How dare you try to shape the good book into a defense for your sin."

"How dare you wield it like a weapon, not against evil or sin but against anything that threatened to take me or George away from you," John argued.

"You will burn for turning your back on your reli-gion, John."

"I haven't abandoned religion, Mother," John said somberly. "I've found a new one, a better one, right here in this house."

"At least I still have one son who loves and respects me," Almadine said, her voice painfully shrill. "One I can be proud of."

"George is not angel, Mother," John said. "Both your sons are just men."

"Fine, fine men," Abby put in, "of whom you should be proud, Alma."

Almadine whirled on a new target. "I don't need you to tell me about my boys! What do you know about raising young black men? Black boys have a much harder path in this life than anybody else!"

"Only when they don't have good parents behind them," Abby said. "I never agreed with your methods of discipline, but I know you did the best you could by John and George. And they turned out wonderfully."

" 'Spare the rod, spoil the child!' " Almadine stated triumphantly.

"The Bible doesn't say to whip your child until he can barely walk just for playing in the park," Abby said softly. "Or 'til you draw blood."

Almadine finally broke, her shoulders bouncing from the force of her sudden tears. "He should have kept his little butt in church like he was supposed to instead of running wild with your little seductress."

Abby chuckled sadly. "If kindness and friendship are what seduced your son, then my Chiara really was a seductress. And so am I, because I did everything I could to let John know that he was welcome in my home any time. That he was just as much a part of my family as if he'd been born to it. I never loved your son more than when he came back to St. Louis for my mother-in-law's funeral." Abby looked upon John with the maternal tenderness he'd never seen on his own mother's face. "That's the kind of man you raised, Alma, despite your dependence on the rod. You couldn't beat out the very thing you tried to—John's love for the folks who loved him."

Almadine started for the swinging door. "I don't have to stay here for this. I won't be persecuted, not by the likes of you, Abigail Winters." She pushed the door, but it wouldn't give. She found out why when Bartholomew and George swung the door in to gain entry to the kitchen. "Take me home, Bart," Almadine demanded. "I won't spend another minute in this house. George, get your coat and let's go."

"Mother, don't," John said, following after her. "I don't want you to go."

Almadine narrowed her cold black eyes at him. "You like it here so much, you can stay. I want you and all of your things out of my house *today*. And don't bother calling me or coming by until you're ready to apologize for what you did to me here today."

"You're being ridiculous, now," John said.

"Moms, come on, that's not right," George said.

"I want him out!" Almadine shrieked, her mouth in a jagged line that made her look like a badly carved jack o' lantern. "He's got no respect for me and I want him out of my house!"

Bartholomew cleared his throat, his huge belly shuddering from the effort. "Actually, Alma, it's my house," he said. "And you are not kicking my son out of it."

Almadine's eyes and mouth fell open, and she spent a good few seconds frozen in that position before Bartholomew spoke again and spurred her into motion. "I've spent the past twenty years hearing about what a good cook Abby Winters is, and waiting for an invitation to this house to see for myself. I'm not about to leave now before I get a crack at that buffet. If you want to go home, get your coat and go. And if you feel like throwing another tantrum, think on Ephesians 5:22: 'Wives, submit yourselves unto your own husbands, as unto the Lord.' "

Almadine's chin quivered.

"John's not the only one who tried to learn your language, Alma," Bartholomew said. "Now what's it gonna be?"

"I…" Almadine smoothed her hands along the sides of her skirt as though unsure what to do with them. "I'm…I think I'll step into the lavatory and freshen up," she said at last. "And then I'll start a plate for you, Bart."

With all the dignity she could muster, which was considerable, Almadine allowed Abby to lead her to the first floor bathroom.

❦

Chiara sat hip-to-hip and shoulder-to-shoulder with John on the steps of Abby's back porch. She held his right hand in both of hers, every so often brushing her lips across his knuckles. They had finished opening gifts and the guests had broken up into smaller groups for conversation and food. John and Chiara had taken that opportunity to sneak away to the solitude of the darkened back yard.

When they were kids, she and John had sat silently in the shade of the big sweet gum tree in the farthest corner of the schoolyard. So they sat now, in silent contemplation of the elemental shift that had just occurred in John's relationship with his mother.

Chiara broke the silence by asking the one question she'd never asked John before. "Did you cry when she hit you?"

He shook his head.

"Mama tried to spank me once," she said, "that time I used her crystal punch bowl to mix up some mud and eggs in the kitchen. She was going to use her bare hand, but as soon as I started crying, she started crying, too. She couldn't hit me. The whole time you were yelling at your mother in there—"

"I wasn't yelling," he said.

"Yes, you were. And the whole time you were doing it, I kept thinking about that one time in the sixth grade, when you showed me your back. There were at least a dozen thick, red, swollen welts criss-crossing your back." Chiara swallowed back the hard lump that had risen to block her throat.

John hung his right arm over her lap and hugged her knees, drawing her closer to him. He remembered that day, and how the sight of his back had sent Chiara into hysterical tears as she'd begged him not to go to the park ever again.

"Why didn't you cry, John?" Chiara asked. "Maybe she would have stopped if she'd really known how much she was hurting you."

"The first time I cried would have been the last time I'd ever have seen you in the park," he said. "My mother would have gotten what she wanted. She never talked about her childhood much, but from what I've seen of her relationship with my grandfather, he kept her on a very short leash. She couldn't wear pants or drink anything stronger than soda. She had to go to prayer meetings every day after school from the time she could walk to when she graduated high school. She wanted to go to college, but her parents thought she would end up 'corrupted,' and they made her get married. They practically handpicked my father for her."

John bowed his head, his hand leisurely stroking Chiara's right calf through her pants. "I can see why my mother has hated your family all these years."

"Then tell me, because I can't."

"Because your mother didn't crumble when she was left alone with five daughters," John said softly. "Because Abby accepted God's plan, and went on and lived her life to the fullest. She taught you and your sisters to live your lives fully, to follow your dreams and pursue your loves and to be good people, not because you're scared that you'll go to hell if you don't, but because that's what you are. She doesn't like you because she's so jealous of how God has blessed you."

Chiara laid her head on John's shoulder, and she wrapped her arms around his. "God has blessed her, too. She's just too stubborn to see it."

"A nod is as good as a wink to a blind donkey," John said.

Chiara laughed in spite of herself. "What's that supposed to mean?"

"Your Grandma Claire used to say that," John reminded her. "It means that it doesn't matter what you do when you're dealing with someone as stubborn as my mother."

"Do you think she'll be better when the baby's born?"

John stared into the purple blackness of the moonless winter sky, and he tried to picture his mother in the role of grandmother. The shadowy depths of the heavens showed him an image of Almadine, dressed in one of her black, brown or green Sunday suits, bringing her first grandchild to church. He envisioned Almadine's claw-like hand clamping on the child's shoulder to make him hold still in the uncomfortable pews, or tugging his ear if he started to nod off.

"I think she'll try even harder to succeed with him where she failed with me," John said.

"So no unsupervised visits," Chiara joked.

"You got that right."

Chiara stroked his arm. "You're paying interest on a problem you don't have yet."

."Grandma Claire speaks again," John chuckled.

"Once she sees the baby, she'll soften up," Chiara said. "She has to."

"I hope so," John murmured, turning his face from the sky to press a kiss to Chiara's head. "For her sake."

The squeal of the back door and the creaking of the floorboards of the patio made John and Chiara both look behind them, and they saw Bartholomew crossing the patio.

"I'm just about ready to take your mother home," he said. "I figure she's been tortured enough tonight."

"Tortured?" John echoed. "No one's been anything but nice to her."

With a loud grunt, Bartholomew lowered himself to the top step, to sit beside John. "You know how your mama is. Folks being nice to her *is* torture." He handed John the shallow white box that Almadine had tossed at Chiara's feet upon their arrival. "You missed this when you were opening the rest of your gifts. It's from me and George and your mother."

"Who picked it out?" John asked, seriously doubting that his mother had anything to do with selecting a gift for him and Chiara.

"You will." Bartholomew's merry eyes sparkled and the left side of his mouth turned up in an impish smile. "Consider it an engagement, wedding and baby shower gift all in one.

John gave Chiara the honor of opening the slim box, which couldn't have measured more than ten by four inches. The inside held what looked like a gift certificate, but what it entitled the bearer to remained a mystery, as Chiara could only cover her mouth with her hand.

John took the certificate and read it himself. "Dad," he gasped. "This is too much. A car from your dealership?"

"Those sporty little things you and Chiara drive are fine for a young couple hiding a marriage and a pregnancy, but you're out in the open now," Bartholomew said. "You're gonna need something practical, something big enough to carry a baby seat, a diaper bag, a stroller, all your groceries—"

"You've given this some thought, huh, Pops?" John chuckled.

"I've lived it, boy! I got two sons of my own, you know." Bartholomew quieted, and his smile transformed from playful to regretful. "I owe you an apology, John. I'd hide out at work on Sundays to avoid going to church with your mother. I grew up in the church, same as your mama, and I thought it was good for you to go to services every week. It wasn't until later, when she dragged me along to keep George, that I saw the truth of what was going on at her daddy's church." Bartholomew set a big, meaty hand on John's knee. "Alma's daddy's got the wrong idea about what church is for, and what his role in it is. He scares folks now. He wasn't so bad when Alma and I first met. It was at a Baptist convention across the river, in Belleville. Your mother was a quiet little thing in a blue skirt and a white blouse with a big lacy collar. She had this sweet little smile and the skinniest legs." He let loose with a rolling laugh that made his belly bounce against his lap. "I was big and loud and had the reputation of being a li'l bit of a ladies' man."

John smiled, easily seeing his father thirty-five years younger and in his prime.

"I think the only reason Alma's daddy let me pursue her was because he was itchy to get her married off. She'd just graduated from high school and he wouldn't allow her to go to Lincoln."

John was stunned. "Mama wanted to go to college?"

"Oh, yeah," Bartholomew said. "She wanted to be a teacher."

"Like my mother," Chiara said.

"Only Alma's folks were hardliners," Bartholomew said. "They count themselves as Baptists, but they make up their own rules as to what Baptist means. For Alma's people, a good Baptist woman stays home and takes care of her husband, children and house, in that order. I would've let her go to school, but her daddy ruled my roost until it was too late."

"It's not too late for her to go to school," Chiara said. "It's only too late when you're dead."

"I hate to say it, but the part of Alma that wanted to go to college is dead," Bartholomew said. "Maybe if I'd gone to services with her, and found out sooner what was going on there, I could have saved her. Saved that part of her."

"Don't blame yourself, Mr. Mahoney." Chiara reached across John to take her father-in-law's hand. "It's not your fault. Trust me on that."

"Every one of the whippings Alma handed out was my fault," Bartholomew said sadly. "And I'm sorry for it, John. I really am. I would never have known if George hadn't told me one Sunday around the time you were thirteen. Why didn't you tell me, boy? Do you think I would have let her keep on with 'em?"

"I guess I thought I deserved them," John said, his voice thick with the emotion he didn't want to display before his father.

Chiara moved to squeeze herself between Bartholomew and John, and she held both their hands. "The whippings weren't your fault," she said to her father-in-law, "and you didn't deserve them," she told John.

"You don't owe me any apologies, Dad," John said. "I don't want to look back anymore. I have too much to look forward to."

"Me, too," Bartholomew laughed. "I'm going to be a grandpappy!"

CHAPTER TWENTY-THREE

Traveling stateside might not have been as exciting as traveling in a foreign country, but Chiara still got the same perks on the East Coast that she'd enjoyed in the Far East. Two days after speaking with Grayson, she arrived at Baltimore-Washington International Airport and disembarked her first-class fight to find a driver displaying a placard with her name on it. He took her overnighter, but she insisted on carrying her briefcase herself.

Her driver led her to the pick-up area at the front of the airport and opened her door for her. Once her driver settled behind the wheel of the dark Lincoln Town Car and started the vehicle toward I-95 North, Chiara propped her briefcase on her knees and opened it.

Along with a few of her personal effects and USITI paperwork, the case contained a complete set of R-GS chips and their master. It also contained another set of chips that would complement the R-GS system in a way that Chiara hoped would ensure her safety and security—and that of the folks she loved—from Emmitt Grayson and Carlton Puel forever.

She stroked her fingertips over one of the small white cards bearing the rebound chips that George had developed and Clara had helped refine. Thin as a sheet of paper, the iridescent chip was nearly clear, and it looked more like a section of a dragonfly's wing than a highly advanced security device.

While Grayson and Puel had turned to mythology to name their major enterprises, George had taken a more straightforward approach, giving his rebound chip the lengthy moniker of Secure Notation Imprinted Transistor Chip. Or SNITCH, for short.

The greenish-black master chip contrasted darkly with the pearlescent SNITCH, and Chiara's heart started to beat loudly in her ears as she closed her briefcase and focused her thoughts on the sale she had to make.

Walter Westcott, founder, head researcher and sole employee of Westcott Technologies, held nineteen patents of his own and had assisted in the research and development of twenty-six more. Dr. Westcott, who held a doctorate in analytical and organic chemistry, specialized in pharmaceutical chemistry. He also held a medical degree and an MBA from Johns Hopkins University.

Dr. Westcott's career achievements included working with the National Institute of Health to create drugs used to treat patients suffering from rare diseases such as cystic fibrosis and Hunter Syndrome.

For the past decade, however, Dr. Westcott had devoted his time and considerable talent to developing a product tentatively called the Nutbuster. Similar to the home lead tests consumers could purchase over the counter at hardware stores, the Nutbuster was a device that could be used to detect the presence of nut oils and nut derivatives in ordinary food.

Grayson had been pursuing Westcott for four long years with no success. This was likely the last pitch Grayson would be allowed to make, and it was certainly the last Chiara intended to make on Grayson's behalf.

She knew more about the Westcotts and Westcott Technologies than the doctor and his wife probably knew themselves. She would use every tool at her disposal, every method in her arsenal, to sell the R-GS system. And then she'd pray to heaven that George's lovely little SNITCH chips could do the rest.

Chiara's investigations into the life Dr. Walter Westcott led outside the laboratory would prove most crucial in formulating her sales pitch. The personal components of a potential client's life always impacted the business aspects, and those were the tools Chiara needed to build a successful sale. Those were the things that made the work personal, and therefore more important to the customer; and as a top-notch salesperson, they were the things Chiara relied on for success.

On paper, Dr. Westcott seemed to be an amazing man dedicated to pursuits that could only benefit humanity, and Chiara felt a nauseating level of guilt over her determination to sell the R-GS system to him. But if George's chip performed as planned, Dr. Westcott would have the privilege of knowing that he'd helped apprehend one of the most successful corporate spies in the history of modern technology.

"Emmitt Grayson's not fighting fair anymore," Orabelle Westcott said after opening the front door of her home to Chiara. Chiara felt the shorter, older woman's eyes on her as she entered the foyer, and she was confident that the soft yet sophisticated Ann Taylor suit she'd chosen gave her the proper balance of professionalism and approachability. The peplum of her white Donegal tweed jacket nicely hid the small swell of her abdomen, and the matching petticoat skirt gave her the right touch of modesty as the hem met the tops of her black calfskin boots.

"That Mr. Grayson's a smart man, sending you here," Mrs. Westcott said as she took Chiara's white mohair and wool coat. "You're young, pretty and sharp-eyed…It's gonna be hard for my husband to deny you just about anything."

"I don't want your husband to agree to anything he isn't completely comfortable with," Chiara said.

"I'm here to do a job, and if I do it well, then Westcott Technologies will be the better for it."

"Nicely put," Mrs. Westcott said, nodding approvingly. She was hanging Chiara's jacket in a closet off the foyer when Dr. Walter Westcott himself ambled down the wide stairway that fed into the foyer.

Stepping forward, Chiara extended a hand. "Dr. Westcott," she smiled. "It's a pleasure to meet you. Thank you so much for taking the time to see me today."

Dr. Westcott stepped onto the pale green marble floor, and Chiara was surprised to see that he was the same height as his wife, who stood no taller than five feet. The doctor's whitened afro contrasted sharply with the deep brown of his skin. Although his hair aged him, the cheery twinkle in his dark eyes gave him a youthfulness that belied his seventy years. He took her hand in both of his and gave it a long squeeze.

"Young lady, may I ask how old you are?" the doctor said by way of greeting.

Chiara happily obliged. "I'm thirty."

Beyond her, she heard Orabelle chuckle. "Miss Winters, I was married fifteen years before you were born," Dr. Westcott said.

"You were nominated for a Nobel prize the same year I was born," Chiara countered, "for your work on the inhaled corticosteroids physicians use to treat asthma and cardiopulmonary disorders."

"I knew you'd be smart, but I didn't realize you'd be so thorough," Dr. Westcott said. "Would you like to join me in my lab, or would you be more comfortable in the sitting room, or the patio?"

Chiara played her first ace. "I'd love to see your lab. My sister Clara Winters is a virologist, and—"

The doctor hesitated. "Clara Winters Holtz, out of California?"

"She moved back to Missouri a couple of years ago," Chiara said. "She conducts a great deal of independent research and lectures throughout the United States. She was jealous about this meeting with you. She admires and respects you quite a lot."

Detailing Clara's work and achievements as though he were her number one fan, the doctor guided Chiara and his wife through their lovely, plantation-style home. Chiara carefully noted the photographs stacked two-deep on the fireplace mantel in the living room, and the ones stacked five-deep on the lid of the baby grand piano gleaming in the sitting room. The doctor had five children and seven grandchildren, but it seemed like more judging from the number of framed photos adorning the walls and surfaces in each room they passed. The understated luxury of the décor revealed more evidence of the love that had once filled the house; Chiara couldn't help smiling when she saw scribbled faces carved on the end of the dining room table, and a section of hallway bearing a large framed crayon drawing that had been

applied directly to the wallpaper by someone less
than a yard tall.

Dr. Westcott led Chiara through the spacious,
airy kitchen that Chiara immediately adored for the
big, wide skylights in the high ceilings. Orabelle
held back to finish preparing lunch, which—
judging by the distinctive scent of Old Bay
seasoning flavoring the air—would be homemade
Maryland crab cakes.

The doctor held the back door open for Chiara,
and she stepped out onto a large enclosed patio.
"Once all my children were married off and settled
into homes of their own, we turned the carriage
house into my laboratory," Dr. Westcott explained.
"Nothing beats a five-second commute to work."

At the front door of the carriage house, Dr.
Westcott lifted a small panel that Chiara would
never have noticed had she not seen him open it. He
punched in a series of numbers and letters, which
deactivated an alarm system and unlocked the front
door. Chiara glanced at the windows and saw that
each was heavily wired. The friendly, one-story
stone cottage seemed as secure as any government
installation.

Once inside, Chiara saw nothing homey or cozy.
The carriage house was for science and research
only, and it was just as sterile and impersonal as
Clara's lab.

Chiara also noticed that the security precautions
weren't limited to readily apparent hard-wired

systems. The windows and skylights had a subtle sheen, a clear indication that they had been treated to deflect radio and satellite interference as well as to prevent photographs or video images from being taken. Chiara smiled to herself, pleased that the doctor was so protective of his intellectual property.

"I like to conduct business out here, Miss Winters, so whenever you'd like to begin, please feel free," Dr. Westcott said, pulling up a tall stool for her at a long, shining stainless steel lab table.

"Quite frankly, Doctor, there's not much I can tell you that past USITI sales reps haven't already," Chiara started. "You're basically a small business owner who interfaces electronically with other individuals and businesses across the globe, and you've told us many times that you're perfectly happy with your current system."

"So you came here for my wife's famous crab cakes instead of to make a pitch?" the doctor laughed.

"Oh no," Chiara chuckled, "although my stomach seems to be doing more talking than I have since we passed through the kitchen."

"Are you married, Ms. Winters?" Dr. Westcott asked.

Caught off guard, Chiara started to give her rote response, which before recent events had always been an outright denial or a clever change of subject. Feeling that she owed the doctor what truths she could divulge, she answered honestly. "Yes."

"How long?"

"Twelve years in March."

"My," he gasped. "You get hitched in the cradle?"

"No, sir," she smiled. "Although it was something like that. We met when we were very young."

"Any children?"

"One on the way. We're due in July."

Dr. Westcott's cheeks bulged in an enormous smile. "Well, congratulations, Ms. Winters!" he exclaimed. "I was never happier than when Orabelle was expecting one of ours. Nothing I do in this lab compares to what's going on under your heart right now. That's the real miracle. That's the closest thing to magic and divinity we get on this planet."

Chiara's nose twitched from the effort of holding back tears at the doctor's lovely words, but she plowed on, determined to make her sale before he broke her heart. She played her second ace. "This is my last assignment for USITI, Dr. Westcott," she said. "I've resigned my position so that I can stay home and take care of my child full-time. My husband and I are fortunate in that we can afford to do that. There are so many other things, though, that I worry about. This is a scary world we're bringing this child into. It's the things you can't see that can be more dangerous than the ones you can."

Dr. Westcott's smile dimmed a bit as Chiara's words sank in.

"I've read the research on your latest break-through," she went on. "I think it's amazing. It'll save a lot of lives. Especially those of children."

"You are quite thorough in your research, Ms. Winters," the doctor sighed.

"I'm sorry about your son."

The sparkle left Dr. Westcott's eyes as he fixed Chiara in his gaze. "You...I rarely speak of...How—"

"My sister Cady has access to a specialized search engine at the newspaper she freelances for," Chiara explained. "She showed me your son's obituary."

Dr. Westcott sat heavily on a stool facing Chiara. "It's been ten years," he said wistfully. "Jonah was the baby. Of course he wasn't much of a baby when he died."

"He was twenty-two?" Chiara offered gently.

The doctor nodded before recalling a story that Chiara already knew. "Jonah was in culinary school, at Johnson & Wales up in Providence, Rhode Island. He wanted to be a chef and own his own restaurant someday. He and some of his school friends went to a chili cook-off in Texas. Jonah was always very careful about what he ate because of his allergy to peanuts. All the contestants in the cook-off were supposed to list all their ingredients at their cooking stations. But you always get folks who don't want to give up all their secrets."

Chiara succumbed to the temptation to set a comforting hand on the doctor's shoulder. The small gesture spurred him on.

"Jonah's friends said that within two minutes of sampling one of the chilis, he went into anaphylactic shock," the doctor said. "He carried an EpiPen with him at all times, and it was used, but it didn't totally suppress the reaction. Jonah died at the hospital twenty-five minutes later. The chili cook had used peanut butter as a thickening agent, but she didn't list it on her ingredient sheet because she didn't want anyone to steal her secret."

The story sounded so much worse coming from Dr. Westcott than it had when she'd read it in the documents Cady had provided her.

"She didn't win the cook-off." Dr. Westcott smiled somberly. "It's been ten years. Jonah would have been thirty-two come February fifteenth."

Chiara swallowed hard to choke back the emotion clogging her throat. This meeting wasn't like any she'd ever experienced. She was used to huge, impeccably decorated conference rooms and boardrooms, used to an audience of trustees, vice-presidents, attorneys, CEOs. She'd never given a sales pitch as personal, intimate and important as this one. She suddenly wanted to admit everything to Dr. Westcott, to confess that he was being made part of a plan to bring down Emmitt Grayson.

But she couldn't. If her plan failed, his knowledge of the R-GS rootkits and master chip intrusion might place him, Orabelle and the rest of his family in jeopardy. Chiara stiffened her spine and placed her trust in her instinct: that the SNITCH would work, and that Dr. Westcott would handle the information it provided quickly and appropriately.

"The Nutbuster is a fitting tribute to your son's life and your life's work," she told the doctor. "You'll spare a lot of parents the suffering you've had to endure."

"And what role could your company's R-GS system play in regard to me and my work?"

"From the information you've already provided to USITI, I can tell you right now that the system you currently utilize is perfectly adequate for your needs," Chiara said confidently. "Essentially, you're a small business owner, but what makes you unique is the number of different types of organizations and people with whom you have to interact all over the globe. USITI's R-GS system is the best there is when it comes to the particular needs of a businessman like yourself."

She set her briefcase on the lab table, opened it, and then flipped open her notebook computer. She had a hard copy of her presentation, but knew that the online version would dazzle the old scientist with its ease of use.

Using her mouse, Chiara guided him all over the site, showing him the simple beauty of the R-GS system. "Each R-GS system is tailored for each client," she said. "Given the sensitive nature of much of your work, Emmitt Grayson personally undertook the challenge of devising a system that would ensure the protection of your critical business and research information, a system flexible enough to accommodate future growth as well as respond to the changing requirements of your customers and work associates.

"The most beautiful part of the system is its simplicity," Chiara finished. "Simplicity improves productivity. Security, simplicity and productivity…those are the things USITI's R-GS system guarantees."

Dr. Westcott spent a long moment quietly pondering Chiara's spiel. This was usually the place where she fielded questions, where her potential clients either challenged her to make a harder sell or to allow them trial use of the system before they made a final decision. Chiara's short time in the doctor's presence had shown her that he was a no-nonsense sort, and that he'd give her an answer, one way or the other, rather shortly.

"Okay, Miss Winters," Dr. Westcott said sooner than Chiara expected. "I'll try your system, on a trial basis."

She stifled a sigh of relief. "Would thirty days suit you?"

"I think thirty days would certainly suffice," the doctor agreed.

"Excellent," Chiara said. "The head of information systems in our new St. Louis office will come here personally to install the R-GS system. His name is John Mahoney, and he's very good at what he does."

"I wouldn't expect anything less than the best from USITI," Dr. Westcott remarked. As if that concluded the day's business, he rose from his stool and offered a hand to Chiara. "I think Orabelle's got some crab cakes on for lunch. Would you care to join us? I won't take no for an answer."

"In that case, I won't waste my breath by faking a polite refusal." Chiara smiled and accepted his hand. "I'd love to join you for lunch." *While you're still on speaking terms with me*, she thought.

❧

Two weeks after John returned from installing the SNITCH chip at Westcott Technologies, a soft knock sounded on the door of his office at USITI-St. Louis. Before he could respond, the door flew open and a flood of strangers in dark blue nylon jackets washed into the room. John saw many more jacketed men filtering through the offices and cubicles beyond his doorway. A man in a dark suit displayed a gleaming badge and identification card as he strode toward John, his face severe.

"John Mahoney," he started in a deep, authoritative voice not meant to be questioned or interrupted, "please step away from your desk and your computer. This office is being seized by the Federal Trade Commission, the FBI and the Missouri State

Attorney's office on charges of corporate espionage
and numerous privacy violations. We have orders to
seize everything in this facility, including but not
limited to all computer systems, hardware, software—"

"He's one of us, Mr. Connor."

John, who'd been rigid with apprehension and
shock, visibly relaxed at the sound of Ciel's voice as
she came up behind the man in the suit. Dressed in
a pale gray, pinstriped skirt and jacket that flattered
her figure, she looked as though she'd just come
from court.

"John," Ciel said, "this is Matthew Connor. He's
with the FBI. He's been working very closely with
the state attorney on this case."

"The SNITCH worked?" John said, his voice
shriveled to an embarrassing squeak.

Ciel grinned openly. "It worked, all right. Three
days ago Dr. Walter Westcott's computer system
reported a series of unauthorized outside invasions.
The dates and times of the breaks were logged as
well as the duration of the visits and the information that was copied. Best of all, the SNITCH
tracked the information back to Emmitt Grayson in
Chicago. The SNITCH performed beautifully."

"Mrs. Clark told me that a college student
devised the secureware that snared Grayson," Mr.
Connor said.

"My kid brother," John said. "He's…talented."

Mr. Connor whistled in amazement. "Mrs. Clark here contacted the state attorney, who got the FBI involved. Quite frankly, in all my years in the computer crimes division, I've never seen anything like that SNITCH." Mr. Connor handed John a tri-fold booklet of papers.

"What's this?" John asked.

"The warrant for the seizure," Mr. Connor said.

John set it on his desk without reading it. "I'm sure everything is in order. What do you need from me?"

"Not a thing," Mr. Connor said. "You've done quite enough already."

John sank heavily into his chair, realizing that it was the last time he'd ever do so. The chair, the desk, everything in the office, would soon be in the possession of the U.S. government. "It worked." He scrubbed his hands over his face. "I have to call Chiara. I have to let her know that…" He glanced up at Ciel, and he wondered if she could see the hope in his eyes. "It's over, isn't it?"

"For Emmitt Grayson, definitely," Mr. Connor said. "You and Chiara Winters executed a masterful sting. The information we gathered on Emmitt Grayson from Dr. Walter Westcott alone will be enough to charge him with at least a dozen domestic and international privacy and fair trade violations."

"This was a team effort," John said. "It wouldn't have happened without the Winters sisters and my brother pitching in."

"Every USITI office is being raided at this moment, with Chicago being our top priority," Mr. Connor said. "At this time, we have no reason to believe that anyone other than Emmitt Grayson has directly and knowingly committed a crime. However—"

"Mr. Mahoney!" A frantic female employee burst into the office and pushed her way through agents and between Mr. Connor and Ciel to get to John. "Mr. Mahoney, there are FBI agents boxing up the computers. They're collecting files and taking everything that isn't nailed down! What's going on? Are we in trouble?"

John looked to Mr. Connor for an answer.

"I was just telling Mr. Mahoney here that no one in this office is in danger of arrest," Mr. Connor explained calmly. "We have reason to believe that United States IntelTech, Inc. is guilty of corporate spying. We're looking at one suspect in this case."

Horrified, the woman looked at John. "What's happening to the company, Mr. Mahoney? Will I have a job in the morning?"

John stood and stepped around his desk, to take the woman by her shoulders. "I don't know exactly what's going to happen to USITI-St. Louis, but as soon as I do, I'll let everyone here know."

The woman's mouth worked, but no sensible sounds came out. "M-Mr. Mahoney...I don't...wh-what..."

"Every employee is insured against this sort of thing," John assured her. "You'll receive your salary for several months even if USITI goes under."

"Why don't you go home, ma'am," Mr. Connor said. "Until further notice, you have the day off."

"Oh God, Mr. Mahoney, is it really that bad?"

"I'm afraid it is," John said. "For Emmitt Grayson."

❧

Chiara sat at a sterile grey table separating her from Emmitt Grayson. A month in the East Moline Correctional Center, where he'd remain until his trial—which was being touted as the biggest in Chicago since Al Capone went down in 1931—had drastically altered Grayson's appearance. His face was more gaunt, his cheeks hollowed by his inability to eat carbohydrate-heavy food that was a far cry from the gourmet specialties he had grown accustomed to prior to his incarceration. His costly tailored suits had been replaced by a state-issued jumpsuit that did nothing to flatter Grayson's naturally slim build.

Although he had none of his usual grooming products, Grayson still managed to keep his steel-gray hair slicked back from his wide forehead. And his icy, unblinking stare remained the same. The only thing that had changed was Chiara's ability to meet his gaze head-on, which she did as she waited for him to speak.

"Thank you for coming," he said softly. "I didn't think you would."

"There's something I want to know," Chiara said. "Something I think you can tell me."

Grayson's lips moved into the approximation of a smile. "Chen Zhou."

"That's right," Chiara snapped, making no effort to mask her anger.

Immediately after the raid on the USITI offices, her life had been turned upside down again, but in a different way. Cady had written an article for her newspaper detailing every step of USITI's downfall, from Chen Zhou's death to Dr. Westcott's discovery of Emmitt Grayson's document theft and the subsequent raids on the USITI offices.

The article, which included two sidebars on George's invention of the SNITCH and Carlton Puel's alleged involvement in attacks on Chiara and John, had been syndicated, and had run in major dailies across the United States.

The world had learned of Emmitt Grayson's downfall at the hands of two USITI employees, and the spotlight had turned its ugly glare on Chiara and John. Chiara had always cherished her privacy, had guarded it ferociously, and the unneeded attention had driven her into seclusion at her mother's house until the day she and John had hopped into John's Nissan and driven to Moline for Chiara's private meeting with Grayson.

She could now admit to herself that Grayson had always scared her a little bit. Until now. The only feelings she had left for him were contempt and anger, and they rose as she faced him in his prison grays.

"Did Carlton Puel kill my friend?" Chiara asked bluntly.

Grayson was first to look away. He dropped his gaze to his hands, which were flat on the tabletop. "No. Carlton is greedy and ruthless, but as far as I know, he isn't a murderer."

"How does he figure into everything that happened?" Chiara asked.

"Carlton and I are old friends," Grayson said softly. "In college, we were something of a team when it came to computers. We shared ideas, innovations. I was the more talented of the two of us, and he knew it. He resented it."

"How did he find out about the master chip technology?"

"That was something I began working on during my undergraduate years. I perfected it once I created USITI. Carlton knew that I was using the system once he read the *American Investors* article." Grayson chuckled mirthlessly. "Back in college, I never won a single college football bet, never mind masterfully played the stock market. He knew that I'd discovered…an advantage. He badgered me until I told him about the R-GS system, and I offered

him a cut. Evidently, he wanted more. Too much
more."

"So he went to Zhou, to get a master chip of his
own," Chiara guessed.

"When you returned from Tokyo, Zhou
confronted me," Grayson said. His hands began to
shake and he removed them from Chiara's view. "He
told me that he knew what the chips did, and how
I'd built my fortune. He called me a thief and
refused to turn over the master chip. I couldn't let
him keep it. I couldn't let him turn it in to the
authorities."

Chiara sat up even straighter in her chair. Her
heart seemed to stop its hard drumming in her
chest. "You…you?" she gasped.

"I only wanted him to sleep, so I could search his
apartment," Grayson admitted. "He wasn't
supposed to die."

Chiara blanched and failed to hold back tears.
"You know we're being taped, don't you? You know
you just confessed to murder?"

Grayson's smile trembled. "Actually, my legal
team has informed me that such an admission falls
under the category of voluntary manslaughter."

Chiara began to shiver despite the warmth
provided by her snug wool jersey dress. "Why are
you telling me this? Why didn't you tell the authorities when you were arrested? You ratted Carlton
Puel out fast enough, when you told the police that

he's the one who sent Anthony Taylor to attack me and John."

"I felt I owed *you* the truth before all others." He gave a tiny shrug. "That, and the full complement of benefits, bonuses and incentives you earned during your tenure as a sales representative for USITI."

"I don't want anything from USITI." She angrily swiped away the tears wetting her cheeks. "I don't want anything from you."

"My lawyers have already transferred the appropriate funds into your bank account, Chiara," Grayson said. "It's the least I can do, for what you've been through."

She slammed her fists on the table as she launched herself to her feet. One of the two guards standing at the doorway took a short step toward her. "It's not just me!" she ranted. "It's John and our families, and Zhou! It's all those people you spied on and stole from, and all the USITI employees who are in limbo now, wondering if they're going to lose their jobs. Do you have any real idea how much damage you've done?"

Grayson accepted her wrath unflinchingly as he gazed at the walls around him. "I believe I'll have lots of time to reflect on that in the near future, Chiara."

Chiara bid Grayson a hurried and impersonal goodbye before rushing into the drab lobby of the minimum-security facility. She threw herself into John's arms and wept into his neck and shoulder.

"Baby, what happened?" John asked, trying to pry her off of him enough to look into her face.

"He did it," she whispered on a sob. "He killed Zhou, all because of that chip."

John's arms slowly went around her, his hands caressing her back. He pressed his lips to her head and comforted her until she was empty of tears. "It's over now, baby. It's all over. Grayson's in here, Carlton Puel's in jail in Arizona, and the whole world knows what we sacrificed to do what's right."

"I just want to go home." Chiara forced strength into her voice. "I want to put all this behind us and get on with the business of building our family."

John clasped her hand and brought it to his lips as he led her through the security checkpoints, out the heavy double doors and into the bright cold of a clear February afternoon. "When you say 'home,' exactly where do you mean?" he asked. "Do you still want to move back to Chicago?"

She shook her head. "No. I want to go someplace new. Someplace sunny."

"Someplace with no news crews and reporters," John added as he opened the door of his Nissan for her.

Instead of climbing into the car, Chiara wrapped her arms around John's neck and drew him into a kiss that took the chill right out of the wintry day. "As far as I'm concerned, I'm home already. Home has always been where you are, John. Whether it's St. Louis, Chicago, or Timbuktu, my home has always been with you."

John spent a long moment tasting her lips before he drew away, smiling. "Now that we're both unemployed, maybe it's time we settled down and found a house. I think I know just the place."

"It's not that mess on Heger Court your mother's been trying to force on you, is it?" Chiara asked warily.

"Nope." John helped her into the car. "It's nowhere near my parents' house."

"Then I like it already," Chiara grinned as she allowed John to close her door.

EPILOGUE

Four months later

Chiara's bare feet padded across the bamboo flooring of the airy living room. She wore the white dress she'd purchased at Soul Hippi, and Ciel had styled her long dark hair in intricate but delicate braids adorned with silvery-white cowrie shells. As she'd imagined, the dress was perfect, thoroughly pleasing Chiara with the way it fell over the vast roundness of her belly.

She stood to one side, partially hidden in the voluminous white sheers pulled to one side of the extra-wide sliding glass doors leading to the lanai and the private beach beyond it. There were more people on the beach than the small bit of white sand had seen since she and John had moved into the renovated plantation house in March.

In the earliest days of his unemployment, John had spent a lot of time surfing the Internet looking for real estate that fulfilled both of their requirements: They both wanted a two-story home someplace sunny and far enough away from both families to prevent surprise visits.

Chiara would have been happy to purchase a small place in Okinawa, Japan, but John had argued that Okinawa was just too far from Missouri. Compromise had come in the form of an old plantation home on the island of St. Kitts. The ten-room stucco house had been a sugar plantation in the late 1700s. After a century and a half of private ownership, it had been used as a tourist resort, but had fallen into disuse and disrepair in recent years. With their house fund and combined severance packages from USITI, Chiara and John had been able to purchase and renovate the house and its twelve acres of land, fully modernizing it and restoring its tranquil, elegant beauty.

The house had seemed big to Chiara, before the Winters and Mahoney families descended upon it. Chiara's older nieces and nephews spent most of their days at the beach, climbing nearby Mount Liamuiga, biking around the island, or simply hanging out at the shops and restaurants in Frigate Bay.

The younger children, Cady's twins, Virginia, and one-month old Jacob, and Kyla's daughter Niema practically lived on the lanai. Along with their unlikely babysitter, Bartholomew, the toddlers took in the island breeze from the covered patio and napped to the lullaby of the ocean softly tickling the shore.

As Chiara peeped from behind the sheers, she saw everyone assembled there on the shore. Every linen-draped folding chair had a body in it. There were a couple of people she didn't recognize, namely the ebony-skinned young women sitting beside Troy and George.

Miss Etheline had done what none of Troy's aunts could, which was break up a successful senior year relationship. Tiffani McCousy had dropped Troy hard soon after her run-in with Etheline Simpson. And George, basking in his newfound glory as the premier secure software designer in the United States, had developed the confidence to spend more time talking to girls in the real world rather than the virtual one to which he'd been so devoted.

USITI's downfall had led to success for every party involved in Emmitt Grayson's destruction. Cady's article had been nominated for several journalism awards, including the Pulitzer. Ciel had been offered, and accepted, a position as a Missouri assistant district attorney while Lee had masterminded a restructuring plan that allowed USITI's employees to purchase the company from Emmitt Grayson, effectively removing him from the organization entirely while sparing their jobs. Clara, in partnership with George, had a patent pending for their SNITCH technology, and not to be outdone, Kyla was in talks with a team of producers from Metronome Films to star in a film account of John and Chiara's story.

As for Chiara and John, they had decided to build a business from home. They were equal partners with George in a fledgling software design company specializing in secureware. George had refused several top-dollar offers from major firms, choosing instead to design for his brother and sister-in-law, the only employers he'd interviewed with who hadn't suggested that he cut his hair.

John, as CEO, would oversee operations and Chiara, once the baby was born, would be the head of technical sales.

Their ownership of the SNITCH had given them a very solid head start on the competition, and sales of that product remained strong; so strong, in fact, that George had purchased his first house—a pretty little three-bedroom on Heger Court.

Chiara watched as the native officiate in the black robes at the shoreline raised her arms, signaling for quiet. A three-piece island ensemble comprised of the *shack-shack*, *baha* and guitar began playing a soft, sweet melody, and Chiara swallowed hard. That was her cue.

She crossed the lanai and stepped out onto the warm sand, burrowing her toes into the powdery surface with each step she took closer to John, who awaited her near the woman in black. John spent so much time outdoors that his skin had darkened two shades, and his informal white linen shirt and loose-fitting drawstring trousers nicely complemented his new complexion.

With each step she took closer to her husband, Chiara felt her heart swell in her chest. John was the love of her life, and now that she was about to renew her wedding vows to him, she was delighted to do it in front of her beaming family. If she could, she would share her joy with the entire world.

She smiled to herself, shaking her head at her past behavior. *Why on earth did I hide my marriage to this man for so long*, she wondered to herself as a gentle breeze made music with the cowrie shells in her hair. *What the hell made me keep so much of my life a secret from my mother and my sisters?*

She took John's hands and spent a moment gazing into his magical eyes before turning to their assembled guests. She forgot all about the loving tyranny of her mother and sisters, and she let go of the resentment she'd harbored for so long. Chiara knew that she'd survived what she'd been through with Emmitt Grayson and USITI because of her mother and sisters. Because of her family, the one to which she'd been borne and the one she was marrying into.

Chiara met John's eyes once more and saw his unasked question. "I'm fine," she said, answering him softly so that only he could hear. "I'm just glad to be here."

John cocked an eyebrow. "On the beach?"

"No." Tears of happiness welled in Chiara's eyes as she glanced once more at her family. "I'm glad to be home."

2010 Mass Market Titles

January

Show Me the Sun
Miriam Shumba
ISBN: 978-158571-405-6
$6.99

Promises of Forever
Celya Bowers
ISBN: 978-1-58571-380-6
$6.99

February

Love Out of Order
Nicole Green
ISBN: 978-1-58571-381-3
$6.99

Unclear and Present Danger
Michele Cameron
ISBN: 978-158571-408-7
$6.99

March

Stolen Jewels
Michele Sudler
ISBN: 978-158571-409-4
$6.99

Not Quite Right
Tammy Williams
ISBN: 978-158571-410-0
$6.99

April

Oak Bluffs
Joan Early
ISBN: 978-1-58571-379-0
$6.99

Crossing the Line
Bernice Layton
ISBN: 978-158571-412-4
$6.99

How to Kill Your Husband
Keith Walker
ISBN: 978-158571-421-6
$6.99

May

The Business of Love
Cheris F. Hodges
ISBN: 978-158571-373-8
$6.99

Wayward Dreams
Gail McFarland
ISBN: 978-158571-422-3
$6.99

June

The Doctor's Wife
Mildred Riley
ISBN: 978-158571-424-7
$6.99

Mixed Reality
Chamein Canton
ISBN: 978-158571-423-0
$6.99

2010 Mass Market Titles (continued)

July

Blue Interlude
Keisha Mennefee
ISBN: 978-158571-378-3
$6.99

Always You
Crystal Hubbard
ISBN: 978-158571-371-4
$6.99

Unbeweavable
Katrina Spencer
ISBN: 978-158571-426-1
$6.99

August

Small Sensations
Crystal V. Rhodes
ISBN: 978-158571-376-9
$6.99

Let's Get It On
Dyanne Davis
ISBN: 978-158571-416-2
$6.99

September

Unconditional
A.C. Arthur
ISBN: 978-158571-413-1
$6.99

Swan
Africa Fine
ISBN: 978-158571-377-6
$6.99

October

Friends in Need
Joan Early
ISBN:978-1-58571-428-5
$6.99

Against the Wind
Gwynne Forster
ISBN:978-158571-429-2
$6.99

That Which Has Horns
Miriam Shumba
ISBN:978-1-58571-430-8
$6.99

November

A Good Dude
Keith Walker
ISBN:978-1-58571-431-5
$6.99

Reye's Gold
Ruthie Robinson
ISBN:978-1-58571-432-2
$6.99

December

Still Waters...
Crystal V. Rhodes
ISBN:978-1-58571-433-9
$6.99

Burn
Crystal Hubbard
ISBN: 978-1-58571-406-3
$6.99

Other Genesis Press, Inc. Titles

2 Good	Celya Bowers	$6.99
A Dangerous Deception	J.M. Jeffries	$8.95
A Dangerous Love	J.M. Jeffries	$8.95
A Dangerous Obsession	J.M. Jeffries	$8.95
A Drummer's Beat to Mend	Kei Swanson	$9.95
A Happy Life	Charlotte Harris	$9.95
A Heart's Awakening	Veronica Parker	$9.95
A Lark on the Wing	Phyliss Hamilton	$9.95
A Love of Her Own	Cheris F. Hodges	$9.95
A Love to Cherish	Beverly Clark	$8.95
A Place Like Home	Alicia Wiggins	$6.99
A Risk of Rain	Dar Tomlinson	$8.95
A Taste of Temptation	Reneé Alexis	$9.95
A Twist of Fate	Beverly Clark	$8.95
A Voice Behind Thunder	Carrie Elizabeth Greene	$6.99
A Will to Love	Angie Daniels	$9.95
Acquisitions	Kimberley White	$8.95
Across	Carol Payne	$12.95
After the Vows	Leslie Esdaile	$10.95
(Summer Anthology)	T.T. Henderson	
	Jacqueline Thomas	
Again, My Love	Kayla Perrin	$10.95
Against the Wind	Gwynne Forster	$8.95
All I Ask	Barbara Keaton	$8.95
All I'll Ever Need	Mildred Riley	$6.99
Always You	Crystal Hubbard	$6.99
Ambrosia	T.T. Henderson	$8.95
An Unfinished Love Affair	Barbara Keaton	$8.95
And Then Came You	Dorothy Elizabeth Love	$8.95
Angel's Paradise	Janice Angelique	$9.95
Another Memory	Pamela Ridley	$6.99
Anything But Love	Celya Bowers	$6.99
At Last	Lisa G. Riley	$8.95
Best Foot Forward	Michele Sudler	$6.99
Best of Friends	Natalie Dunbar	$8.95
Best of Luck Elsewhere	Trisha Haddad	$6.99
Beyond the Rapture	Beverly Clark	$9.95
Blame It on Paradise	Crystal Hubbard	$6.99
Blaze	Barbara Keaton	$9.95
Blindsided	Tammy Williams	$6.99
Bliss, Inc.	Chamein Canton	$6.99
Blood Lust	J.M.Jeffries	$9.95

Other Genesis Press, Inc. Titles (continued)

Other Genesis Press, Inc. Titles (continued)

Eve's Prescription	Edwina Martin Arnold	$8.95
Everlastin' Love	Gay G. Gunn	$8.95
Everlasting Moments	Dorothy Elizabeth Love	$8.95
Everything and More	Sinclair Lebeau	$8.95
Everything but Love	Natalie Dunbar	$8.95
Falling	Natalie Dunbar	$9.95
Fate	Pamela Leigh Starr	$8.95
Finding Isabella	A.J. Garrotto	$8.95
Fireflies	Joan Early	$6.99
Fixin' Tyrone	Keith Walker	$6.99
Forbidden Quest	Dar Tomlinson	$10.95
Forever Love	Wanda Y. Thomas	$8.95
From the Ashes	Kathleen Suzanne	$8.95
	Jeanne Sumerix	
Frost on My Window	Angela Weaver	$6.99
Gentle Yearning	Rochelle Alers	$10.95
Glory of Love	Sinclair LeBeau	$10.95
Go Gentle Into That	Malcom Boyd	$12.95
Good Night		
Goldengroove	Mary Beth Craft	$16.95
Groove, Bang, and Jive	Steve Cannon	$8.99
Hand in Glove	Andrea Jackson	$9.95
Hard to Love	Kimberley White	$9.95
Hart & Soul	Angie Daniels	$8.95
Heart of the Phoenix	A.C. Arthur	$9.95
Heartbeat	Stephanie Bedwell-Grime	$8.95
Hearts Remember	M. Loui Quezada	$8.95
Hidden Memories	Robin Allen	$10.95
Higher Ground	Leah Latimer	$19.95
Hitler, the War, and the Pope	Ronald Rychiak	$26.95
How to Write a Romance	Kathryn Falk	$18.95
I Married a Reclining Chair	Lisa M. Fuhs	$8.95
I'll Be Your Shelter	Giselle Carmichael	$8.95
I'll Paint a Sun	A.J. Garrotto	$9.95
Icie	Pamela Leigh Starr	$8.95
If I Were Your Woman	LaConnie Taylor-Jones	$6.99
Illusions	Pamela Leigh Starr	$8.95
Indigo After Dark Vol. I	Nia Dixon/Angelique	$10.95
Indigo After Dark Vol. II	Dolores Bundy/	$10.95
	Cole Riley	
Indigo After Dark Vol. III	Montana Blue/	$10.95
	Coco Morena	

Other Genesis Press, Inc. Titles (continued)

Other Genesis Press, Inc. Titles (continued)

Naked Soul	Gwynne Forster	$8.95
Never Say Never	Michele Cameron	$6.99
Next to Last Chance	Louisa Dixon	$24.95
No Apologies	Seressia Glass	$8.95
No Commitment Required	Seressia Glass	$8.95
No Regrets	Mildred E. Riley	$8.95
Not His Type	Chamein Canton	$6.99
Nowhere to Run	Gay G. Gunn	$10.95
O Bed! O Breakfast!	Rob Kuehnle	$14.95
Object of His Desire	A.C. Arthur	$8.95
Office Policy	A.C. Arthur	$9.95
Once in a Blue Moon	Dorianne Cole	$9.95
One Day at a Time	Bella McFarland	$8.95
One of These Days	Michele Sudler	$9.95
Outside Chance	Louisa Dixon	$24.95
Passion	T.T. Henderson	$10.95
Passion's Blood	Cherif Fortin	$22.95
Passion's Furies	AlTonya Washington	$6.99
Passion's Journey	Wanda Y. Thomas	$8.95
Past Promises	Jahmel West	$8.95
Path of Fire	T.T. Henderson	$8.95
Path of Thorns	Annetta P. Lee	$9.95
Peace Be Still	Colette Haywood	$12.95
Picture Perfect	Reon Carter	$8.95
Playing for Keeps	Stephanie Salinas	$8.95
Pride & Joi	Gay G. Gunn	$8.95
Promises Made	Bernice Layton	$6.99
Promises to Keep	Alicia Wiggins	$8.95
Quiet Storm	Donna Hill	$10.95
Reckless Surrender	Rochelle Alers	$6.95
Red Polka Dot in a	Varian Johnson	$12.95
World Full of Plaid		
Red Sky	Renee Alexis	$6.99
Reluctant Captive	Joyce Jackson	$8.95
Rendezvous With Fate	Jeanne Sumerix	$8.95
Revelations	Cheris F. Hodges	$8.95
Rivers of the Soul	Leslie Esdaile	$8.95
Rocky Mountain Romance	Kathleen Suzanne	$8.95
Rooms of the Heart	Donna Hill	$8.95
Rough on Rats and	Chris Parker	$12.95
Tough on Cats		
Save Me	Africa Fine	$6.99

Other Genesis Press, Inc. Titles (continued)

Other Genesis Press, Inc. Titles (continued)

ESCAPE WITH INDIGO !!!!

Join Indigo Book Club©
It's simple, easy and secure.

Sign up and receive the new releases
every month + Free shipping
and
20% off the cover price.

Visit us online at
www.genesis-press.com or
call 1-888-INDIGO-1